Three Months in Florence

2/20

Books by Mary Carter

SHE'LL TAKE IT

ACCIDENTALLY ENGAGED

SUNNYSIDE BLUES

MY SISTER'S VOICE

THE PUB ACROSS THE POND

THE THINGS I DO FOR YOU

THREE MONTHS IN FLORENCE

Published by Kensington Publishing Corporation

Three Months in Florence

MARY CARTER

KENSINGTON BOOKS
www.kensingtonbooks.com

KENSINGTON BOOKS are published by

Kensington Publishing Corp.
119 West 40th Street
New York, NY 10018

ISBN-13: 978-0-7582-8470-9
ISBN-10: 0-7582-8470-5
First Kensington Trade Paperback Printing: August 2013

eISBN-13: 978-0-7582-8471-6
eISBN-10: 0-7582-8471-3
First Kensington Electronic Edition: August 2013

10 9 8 7 6 5 4 3 2 1

Printed in the United States of America

This novel is dedicated to the people of Italy

ACKNOWLEDGMENTS

First, I'd like to thank the Kensington team: my editor, John Scognamiglio, my publicist, Vida Engstrand, and Kristine Mills and Judy York for bringing stories to visual life with the covers. Thank you to everyone behind the scenes at Kensington as well. I'd also like to thank my agent, Evan Marshall.

Thank you, Janice B. Rimler, and Franceso Giuseppe Filecci for helping me out with most of my Italian phrases. Any last-minute errors are mine alone.

Thank you to the wonderful people of Italy I met while traveling in 2012. Especially Marco and his lovely family at the Villa San Lucchese in Poggibonsi (Tuscany). It's a wonderful place to stay, and he primed my curiosity for Florence when he put his hand on his heart and proclaimed, "Firenze. The heart of Italy!" From the cab drivers to the waiters (bar a few testy shopkeepers), it was a wonderful experience. I hope all my readers get a chance to go. In the meantime, I hope you feel as if you're there for a bit in between the pages of this novel.

As always much love and thanks to my family and friends. The only thing better than an espresso in Italy would be sharing it with all of you.

CHAPTER 1

"How did you two meet?" is the question everyone asks when you're in love. This is:

The Story of Us

It's my first week of grad school. I carry sketchbooks and even have a paintbrush tucked in my bra, and I've stuffed my schedule with all things "art." I walk into the auditorium, bounce down on one of the plush red seats, and when I look up, there's this tall man standing on stage under the spotlight. He's so good-looking I wonder if he thinks he's here for theater practice, or maybe I'm here for theater practice, and the last time I was in a play was in the third grade where I played a tree, and had stage fright so bad I plucked all my leaves off backstage, so by the time I was literally shoved under the spotlight for my fifteen seconds of fame, my branches were as bare as the day I was born, and my first line was supposed to be: "Summer, beautiful summer. You make my leaves so green." Instead of delivering the line, I peed my pants the second the curtain went up. I've never graced the stage again.

I glance at my schedule to make sure I'm in the right place, and yep, this is it, Fifteenth Century Renaissance Sculptures. Alex Wallace, TA. Welcome to my favorite class, I think, as I settle back, plant my flip-flops on the seat in front of me, and start sucking on the end of my pen. In my mind, I am painting him.

He has a soccer player's lean but strong body. Dark hair and dark eyes, and I really like his facial structure. It is the first time in my life I've ever noticed, really noticed a man's chin, and I have been sketching nude models since undergrad. Nevertheless, the rest of him isn't bad either. His olive skin glows, and his cheekbones look as if they've been sculpted from marble, which is ironic given the subject. I wonder what our kids will look like.

I'm from hearty Nordic stock, with fair skin, white-blond hair, and eyes some people accuse of being aqua. We are two opposite but beautiful things. I want two kids. Our first will have his dark hair and my eyes. The second, my blond hair and his eyes and cheekbones. I continue thinking of combinations while he meticulously sets up a slide show. He's dressed in a shirt and a tie. The professor doesn't even wear a tie. He is trying too hard. I imagine my fingers touching his neck, loosening his tie, unbuttoning his shirt. Maybe a kiss or twelve for luck. I wish our culture wasn't so hung up on clothes. I would love to sketch him in the nude while he works.

But it's not until he speaks, or should I say, performs his lecture, that I lift right out of my seat. He's not just a pretty face; Alex Wallace is electric. The words and phrases that pour out of him startle me.

Sculpted, chiseled, formed. Carved busts. Young virgins. Ideal images. Unbaked clay. Fired bronze. Rough stone. Flat chisels. Toothed chisels. Clawed chisels. Glazed terra-cotta. *Putto Poised on a Globe.*

By the time he finishes, I have to look around to see if anyone else is this turned on. Except for a girl a few rows ahead leaning forward and chewing on her hair, and a slim boy at the aisle with his fingers clasped under his chin like he's praying, everyone else seems unfazed. When the lecture is over, I remain seated and wait until the place empties out. Alex Wallace gathers up his things and is gone. He doesn't even glance at me on the way out. Interesting. I take a deep breath. I am the only person in the auditorium. A peaceful, almost holy anticipation hovers above the sea of red seats. The overhead lights click off one by one, leaving just a single halo spilling out from the ghost light standing center stage.

What, exactly, just happened here? I feel as if I've been sculpted, and chiseled, and formed, and roughed, and toothed, and clawed, and my terra-cotta glazed. And I remember nothing of the lecture. Because while the rest of the class was furiously taking notes on *The Rape of the Sabine Women,* I was staring at Alex Wallace, and thinking: That's the man I'm going to marry.

Huh.

It is quite disturbing given my proclamation on day one: "I'm going to marry my art and let boys be my playthings!" I leave the theater in a daze and pretty much wander around the same way until I know Megan will be back at the dorm. I plop down on my bunk and harass her until she agrees to help me formulate a nine-point plan of attack to get Alex Wallace to marry me. Because that's what descendants of Vikings do; they plan their attacks. I am cocky and in the bloom of my beauty. He doesn't stand a chance.

> Lena and Alex date. The CliffsNotes:
> Courtship, courtship, courtship, young love, hot sex, young love, hot sex, dorm rooms, sweatpants, breakfast cereal, jealousy, fight, fight, fight, young love, hot sex, pregnancy scare, false alarm, back to using condoms religiously, fight, break up, go out with a jerk and see Alex's jealous side, back together, hot sex, jealousy, marriage proposal—sealed with Froot Loops and a kiss in the cafeteria.

*   *   *

We marry right after Alex finishes grad school. I decide not
to finish because LOVE is my future. I don't need school to be
an artist; the world will be my canvas. Neither of us is working
yet, so it's the perfect time for a honeymoon. We are going to
be that couple, educated and artistic; we are going to travel. We
look at each other and say, "Florence!" Then, "Jinx. You owe
me a Coke!"

All the major works of art and architecture Alex loves are in
Florence. And I get to be the girl who takes him there. And of
course, I'm still an artist too. Just an artist a little more in love
with her husband than she is with her canvases. Between my
parents, his odd jobs, and credit cards, we scrape enough
money together for three blissful weeks. We'll spend most of
the time in Florence, but take side trips to Rome, Milan, and
Venice. Our flowered-vinyl suitcases are packed and waiting at
the edge of the bed.

Picture this. I am dressed in my honeymoon slash airplane
outfit (sweat suit with lacey red bra and panties underneath),
reaching for my suitcase, when the phone rings. Maybe it wasn't
that close of a call, but if you think that's pushing it, sometimes
I imagine it as us sitting on the plane; Alex is just starting to
reach into my sweat pants when the stewardess (that's what we
called her back then; get over it) snatches up a ringing phone
from the back of one of the seats, holds it out to Alex, and says,
"It's for you."

However it happens, it is the university; they have a professor
position to fill, and they want him to start yesterday. They definitely aren't going to wait for a honeymoon. Italy is going to
have to wait.

"We'll go winter break," Alex says. I am determined to be a
Perfect Wife, and I agree. But by the time winter break comes
along, we have purchased the perfect little "starter home" (still
live there to this day), and we are strapped. And nobody can
tell me our bodily fluids don't have a warped sense of humor,
because this is the exact time his sperm and my egg pick to
dance the tango. Now I am pregnant. Alex is terrified of raising

a family on such a meager salary. I know he is thinking of our honeymoon.

"What's the use of going to Italy if I can't drink wine or eat soft cheese?" I say. "We'll go next year."

Alex gathers my hands in his and gazes into my eyes. "Are you sure, Llama?" he says. "Are you sure?" My name is Lena, but Alex always calls me Llama. Drama Llama, if I get particularly worked up about something.

"Of course I'm sure," I say. I'm not at all. I am confused. I am terrified that if we don't go now, we'll never go. Does he want me to insist? Why doesn't he insist? I want him to insist. Will this set a precedent for the rest of our marriage? I wait, and he does not insist. It's a definite chink in his armor. I make a conscious decision to play the martyr. "Next year we'll take our child with us and properly introduce him or her to gondola rides, savory pasta, and cobblestone streets," I say.

Alex kisses me and says, "Our child will love it. And we'll still find plenty of time to be alone. After all, Italy is the country of *amore.*"

"Let's practice," I say. "We'll get wine and cheese, overflow the bathtub, and pretend it's Venice."

But when our daughter Rachel is a year old, instead of Italy we take her to a petting zoo where she promptly develops an irrational fear of tiny goats. I never imagined motherhood would be so time-consuming and exhausting. Why in the world would I want to take an infant to Italy? I showed her my favorite Monet painting in a lovely book I purchased, and she spit up on it. If we went to Italy now, Alex would enjoy it, and I would be on baby duty.

And then, just when Rachel is getting old enough to appreciate more than the primary colors, I secretly start to plan another trip. I throw up from excitement. At least that's what I think. But no. I am pregnant again. We're already in debt, and I just got over the baby stage. This is the American Dream? It's going to kill me. God does not want me to go to Italy, I think. He is tormenting me. And of course, I love our son, Josh. But once again I am exhausted, and we are in more debt, and no

matter how much I clean, our home still looks like the site of a
toy factory explosion. Alex works long hours, and one kid or
the other is always at the doctor, and one day Alex brings home
a golden retriever puppy, and I say no because who else is going
to end up walking it and picking up its poop, and taking it to
the vet, but it is a cuddly ball of orange fur, and she makes
Rachel belly laugh like an old man. Most days, by the time the
kids are in bed and the dog is sleeping, I'm too wrecked to do
anything but watch television. Some days I wonder what my life
would have been like if I had never met Alex Wallace. The only
paints I touch are finger paints. Even my macaroni sculptures
suck. Rachel's are way better. Alex is still himself, still pursuing
his love of all things marble and stone, yet I am turning into
someone else, someone I don't always recognize and don't always like. I am so far from the girl I used to be, and I am jealous
of her, as if she is an entirely different person. I still love Alex,
but I no longer imagine painting him.

When vacation times come around, we go to Gettysburg, and
New York City at Christmas time, and New Hampshire one summer, and Disneyland. We can't afford to go to Europe, but we
do make it to Toronto one year and let the kids gorge on maple
syrup. Gradually, we even stop speaking of Italy; neither of us
wants to admit that we have become those people—the kind
who do not do what they say they are going to do. Until the day
Alex comes home from work, asks my mother to babysit, and
takes me to the Olive Garden.

It's so rare that the two of us go out, especially on a school
night. I feel a little naughty and thrilled. Even if it is a chain
restaurant near the mall. I finish two family-sized bowls of salad
and an entire basket of bread by myself. Alex orders the soup
(the soup!) and barely takes a bite.

"What's going on, Alex?"

His drops his spoon into the bowl. It sends ripples through
his Pasta Fagioli. "I've been offered an incredible work opportunity."

"Okay." I know from his tone, he doesn't think I'm going to
like it.

"It's in Florence. Teaching Renaissance art at the American university."

"Are you kidding me?"

"Llama."

"You're serious?"

"As a heart attack."

"Oh my God. Oh my God." It feels like Christmas. Which is also my birthday. Excitement times two. It's taken us sixteen years, but we are going to do it. We are all going to Florence. "Oh my God," I say again. I wish I hadn't eaten all the breadsticks so I could make them do a happy dance. "When do we leave?"

Alex gently takes my hands. Why isn't he smiling? "Just one semester."

"A whole semester?" I whoop. A whole semester? That's a long time. That's like living there. Just when I thought my life was stale and monotonous and never going to get exciting ever again. I am a new woman. You just never know what's around the corner. I used to hate when people said that, but now I see they are right. Oh my God. I am going to live in Florence. I am going to start painting again. This *is* the dream. We are going to be living the dream. I am going to have sex with him tonight no matter what. "Let's go. We have to start packing." I throw my arm up like I'm going to catch a cab, hoping our waitress will see me, since I can't tell which one was ours in the sea of striped shirts.

"I have to leave next week."

"I'm a fast packer."

"Llama. Listen to me."

"Why aren't you more excited?"

"I'm going to Florence. Not all of us. Just me."

My hand falls to my side. My heart thumps. An immediate lump forms in my throat. I did not just hear him say that. "What the hell are you talking about?"

"We can't just yank the kids out of school."

"Why not? Art. Architecture. A new language and culture. They'll learn more there in one semester than they would the entire year in school."

"What about soccer? And dance? Josh has a tournament, and Rachel has a big recital coming up."

"They'll get over it." I know, the second I say it, it isn't exactly true. Josh is obsessed with soccer, and Rachel with dance. But truth be told, neither of them are very good at their respective sports, so it's not like I'm stunting the next Beckham or Baryshnikov.

"They're putting me up in a dorm. Not even a hotel. A dorm."

"We'll look for a place on craigslist or something."

"What about Stella?"

"My God, Alex. She's a dog. We board her. You don't want us to go; is that it?"

"It's just not logistically or financially in our best interest."

I cannot believe he is sitting across from me, saying this. There is no way, no way, he's going to Florence without me. "It's Florence, Alex. Florence." I give him the look, the one that says, *I gave up my honeymoon for you.*

"Here's what I've been thinking. You guys will come at the end of the semester. When I've made some money, and actually have time to show you guys around. We should be able to afford four or five days."

"No, no, no," I say. "We all have to go together."

"It's work, Lena."

"It's Florence, Alex," I say. We spend the entire time up until he leaves arguing about it. But the kids don't want to go, and when I try and talk to the teachers they don't see how there is enough time to arrange "homeschooling" or any viable alternative. When Alex actually goes, I am stunned, truly stunned. It feels like I've been deeply betrayed. I try and convince myself he's right—it's just work. It doesn't help.

I want to stroll the piazzas, tour the Uffizi Gallery, and drink Tuscan wine on a rooftop overlooking the undulating hills. I sit in Alex's office, staring at him on the computer screen. He's been there almost two weeks now, and he keeps saying how fast it's going, but he's a liar. Tranquilized sloths move faster. He looks so happy, and really tan, and I feel as if I have a mouthful of glass. He's talking, and I'd better start listening, because so far I haven't heard a word he's said.

"So I took the class, on the spur of the moment, just said, 'Right, everybody up,' and we caught a bus back to the center of the city, and our timing was perfect, Llama, it was like it was meant to be."

"Wow."

"We stood back and just gazed at it. The surface was shiny and white, but then as the sun slipped down, it was true, the marble glowed pink. It was incredible."

"Where was this?"

"What do you mean?"

"What glowed pink?"

"The marble."

"I got the marble part—but the marble where?"

"You weren't listening."

"Just tell me."

"The Duomo." He sounds frustrated. With me. I hate him in this moment. The only thing glowing pink around here are the towels I just put in the dryer because when I asked Rachel to throw them in the laundry, she didn't notice the red kitchen towel hiding in among them. And he's frustrated with me? Why would he go on and on about how great it is when he knows I want to be there? Doesn't he want us there? How much am I supposed to take?

"I really don't care," I say.

"Lena."

"I mean it. Good for you. I have to go."

"Don't hang up mad."

"Do you even miss me?"

"Of course. How can you ask that?"

"I can't stand that you're there without me."

"You're going to be here soon, Llama. Look how fast these two weeks have gone by."

"Right." So I try. Because he's right. We will be there soon enough. I might as well make the best of it. Soccer practice. Dance lessons. Homework. Taking care of the dog, cooking all the meals, doing all the shopping, all the yard work. The kids miss their dad. They blame me, and although I know it's mis-placed—just transference—it's not fair. Some nights I yell at them for the same reason. Rachel turned fourteen without her father at her birthday party. I let her have a sleepover with all her friends, and I made a special cake, and bought her an iPod, and all she could talk about was the top he bought her in Italy. The next morning after dropping all of her friends at their homes, she asked if we could go shopping so she could find something new to match her new favorite shirt, and I had the gall to say no, that we had a house ravaged by teenagers that needed cleaning.

"I wish Dad were here instead of you!" she said.

Josh, who is only nine, hurt my feelings too, although he's too young to do it on purpose. We were at one of his soccer tournaments, and just before the game Josh handed me a pic-ture of Alex. "Hold this up during the game," he said. "It will be like somebody is here." As if I didn't count. As if without Alex, I am half of nothing. I record as many of their games and dance recitals as I can, and Alex watches them, but I get the feeling that he's just doing it politely, waiting for the chance to tell an-other story about how wonderful it is to live in Florence. For the next few calls, I make a concentrated effort to listen and be truly happy for him. The closer the time draws to us joining him, the more my excitement grows. I call Alex, determined to nail down our travel plans.

"I have to book our plane tickets. When is your last day at the university?" There is a moment of silence on his end. I can't tell if it's a long-distance delay or if he just isn't responding. It feels like forever before he speaks.

"Llama. Keep an open mind."

"No."

"They've asked me to stay for a second semester."

I don't answer right away. Verbally, anyway. But my head is shaking, and I know I'm sporting an "I knew it" expression. I hate him. I hate myself. I can't take one more second. "No," I say. "You're done. We're coming."

"It doesn't change anything. It just delays it a semester."

"No."

"Hear me out. By the time the second semester is over, it will be summer. Instead of a few days, we could spend a month here if you want."

"We can't afford a month."

"That's the thing. They really, really want me. There's a bonus in it for us."

"How is living in Italy without us 'for us'?"

"The bonus would allow us to stay in Italy for at least a month. Maybe more."

"We're coming now. Tell them no."

"Ten thousand dollars. It's a ten thousand dollar bonus."

"Ten thousand dollars?"

"Yes. It would pay for our entire trip."

"Damn it."

"You can start researching—I'll leave it up to you. If you can make the ten thousand stretch the whole summer, we'll stay the whole summer."

I do like to plan. And if we're there the entire summer then it will feel like I got to live there too. "If I can make it stretch—you swear we can stay the whole summer?"

"I want us to stay the whole summer. I love it here."

I ignore that part. "Swear on it," I say. "Swear on our lives."

"Lena."

"Per favore." I've been learning a few words here and there.

"I swear on your lives."

A few days now, or the whole summer. It kills me, but so does the prospect of missing out on an entire summer, so I agree to wait.

But the next three months change me. My single-parenting life is stuck on an endless loop. All the cooking, all the cleaning, all the dog walking, all the driving to soccer practice, dance lessons, doctor's appointments. Alex starts calling me less and less. Sometimes, when he talks, he slips into Italian. He looks happy, so damn happy, and I am turning mean, and ugly. Most days I miss him: his smell, his presence at the dinner table, his beautiful body in bed (I can't handle the big empty spot where my husband should be)—him running into the kitchen late at night, throwing open an art catalogue to a centerfold of a naked statue, and exclaiming, "What I wouldn't give to get my hands on that!"

But some days I look around and think, "We've done pretty well without you." It's true too. He's been gone almost six months, and we haven't fallen apart. Lately I've been noticing men noticing me. Dads at soccer games and what not. Not that I flirt with them or anything, but it's nice to have male attention, any attention at all. Alex should be thinking about this. He should be dying to get me there or to get back home. But he doesn't seem to miss me at all. Why is that? How can he be fine going six months without making love to his wife? What does that say about our marriage? What is he doing in Italy and whom is he doing it with? I start to think of Italy as the enemy, Florence as my husband's mistress. I would have had more access to Alex these past six months if he'd been in prison. Alex calls me on a really bad day, in the middle of another really bad mood.

"Llama. When you guys come, we'll—"

"We're not coming. You're coming home."

"Come on."

"I mean it. I can't take this anymore. You are coming home."

"We'll talk about this later."

"I will never, ever set foot on Italian soil." And there it is. I've planted a flag. I know the minute I say it, it is a huge mistake, but now it is up to Alex to make me come around. Reassure me how much he loves me. A little begging would be nice.

"You're being ridiculous." This is what I get instead. He loves Florence more than he'll ever love me. I lash out.

"You know, I never expected you to be Husband of the Year, but what kind of father leaves his own children for six months?" There is that interminable silence again. I can hear him breathing. I should stop. "You should have insisted we go sixteen years ago. You couldn't stand up to the university then, and you can't now. You're not a man at all. You're a coward. You've ruined

Italy for me. Why don't you just stay there and never come home?"

He looks me in the eye as his right hand moves the mouse, and the next thing I know, we are disconnected. He hung up on me. He actually hung up on me. In our sixteen years of marriage, he has never hung up on me, ever.

He's a good father, a great father; I never should have said that. When he's here he doesn't miss a soccer game or a dance recital, and at least three times a week he's home for dinner, and if you ask the man to pick up tarter sauce on the way home, he picks up tarter sauce on the way home. He has to know I didn't mean it. There is something wrong with me. Some nasty fighter in me that always has to come rushing out, swords drawn. And then I strike. That's the problem with knowing where someone's wounds are; once you open them up, you're going to make them bleed.

I feel really, really bad, and I'm ashamed of how petty I've become.

But he's the one who went without me in the first place, and he should have insisted we go sixteen years ago, or at least found some time to take us before now, and how would he have dealt with it if I had been the one to go without him? Then again, I knew who I married, didn't I? Nothing excites that man like fifteenth century sculptures, not even me. I just want my husband back. I want everything to be okay. Starting tonight. That's right. Alex is coming home. Tonight. And even though I'm still bitter, I want to work on my marriage. Maybe we can go to counseling. Because, "Where did you two meet?" is the question everybody asks when you're in love. But "Didn't you see the signs?" is what they say when everything goes to shit.

CHAPTER 2

I'm a wife on a mission. I'm throwing a welcome home party, and it all begins with hanging the welcome home banner. The ladder wobbles as I climb. It is an outside ladder, meant to sink into soft, packed dirt, and it does not like the uneven slate tiles in my kitchen. We have that in common; I've been dying to get these tiles repaired for years now, but I will not greet Alex with a honey-do list. I've done enough damage already. My cell phone sits on the kitchen counter cold and unblinking, like a silent assassin. Of course he can't call from the plane, but I wish I could talk to him right now, tell him it's all going to be okay. He's still upset that we didn't come. But this is for the best; I don't want to go to Italy right now, but maybe after he's home and we're in a better place we can revisit the subject with a caring therapist who will make him see what a horrendous thing he did by going to Florence without me.

In one hand I grasp the banner, in the other a hammer, which leaves me no choice but to put the two large nails in my mouth. When I reach the top step, the ladder teeters and shakes, a mini-earthquake beneath my feet, and the five-foot banner ripples as if startled by a burst of unwelcome wind. I freeze, and envision swallowing one of the giant nails, seeing an X-ray, a ghostly imagine of the steel shank puncturing my lungs. I will be laughed at, the human equivalent of Stupid Pet Tricks. Why didn't I put them in my pocket? Because I am a Florence Widow, and it's done damage to my brain. It's like being a Football Widow, only a thousand times worse. At least Football Widows can eat leftover chicken wings and cuddle up to their husbands at night, whereas I struggle to fall asleep, alone, convinced he's strolling piazzas with a bottle of Super Tuscan in one hand and an Italian supermodel in the other.

Steady now. I breathe slowly, through my nose, and the ladder settles. Moving my arm as if I am performing major surgery, I place the right-hand side of the banner just above our kitchen window. It's the perfect spot; Alex will see it the minute he walks in. I remove one nail from my mouth, carefully place it in the corner, and hammer it in. Plaster flakes off, and a speck sticks in my eye.

It hurts; it hurts; it hurts. I squeeze my eye shut. It's like a paper cut in my pupil. I just have to get through this. I will wash my eye out soon. Just keep going. What irony, if I were to go blind today of all days. Today, when he is finally coming home, will be the day I swallow nails and go blind. My own personal apocalypse. Can I get some kind of metal poisoning from nails in the mouth?

Roses go in the mouth; nails do not. I would have asked the kids to help, but they don't know he's coming home tonight. It's a surprise. I can't wait to see their faces. This is indeed a banner day. I am trying to do too many things at once, but that's typical when you're raising two kids by yourself. But they're in no danger of wandering into the kitchen and spoiling the surprise, for they scattered far and wide the minute I asked them to help with dinner. Well, not far enough actually, for Josh is in the living room playing that zombie video game that I hate. Grunt, grunt, grunt, scream, scream, scream. That can't be good for him. But he's getting away with it tonight. Everything goes tonight. I am grateful they do not realize this, for they would be at my feet begging me for a puppy.

"Sorry, Stella," I say, although our aging golden retriever is nowhere to be seen. I'm sure she's under my bed; there's a storm coming, or so they say, but aren't they wrong like 99.9 percent of the time? Tonight would be the night though, wouldn't it, that they're right? Alex's plane will be fine, I tell myself, and on time.

I blink my one good eye and slowly go back down the ladder. I take the remaining nail out of my mouth, quickly rinse out my bad eye, then scoot the ladder over four feet and repeat the process on the other side. The banner has been hung. I climb down, and survey my work.

BENTORNATO A CASA ALEX!

It's perfect. A welcome home sign and an Italian lesson for the kids rolled into one. It's a little crooked, but I don't care; it's perfect. I clasp my hands to my lips and tears spring to my eyes. *Good people come home to those who wait.* I open the fridge and check to make sure the champagne hasn't run off with the Brie. They're both where I left them. They'd better be, given what I paid for them. I shut the fridge, then open it again and point at the champagne and Brie with a "Gotcha!" look. They don't respond. I am giddy, drunk on the anticipation of seeing my handsome husband again. I didn't think this day would ever come; I didn't think I'd survive this, and now here it is. I know this is going to be one of the best days of my life, one of those days I will tell our grandchildren about. Maybe in the retelling I will leave out the near lung-piercing, potential mouth-poisoning, and self-blinding bits. Absence does make the heart grow fonder, and as I've discovered during this time—wiser. I am going to be a better wife than I was when he left; I am going to make up for not being a particularly good sport about this latest adventure. And, I am going to have to tread very, very lightly around certain subjects, because I am still furious with him for going, even if it's not logical, and if I don't get a handle on my resentment I'm going to strike when we all least expect it.

I look at the clock. It is nearly five p.m. Two more hours. That's all I have to wait. I can hardly believe it. Right now, he's sitting on that plane, thinking of us. Thinking, *In just a few short hours I'll be having dinner with my family.* He's thinking of how good it will feel to see Josh and Rachel, to have them squeal with delight when he walks in that door, and then to kiss his wife like it's the first time. And then there's this evening. Back in my bed, back in our bed. I can only imagine what satisfying six months of pent-up longing will be like. Maybe we can have angry sex, make-up sex, and I-really-missed-you sex all rolled into one. *Mama Mia!*

But now I wish we were waiting at baggage claim with the banner, and flowers, and hugs, and kisses, a forty-piece band. Although I'd be tempted to have the banner say: DON'T YOU EVER LEAVE ME AGAIN. I wonder if Alex suspects this, which is why he came up with the idea of surprising the kids. He wants to come in the door and casually sit down to dinner like in one of those heart-warming videos of a soldier coming home from war. Alex teaching Renaissance art for two semesters is hardly the same as a man returning home from war, but we've missed him nonetheless, and the kids are going to freak. I'm going to freak. Okay. I'm already freaking.

But now I have the strongest feeling that I should have insisted on the airport thing instead. I will distract myself by making Spaghetti Bolognese and practicing my Italian love phrases. I'm hoping a familiar dish and romantic utterings in a foreign language will ease his transition back to us. I just didn't know there would be so many to choose from. The Italians have a hundred ways of saying "I love you."

I study the list of amorous words I pulled off the Internet, convinced that the fate of my marriage depends on picking the exact right one. Something that also says, *Sorry I didn't handle you being in Florence without me very well.* But what wife would?

I will make it up to him; I will be nicer, more romantic, starting right here, right now. Listen to this. *Sono sopraffatto da te. I am drunk with you.* Isn't that beautiful? My tongue literally tingles when I say it. Never, ever would it have crossed my mind to say, *I am drunk with you.* Why not? What's wrong with me? It's love! Listen to this one. *If you weren't, I'd invent you.* If some man, and of course by that I mean my husband, looked at me and said, "If you weren't, I'd invent you," I would die of happiness. I would never get angry with him for anything again ever. Not all of the phrases are so poetic, but the sheer number of them just proves that the Italians know the ins and outs of *amore.* I don't know how this squares up with the Mafia and their history of investing in cement shoes, but it's not what I choose to focus on. Violence is that same fiery passion turned inside out I suppose. But my husband is coming home, and I want to think only of love.

I am dazzled by you.
I am weak for you.
You're everything I want.
You have bewitched me.

Alex will probably think I've been abducted by aliens if I say any of these. Gaze into his eyes and say, *I am weak for you.* But being romantic for a change might do the trick. *Alex, you're back. Thank God. I am weak for you.* Quietly, I try whispering it out loud, but it comes out with an accent closer to French than Italian. I try it with a German one. *I am veak for you. My heart is like flopping fish.* My laughter echoes through our outdated kitchen. But nobody is here to witness my mirth, so maybe it doesn't really count. Another loud grunt, followed by eerie music, punctures my thoughts.

"Josh!" It's impossible to practice even something as simple as *"ti amo,"* when he's harpooning zombies in the background. I look to the living room and I open my mouth as if I'm going to yell again, but in the end I shut it, listening now to the sound of my jaw creaking. When did it start doing that? I open and shut it several more times, noting the creak about every other time. From the other room comes a bloodcurdling zombie scream.

"YEAH MAN!!!" Josh says. I creak my jaw again and glance at the big clock above the stove. It always reminds me of a train station, and I have the urge to go somewhere, anywhere. Flee! I glance at the ceiling, wondering what our fourteen-going-on-thirty-year-old, Rachel, has been doing in her room for so long. Most likely entombed in earphones and social networking. What if she's chatting with a predator? I've put restrictions on the computer, but I certainly don't trust that it's a hundred percent safe. I've talked to her of course, but that doesn't mean she's listening. Since she turned fourteen she has taken to pretending she is a stranger in her own home, like a polite but distant exchange student from Finland.

"Torna a casa. Ho bisogno di te," I say to the ground beef sitting on the counter. *Come home. I need you.* The ground beef does not answer.

I use a meat cleaver to chop baby carrots for the salad. I love the heft of the giant blade, like pushing down on the handle with the heel of my hand, working up a slicing rhythm. Meat sauce simmers in a large red pot on the burner, and thick slabs of garlic bread sit on the counter awaiting the warming stove. It smells spicy, and fresh, and close enough to homemade. Alex will be impressed, and maybe it will make up for my bad attitude. Stella trots into the room and within seconds is at my feet. Snout in the air, eyes pleading.

"They're just carrots," I say. "You won't like them."

I will. I will like them. Try me.

I nudge a carrot over the edge, and Stella dives for it. She chews for a second, then looks at me. Horrified. Betrayed. *How could you do that to me?* She spits the orange mess on the floor.

"Told you," I say. But I feel bad. I love this dog. I could probably come up with a hundred ways to say *I love you* to her. That doesn't say much for me, but I was raised by stoic people who found it much easier to love animals than people. I reach for the paper towels on top of the fridge, and at the same time pull down the box of dog treats. Stella accepts my apology, then glances at the stove where the meat sauce is simmering.

"Not a chance," I say. "Shoo." I am pouring myself a glass of wine when the doorbell rings. Just as I reach the foyer, Josh gazelle-leaps in front of me, and throws open the door. A gust of wind blows in, rattling my empty flowerpots in the corner of the porch. A large cardboard box sits on the welcome mat, and a deliveryman hurries back to his truck. His brown uniform recedes into the darkness, his truck roars to life, and he is off.

"Till we meet again," I call after him.

"You're weird," Josh says.

"I know." The smell of the strong summer wind mingles with garlic from the kitchen, and I suddenly think of Halloween even though it is the end of May. It's not normally this dark this early, but they have been predicting this storm for days now. Not a single streak of afternoon blue remains. The heavens have been slashed with broad strokes of dirty gray. In the near distance, rectangular patches of black clouds steadily move in, like ocean barges plodding their course. The tips of the oak trees that Alex planted in the yard, one after each kid was born, whip their leaves back and forth, and the wind chimes that came with the house dangle and plink above our heads. "FTD," Josh says with his face kissing the box. "Is that like the fire department?"

"Flowers," I say. Josh maneuvers the box about a foot inside the door and tears into it. I shut the door just as Rachel bounds down the steps wearing what appears to be a red tube top as a dress. She is a siren; she is a stop sign; she is only fourteen.

"What's that?" She leans over the stair rail and stares at the box. Her breasts bulge out of the tight dress, boosted by the wooden bannister on which they rest. Seemingly overnight, she has the body of a woman, and nobody asked me if I was ready, and I am not, and she is definitely not, and I want to stop it.

"Rachel Anne Wallace, what are you wearing?"

"Like it?" She comes to the bottom of the steps and twirls around. "It's what all the women in Florence are wearing."

"Go, change. Now." *Is that what all the women in Florence are wearing?*

"Dufus!" Rachel says. "You can't use that!" I am just about to reprimand Rachel for calling her brother a dufus when I notice Josh towering over the box with my meat cleaver. He's definitely my son. Next he'll be chewing on nails.

"Give me that," I say. I take it out of his hand.

"I couldn't find the scissors."

"Well, this was an excellent second choice." I should probably look for the scissors myself, but I have no idea where they are, so I slice through the tape with the meat cleaver and allow Josh to rummage inside.

"You're right! Flowers!" Josh lifts up a dozen long-stem roses. They explode from a tall green vase strangled with a big red bow. I have never seen roses so fat and gorgeous. They must have cost a fortune. My mother's voice hovers inside me. *Men only give flowers for two reasons: It's your birthday, or they feel guilty about something.*

"It's from Dad!" Josh says. I take the card out of his hands and open it.

I'M SORRY.

The words echo in my head, and my heart becomes a pattering drum. *He's sorry? Why is he sorry? I'm the one who's sorry. Get here quick so I can tell you. And kiss you. And feed you. And take you to bed. I miss you, Alex. You don't need to be sorry. You're coming home. Why are you sorry? What did you do?* Josh is looking at me so expectantly that I force a smile.

"What does it say?"

"It says, 'Just because. Love Alex.' " I shove the card in my pocket.

"Grandma says—" Rachel starts.

"Go upstairs and change," I say. I do not need my daughter quoting my mother. Why didn't he just bring the roses with him?

Thunder cracks and lightening flashes through the room seconds before the rain tatters on the roof and slashes at the windows. Will his flight be delayed? Where is it right now? Is he safe? *Don't be sorry, Alex; just be safe. Why are you sorry?* If he's not on that plane, for any reason, any reason at all, I am going to kill him.

"Everyone look for open windows." I run into the den. Sure enough, two of them gape at me. I heard the weather report this morning. Why didn't I think to close them? Alex is the one for details, not me. I slam them shut and return to the hall. Josh holds a piece of paper in his right hand, and Rachel stands over the roses, hands on hips.

Josh shoves the paper in my face. I move it away so I can see it.

"Look at it," Josh says. He moves it back.

Again, I thrust it away. "I can't focus if it's jammed up against my eyes."

"Weird," Josh says.

You don't know the half of it. My mandible is creaking too. The piece of paper is actually an eight by eleven-inch picture. A tell-tale purple streak in the upper right-hand corner tells me Josh has been using Alex's printer. It's facing the wrong way. I turn it to landscape. There stands Alex with a group of young students posing in front of the Duomo. Josh jabs at it. His fingernails are dirty. When was the last time he had a bath?

"It's Dad. Standing in front of the Dumbo."

"The Duomo."

"Whatever."

"Not whatever, *mio amore*. One's an architectural marvel; the other's a little elephant with big ears." I place my hands by my ears and scissor them out as far as they can go.

"A man only gives you flowers if it's your birthday or he feels guilty about something," Rachel suddenly announces as if she's just worked it out. I trace Alex's face with my fingertips. He is grinning ear to ear.

"Is it your birthday?" a muffled voice says. I glance over. Josh is wearing the box on his head. I should probably tell him to take it off, but as long as he can talk, he can breathe.

"Mom's birthday is on Christmas, dufus," Rachel says.

"Find the dog, now," I say. "And don't call your brother a dufus." I glance at the picture again. My stomach is hit with that "Why did I get on this rollercoaster?" feel. I look closer.

Josh thrusts his index finger in the air. "That's right! I forgot! Merry birthday, merry birthday, merry birthday," he starts to sing to the tune of "Jingle Bells."

Rachel gives me another look. *You're telling me he's not a dufus?* How can Alex stand there smiling and leave me here all alone? His right hand is cupped over his eyes, and his head tilts to the left as if the person next to him is whispering something in his ear. I look to see who this mystery person is, but she has been cut out of the frame. On purpose? All that remains is a long strand of wavy black hair, resting at the nape of Alex's neck. It seems so intimate, even though it is just a wisp of hair. Alex probably didn't even feel it. But boy do I feel it. I have a sudden desire to grab the rest of her hair out by its roots. Another crack of thunder, even louder than the one before, jars me from the picture.

"Stella," I say to Rachel. "Now."

Rachel rolls her eyes, but then turns on her heels and runs up the stairs. "She's probably already peed."

Probably. But I want her to know she is not alone. "Where did you get this?" I say, bouncing the picture at Josh even though he cannot see me from inside the box.

"Dad's Facebook page," he says.

I am impressed he can still follow the conversation. "Dad doesn't have a Facebook page."

"He does! He even has friends."

"Does he now?"

"Not very many though. Less than two hundred."

Less than two hundred? Alex has two hundred friends?

"It's pretty much all girls."

"Really?" I try to keep my voice light. Since when? Why didn't Alex tell me? I don't even have a Facebook page. I kind of want one, but Alex and I always make fun of people with Facebook pages. It's our thing. Like those people who have never eaten at a McDonald's and so the first thing they tell you when you meet is that they've never eaten at a McDonald's.

That's Alex and me with Facebook. We love to go to faculty parties and announce it at the first opportune moment. Then we find each other in the crowd, lock eyes, and grin at each other in smug solidarity. Yes, it's obnoxious, but it's our thing. We're horrified when we see families at restaurants all texting at the table instead of talking to each other, and by about the fourth time we witnessed this, we looked into each other's eyes and we vowed we would never, ever get a Facebook page, and I fell for it! Was he keeping secrets or had he forgotten to mention he was now one of those people we like to make fun of, and by the way, he has two hundred girlfriends?

Rachel pounds back down the stairs. "Found her! She was under your bed!" Stella is perched on the top stair, peering down at us, but she refuses to come any closer.

"It's all right, girl," I say. I wonder how you say *Without your big orange head, I am nothing,* in Italian?

Rachel picks up the envelope that came with the flowers. "It doesn't even have your name on it," she says.

"Maybe they're for all of us," I say. Maybe it is for all of us, and maybe it's not so ominous. It just means he feels guilty he hasn't been there for us, and he can't wait to come home.

"Or maybe he's afraid of calling you by the wrong name."

"The wrong name?"

"You know. Like he has a girlfriend, and he sent her flowers too."

"Rachel Anne!"

"I'm kidding. I'm kidding."

"I don't care. That's not nice."

"You're yelling."

She's right. I am yelling. I'm shaking too. And my mandible is creaking again. "Go upstairs and change. Now."

Rachel drops the envelope. It lands on top of one of the roses. She turns on her heels and pounds up the stairs. "Okay, okay. Gawd. It's not my fault if Dad has a girlfriend." I let out a cry, and Stella is a tornado of orange down the stairs. I drop to my haunches and throw open my arms. Stella barrels into me and tucks her big orange head into my stomach. She is shaking too.

"Okay, okay, sweetie. It's okay."

"You talk nicer to the dog than you do to us," Rachel says. Stunned, I glance up at my daughter who is watching me from the top of the stairs. And then she disappears as another crack of lightening lights up the roses. Stella whines, and soon the smell of piss reaches my nostrils. I step back just as a puddle of urine begins to spread from underneath Stella, who, keeping her body as low to the ground as possible, starts to slink away. I look at the flowers again.

"Eww," the box says. "Who peed?" One more flash of lightening is all it takes to jar something in me, and suddenly, I see it in my mind's eye. I grab the picture, and look at it, really look at it, zeroing in on Alex's left hand. The sun is shining, oh so bright, which is why his hand is cupped over his eyes (he's always leaving his sunglasses and reading glasses somewhere), and that's when I notice what's missing. There's no glint, no shiny reflection from the hot Italian sun off his ring finger. And why would there be? It's naked as the day he was born. For the first time in sixteen years, Professor Alex Wallace isn't wearing his wedding ring.

CHAPTER 3

I feel as if someone has punched me in the stomach. And that's when I know the right phrase, the only phrase. The phrase I would use if Alex were standing before me right now. And it is not, *I am drunk with you,* or *I am dazzled by you,* or *You are the man of my dreams,* or even *If you weren't, I'd invent you.* It's much, much closer to the truth. And isn't that what love is all about? The truth? Opening our hearts and our veins to the ones we love, handing them the razor, and begging—please don't open me up and let me bleed? This is what I would say to my Alex, my husband, my absentminded professor if he were standing before me right now.

Senza di te la mia vita è un inferno.

And I mean it. I really and truly mean it, Alex, and please don't let this be anything other than a simple misunderstanding. *Senza di te la mia vita é un inferno.*

Without you, life is hell.

"What's burning?" Josh says.

In the commotion I've forgotten all about the meat sauce. It gurgles on the stove and bubbles up like a volcano threatening to erupt. I race into the kitchen and turn down the heat before dipping my spoon into it and tasting it. Oh God. Too quick, too hot! It scorches my tongue, and I can already feel it swelling to twice its size. I don't want to finish dinner, especially since Alex is not going to burst through the door and casually sit down at his rightful place at the table.

I don't want to eat; in fact, starting now, I am going on a hunger strike. All I want to do is check out Alex's Facebook page. But not with the kids hovering around waiting to be fed. I hurry over to the sink, turn on the faucet, and ferry cool water to my mouth. Why aren't they in here setting the table? I think I've asked them twice. Nicely. I can't always be the bigger person. I should just let dinner burn, and they can come and eat off the counter like savages.

Oh God, I'm a horrible mother and I'm having a nervous breakdown. I pick up the cell phone. There is no call from Alex. That is because he is on a plane? Right? I quickly dial his number; there are a lot of digits, but I memorized them a long time ago.

You've reached Professor Wallace—

"Alex," I say, "you're on the plane, right?" I hang up. I head for the den with Stella at my heels. I will check his flight status. The meat cleaver is still lying in the foyer next to the roses for anyone to trip over or slice off a limb. I will not be winning Mother of the Year anytime soon.

"Kids. Set the table," I yell. "And somebody put the garlic bread in." There is no reply. I swipe up the meat cleaver then continue into the den. I sit at the computer, and it hits me that Alex never gave me his flight info. He probably flew out of Rome, but he could have flown out of Pisa. Why didn't he give me the exact information? I call him again.

You've reached Professor Wallace—

God I hate that message. Why can't he just say Alex? "Why didn't you give me your flight information?" I say. "And the flowers are gorgeous, but to be honest they've made me a little confused. A lot confused. Why are you sorry? You'd better be coming home—"

His phone cuts me off, hangs up on me. Damn it. I bang my cell phone against the desk, then toss it onto the floor. I bring up Skype and wait for my image to appear in the left-hand corner. When it does, I almost hang up. I look horrible. Dark circles underneath my eyes, mascara smeared, hair shaggy. I'm wearing a faded old sweat shirt of Alex's because it smells like him. I have a dress waiting on the bed, a sexy black number, but I didn't want to get Bolognese sauce on it. Should I change first? No. Because he's not going to answer. He's on a plane. *Snakes on a Plane!* But Alex is not a snake. Right?

I take a deep breath and click on the CALL button. When the call connects, each ring makes my heart feel like it's skipping rope. And then, it answers. Something squeezes at my heart. Why is he answering; do they let you use videophones on the plane? I'm so flustered I almost hang up. But when the picture comes in, I don't see Alex or the interior of a plane.

There on the screen is an arresting young woman. She has flawless olive skin, dark brown eyes, and wavy black hair that falls past her breasts. I instantly see the strand of hair lying at the nape of Alex's neck. It's a match. She is wearing a tight, low-cut top that somewhat resembles Rachel's tight dress, only she is sporting twice the cleavage.

"Pronto?" she says. Italian. The girl is Italian. I've dialed the wrong number. I glance at the screen. It says I am connected to Alex Wallace.

"Um, hello? Do you speak English?

The young woman looks me in the eye, her pretty little chin tilts up, and she keeps her gaze steady. "Yes. I speak English." She sits back in her chair and waits. Now that her face isn't taking up the entire screen, I can clearly see that she isn't in Alex's dorm. Gone are the plain white walls and the Michelangelo calendar perpetually open to the statue of *David*. Here I can make out a kitchen behind her with a squat white refrigerator covered in pictures, and a counter littered with empty bottles of wine, their corks bobbing next to them like murder weapons carelessly dropped next to dead bodies. Besides the wine there is a large basket of fruit and a hunk of yellow cheese sitting on a cutting board. It's like an Italian still-life painting, and it feels as if I can reach out and touch it.

"I'm sorry. I must have the wrong number." I reach up to end the call.

"Lena?" Startled, my head jerks up. "You are Lena. No?"

No, I want to shout, but I am struck mute. She knows my name. My heart has caught on before my mind and is beating through my chest as if to say, "Let me at her!" Wait. My name appears on the screen, just like Alex's. She knows my name because of caller ID; that is all. Maybe she is a student and she borrowed Alex's computer. He is that kind of guy, isn't he? The type willing to loan his laptop to busty young Italian girls. Or maybe she stole it. Maybe she has his cell phone too. There are a lot of scam artists in Italy. Gypsies, thieves, you name it.

"Would you mind putting that down?" the girl says. She is pointing at me. My mind is blank. What is she talking about? "The big, big knife. How do you say? It's kind of 'freaking me out.' " She uses air quotes, then laughs. I glance at my hand. I am holding up the meat cleaver. I look like I should be hiding in a cornfield late at night waiting for little children.

I drop it on the desk with a clank. Stella leans forward to sniff it, and I gently push her away. "Sharp objects and soft snouts do not a match in heaven make," I say.

"What?"

"I'm talking to my dog."

"Mom?" Rachel yells from outside the door. "Are you talking to Dad?"

"No," I yell back. "Go set the table. Please." Do I add "please" because I want this girl to think I am civilized and polite? I glance at my image again. I think that ship has sailed.

"Is that Rachel?"

Oh God. That is not good. That is *so* not good. "How do you know our names?"

The door to the den rattles. "MOM. Why is the door locked?"

"SET THE TABLE NOW." I'm doing it again, screaming. I hate when I turn into crazy mom. Why can't I just get a break?

I really need a break. The girl on the video looks terrified, without marring even a speck of her beauty. I want to apologize, explain that somehow I have raised children who don't respond unless I yell. Something wet trickles onto the top of my right bare foot. Stella hangs her head and thumps her tail.

"Stella. No, no, no," I say. I whisper it, but it is too late.

"Stella? The dog that pees when you yell? Alex says she pees a lot."

"Who the hell are you?" *And how did you know that?*

"Alex named her, no? I do not understand this naming. Tennessee Williams? Desire? He wants to shout her name very loudly?"

Alex. Desire. Hearing this girl say those two words makes me want to reach through the screen and strangle her. I wipe my foot on the carpet. "You need to tell me who you are, right now."

"I'm Alexandria. Does my name mean anything to you?"

"Alexandria? Very funny." The name solidifies it; this is some kind of prank, some kind of scam. I feel better. I still want to kick her ass, and I'm worried about Alex, but I feel better. What kind of scam artist is she? And how does she know all of our names? And nobody could guess that Alex wanted to name Stella after *A Streetcar Named Desire* just so he could bellow her name like Stanley. Scared the poor dog to death even though he didn't mean to. He's the reason Stella pees, not me. But it's hardly the moment to be clarifying any of that.

"If you're one of his students, you are in serious trouble. You could get expelled. Do you understand—whatever your name is?" She can't be one of his students; his students are all American.

"Ah, because I am Alexandria, no? I understand. It is wild. Like fate." The girl disappears from the screen, and when she pops back up she is holding a purse. It looks designer and expensive; I can practically smell the leather through the screen. She roots through it, finds what she's looking for, then triumphantly hoists up an ID. She holds it way too close to the screen. "See? I am named after Alexander the Great." For the first time I notice that it's not just her accent that is difficult to understand; she is also slurring her words. And swaying as if listening to music only she can hear. She's drunk. That's what this is. A drunk girl, playing games. I can't even read the ID without my glasses, but I'm not about to admit that. "Alex was named after his great, great grandfather, right? Both of us named after 'Greats.' "

"I don't have time for this. Is Mr. Great there? You know—my husband?"

"He's not here."

A thousand pounds lift off me. "So you borrowed his computer?"

"Borrow? No, no, no. And he told me never to answer it, so he will be very angry. But he is already very angry. We had big, big fight. Our first, big, big fight. He slam all the doors. Slam! Slam! Slam! He do this to you?"

Fuzzy clouds swarm me as I see a montage of Alex slamming doors over the years. I yell; he slams. It isn't a perfect system, but it has carried us through numerous arguments. "Where is my husband?"

"I told him he must tell you. About us. About me. It is time. If we are going to live together for the summer."

"No. Alex is coming home tonight." I emphasize "tonight," for that is very specific and cannot be refuted. Even if he hasn't exactly given me his flight number and arrival time, he is coming home tonight. Even though he sent me roses and it's not my birthday, and it said SORRY in capital letters, he is coming home tonight.

"Alex is here. So I cannot see how he can be there. He is not coming home tonight, or tomorrow night, or even next week. He is staying for the summer with me."

"STOP LYING." I slam my hand into the desk. Stella trots for the door. Someone pounds on it.

"MOM?"

"Rachel. Honey. I mean it. Go away."

"You hate me," the girl says. "I understand. But I am with Alex. I am with him many months now. He loves me. He is sorry because he is so sensitive for you. This is why I love him.

My friends say this is not possible, a sensitive American man. But you know this is him, no?"

"You are a very sick girl. A very sick, lying, little girl."

"He says, 'Oh God, oh God, oh God,' when he comes. And his penis is a little bit curved on the end. Like this." She shapes her finger into a very familiar curve. I feel sick. This girl is making me sick. What man doesn't say "Oh God, oh God, oh God" when he comes? A roar fills the space where I used to have thoughts.

"Lies, lies, lies. Vicious lies."

"It is the truth. I am how you say—'Fucking your husband.' " She slaps her hand over her mouth as if she is the one in shock. "I'm sorry, I'm sorry, I use the wrong word. It is not fucking. We make love. Alex and I make love. I'm just so drunk."

I am drunk with you.

I am drunk because of you.

She hangs her head, and all I can see now is a pile of hair, sobbing. "He promised to tell you. He promised, he promised, he promised."

My hand guides the mouse over the END button. Push it. Just push it. Why can't I push it? There is a tiny, tiny, tiny part of me that fears it is true. I am staring at a car wreck, and I cannot look away. "Prove it," I say.

Alexandria's head snaps up. She looks totally wild and beautiful. I have never hated someone so much in my entire life. I watch her scan the room. Suddenly she picks up the computer. "Come," she says as if I am in the apartment with her, and she is giving me a friendly tour. The images on the screen jerk as she walks. I see a large bed with voluptuous red covers thrown back, a leopard-print chaise lounge with women's clothes draped over it, another chair piled with clothing, a window thrown open, a sheer curtain undulating in the breeze. I imagine pushing her out of it. This has to be a hoax; the place is a pigsty and Alex is a neat freak. She approaches a closed door and throws it open. I am afraid she is going to drop Alex's laptop. I am looking at a closet filled with men's dress shirts and pants. The kind Alex wears to work.

"Recognize these?" She runs her red-tipped fingernails down a pair of gray pants. I imagine Alex in them, her hand running down his leg.

"They're just clothes. Just men's clothes," I say. The screen bounces again, and we are in a tiny bathroom. Alexandria's hand reaches for a leather toiletry bag on the sink. She brings it into view. I stare at the big silver A. Underneath, it is engraved. LOVE, LLAMA. I gave it to him last Christmas. My birthday. That Christmas I actually had two presents for him. The leather toiletry case in case he forgot to give me a separate birthday present, and an iPad in case he remembered. The iPad is sitting in the back of my closet. A wave of guilt hits me. I can be so petty, and I'm not proud of it; I'm really not. I always vow to change, and then something happens and I get angry, and I can feel myself locking up inside, like a stuck gearshift.

Alexandria shoves her face in the camera. "Believe me now?"

"I'm going to kill you," I say. I have never said this to anyone. I've thought it of course, mostly about Alex, but the words have never come out of my mouth. Alexandria's head jerks in the opposite direction. Then, she looks at me, and a slow smile breaks over her face. She puts a finger up to her pouty lips.

"*Oh Dio mio.* He's back." She drops the laptop on the sink, facing out. Now I can see another door. She reaches toward the screen. "Muting you. You can hear us, but we can't hear you," she says, as if she is holding me captive. And she is. I could no more turn away from what is about to happen than I could cut my own arm off. Alexandria walks to the door, and I look at her ass. It is perfectly shaped, and it wiggles. Even drunk she has no problem walking in heels. And then, the front door opens, and in walks my husband.

"Alex!" I cry. Maybe she didn't mute it enough. Maybe he can hear me. "Alex!" But he does not look at me. It's him. He's right there. He's not on a plane. He's not coming home. This evil, lying bitch was telling the truth. I want to touch him, hear his voice, cover his lips with mine. I will forgive him everything if he will just look at me. I will give him the iPad. I will learn a hundred ways to say I love you. Alexandria launches herself into his arms. No. This isn't happening. Alex. No. Push her away! But he doesn't. I watch, horrified, as Alex wraps his arms around her. My husband.

"I'm sorry," I hear Alex say. He is apologizing to her. Not me. His wife. He is apologizing to her.

"You're going to be," I say. "You're going to be very, very sorry." What is he saying? He's speaking into her neck, and speaking Italian to boot.

"Speak English! Alex, Alex, Alex, Alex." I keep yelling, but he can't hear me. He doesn't glance my way once. He leans in and kisses her. It is a long, passionate kiss; in fact, it might not ever end. I'm sure tongues are involved. It is a horror show. I reach for the meat cleaver. Stella lets out a series of high barks.

"Alex. Please. Please. Please," I say. This is some kind of horrible nightmare. I am asleep. This is a dream. "ALEX, ALEX, ALEX."

"Mom?" Rachel's voice comes from outside the door again, but it is almost a whisper.

My kids are in the house. What kind of mother forgets her kids are in the house? A searing pain stabs me in the throat; shame spreads through the center of my chest. Alex pushes Alexandria against the door and continues to ravage her.

"MOM?" It's Josh this time.

"It's okay, kids," I say. "I'll be out in a minute." I try to sound normal, but it's too late. I hear a series of thuds on the door as if they are ramming into it. Suddenly it breaks open, and Josh and Rachel stumble into the room. I am looking at them before I realize they are looking, wide-eyed and startled, at the computer screen.

"Mom?" Rachel says. She wants me to explain why she can see her father kissing another woman. I truly wish I could.

"What is that?" Josh says. He steps forward. "Is that Dad? Who is the girl?"

"Oh my God," Rachel says. "Oh my God."

Alexandria is taking off her clothes. Her bare breasts spring forth. Oh my God. My son. His eyes are glued to the screen. Is he old enough to be lusting after his father's mistress too? Rage

I never knew possible floods me as I lunge for the computer. I grab the monitor and shut it off the wrong way, the way Alex told me never to shut it off, pressing the power button until the screen snaps to black.

"What's happening?" Josh says. "What's happening?" I shake my head, walk toward the busted door, then remember to go back for the meat cleaver.

"Mom," Rachel says. "I didn't mean it. I didn't know."

"Was that some kind of show? Who was that girl? Was that some kind of an art show?" Josh says.

"You are not that stupid," Rachel says.

"It's okay, kids," I say. "It's going to be okay." I walk out of the den, and they follow at a distance. Even Stella doesn't get that close. It might have broken my heart if I still had one. I grab the vase of roses on the way to the kitchen. Once I hit the ceramic tiles, I hurl it to the floor with all my might.

"Mom!" Rachel yells.

"Let's set the table," Josh says. "Mom. We're setting the table. We're setting the table." I stare at the vase on the floor. It made a loud thud, but didn't shatter. I can't even get that right. Water is gushing out, and the roses have slid out of the vase. Maybe it's me. I'm bringing this all on because I am not loving enough. Maybe if I am nice to the roses, they will be nice to me. I drop to my hands and knees and crawl toward them.

"Mom!" Rachel says.

I reach the roses, pick up a handful, and squeeze them until I feel the thorns digging into my palms. I want to drive them deep inside.

"Something is burning," Josh says. I jerk my head up. Soon, the stench of burnt garlic overwhelms the room, and wisps of smoke curl out from the stove like snakes being charmed.

"The garlic bread. Josh, you forgot the garlic bread."

"You told me to put it in," Josh says. "You didn't say anything about taking it out." The smoke alarm sounds.

"Turn off the stove, Josh. Don't open it. Just turn the knob to off."

"Mom," Rachel says, clapping her hands over her ears.

"Stella just peed." It must be a world record. How can it be possible to pee that many times? Josh removes the broom from the tiny closet in the kitchen and begins jabbing it into the fire alarm on the ceiling.

"Mom?" Rachel says.

I haven't moved from the floor. Why haven't I moved? That's right, I am here to be nice to the roses. "Hit it harder," I yell to Josh. He whacks it a good one, and the fire alarm breaks open. Its shell clatters onto the kitchen floor, and the batteries swing from the disconnected wires like hanged men. I am proud of him. The phone rings, and despite all the competing noises, it makes me jump. "Nobody answer that!"

"It's Grandma," Rachel says.

Of course. My mother. Apparently, her new boyfriend has let her up for breath. But not Alex. No. Alex is not calling. He does not even know we exist. Maybe being nice doesn't get you anywhere. I lift the cleaver above my head. "Do not answer!"

"Grandma?" Rachel says. "Help."

Just once. Just once I wish they would listen. I bring the cleaver down on the roses, and one-by-one begin chopping off their silky little heads.

FIRENZE
MONTH ONE

A coloro che vuol perdere, Dio prima toglie il senno.

Whom God will destroy, he first makes mad.

CHAPTER 4

We are here, in a taxi that picked us up from the Santa Maria Novella train station, navigating the narrow streets. Alex was right. Florence is beautiful; it is everything I ever imagined. Thick stone buildings support medieval arched doorways, and statues rest in the crevices, as if watching the people and cars passing on the cobblestone below. Little shops, and sidewalk trattorias, and people are everywhere. Colorful scooters and bicycles with baskets weave effortlessly in and out of the lines of compact cars. I imagine myself zipping around in a Vespa. It would be red, and I would have a helmet to match. My basket would be stuffed with a thick loaf of bread and a bottle of wine. I'd be racing home to a dinner party Alex and I would be throwing on our outdoor patio covered in blooming lavender vines and twinkling lights. With my husband. Holding hands, entertaining our friends. Delaying the cleanup afterward so we can make love on the rough bricks of the patio still warm from the afternoon sun. We are actually here, in the city I've always dreamed of, taking a bumpy cab ride to the university, and it's all tainted by the balled-up fist in my throat and the constant threat of tears. I want to stick my head out the window and scream. It is a miracle that I have so far resisted this temptation.

Our driver is young and endlessly enthusiastic about all things Italian. Lighter skin than I thought most Italian men had and soft brown curls that you want to run your fingers through. I think all three of us had our eyes glued to his biceps when he was lifting our luggage into the trunk. The only thing odd about him is his mustache. It is thick, and it looks as if *Magnum, P.I.* has just hit the Florence airwaves and he is a big fan.

"You are here, Firenze." He has a booming voice, and he pauses after the declaration as if waiting for a band to strike up. When we don't reply, he puts his hand over his heart and checks us out from his rearview mirror. He doesn't stop looking until I meet his eyes, and I only do so because I want his attention back on the crammed road. Rachel and Josh are each hanging out a window as if they are a couple of retrievers, and the real retriever is sitting next to me in the middle, with her head planted squarely on my chest. Either she is still woozy from the sedative, or she can smell grief on me the way some dogs can smell cancer. I pulled up to the doggie daycare to leave her behind, but at the last minute was gripped by this notion that the entire family had to be here to confront Alex, and Stella is family.

Each bump the driver races over (and he seems to delight in finding every one) sends a shock through my tailbone. Stella whines each time I wince, and she attempts to lick the entire side of my face with her lethargic, wet tongue.

"Firenze!" he says again. "You are here."

I know, I want to say. I realized it the minute we got off at the train stop that said FIRENZE.

"The heart of Italy. The most romantic city on all of the earth." He grins.

So romantic, you can end sixteen years of marriage in a few short months. Put that on the brochure. Rachel turns and gives me a look. It is as if she is reading my mind, and I feel violated. I need to be alone with all of these dark thoughts swarming around. I should have asked my friend Megan to watch them. I wasn't thinking anything through. I would have asked my father, but he is not long out of the hospital recovering from a heart attack. Although he and my mom divorced two years ago, I know the heart attack was brought on by my mother's going on a cruise with her new boyfriend Frank. My father has nurses, and friends from the Elks club, but I feel horrible that I'm not there. Some pair the two of them, my mother and Alex, but I won't think about my mother now either; all of my anger needs to be focused squarely on Alex. Rachel is still watching me. I pretend not to see her. She will grow up taking her cues from me. I need to hold it together for them. I need to stop thinking of that woman bearing her breasts on my computer screen, and Alex lusting after her. I don't know how people survive this. I am starting to think I will not be one of them.

"Your first time, no?"

Seeing my husband with a naked twenty-something? Yes, my first time. Although that doesn't necessarily mean it was his first time. Oh God. I have not considered this. Has he cheated on me before? With how many girls? How many times? How could the father of my children do this to us? I can see the sensationalized headlines: PROFESSOR OR PERVERT?

I am going to be sick. I hate sitting in the middle. "Are we almost there?"

Josh laughs, an innocent, happy laugh. Is it odd for him to be so happy? "You tell us not to ask that," he says. I force a smile at Josh, then look at the driver.

"In Florence, no matter where you are going, you are almost there," the driver says. "Except when there is traffic. There is always traffic. So even though we are almost there, we are sitting here."

"*Grazie,*" I say, although I don't know what I'm thanking him for.

"Grassy?" Josh says.

"*Prego,*" the driver says.

"Huh?" Josh says. He looks at me with his eyebrows all tensed up. Despite myself, I laugh.

"*Grazie* means 'thank you' and '*prego,*' I'm assuming, 'you're welcome.' "

"Oh. It sounded like grassy and Prego. You know like grass and spaghetti sauce."

"That's Ragú, dufus," Rachel says.

"Don't call him that," I say.

"So you here before? In Firenze?" The driver is like a broken record skipping and starting over. Oh God. Even my analogies age me. Alex's mistress is so young she's never even owned or played a record. It makes me want to smash one over her head.

"It's our first time," Rachel says. "But our father has certainly been here."

The driver grins and bobs his head. "Ah. *Si, si.*" He doesn't have a clue, but he's very happy.

Josh brings his head in from the window. "I think Dad was tricked," he says. "I think that girl tricked him with her boobs."

I don't know what to say. He's obviously processing it. Should I tell him not to say 'boobs'? It hardly seems like the point now. Yes, poor Dad, tricked by a girl half his age and her perky, big boobs.

"Do Italian girls like to trick men with their boobs?" Josh asks the driver. I lean over Rachel to roll the window down, but it's already down. We've literally only moved a few feet in the past twenty minutes.

"I do not know," the driver says, twirling a corner of his mustache with one hand while stretching his other over the back of the passenger seat and driving with his knee. "It is possibility."

Josh takes this in, then nods earnestly. "I think they do," he says. "I think they do."

I continue to stare out the window. Italy smells like car exhaust and lavender, and I could swear Parmesan cheese, but I wouldn't dare say it out loud; I don't want to stereotype. To my right, an old man stands in the doorway of a shop. He has suspenders and a long-sleeve shirt with the cuffs rolled up.

"Hoomiditity," the driver shouts. He's watching me watch the sweating old man, and he's trying to say "humidity." I suppose it is a hard word to say, and I should applaud his effort, but if I'm not careful he's going to crawl back here and sit on my lap.

"Yes," I say, and go back to looking at the old man. Poor guy, it's sweltering, and he's trying to fan himself with a sandwich. His face looks like he's survived a few big storms. In the short time I've been here, I've noticed that Italy has some of the most beautiful young men, but some of the ugliest older ones. I'm not trying to be mean; in fact, their faces have so much character it makes me want to sit down with them and hear their stories, but something definitely seems to happen in the transition; they age hard, as if plunging off the cliff of youth. Maybe, in a way, we all should. Wear our outrage at the aging process on our face. Next to the man is a scruffy-looking dog. Stella notices too and walks over Rachel's lap so she can hang her head out the window and gaze longingly at him, but the tough old dog doesn't even acknowledge her. He rests his chin on his paws and stares off into the distance as if life in this gorgeous city were an endless bore. Less than an hour in Italy and even my dog is trying to pick up a lover. I push her large rump down.

"Sit," I say. Stella sits half on Rachel, half on me.

"Ow, Mom. It's hot. I can't have this fur ball on me." Rachel shoves Stella gently until she is lying all on me. Suddenly, I feel a sweaty hand grasp mine. Josh is running his fingers over my diamond engagement ring. I feel a sense of desperation in his touch. It reminds me of how he used to grasp my finger with his tiny hands as a baby. I want to howl on the spot. My kids are going to grow up, and my husband is going to leave me, and this is not the life I dreamed up when I sat in that auditorium and fell madly in love with Alex Wallace. I willed him into life; I manipulated this marriage into existence. The thought that it was a foolish thing to do has never crossed my mind until now. He doesn't even know that we are here. He doesn't know that he's squeezed my heart to a pulp and regressed his son to an age where he wants to cling to his mother. I give it a minute so that he doesn't feel rejected, then move my hand. I am reminded that whatever happens to Alex and me will drastically affect these kids. It's not just the couple who is married; it's the whole family. They don't get a choice in this; they must be terrified. I will have to think of them first, always.

Is it weird that I'm still wearing my rings? Well, why would it be? Alex had them specially made, a thick platinum band and an engagement diamond surrounded by little silver spikes. It's gorgeous, and looks a little bit like a weapon.

"Perfect rings for the perfect Viking wife," Alex teased when he first slipped them on my finger. They feel as if they are a part of my body. Should I rip them off and throw them at Alex's feet? Hock them? Buy a Vespa instead? Or take a hammer to them? Throw them into the Arno River. Swallow them and choke to death. Shove them down Alexandria's throat and make her choke on them. I might not even be able to get them off. My fingers are swollen from the heat. I want out of this car. I think we could walk faster than this.

"Kids like to see city, no? They should see everything. You, boy? You like sports? You play football?"

"No," Josh says. "I play soccer."

"He meant soccer, honey. They call soccer 'football' here."

"Oh," Josh says. "Yes," he says to the driver in a volume three times his normal voice and much slower. "I like. Football." He turns to me and whispers. His breath is bad. "What do they call football then?"

"American football, probably."

"That's what I mean." Josh is getting frustrated now, and that's when I realize how tired we all are. They need bed, and food, and bathing.

"That's what Mom meant, dufus. They call American football, American football."

"She called me dufus! Mom said DON'T." The driver is raising his eyebrow now. He is going to post on his Facebook page about my rude American children and me. I reach over, and I pinch Rachel on the back of the arm.

"Ow, Mom!"

I lean in, and I mean business. "If you call your brother that one more time, you are going to seriously, seriously regret it," I say.

"Florence," the driver says. "The best city in the world. Art.

Masterpieces. Architecture. *Magnifico!* We are a living museum, everywhere you see. And Tuscan cooking!" He kisses his fingers and throws them up. They hit the roof of the compact car, and it must hurt for he jerks his hand back and shakes them in the air. I hope it will subdue him, but no, he picks right back up with a shrug and a grin. "You like really nice wine? You like shopping? You like gelato?"

You, like, ever shut up?

"You like beautiful scenery? See the hills?"

"Yes. Florence is very beautiful." And I mean it; it is. It truly is. It's not his fault I can't appreciate any of it right now.

"*Buono!* You will love my Firenze. And golden-haired woman like you, Firenze will love you back."

"Oh my God," Rachel says. "She's married, you know." She turns to me. "Aren't you?"

"Enough," I say. More tears. Thank God I am wearing sunglasses. My eyes are swollen to the size of golf balls. I am not wearing any makeup. Big sunglasses and white-blond hair, I guess that's all I need to still attract a man. Only I don't want any man but Alex. For a second I want to take my sunglasses off and show him my streaked face, my swollen eyes, my overpowering grief.

"You married?" he says. "Of course you are. Golden beauty like you." He is openly leering at me through the mirror and seems to have no problem with the fact that I'm married and my kids are in the car. What is wrong with these people? Why are their libidos so raging? Is it all the olive oil? The exuberant hand gestures? Salami hanging from the ceiling of every food market? Or the Italian language itself? *Mangi, mangi, mangi!* Even that sounds sexual. He's still talking. Maybe he thinks we won't tip him if he doesn't play tour guide. Normally I would appreciate it. Now it's like nails on a chalkboard. If I had a Post-it note I would write; *There's a hundred euro in this for you if you would please shut the fuck up.* But that's a lot to write on a Post-it, besides which, I don't have one. I wonder how you say "shut the fuck up" in Italian? I could probably convey it with a few hand gestures. He slaps the steering wheel with his hand, startling me.

"Lucky man," he says. He slides his sunglasses down and once again leers through the mirror. His eyes are a beautiful shade of hazel. He wiggles his eyebrows. They match his mustache. "Lucky, lucky man." Rachel bursts out laughing and then covers her mouth with her hand. Every fingernail is a different color. When did she do that?

"What?" Josh says. "What's so funny?"

Nothing is funny, I think. Nothing will ever be funny. The tears start again. This is a mistake. A huge mistake. I hate crying. I am not a crying type of person. Vikings do not cry. Tears freeze in sub-zero temperatures. Somebody forgot to tell my tear ducts. Shit. I'm out of tissues. I should have stolen a roll of toilet paper from the plane. What's wrong with me that I can't remember to do anything? I sniff and casually bring my sleeve up to my nose. The driver jerks his head up as if I'm about to say something profound. Stella moves over to Josh and hangs her head out his window. Josh puts his arm around her and does not complain about her being a big, hot fur ball. I am grateful. I am going to start sobbing if I'm not careful.

I wipe my nose on my sweater. I don't even know why I brought it. It's hot in here, way too hot for a sweater, not that I've been wearing it, just sitting on it. Screw it. I can use it as a tissue. Is the driver looking at my cleavage? Guess American women can trick men with their boobs too. I'm wearing a little black dress. I thought it was appropriate: dress for a funeral. But now I'm attracting the sun like sixty feet of asphalt. My thighs are sticky. I spread my legs slightly and fan myself with an Italian newspaper sitting on the seat. The cover has some kind of showgirl. Sex fiends. All of them.

The driver leans forward as if trying to look between my legs. "Your husband? You meet him here?"

My right temple is throbbing. I have decided if I weren't terrified to drive here, I would kill the driver just to shut him up.

"You bet your ass we're going to meet him," Rachel says. "You've been served!"

"Rachel."

"What are we going to serve?" Josh says.

"His head on a platter," Rachel says.

"Rachel!" I sigh, close my eyes. The heart of Italy. Maybe it is appropriate to be in the heart of the country at a time when mine is broken and black. Maybe I should rip open my chest and let Florence inside, allow the city's heart to beat in place of mine. The driver slams on the brakes. He beeps at the car he almost rammed into, then shakes his fist in the air. He quickly recovers and resumes chatting us up.

"While you are here you must see it all. Rome. Venice. Pisa. Milan. Cinque Terre. You know Cinque Terre?"

I laugh. Did I know it? The five connected villages on the edge of the Mediterranean? Where you could walk from one to another? Where the world soars from the side of a cliff? That Cinque Terre? Where I couldn't wait to honeymoon with my husband? "Yes," I say. "I want to see everything." Including my husband's mistress. I, definitely, maybe, want to see her.

"How can we see everything?" Rachel says. "We have to be back for dance camp."

I should have never let Rachel watch *Dirty Dancing.* Rachel likes dancing, but she doesn't love it, and she doesn't practice, and sometimes she is downright clumsy. Last recital the poor kid tucked her right foot behind her left while attempting a pirouette, and she ended up tripping herself. That would have been embarrassing enough had she not fallen sideways and taken five other ballerinas down with her like a line of tutu-clad dominoes. She's yet to attend another dance function where that story hasn't been dragged out and repolished. Not that it matters to me; I'm far from a stage mom or even a soccer mom; I just want my kids to try different things and have fun. But Rachel is acting as if missing dance camp would be the end of life as she knows it. Don't these kids realize that my life feels as if it's about to end? No. No, they don't. And I cannot forget that.

"And I have a game next week," Josh says. This coming from the kid who prefers to stare at the sky instead of the soccer ball.

"Where I pick you up? The train station? The Santa Maria Novella. Easy to take the train. Rome? Venice? Pisa? Milan? You go there. And that way, see, that way?" He waits until I look in the direction he's pointing. "That way is the historic district. And over there. You like shopping? Gucci? Prada? Via Tornabuoni."

"I know all those shops except Via Tornabuoni," Rachel says smugly.

"Via Tornabuoni is the name of the street," I say. Where does Alexandria live? Via Mistress Lane?

"I know that," Rachel says. "It was a joke." She smiles at the driver. Is she flirting with him? Please, don't let Rachel get out of control. I can't handle one more thing.

"Florence, you walk everywhere," the driver says. "You no drive."

"Then how come you're driving?" Rachel says.

"*Si, si,*" the driver says. "University not far now."

"Forget the university. Gucci? Prada?" Rachel says. "Where?"

"Hush, you," I say. Not far now. Alex is not far now. For a split second I'm excited to see him. Smell him. Touch him. My Alex. My husband of sixteen years. Together in Florence like I've always dreamed. And then it hits me. I won't get to touch him. Kiss him. Nuzzle his neck, inhale the essential scent of him.

I'm not ready for that. I'm not ready to let him go. This isn't fair. Why did I have to find out? Why can't I have just one unadulterated moment with my husband in Florence? Unadulterated. Nice. It's over. Isn't it? He's ruined everything. I'm never going to have a husband again. Why, why, why? How could he? A panic is growing on me, like moss up a tree. How can I make this NOT be happening?

"The streets? The buildings? Thirteen, fourteenth century. You have nothing so old in America."

"Sure we do," Josh says. "Grandma and Grandpa!" He throws his head back and laughs. It's the kind of joke Alex would have laughed at. My two men, laughing at anything. That's what I used to say. And now there is one.

We come to the end of the street. The driver can only turn left. Instead, he idles, and points out the window. "Ah, here, here. Look. Duomo, you see? Big, big for tourists. Beautiful, no?"

"From the picture!" Josh says. "Dad was standing right there!" Yes. With his whore.

"It doesn't look real," Rachel says. She's right. The marvelous domed church stretches out in all directions, up, down, and sideways. It's like something out of a fairy tale.

"That was Brunelleschi's architectural marvel," I say. "It's the largest brick and mortar dome in the world. When we see it again you'll be amazed at all the statues, and frescoes, and marble. Dad says the marble turns pink at night when the sun sets on it." As soon as I say it, I'm instantly furious. *What else is Alex looking at at night that is pink?* I feel the threat of tears and silently admonish myself. *Look at the dome! You are here, in Florence. You have always wanted to come here; this is your dream. Do not let him destroy your dream.*

"Cool," Josh says.

It is. It is cool. Everything is cool. "At the time this was built, they didn't even know how they were going to pull it off, just that they were determined to do it. It's called technology forcing. Like putting a man on the moon. They decided they were going to do it first, and then they did it. They made it happen." I don't know why, or even how I've switched to tour guide mode, but it's good for me. I need something to take my mind off the war in my head.

"How do you know all this?" Josh asks me. He sounds impressed.

"She reads, duf—dearest Joshua," Rachel says.

"I do read," I say, letting this "dufus" slide. "You two should try it." Besides trying to squeeze a little education in on my kids, is there a lesson for me in that little speech? It looks impossible at the moment, but what if there is a way to save my marriage? What if I just decide I am going to do it, just like men decided they were going to build the Santa Maria Fiore, just like they decided they were going to put a man on the moon? Decide first and then do. Marriage forcing. Is it possible? What are my options? Lose my kids every other weekend for the rest of their childhood?

The taxi idles at the curb. The driver rests one elbow out the window as if he has all day. He points to the line stretching along one entire side of the church.

"You want to climb to the top for such a nice view. Tuscan hills and the city skyline. *Belissimo!*"

I nod. I will do it. Climb to the top for the view. Enjoy the beauty, and then jump off. After I leave the kids with their father of course. Between the stop and start of the traffic, and the heat, and my throbbing temples, and the evil thoughts that keep attacking me, I am going to be sick. I am going to be sick on the fourteenth-century sidewalk.

"Stop," I say. He looks at me funny. Right. We are already stopped. I pull out my wallet. Hand him double the fare.

"I take you all the way," he says. "You want the American university, no?" I glance out the window again. The area around the Duomo swarms with tourists. They stand with maps, and cameras, and gelato, and bags that scream Ferragamo, and, of course, their lovers. *If you weren't, I'd invent you.* Look at all the lovers. Are Alex and Alexandria nearby? Strolling hand in hand? How much would I have to pay the driver to run them over?

I manage to find my voice. "What do you think of ex Prime Minister Berlusconi?"

"He is no longer retired," the driver informs me.

I don't bother to correct his English. It's much better than my Italian. Besides, I know what he's trying to say. "I know—but what did you think of how he behaved?"

"I bet you American can't even tell me who is Prime Minister—"

"Obama," Josh says.

"President of the United States," I correct. "But we're talking about the ex Prime Minister of Italy."

"So there's no Prime Minster right now?" Josh says. I wish he wasn't listening to this conversation.

"There is. Prime Minister Mario Monti," I say.

"*Si, si! Buono!*" The driver claps his hands. "Oooo," he adds as if I am a seal who has just performed a trick.

"Back to Berlusconi. When he was parading around with very young women. Did you approve?"

The driver shrugs. Grins. "Italian men. We like beauty. We like beautiful women. Like you. I like you. Both of you," he says, glancing at Rachel.

"She's married," Rachel says.

"And she's fourteen!"

"I can still like."

My thermometer pops. "No. Not a fourteen-year-old you can't."

"He can too! He already said it!" Rachel is thrilled.

"Sorry, sorry, she look much older."

"See?" Rachel says.

"*Sì!*" the driver echoes.

"Are you married?" I demand.

"Married. Yes. I have wife. And daughter."

"Where is your ring?" Rachel says.

He absentmindedly rubs his finger. "Italian men. We don't always wear. It's tight. Like it's strangling me."

"Does your wife wear her ring?" I say.

"Of course! Of course! Others, they must know. She is married."

"Do you have a mistress?" Rachel says.

"What's a mistress?" Josh says.

"Pardon?" the driver says.

"Never mind," I say. "We're going to get out here."

"A mistress," Rachel says. "You're sure you don't have one?"

"Rachel enough."

"No, no, no. I am married man."

"What's a mistress?" Josh pipes in.

"You know that girl we saw with Dad?" Rachel explains.

"Rachel! Enough!" Me again. I'm always the one reprimanding.

"Is she a mistress?" Josh says. He is confused.

"Josh, this isn't happening right now," I say as gently as I can.

"What isn't?" he says.

"This conversation. Everybody out of the car."

"Are we there?" Josh says, looking at the Duomo. "Is this where Dad works?"

"No. But we're getting out anyway. I have to get out of this car."

I throw the euro at the perverted driver, demand that he open the trunk, and hustle everyone out. This time he does not get out and flex his biceps for us. I heave all our suitcases onto the street. "I no like her," the driver yells out the window. "I only like you!" I shake my head. Rachel stomps her foot. Stella strains at the end of her leash, wagging her tail so hard she's going to leave bruises on my thigh. I will welcome them. The taxi driver tugs on his mustache and gives me what looks like the Italian equivalent of the middle finger before screeching forward a few feet. I take pleasure in the fact that he really can't go anywhere, but we are free. We all grab our luggage and move onto the sidewalk.

"Happy now, Mother?" Rachel says.

No, I think. I'll never be happy again. In unison, we turn to the Duomo, towering all around us. Yes, like something out of a fairy tale. Or a nightmare.

CHAPTER 5

We stand and take it all in. The city is buzzing. Tourists snap pictures of the buildings, the statues, the sky, each other. Directly across from the Duomo is the Baptistery. It's noted for its three sets of bronze doors and relief sculptures. It makes me think of the age-old philosophy riddle—which door will I choose? What's behind door number one? How in the world did I open the one with the mistress? Does it even matter? Because we all know, once you open a door, you can never go back. But you don't have to go through. I force myself to focus on something else. The sculptures are magnificent. Life-sized men holding books and quills. Men in robes, men huddled together, angels flying overhead. Alex would know whom the sculptures represent and all the interesting stories that go along with them.

Also nearby is the Giotto Tower. If you don't want to stand in line to climb to the top of the Duomo, the Giotto offers similar views. I am proud of how much I remember from my guidebooks. But Alex is the one actually living here; he should be giving us the tour. People are gathered in front of the steps of the Baptistery, and congregating in the space in front of and alongside the Duomo. There is a definite energy to the city; Florence has a soul. Vendors sell their wares from small foldout tables, and drivers stand next to regal horse and carriages, calling out to tourists. They spot us immediately, a single mother and two ragged children.

"Lovely, lovely lady," a carriage driver calls to us. He gestures to his horse, wearing a red plume and adjusting his legs, making little clacking sounds with his hooves on the stone streets. The horse looks at Stella and whinnies.

"He likes you!" the driver says. "A ride for you and your *bambinos*." He glances at Stella and shakes his head as if she smells bad. Which she very well might. My senses are dulled from all the crying. "But no dogs. Just you and your *bambinos*."

"What are your *bambinos*?" Josh says. "Your boobs?" He whispers it, but just barely. I want to throttle Alexandria. Ever since seeing hers, he's been obsessing about breasts.

"Josh," I whisper, "*bambinos* means children. You and Rachel are my *bambinos*. But please stop saying the word 'boobs.' They're breasts. But I think we've heard enough about them for quite a while, okay?" Josh shrugs, paws the ground with his tennis shoes. The horse cocks his head sideways as if sizing up the competition.

"Another time," I say. "Come on kids."

"Are we going to a hotel? With a swimming pool?" Josh says.

"Probably not," I say. "This way."

"I'm hungry," Josh says. "Are we going to eat?"

Eat. Swim. Watch television. My son's life is still going on. "We'll get some gelato first. How about that?" I say.

"What's that?" Josh says.

"It's ice cream, stupid," Rachel says. Seriously. What do I have to do? Gag her? Get a stun gun and zap her every time she is mean to her brother? I grew up an only child. Is this a right of passage, a strength-building experience? Or is all this going to damage Josh? Will he end up marrying a big-breasted woman who does nothing but put him down and call him stupid? The

THREE MONTHS IN FLORENCE

thought makes me furious. But I can't come down too hard on Rachel. She's the daddy's girl. And she is feeling his betrayal every bit as much as I am. Rachel felt abandoned by Alex before this. She didn't like his missing her dance recitals any more than Josh liked his missing his soccer games. It's a family affair. It will affect us all in our own ways. Create rips in our family seam where before there were only little tears. Did Alex think about any of this? Of course not. Giving in to your animal needs is much easier than facing up to the damage it does.

Alex used to represent the ideal man to Rachel. Handsome, smart, funny—the family guy. Who will Rachel choose for a mate now? Will she purposefully go after the opposite of Alex? Land some uneducated motorcycle gangster? As we walk, unsure of exactly where we are headed, I wonder if they have gelato laced with alcohol.

It doesn't take long to find the creamy dessert. There is a shop on the corner of the first street we turn down. I tie Stella's leash to a nearby streetlamp. She sits, tongue hanging out, as if it's the most natural thing in the world that we are in Italy. She doesn't care where she is, as long as she is with us. Why can't Alex be more like her? It's really not apropos, calling men "dogs." Dogs are loyal. Dogs love you unconditionally. I pat Stella on the head.

Josh points at her. "Stay," he says, even though she already is. The shop smells sweet and welcomes us with a winding display case packed with colorful mounds of gelato. I can't help but compare it to American ice cream parlors. With their fluorescent lighting and plastic buckets of ice cream that scowling teenagers disappear into while wielding silver scoopers. But here, everything is on display like an art show. Not a single flavor is scooped down to the last bit. They are overflowing and proud of it. Some are topped with bright berries; others candy. All the servers are standing up straight and smiling. Their black aprons are pressed without a drop of gelato on them. It is classy and beautiful. I want to live here. Where just going for dessert lifts you into the realm of a pleasant experience, like a night out at the opera. Is that the difference between Alexandria and me? Is she exotic gelato, while I am unappreciated ice cream? The Devil isn't in the details, I think, looking around. Beauty is.

"Are you crying?" Rachel says. I have my sunglasses on. How can she tell? I shake my head and steer the kids closer to the case. Gelato seems to come in a thousand flavors, and every color in the crayon box. Josh puts his hands on the case and presses his nose against it. I gently pull him back, then clean the case with the sweater wrapped around my waist. Then I remember I wiped my nose on it, so I move us farther down. Americans in Florence. Bulls in a china shop.

Josh orders raspberry and chocolate, and Rachel gets caramel and peanut butter, but when I go to order it hits me that I have zero appetite. Putting anything into my mouth and swallowing seems impossible. Instead I order a scoop of vanilla for Stella. Once I take it outside, she only takes a few licks. The poor girl is exhausted. I need to find us a place to stay.

"What's going on?" Rachel says. A crowd of people is circled around something on the sidewalk across from us. We cross over and squeeze our way in. Laid out before us on the patch of faded cobblestone is a life-size face sketched in vibrant colors with chalk. It's the face of a stunning woman. She has long red hair flowing out behind her, purple eyes, pink cheeks, and neon green lips. The face looks as if it's glowing in the dark even though the sun is shining overhead. The face looks familiar. As I stare at the drawing, the lips seem to move.

"I am fucking your husband," it says. I want to spit on it, stomp on it, dump gelato on it.

I take Josh and Rachel by the arm. "Let's go."

"It's so cool," Rachel says. "It's like the stuff you used to do." I stop in my tracks. Rachel was so little when I was dabbling in art. It was true. I sketched a lot of faces while Rachel played in her high chair. I used to draw them on the breakfast napkins, show them to her, and she would squeal with delight. Sometimes she just threw peas at them. I started keeping the ones that made her squeal and throwing out the ones with mashed peas on them. Even then, I never took my work very seriously.

"I can't believe you remember that."

"You were good. Not as good as that." We look back at the chalk drawing.

"I mean making love," the face taunts me. "Alex and I make love."

"She looks like the girl with the boobs," Josh says. "I mean breasts."

"Oh my God," Rachel says. "She does. She totally does." I elbow through and glare down at it again. It wasn't just my imagination. It looks like her. I aim for the middle of the face, then dump vanilla gelato on top of it. Smack. The gooey cream clumps underneath the nose and above the neon lips. There is an immediate reaction from the crowd. Gasps, and phrases uttered in different languages, and looks of horror.

"Mom," Rachel says. She pulls on my arm.

"*Scusi,*" a man in a dress shirt and a black cap, carrying a stack of brochures, says. He pushes past me and stares at the drawing. He whirls around, looks at the empty, dripping carton of vanilla in my hot little hands, and begins sputtering in Italian. Hands flapping, mouth moving, I can't understand a word. But I definitely get the vibe.

"Sorry, sorry, *scusi, grazie,*" I say. *Capisce?* "It was an accident."

"I saw you," he says switching to English. He mimes me dumping the gelato on the drawing. "No accident!"

"I have a twitch," I say. "I twitched." Stella lunges forward and begins furiously licking the gelato. Great. Now she wants it. I yank her back. She sticks out her tongue. It is foamy white and neon green.

"This is a walking art tour!" the man shouts. He shoves a brochure at me. I have no choice but to take it. "This is a popular living exhibit. You destroy an artist's work!"

"I'm sorry," I say. "*Scusi.*" I shove the brochure in my purse.

"Our father is having an affair," Rachel says.

"She has big BREASTS and looks like her," Josh says.

"They're coming," the man says. I look up to see another group, headed for the drawing. In the lead are men carrying cameras and microphones. The man with the brochures straightens his cap and his spine. "You stay," he says. "We have to tell them your name. The media will want to know."

I grab Rachel and Josh. "Run," I say. "Fast." For once, my children don't argue with me. We take off at top speed, gelato jostling, dog collar jingling. Stella gets a second wind and takes the lead, yanking us through the crowds. I can hear the man in the dress shirt shouting after us. We don't stop until we round a corner and make it to the end of that street as well. We lean against a nearby building to catch our breath. Gelato drips from the arms of my *bambinos.* We are all gasping for air. The soles of my feet burn from running on the pavement. My heart trips in my chest.

"Now what?" Rachel says.

"Are we in trouble?" Josh says.

"No," I say. "Wasn't that fun?" And I mean it. It was the most fun I've had in a long time. At first the kids just stare at me. Then Josh nods. Rachel lets out a little smile.

"Kinda," she says. "It kinda was."

"It really was," Josh says. "Except this." He holds up his arm, sticky with cream.

"We'll get more," I say. "Tomorrow." I throw my arms around them and steer us down the next street. I look up and see a red brick tower with a top that looks like a crown. The Palazzo Vecchio. It is a sign. The town square. Where they used to have public hangings. It is the perfect place to rendezvous with Alex.

We step into the square. I know a lot about this place, the Piazza della Signoria. This used to be the center of the Florentine Republic. They were ruled by a council called the signoria. Years of upheaval followed, dominated by coups, various factions attacking and overthrowing the ruling party, only to be attacked and overthrown themselves. Florence, the city established by Julius Caesar in 59 B.C., would go through much turmoil as men fought to possess and control her. The Medici family gained power in 1434. Cosimo de' Medici led the coup against the coup leaders that exiled him the year before. Standing here, on such a pleasant day, I try and feel the drama and the violent history, but all I see now is beauty. It is hard to imagine they used to hang men in this very square. It is also known as Palazzo Vecchio, for the red brick tower that can be seen almost anywhere in the city. Palazzo Vecchio means "old palace." What pretty names the Italians have for everything, what a beautiful language. Every time I try and pronounce something, I feel as if I'm reciting poetry. It is a massive fortress, and one of the most impressive public spaces in all of Florence.

Here, in the square is a replica of Michelangelo's statue of *David*, as well as the Loggia dei Lanzi, a building at the corner of the square, adjoining the Uffizi gallery. It boasts three soaring stone arches, and underneath them stands a parade of statues. Even though they are all replicas, I cannot believe they are out here, for all to see and touch, a museum in its own right. The loggia's outside vestibules house sculptural depictions of the four cardinal virtues, right underneath the parapet. The seated statues rest in a threefold shape that to me looks like a cross between a clover and a star. They each have wings, and a lion at their feet: *Fortitude, Temperance, Justice, Prudence.*

I need all of these virtues; I need all of their strengths. But most of all, I want justice. For me, for Stella, for the *bambinos.* I don't know how to bring Alex back into our fold, but I know I cannot let this woman, this mistress, destroy my family. She has staged a coup, and now it is time for me to counter. And I know just the location within this square. The *Fountain of Neptune.*

Alex and I have talked a lot about this fountain. It was the work of Bartolomeo Ammannati and his assistants. Commissioned for the wedding of Francesco I de' Medici to Johanna of Austria in 1565. The original artist hired to do the work was Baccio Bandinelli, and he succeeded in designing the model, but died before he could begin sculpting the marble.

The Neptune figure has a face that is supposed to resemble Cosimo de' Medici. The work is meant to represent Florentines having dominion over the sea. The Neptune poses on a raised pedestal in the center of the fountain, flanked by the mythical figures of Scylla and Charybdis. The Neptune is a replica, and the original rests in The National Museum.

It is not the history or even workmanship that so draws Alex to this statue, but the story and characters surrounding it. While it was being worked on, many Florentines were not pleased with the fountain. They named it Il Biancone, The White Giant.

Despite the criticism, Ammannati continued his work, assisted by the best sculptors and casters in Florence. He added bronze river gods, laughing satyrs, and sea horses rearing out of the water.

Over the centuries, this fountain has taken a lot of abuse. In the sixteenth century, locals used it to wash their laundry. It was vandalized in January of 1580. Damaged again in 1848 during the Bourbon bombardments. During a carnival in 1860 a satyr was stolen. In recent times it has been climbed by teens, and you guessed it, damaged. I read a shoulder was painted blue once after Italy lost a football game. Or maybe they won. I don't remember the details. All I know is this fountain has been through a lot. But the story Alex loves to tell about this statue, demonstrating the surly and jealous rivalry between artists of the time, revolves around Michelangelo.

He is purported to have looked at the fountain and exclaimed, "Ah, Ammannati, what a beautiful piece of marble you have ruined." I empathize with Ammannati. Forging on, despite others trying to tear him down. Taking abuse, and still standing. It is here where I want to face Alex. Because I, like this fountain, am damaged. He is the only man on earth who will understand the significance of the location. Sometimes, when someone is going through a hard time, like a celebrity, or a politician getting unwanted attention, Alex will look at me, shake his head, and say, "Ah, Ammannati." It is my turn. Soon, Alex will meet us here. I will face him. I will look him in the eye.

"Ah, Alex," I will say. And the rest will be understood. *What a beautiful piece of marriage you have ruined.*

CHAPTER 6

But was it? Was our marriage beautiful? The Friday before Alex left for his first semester in Florence, we all went out to dinner at Friday's. Josh and Alex thought it was a hoot that we were eating at Friday's on a Friday. I told you; it doesn't take much to amuse those two. Alex and I ordered steak. When I cut into mine, the piece flew off the plate and landed on Alex's cheek. He didn't miss a beat. He began moving his face side to side, talking as if it weren't there, until we were all in stitches, even me, and I usually don't go for the same slapstick they do. Alex and I had milkshakes with alcohol—these days it's our version of partying. Were we perfect? No. But I didn't have any clue we were in this kind of danger.

Even though it only took me forty-eight hours after finding out about Alexandria to get us to Florence, my bigger record was in opening my mouth. There isn't any human way I could have kept it shut. If a bomb suddenly went off in the middle of your house, would you keep quiet?

This is how my friends, and the checkout lady at the grocery store, and the teller at the bank, and the librarian, and the mailman, and best friend Megan, and maybe a few others, reacted when I told them my husband, professor of Renaissance art, father of my two beautiful children, had a mistress in Florence, Italy:

Oh my God. What do you mean?

Alex? Your Alex? Like. A mistress?

Really? Does he buy her things?

But you two are the perfect couple! You've been married sixteen years. You have two kids. That rat bastard. I would kill him. You'd better lawyer up and take him for every penny he's got. I'm here if you need me. Except Tuesdays and Thursdays. I'm off on Tuesdays and Thursdays. Don't even worry about your overdue books, doll. Seriously, you know you owe like four dollars and thirteen cents, right? It's on me. And he won't be allowed to so much as borrow a periodical when I'm on duty. Do you want to check out the books on marriage? You never know, doll. Plenty of dirty dogs out there; someone has to have some advice.

Would you like paper or plastic?

How old is she?

Where does he keep her?

That's horrible. Darn tootin' I would comb through his bank accounts. But unfortunately, you're not on the account, so I can't print those records for you.

Are you sure?

I don't believe it. You shouldn't either. That woman could be mentally ill. You can't just take her word for it.

No. Not Alex. How did you find out? I wish I were there. Do you want me to check flights? I can't believe this. Not Alex. I was there when you two first met. I literally saw him fall in love with you. You are not alone. We will figure this out together.

An affair, you say? How delightful. Was it themed?

Are you serious? But you're so pretty for your age!

I'm not surprised. I told you it was insane to let that man be alone in such a provocative country.

Did you suspect?

Did you suspect?

Did you suspect?

Dis you sushpect? (Drunk coming out of a bar)

Did you see the signs?

Did you see the signs?

Did you see the signs?

Did you see the signs?

Did you see the signs?

Welcome to Alitalia. Three first-class tickets and a dog. I see. Yes, there will be wine on the plane. No, our in-flight movies are much more current than *Fatal Attraction*. Why do you ask?

Here are a few of my replies:

I mean he has a woman, who he dates and buy things for, and has been sleeping with behind my back.

Yes, Alex. My Alex. Yes. Like. A mistress.

What does that matter? You think he did this because I'm too old? I'm thirty-eight. He's forty-two. I'm telling you age has nothing to do with this. Right? She's—what? Twenty-three? Oh God. She doesn't look any older than twenty-three. Rachel's going to be twenty-three. In nine years. Typical. Just dump the old wife over for a new foreign model. I can't breathe. I changed my mind. I'll take paper. Give it to me now!

What is she, a kitten under his desk? I don't know where he keeps her. I mean she probably lives somewhere, and he lives in the dorms, and they get together in freaking olive groves or something. I don't know! Her apartment I guess.

How could I? He's in another country. There are no clothing pockets to rifle through, no cell phone to check, no lipstick on the collars he left behind six months ago!

No!

No! I didn't. Honestly. Our marriage wasn't perfect—I have a bit of a temper sometimes, and we have two kids, and a dog, and a mortgage. And he works a lot. I mean like a lot. But I'm a stay-at-home mom, so we made time. And no matter how much we were fighting, our sex life was always robust. I am telling you the truth. We still did it standing up even. If this is about sex, then I definitely didn't see the signs, because before he left we never had a problem in the bedroom. In fact, if we hadn't been so good at sex we might never have gotten married in the first place. I don't know what I'm saying—I'm talking too fast to think about it.

Yes. Now that I look back. His voice started to change. He was more withdrawn. He called me less. He wouldn't tell me exactly when he was coming home. At some point he stopped calling me "Llama." He got a

Facebook page and two hundred girlfriends. He stopped wearing his
wedding ring. He sent me flowers, and it wasn't my birthday.

I stand before the *Fountain of Neptune,* dig in my pocket, and
take out a dime. I toss it into the fountain without making a
wish. Wishes are for fools. The kids are strolling around the
square, and they are still in my sight, so I am letting it happen.
I stand, unable to move, forcing others to maneuver around
me. I don't even budge when a young couple on their honeymoon wants to have their picture taken in front of the fountain,
right where I'm standing. Josh and Rachel are taking in the
sculptures, the people, the unfolding scenes of the city. They
are going to be all right. They have their whole lives ahead of
them, unlike me. Mine is behind me. They are still going to get
to love Alex, to hug him, and kiss him, and be a family with
him. And Alex will be all right too. He has his job at the university, his kids, and his mistress. If I do nothing, everyone will be
all right except me. I always used to wonder how women could
take men back after an affair. Now I wonder how they couldn't.
How they could stand to lose everything rather than fight like
hell to forgive, to work it out, to not be the only one in the family completely left with nothing?

I take out my cell phone and stare at it. I added an international package before I left, and I'm charged up, so technically
I could call him right now. I have listened to the first five voice
mails from Alex. The first one came in while we were watching
him on the computer screen. I figure he left it right before he
walked into Alexandria's apartment. I can tell from the sound
of his voice in the messages that he doesn't know we know
about his mistress. He thinks I'm just upset because he didn't
come home. Which, of course, I am. The rest takes my rage to a
whole new level. I don't need to listen to the messages again; I
know them all by heart.

"I'm sorry, Lena. I will explain everything. Just not on voice
mail. Will you please call me back as soon as you get this?"

"Lena? I know you must be furious. Please call me back, okay?"

"You have to talk to me at some point. I need to speak with the kids too. Call me."

"I'm going to keep calling you until you answer."

"I mean it. I'm going to call and call and call. So call me back." I shut off the phone after this one. There are fifteen more I haven't bothered listening to, and I've deleted his twenty-some text messages. I like the thought of him churning up with guilt. Wait until he finds out that his little secret is out. This is an ambush, and it gives me a secret jolt of pleasure, turning the tables on him. The element of surprise. Obviously, Alexandria hasn't confessed. What a stupid girl. Does she really think Alex will forgive her for making his family watch their adulterous, amorous activities live? She has to know I will confront him—so why hasn't she told him?

She's a coward; that's why. Either that or such a psychopath that she somehow thinks Alex will still choose her over me when I tell him what she's done.

I hope Alex knows how lucky he is that I'm not standing in front of the university with an axe, chopping down olive trees and shouting out his betrayal for all his colleagues to hear. It's not that I haven't fantasized about doing it; I have. Many times. But it would probably cost him his job. And I have been a stay-at-home wife and mother for the past sixteen years. One of us needs to keep his or her paying job. Eventually, I will have to get a job. I can't think about this now. With all the recognition lately about how being a mother is one of the toughest jobs in the world, the one thing nobody mentions, or forgets to tell you, is that one day you could lose it all, and toughest job in the world or not, good luck going back into the job market with nothing else on your resume.

"Mom?" Rachel says. My two kids are back in front of me, already bored. "Why are you just standing there?"

"I need a minute," I say. It's a lie. I need a couple of years.

"Are you going to call him?"

"Yes."

"I don't want to see him."

"I do," Josh says. "I want to see Dad."

"Of course you do," I say. I have to force each word out of my mouth, and my voice cracks.

"He's clueless," Rachel says.

"Hey. I am not. About what?"

"Rachel. No matter what, he's still your father." I have to say this because that's what a good mother will say. But I don't want to. I want to wind her up like a weapon and unleash her on Alex.

"I hate him," she says.

Me too. "Please don't say that. This is between him and me. He's still your father."

"You can't tell me how to feel!" Rachel grabs the cell phone out of my hand. Before I can stop her, she's already dialing Alex. How do kids work these gadgets so effortlessly? I go to reach for the phone. I've decided I'm going to toss it into the fountain, but she's already talking.

"Dad? It's your daughter. Rachel. We know about your girl-friend."

"Oh God." I sink to the ground. Stella barks and sniffs at me. I push her away. She sniffs the fountain, then jumps into it. People look at me, look at her, look at me, take pictures of me, take pictures of her, look at me, and wait for me to do something—*Your dog is in the fountain!*—but I do nothing. Perhaps I have the soul of an ancient Florentine in me and I do not care that my dog is in the fountain. Or perhaps I have just realized that I am asleep, in the middle of a nightmare, and I am tired of pretending that anything I do will make any difference or even any sense. And so I sit. And Stella pees in the fountain. And Josh points.

"She's peeing in the fountain," he says. "I have to go. Can I pee in the fountain?"

"Go ahead," I say. Josh starts for the fountain. Rachel pulls him back. We have only been here a few hours and have managed to vandalize two public works of art. I'd say that's pretty impressive.

"We saw everything, Dad. We saw you kissing her. We saw her take her top off. Josh is obsessed with boobs now!"

That's my girl, I thought. Then: I wanted to tell him.

"We're here, Dad. In FLORENCE. We're at some square with naked statues."

"Piazza della Signoria," I say. It rolls off my tongue like poetry.

"Tell Dad that Stella just peed in the fountain and I have to go too," Josh says.

"Yes. The clock tower. She's right here. On the ground." Rachel holds the phone out to me. I shake my head. Rachel takes the call back. "I don't know. Fine. I'll ask. Why are you on the ground, Mom? Did you fall?"

I shrug.

"She's sad. That's why she's on the ground. How could you, Dad?" Rachel is on the verge of tears; I can hear it in her voice. Stella jumps out of the fountain and shakes, spraying urine-soaked water in every direction. The crowd exclaims and moves back, still filming her and us. I should take the phone from Rachel. I should get off the ground. But I can't. "I don't know. Did you tell anyone about this, Mom?"

It lifts me off the ground and onto my feet. "That's what he wants to know? Did I *tell* anyone?" My emotional mind lashes out while my practical one starts listing everyone I've told. My best friend Megan, of course. The lady at the grocery store. The librarian. The mailman. Most of the Alitalia crew. That was it. Wait. The cab driver. The chalk-drawing tour guide. He's lucky we didn't tell the horse and carriage guy. What the hell does it matter? Did I tell anyone? The Alex I knew is gone. I am going to shout it from every Tuscan rooftop I can reach. I grab the phone and toss it into the fountain. I don't hear a thing after that, but I imagine I can hear his voice, calling from the depths of the water.

Forgive me! Forgive me!

I do not.

"Let's go, guys," I say.

"Where?" Josh asks.

"To a hotel. Where you can pee. And eat. And sleep."

"And watch TV?"

"And watch TV."

"What about Dad?" Rachel says. "I'll bet he's on his way."

"I really have to go," Josh says.

"We'd better find a place then. Other than this fountain."
Yes, we had to get away. From the people still staring, the cameras still flashing, and Neptune, on his high horse, rearing above us. I glare at people as we shove by them. *We're just a normal family. On holiday. In Italy.* Capisce?

Josh has been allowed to use a restroom in a nearby restaurant. I don't leave the square, like I planned. I can't do this alone. Alex will have to take the dog, and the kids, and I don't know where I'll go, but I can't do this alone. I see him right away, standing by the fountain, staring into the water. I guess he spots my cell phone. He is as familiar to me as my own reflection. For a second I am relieved he is on his own, as if he would dare come with her. When our eyes meet, I am jolted by his expression. He looks lost. And grief stricken. My heart squeezes, and I want to run to him, throw my arms around him, make all of this go away. For a second. How dare this hurt him when he's the one who caused it? Josh and Stella make a run for Alex. I wish to God I could be one of them. I wish I could be anyone but me. Rachel and I hang back.

"You brought Stella?" He sounds surprised but not argumentative. I don't answer. Josh runs into his father's arms.

"Hey, buddy," Alex says, embracing our son. It must feel so good to hug Alex after six months. I had imagined the exact moment so many times. I've been robbed of my moment! BA. Before Alexandria. I've never felt so much hatred toward another woman in my life. I should be more angry with Alex, but right now it's her I blame. The sight of Alex being loving is too painful to watch. Alexandria's words come roaring up at me.

I told him he must tell you. About us. About me. It is time. If we are going to live together for the summer. . . .

Alex breaks the hug and steps forward. He holds his arms

open to Rachel. He is crying. I can't remember the last time I saw Alex cry. When his father died. And again, when his mother passed shortly after. His parents were in their forties when they had him. He was a surprise baby. Their miracle baby. They loved me. They loved us. They would be so ashamed.

"She died of grief," he said at his mother's funeral. "She loved my father that much. Just like I love you."

We are dying of grief too, just not the loving kind. His tears will not move me. They cannot. I keep seeing her. Kissing him. Him apologizing to her. Her hair lying on the nape of his neck.

"Rachel?" Alex says. He is still waiting for his hug.

"Not on your life," Rachel says. I am ashamed. And proud.

"Hit him," she says. "Hit him, Mom."

"Rachel," I say, "nobody is hitting anyone." I did want to hit him. Slap him across the face in front of everyone. If the kids weren't here, would I do it? Would I slap him? Life wasn't like the movies. You can't just walk up and slap people. Can you? Alex is looking at me. I wonder what he sees? Does anyone ever really know what another person truly thinks of him or her? Am I the tired, old wife? What does he see? The large sun-glasses? The black dress? *I spread my legs for the taxi driver,* I want to tell him. *And he really liked me. Or Rachel. We weren't sure which.*

Alex glances at the fountain. "Ah, Ammannati," he says quietly. He gets it, right away. He's still my husband. The boy I fell in love with at first sight. The man who knows me better than anyone on this earth. I am not prepared for how much this hurts.

CHAPTER 7

I can't take any more; I'm too tired, too overwhelmed, too stunned. Seeing him is like taking a thousand volts of electricity to the heart. This can't be happening; it can't. The unfairness of it outrages me, but grief is the clear victor, and it is stamped on both of us. I break into sobs, and once I start, I can't stop. I think Rachel is yelling at Alex, and I think Stella is barking, but I'm not sure because it's impossible for me to hear anything over my cries. "Lena, Lena, Lena." Alex puts his arms around me and pulls me into him. I don't touch him back, but I let him fold me against his chest. I have always fit so nicely into him, and I need his touch, if only for a few seconds. I want to remember what his heartbeat feels like against my breast, smell him, feel the weight of his arms around me. And I am too, too tired to fight.

"Dad," Josh says. "You shouldn't have kissed that girl. Mom cries all the time now."

"I'm sorry, I'm sorry, I'm sorry," Alex says. "I'm so, so sorry."

"Sorry you did it, or sorry you got caught?" Rachel says.

Her zinger gives me the strength I need to pull away. Alex

runs his hand through his hair. "I'm truly sorry for everything," he says, without directly addressing Rachel's question.

"Did she trick you with her boobs, Dad?" Josh says.

"What?"

"Did she?"

"I . . ."

"We all saw them," Rachel says. "On the computer."

"Oh God," Alex says. "Lena. Lena. I . . ."

I find my voice. "I called you on video chat, and she answered. She purposefully set the computer screen up so we could see you when you came to her door. She didn't tell you?"

"No. Of course not. Of course not."

"That says a lot about her right there. Don't you think?"

"I can't tell you how sorry I am. Kids. Your mother and I need to talk. And after that, I'll speak with the two of you. But not here, okay? Let's get you guys checked into a hotel. I'm sure you're starving too, right?"

This is the Alex I know. Sensible. Take charge. And it's fine with me; I don't want to be in charge anymore. But I'm furious too. Let's get *you guys* checked into a hotel? Like he's not joining us? Like we're already split apart, like he thinks he gets to just walk away?

"We had really cool ice cream," Josh says as we walk. "We smashed some into the ground." He does not mention the art exhibit, the chalk drawing that looks like his father's mistress.

"It was gelato, dufus," Rachel says.

I need someone to give me a horse pill of a sedative. "Take the kids," I say. "I'll find my own hotel."

"I'm going with you," Rachel says.

Alex starts to touch my arm. I flinch. He pulls back. "Lena, please. Let me get the three of you settled."

"How noble of you," I say. I really want to ask him to kill me and throw me in the river. I'm about to say something of the sort when I catch Rachel in the corner of my eye. She is crying now too, watching to see what I will do. If I throw a fit in front of them, right here, right now, it will be seared into their memories for the rest of their lives. They may even end up in therapy.

Our mother lost it in the town square. She completely flipped out. Luckily, our father was there to take care of us when the Italians came to take her away.

"You're right," I say. "Let's find a hotel." I want to sink into a bed and never wake up.

"Why don't we go to Dad's place," Josh says. "The one on the video." I watch Alex cringe.

"It wasn't his place; it was hers. Right, Dad?" Rachel says.

Alex is truly squirming. I am in love with my kids right now. But also angry that they are in this position. Alex focuses on something in the distance. Maybe he will find wisdom in the hills. If so, it's not going to come soon enough. "I know of a really nice hotel," Alex says. "Not far from here."

"Does it have a pool?" Josh asks.

"No, buddy. And it's a little older than the hotels back home. But it has beds, and running water, and air-conditioning."

"What about TV?"

"Yes. But not as many channels as you're used to. And I don't know how many of them are in English."

"Video games?"

"Definitely not," I say.

"We're not on vacation," Rachel says.

"But we could be," Josh says. "I mean, we're here."

Alex puts his arm around Josh. "We'll try and make the best of it," he says.

The hotel is right near the Santa Maria Novella train station. It is a four-star, in an older building with an extremely modern lobby. Everything, from the leather sofa and chairs, to the flowers, walls, and marble tiles, is white. Like they want you to think you've stepped into heaven. *Sorry,* I want to shout, *we're meant to be in hell.* It's geared to tourists. I'd much rather a more authentic-looking place, but this looks expensive, and I've no problem making Alex pay. But they won't take dogs. Alex speaks Italian with the girl at the desk. She smiles a lot. Everyone is so in love with Alex. Maybe that's his curse. Or mine, depending on how you look at it. Alex is not only good-looking; he just has it. Charisma, charm, animal attraction. Wherever he goes, women are drawn to him.

I used to be proud of it. And to be honest, I have the same affect on men. Or *had*. Somewhere along the line I started looking less sexy and more mommy. Dashing out of the house
without makeup. Wearing sweats and T-shirts. Not giving off
any vibes at all. And why should I? Alex was never the type to
swivel his head around if a better-looking woman came into the
room. I always loved that about him. I thought he was above
such trappings. I have been naïve.

Maybe that kind of attention is just too hard to ignore. We're
animals. We've tried to domesticate ourselves, but deep down
we're still just wild animals. Stella is better behaved than we are,
and they won't take her. We move on. Josh chatters excitedly,
and speaking of swiveling, Rachel's head is moving nonstop. At
first I think she's taking in the architecture, and the shops, and
the culture, but then I notice she's checking out all the men
and boys in the vicinity who are openly checking her out. Alex
is leading us hesitantly and constantly glancing at me. I never
look at him directly. We are getting away from the center of
town, away from the bustle and the shops. The buildings look
older, and the streets are narrower.

"We're in the historic district," Alex says, reading my mind. I
am suddenly glad we have Stella. I'd much rather stay at a hotel
with history and character. I bet Alexandria prefers the expensive white one. Oh my God, has he taken her there? He stops in
front of a faded yellow building with a giant arched wooden
door. "This is it," he says.

"Cool," Josh says. Everyone looks at me. I nod. We step in.
Faded brown carpet and a couple of high-backed ivory sofas
make up the lobby. A few steps beyond the reception desk is a
winding staircase. Alongside the desk is a hall that ends in a
door. It is propped open, and beyond it I can make out a patio
with blooming flowers and outdoor tables. As we approach the
desk, I take out my credit card.

"I'll get it," Alex says, reaching for his wallet.

"No," I say. "You won't." I turn to the girl manning the desk.
"Room for three," I say, pasting on a smile. "Two children, one
adult, and one golden."

"What about Dad?" Josh says.

"Kids," Alex says, pointing to the patio. "Why don't you two go check it out?"

"Cool," Josh says. "Maybe they have a pool too."

"Clueless," Rachel says.

"Be careful not to touch the flowers. *Vespas,*" the girl says.

There are scooters on the patio? Hiding behind flowers? I must look as confused as I feel. Alex laughs, then quickly covers his mouth and coughs. The girl behind the desk raises her hands into wings and makes a buzzing sound.

"Wasps," Alex says, still trying to keep a straight face. "They're bad this season."

"Don't get stung, kids," I say as I imagine Alex's body covered in them.

"Great," Rachel says.

"You'll be fine. If you don't bother them, they won't sting you," Alex says. He probably wishes he could say the same thing about me, but it's too late, I'm already bothered. I watch them go. They would never have listened to me on the first try. Maybe Alex should get full custody. The urge to walk the other way, out the front door, and never look back is stronger than I could have ever imagined. I no longer think parents who abandon their children are cruel. Now I just think they feel like I do. Incredibly sad. Hopeless.

"I don't have to stay," Alex says. "But I'm paying for the room."

"Save your money for your mistress." The girl behind the desk is openly watching us, wide-eyed.

"Please," Alex says. "I'm begging you."

I put my credit card away, lean on the counter, and smile at the girl. She is very pretty. In her twenties. Does she sleep with married men? "I'd like the honeymoon suite," I say. The girl raises an eyebrow and glances at Alex. I hate her.

"Lena," Alex says.

"Might as well make the best of it. Right? After all, this is the honeymoon we never had."

"I have one suite," the girl says. "And I can order champagne and roses."

She's back on my team. *"Brava!"* I say.

"My God," Alex says.

"But there will be noise from the streets," the girl says.

"The noisier the better," I say. This way I can yell at Alex all I like.

The suite is large and quite perfect for us non-honeymooners. We enter into a living room with two sofas, and straight ahead, two human-sized, arched windows overlook the street. There is a giant master bedroom with a balcony. We can take our fight outside while the kids stay in the living room with Stella. The biggest problem with the suite, besides the fact that there isn't cable, or a swimming pool, or video games, is the thick, humid air. It clings to us. The "air conditioner" is a tall, tower-looking thing with a hose sticking into a hole by the window. It gurgles when I turn it on and gives off a swampy smell but not much else. I turn it off and fling all the windows open. They are the kind that latch at the top and open like doors. I love them. Under different circumstances, I would have loved Florence.

Noise from the street filters in. The voices are festive a rallying cry. There must be some sort of sports game on, for every once in a while we hear men cheering, their deep voices rising in unison.

"Football," Alex says when another round rings out. "Sounds like the Italians are winning." If we weren't here, would Alex be watching the game somewhere with his mistress?

"American football or soccer?" Josh asks.

"Soccer," Alex says. "It's the World Cup."

"Can we watch?"

"You'll have to see what channels you get, buddy. But I can't promise anything."

"Will you watch with me?"

"Mom and Dad have to talk," Rachel says. "I'll watch with you. Except no talking and no soccer."

I am grateful, for once, that I can depend on Rachel. She is happy because the living room has two couches. I long for the days where simple things like that could make me happy. I am thankful that my kids are still at an age when two couches is an incredibly exciting thing. Seeing Rachel here, dressed in age-appropriate jeans and a pink top, she once again resembles my innocent little girl. I am going to fight like hell to keep her this way for as long as possible.

It doesn't take long before we are all sweating. I encourage the kids to put on swimsuits and stand under the cold shower. Josh is over the moon at the suggestion, and Alex and I laugh as he jumps about the room in his swim shorts, snapping his towel. And then we glance at each other, and the laughing comes to a slamming halt. Once inside the bedroom, I take off my dress without even thinking about it. I am about to remove my slip as well when I realize Alex is in the room. This is the first time in sixteen years that I feel there is something wrong with undressing in front of him. It's been six months since he's seen me in person. I am here to confront him about his infidelity, and here I am, minutes into it, taking off my clothes. But it's way too hot to put the dress back on.

I turn and face my husband. A familiar pang of desire hits me as he takes me in. We have always had a great sex life. Granted, I only had two other partners before Alex, both in college before I captured the man of my dreams. But I can't imagine sex being any better with anyone else. In bed, as in everything else, Alex knows me like no other. If things were right between us, he would be making a move on me, pressing against me, murmuring things into my ear while we tried to keep it down for the kids.

"What are you looking at?" I say. I've put tremendous effort my entire life into keeping in shape for my husband. And he still threw me over for a younger girl. I hate that I still care what he thinks, that I want to look good for him. I hate that I'm not going to make other feminists proud, because the truth is, he's still my husband and I want him back.

"You're beautiful," Alex says quietly.

My eyes tear instantly at the compliment I so crave. "Look where it got me," I say. I step out onto the balcony. The old me wouldn't have dared bare myself in my slip to the world. The new me, it seems, is an exhibitionist. The old Alex would have made a comment or joke about my being on the balcony in a slip. The new one follows me out, but doesn't say a word. I can see people strolling the streets below, and even though I can still hear cheers, I can't tell exactly where they are coming from. I stay facing the street, and Alex takes one of the patio chairs behind me. He's usually so talkative. Now he's as mute as the stone statues that cover this city. The ones that will outlive us all. Alex and I will one day be gone forever. This lifetime is so short. Who says I can't forgive my husband an affair. Who says?

The air is sweet and cloying. "How long has it been going on?" I say without turning around.

"Not long."

"How long?"

"Two months."

Two months of sleeping with another woman was not long? It feels like a lifetime to me. "So if you had come home after the first semester?" I say. He doesn't answer. He doesn't have to. "Did you stay because of her?"

Alex lifts out of his chair. "No," Alex says. "It wasn't going on then."

"Where did you meet her?" I am asking the questions I think I am supposed to ask; only I don't really give a shit. There is nothing he can say, I realize. It's too late. He's done it. It's done.

"Through the university."

If he had come home when he was supposed to have come home, or if I had come to Florence, we would still be a happy family. "Two months," I say. "You've been sleeping with, kissing, touching, laughing with, and having sex with another woman for two months." I don't know what bothers me more. Alex having intercourse with her, or Alex cuddling up to her in bed, both of them falling asleep content and entwined. "And you were going to live with her for the summer."

"That hadn't been finalized."

"What a relief." My voice is dripping with sarcasm. Alex

hangs his head. I don't know what else to say. Everything I do say is going to come out nasty, and he deserves it, but it's going to leave an icky film on me. I can feel the blackness growing on me. I am totally unprepared to ask him anything. I don't have the rule book on how to confront your husband about an affair. What am I supposed to ask?

"Do you love her?" I say. That's the one thing I want to know. *Was the sex better than it was with me?* That's the other.

Suddenly, the bedroom door springs open, and Josh leaps onto the balcony. He is clutching a bag of chips.

"Can we eat out of the minibar?" Oh God. Food. I forgot about food. Just because I can't imagine eating ever again doesn't mean that they don't need to eat.

"No," Alex says.

"Let them," I say. "They're starving."

"We'll go get dinner. A proper meal."

"You take them," I say. "I can't eat." Ever again.

"Josh, go get dressed. Tell Rachel. Give me just one minute, okay, bud?" Josh nods and hops out of the room. Alex is right; the kids should have a proper meal. He is the better parent.

"How about this," Alex says. "I'll take the kids to dinner, and I'll call Harold and Jean. They can probably take them for the evening." Harold is a colleague of Alex's, and Jean is his wife. They have five kids of their own. I've always thought Harold was a pompous windbag, but I like Jean. She's very outgoing and brassy. They are a decade older than us, but have twice the energy.

"The whole family is here in Florence?" I say.

"Yes," Alex admits. He's wincing again. He's been doing this a lot this evening.

"Because Harold was asked to work the summer semester too."

"Yes." Even though Alex knows where I'm going with this, he's going to make me lead him there step-by-step. I realize he doesn't know what the rules are anymore either.

"So Jean and the kids are here in Florence."

"Jean got a job too. She's curating a group of public artworks."

"Well, good for her." The tears, the tears, the tears. They're just making me angry now. I seem to have an endless capacity to be freshly hurt. For the first time it occurs to me that I may not survive this. "Did they ask if I was coming for the summer? With the kids?"

Alex looks away.

"Of course they did," I say. "Of course they did." He is just standing there looking like a wounded animal. I brush past him and into the bedroom. I want to throw something at him. I want to physically hurt him. "Do they know about her?"

"They know who she is," Alex says. "But that's it."

"Are you sure?"

Alex throws out his arms. Runs his fingers through his hair.

"She's very pretty," I say. "And very young. And very evil." A cheer rises from the revelers, the loudest yet.

"I can't believe that thing with the video," Alex says. "It definitely wasn't her best moment. She was upset with me—"

"Oh my God. You're defending her? Are you actually standing here in front of me—your wife—and defending her?"

"Please. I can't think with the kids here. I can't talk about this with them in the next room."

"What will you tell them?"

Alex is confused.

"Harold and Jean."

"The truth. That my wife is here. That we need some time alone."

His wife. He called me his wife. I want to ask him to say it again. I want his words to save me, bring me back to life. For this moment, this little passing slice of time, I am still Lena Wallace, somebody's wife.

"Call them," I say.

CHAPTER 8

Alex calls Harold and Jean right before he takes the kids to dinner. I can tell he's talking to voice mail rather than live people. He sounds so normal. He's using his "entertaining" voice. He has a professor voice, a dad voice, a husband voice, and this put-on-the-charm voice that he's employing now. Does he also have a mistress voice? His entertaining voice is louder than normal. He sounds like he's trying too hard. It's the voice of a man trying to pretend everything is okay when he knows that it's the exact opposite. It tugs at my heart.

His professor voice is passionate and knowledgeable. As a father he knows how to switch between loving and scolding. My favorite has always been his husband voice. Even when he's angry with me, there's a softness to it, a protective quality. Llama. Or Drama Llama. He likes to tease me. Maybe I shouldn't say husband voice; maybe it's his lover voice. Because it's the first voice he used on me.

"What will it take to get you to go out with me?" We stood in the quad, each with a handful of books. Little did TA Alex know, I was the one in control of this. I was the one who had been doing everything under the sun to attract him. Part of my nine-point plan was to make him think he was pursuing me. And it was working.

"Get a Viking cap tattooed on your ass," I said as I walked away.

Back in the hotel, I glance at Alex's ass as he talks on the phone. I wonder what he's told Alexandria about that tattoo? Or has he had it removed? Or replaced. Is there now a giant Italian flag on his ass instead? I couldn't believe that he actually went out and did it. He dropped his pants in my dorm room. There was Alex Wallace's perfect ass with a tattoo of a Viking cap. Horns for a horny boy.

"If you can't do it, we'll understand," Alex was saying. "But we'd love to at least all get together."

We would? Has he forgotten that they have five kids? Since when did my husband become such a consummate liar? "The more the merrier," he says, before hanging up. *Does that include his whore?*

He gives me a long look when he is done with the call, as if he knows what I'm thinking, and he probably does. I have an urge to ask him to drop his pants, as proof of his love for me. The tattoo has faded over the years; each wedding anniversary he has joked about getting it redone. Last year he joked about adding a fleet of Viking ships. It's a good thing he didn't; they'd be sinking.

"I don't think it's going to happen tonight," Alex says. For a second I think he's talking about sex. Of course it's not going to happen. Right? Or should we just do it, get it over like ripping off a Band-Aid?

"What?" I say.

"Harold and Jean."

"Oh. Well. You tried." He gives me another strange look. It feels like a series of mini victories, these looks. He doesn't know what to say or do. Alex is used to asking a lot of questions. I should start counting them, these confused glances, collect them like tacky porcelain owls.

"I'm going to take the kids to dinner. Are you sure you won't join us?"

"I can't." How can you eat? How dare you eat?

"Okay. I'll bring you something."

"Don't."

"I will anyway. What about Stella?"

"I'm sure she'll eat anything."

"Do you want us to take her?"

"I don't care." I can't make any more decisions. Not a single one.

"We'll take her. Plenty of alfresco dining. She can sit under the table."

"Great." So they'll still be a happy family of four. Do they need me at all? I kiss the kids good-bye and try to sound cheery. I stand by the window and watch them as they exit the hotel and start down the street. Josh puts his hand in Alex's. Rachel lingers behind. If I could go back in time and know what was coming, I would have kept this from them. Rachel wouldn't have to be feeling this way. Sports fans continue to cheer; punctuated voices, origins unknown, rise and fall as if the streets themselves are crying out for joy. Italian men sure do seem to love their sports. I cross through the living room and enter the bathroom. It is small. The shower is simply a nozzle that you lift off the fixture. There is no bidet. Several hanging white towels look barely large enough to cover a small child. The mirror is streaked. There is, however, a towel warmer. Just what we need in hundred-something-degree weather, warm towels. Everywhere I look I imagine myself here with Alex on our honeymoon. We would have definitely showered together. Maybe it's the first thing we would have done. Drop our bags on the couch then race hand-in-hand into this small shower. "Warm towels," I would have said. Alex would have laughed, pulled me into him, kissed me.

"Warm bodies," he would have said.

"Wet bodies," I would have said. With one hand Alex would have reached and turned on the shower, while undressing me with the other. I touch the towel warmer as I watch our younger selves shower. So happy. So in love. So many wonderful things ahead of us.

Maybe, if we had come here on our honeymoon, Alex wouldn't have been able to cheat. Everywhere he went, there would have been reminders of our love. Instead, there hadn't been a trace of me anywhere. No memories, no lingering love, no stone walls where we carved our initials. A loud rap on the door interrupts my thoughts. Did Alex forget his key? I pad over to the door and open it without even looking out the peephole. Another strange benefit of life at its worse, I am no longer afraid of knocks on the door. I do, however, forget I am wearing only a slip until I see a young man standing before me with roses and champagne.

"I do," I say. He just looks at me, or rather, stares.

"For the honeymooners," he says after a while, lifting the bottle of champagne.

I lean in, put my index finger to my lips, then whisper. "They're in the shower." His eyebrows go up, and he glances in the direction of the bathroom, then his eyes slide down my body.

"Kidding," I say. I laugh, back up, and gesture for him to come in. He stands awkwardly like a teenager waiting for his prom date. I indicate that he can set the roses and champagne on the coffee table, then change my mind and point to the bedroom. When he returns, he once again stands awkwardly at the door, and I don't know if he's waiting for a tip or just trying to prolong seeing me in my slip.

"I don't have any euro, and my husband is having an affair," I say.

"It's okay," he says. He is handsome. Shaggy brown hair and brown eyes. Tall and muscular. I wonder if his English isn't very good or if he really thinks it's okay that my husband is having an affair.

"Enjoy your stay," he says.

"His mistress is Italian," I say. An eyebrow shoots up. I think he understands me; he just doesn't know what to say. I can hardly blame him. What can you say?

"Please enjoy your stay. *Ciao, bella.*" He reaches for the door-knob.

"Wait," I say. He turns, hands by his side, and waits. I grab his shirt collar, pull him into me, and kiss him full on the lips. At first he doesn't respond, and I am afraid he is going to call the police. *Scandalosa!* Another American woman accused of a sex crime in Italy. But then he puts his arms around my waist and begins to kiss me back. Take that, Alex! But when I feel the tip of his tongue probing my lips, I jerk away as if scalded. He stands, panting, mouth open. I glance down and see that his pants are unzipped. Oh God. When did he do that?

"*Ciao,*" I say, and propel him out the door. I shut it, lock it, bang my head against it several times. I think he is still standing on the other side, waiting for me to change my mind. What am I doing? If I want to get back at Alex, shouldn't I aim higher than a bellboy?

How could he do it? How could he carry on an affair? I don't have it in me. I wish I had a baseball bat. I want to hit something. Maybe when I'm back in the States I will rent out a giant warehouse, fill it with glass—ugly bottles, ceramic vases, Hello Kitty figurines and order baseball bats and goggles. I'll pump the place full of music by female artists raging against men, and charge pissed off women to come in and smash the crap out of everything. Wedding rings too! They can smash those if they'd like. I think it's a genius idea. It's good to have a plan. Just imagining a hundred baseball bats smashing glass and ceramic and tacky Asian cats calm me down. Hello Kitty? Try, Good-bye Kitty. I will make a fortune. I can see the headlines:

HOUSEWIFE TURNS INFIDELITY INTO INCOME . . .
WIFE HAS SMASHING TIME AFTER HUSBAND'S AFFAIR . . .
BETRAYED WIFE HITS A HOME RUN . . .
HELL HATH NO FURY FOR A WOMAN SCORNED, BUT AT LEAST NOW IT HAS A PLACE . . .

I enter the bedroom and stare at the roses. He placed them on the bedside table. I think of the roses Alex sent recently.

SORRY. I begin ripping petals off the roses by the handful. I sprinkle them on the bed. More romance for the honeymooners, right? I crawl on top of the bed and arrange the petals into a giant heart. I am capable of creating public works of art too. I take the stems, snap them, and make a jagged break in the middle of the heart. Should I do it? Should I create my broken heart all over Florence? Place them next to the popular chalk drawings? I stand back and survey my work. Michelangelo might not have been impressed, but I like it. I grab the bottle of champagne and take it onto the balcony. Three young men pass below, chatting animatedly in Italian, wearing soccer jerseys. I hold the bottle of champagne over the rail.

"*Ciao,*" I say. The boys stop and look up.

"*Ciao,*" they say. All grins.

"Want some?" I shake the bottle.

"*Si, si,*" they say.

I pop the cork. It flies up, then bounces off the balcony rail. The boys cheer. "Ready?" They laugh, fling open their arms, and nod. I upend the bottle and let it rain down on them. They dance in the champagne, catch some in their mouths, let it coat their lean bodies. More cheers, pats on the back, they are so happy for their team; they think I am happy for their team; they blow me kisses and disappear into the night. I stare after them long after they are gone, wishing I had saved some of the champagne for myself.

Shortly after, Alex returns with the kids, and Stella, and bags of food. The kids plop on the sofas and immediately turn on the television. Stella follows the bags of food as Alex begins taking out containers and setting them up on the table.

"I thought you were going to eat out," I say. He glances at me, then at Rachel. Her eyes are red and furious.

"We decided to stay in," he says. "We have plenty. I hope you join us." The television stations flicker by, one by one.

"Dufus," Rachel screams, "would you stop changing channels?!"

"Dufus," Alex says, shaking his head and laughing. Rachel gives me a satisfied look. So this is how it would be. If Alex and

I divorced, I would spend all week trying to instill manners and respect into the children and Alex would undo it in a single weekend by laughing and encouraging their bad habits. I storm over to Rachel.

"Look at me." She tries to look around me. I nudge her with my foot. "Look at me." Reluctantly, she meets my eyes.

"If I hear the word 'dufus' one more time, under any circumstances, you are never taking another dance lesson again." Rachel swallows, then her eyes quickly slide over to Alex.

"Lena," Alex says quietly.

I do not acknowledge him. "I am not joking. Do you understand?"

"Dad?" Rachel says.

"Let's just all calm down," Alex says.

"Do you understand?"

"Whatever."

"Just try me."

"It's all in Italian," Josh says, still flipping through channels.

"Duh," Rachel says. I lean down until there is barely an inch of space between our eyes. "What? Mom. Don't be weird."

"That goes for any word with attitude," I say.

"Jesus, Lena," Alex says.

I whirl on Alex. "What was that?"

"Let's just—"

"Calm down? Let's just calm down? Have you had to listen to this smart mouth for the past six months? She's emasculating your son. Is that okay with you?"

"What does that mean?" Josh says.

"I'm sorry, Mom," Rachel says.

"You have a lot of nerve, Professor Wallace. Here in Florence with your young, young, YOUNG little mistress. How dare you."

"Lena."

"Get out." I point to the door. My hand is shaking. Tears are coming. I do not like myself right now, and it's all his fault. I should have never brought the kids. Obviously I'm a horrible wife or Alex wouldn't have dreamed of doing this to me, and now I'm a horrible mother too.

"What did she do to me?" Josh says. "What was that word?" He looks terrified. Rachel is crying. I am crying. Stella has slunk into the bedroom. Alex is standing still, as if we are in an earthquake and he is waiting for the ground to stop shaking.

"I'm sorry, Josh," Rachel says. "I'm sorry, Mom."

"It's okay," I say. I sit on the sofa with Rachel and pat the space next to me until Josh comes over. I ruffle his hair. He is hot and sweaty. He shrugs, never taking his eyes off the television. Rachel starts to sniffle. I reach over and take her hand, then Josh's hand. Such little hands. They are children. "I love you both," I say. "I love you both very, very much."

"It's been a long day," Alex says. "We'll all feel better tomorrow." I wonder how he can lie like this. Rachel flings her arms around me and squeezes.

"I hate him," she says.

"Don't say that," I say. "It's not true." I don't dare look at Alex, because I can't imagine how he is feeling. She is his little girl. He would die for her. "It's okay that you feel angry. And hurt. But he's still your father. The only one you'll ever have." A sob breaks from behind me. We all look at Alex; it's horrifying to hear him cry.

"I'm sorry," he chokes out. "Rachel, baby. I'm sorry."

"Please eat," I say to the kids. "You'll feel better." I turn to Alex. "A word?" I point to the bedroom. He nods and then heads in. I follow, shut the door, and turn the radio on full blast. Italian voices filter out. They are speaking rapidly, animatedly over each other. It sounds like a talk show. There is something comforting about not knowing what's being said; it lifts the burden of listening. Alex stares at the broken heart on the bed. I am prepared for a fight when another sob breaks from him. I have to harden myself; I cannot feel sorry for him. He has on a dark green shirt, and the top four buttons are undone. I've never seen the shirt before. It must be MADE IN ITALY. Did she buy it for him? Or did he go on a shopping spree when he landed the beautiful young thing? His hair is curling at the ends from the humidity. He wipes his eyes, and takes a deep breath, and straightens up. Sweat glistens on his forehead. His cell phone rings. He takes it out of his pocket, and the two of us stare at it. He glances at the screen, shuts it off, and then shoves it back into his pocket. How many times has he done that with my calls? How many times did Alexandria witness him ignoring me, his wife, for her? He won't even look at me.

"Was that her?" Alex doesn't move or answer. I ratchet up the volume. "Was. That. Her?"

"Yes."

Smash, smash, smash, smash. "Have you talked to her since we arrived?"

"No."

I wonder if she is expecting him. What is their routine? Is this date night? The hour they stroll the streets of Florence? Go for a glass of wine? Or just make love at her place?

"Is she a student?" It doesn't make sense because his students are all American, but I ask anyway. I want to emphasize that she is young. She looks like she could be a student. And who knows, maybe some Italians take classes there too; what do I know? I've proven over the last six months how little I know.

"No." His answers are curt, but I can tell it's because he's afraid he will start crying again. Well, let him cry. I have certainly been crying a lot lately, will probably be crying for the rest of my life.

So she isn't a student. Do I feel any relief? At least this affair will not cost him his job. Then again, if he were screwing a student, I could use it as leverage. *If you don't cut it off right now, I'm going to tell the university that you're screwing a student.* Is this what I've come to? Needing leverage?

"This is your one shot," I say. "Start talking."

Alex sits at the edge of the bed with his hands clasped and head bowed. "I'm glad you know," he says. "It's been eating me up inside."

So many nasty retorts are on the tip of my tongue, but I keep them in. I will never hear what he has to say if I start down that road. In my mind I am listening, but I am also smashing Hello Kittys.

"Remember the public art show that I told you Jean is curating?"

"Yes."

"It's a walking tour of chalk paintings—"

"What?

"They're quite the rage right now. They're on the streets, on stone walls, on trees—all through the touristy parts of Florence."

"I've heard of it."

"So soon?"

"Someone handed me a brochure." *Right after I dumped gelato on the slutty chalk face. If I'd had unappreciated ice cream, I would have dropped that too.*

"She's working on the project. She's—um—the subject of the project actually."

"Oh my God." *The face didn't just look like Alexandria; it was Alexandria. She's like the Angelina Jolie of Florence. I am Jennifer. This is not happening.*

"They're working out of a space at the university. That's how we met."

"So Jean knows about this. And, I assume, Harold too." I am not going to say a word about her being the "subject" of this fad art exhibit. I'm not going to act like it matters or like I care. But I am going to dump gelato on every single one I come across; in fact, I am going to dig out that brochure and purposefully come across every single one. Let them throw me in an Italian jail. I'll tell the world that the face of Florence is a husband-stealing shrew.

"None of us have ever discussed it," Alex says.

"But they know, don't they?"

"They might. Alexandria has been working closely with the artist. Giovatti. He's quite good. And if the chalk paintings are any indication—I guess you might call her his muse."

Chalk drawings. Not paintings. Drawings. But I hold my tongue. No matter what, I will never admit to my seething jealousy. I will not acknowledge her beauty or her youth. Alex sounds bitter enough for the both of us. He is jealous of this artist and Alexandria. "He has all of Florence under his spell," Alex adds, cementing my suspicion.

"I don't care about some stupid artist. Stop deflecting!" Alex gets up, and I throw myself on the bed on top of the broken heart. I wiggle my way up so I can lean against the headboard and swish away the petals with the tips of my toes. "Just couldn't keep your hands off her, could you?"

"I'm so sorry. I never wanted you to find out this way. But please. Is there any way we can discuss this without the sarcasm?" Dumbfounded, I open my mouth. Alex crosses to me and stares down at me intensely. "I want us to talk. Really talk. And even though your anger is well deserved, I want to make sure we are really listening to each other." I wait. I am not going to make this easy on him. "I didn't plan this, I swear. And I told her, right away, that I was married." Alex stops, looks me in the eye. "Lena. There is absolutely nothing I can say that's going to make this okay, or any easier."

"I need to hear it," I say. "All of it."

"Like I said. They were working at the university. Giovatti was attracting so much attention that I had to check out his work for myself. Alexandria was flirtatious. I'm used to that. I didn't think anything of it. But if I'm to be honest, I should have stopped going over to see her. I told myself nothing was going to happen. And I was never alone with her—if we went out socially, we were always in a group. I guess I started to feel too comfortable. Then one night, everyone else left early—"

"Stop," I say. I get as far away from him as I can. "I don't want to hear anymore."

"She had a family tragedy. I was there to comfort her. It just happened."

I do not take the bait about the family tragedy. I could care less. "It just happened."

"It's happened, and I'm so, so sorry, but it's happened, Lena."

Pain roars through me like a locomotive barreling down

tracks. "What's happened?" I say. Oh my God. Oh my god. "Are you in love with her?" Alex looks away. "Look at me. Are you in love with her?"

"I'm sorry," Alex says.

"Say it."

"I never meant for this to happen."

"Say it."

"Lena, please."

"Say it."

"You know I've always tried my best to be a good husband and a good father. But something happened to me here. I feel like a different person. It's not an excuse, but—"

"SAY IT."

"I love her. I wish to God I didn't, and I'm sorry. But I love her."

CHAPTER 9

I leap off the bed. "You love her? You've known her, what? A few months?"

"Okay, okay. Infatuation? Passion? I don't know what to call it. I'm confused."

"Stop."

"You asked, Lena. I didn't want to say it. I'm trying to be honest."

"Sixteen years of marriage. I am your wife." I point to the door. "Those are your children out there." I glance at the bushy orange tail sticking out from under the bed. "Your dog. We're your family, Alex."

"I didn't plan this. Am I flawed? Weak? Ashamed? Yes. To all of it. Yes."

Baseball bat, baseball bat, baseball bat. He loves the other woman. My husband loves the other woman. Not me. He doesn't want to stay married? This honestly never occurred to me. Husbands never leave the wife for the other woman. They just don't do it! I'm struck mute. All of my revenge fantasies since finding out about his mistress have revolved around Alex's begging me for a second chance. This scenario, that he loves her, that he still wants to be with her, never, ever occurred to me. How could it not have occurred to me? How many times am I going to be blindsided? This cannot be happening.

"We said 'til death do us part, Alex. You don't get to do this to me."

"I know you don't want to hear this, but I've changed, Lena. I haven't been fully who I want to be. Not until I came here."

"Do you think I'm who I 'want to be'? I gave up who I thought I was going to be for you. For the kids."

"It shouldn't be that way. Don't you see? We haven't been living authentically—it's not real life, the way life is meant to be lived."

If he says *la bella vita,* I will kill him dead. "Are you saying the past sixteen years of our lives haven't been real? Go out there and say that to your children, Alex."

"Of course they've been real. But I've changed. I still love my kids. I still love the years we shared. But here? I'm the man I'm meant to be, Lena. Not the man I've been trying so hard to be."

It feels like someone is clawing my stomach out.

"I'm not the only one," Alex says quietly. "My wife hasn't been happy in a long time either."

My wife, he says, as if I am not that person. Who the hell is he to tell me I'm not happy? Who the hell even has time to be happy? I'm busy, that's all. Very, very busy. And I certainly was a lot happier than I am right now. It's all relative. "We should have been here with you," I say. "You should have seen to it."

"You're right. I should have. I'm sorry. I will regret that the rest of my life."

"The rest of your life with her you mean?"

"And the fact that you're here now and can't even enjoy it? That kills me, Lena." Lena. Not Llama. It's true. My husband doesn't love me anymore. It's like waking up to find your left leg amputated. I still kind of feel it, but it's not there. "I know this is hard."

"Hard? If you took a knife and stabbed me in the heart, that would be hard. This is way, way beyond that." Alex looks at me, and for a second I think he is going to say, Drama Llama. But he doesn't.

"Believe it or not, I want you to be happy. I want us all to be happy."

I laugh, and it sounds like a crazy laugh coming from a crazy person. "I'm never going to be happy again." I reach for the nearest object. It's a bedside lamp. Perfect for reading a little romance novel before slipping into bed with your husband, or lover, or married man you're having an affair with. I yank the cord out of the wall and hurl it across the room. It smashes, and the bulb pops and then shatters, but it doesn't make near enough noise. "You think I'm going to let you get away with this? Abandoning me? Our children?"

"Keep your voice down. I am not abandoning the children. I am still their father."

"We're a package deal!"

"Shhh."

"I'LL YELL IF I WANT TO YELL." Stella streaks for the door. Alex opens it and lets her out. His shoulders are slumped; his breathing is labored.

"See? You call this happy?"

"You made me like this. No matter how fucking unhappy you are, you don't have the right to fuck another woman!" I've lost it. My Viking is raging; my controls are loose; I am grasping at vines and slipping down each and every one. All that waits below is a fiery pit. And then I hear it. Silence. I can no longer hear the television in the next room. The kids have turned down the volume. To listen to us. I open the bedroom door. Josh and Rachel tumble in.

"Mom," Rachel says. "Did he hurt you?"

"Rachel!" Alex says. A look of extreme anguish crosses over Alex's face, and it gives me a jolt of pleasure. Until I look at my daughter. She is in pain, and she is masking it with her defiance. She knows Alex would not physically hurt me; she is bringing out her arsenal. I don't want her to take on this role; I don't want my children to witness this. Children of war, I think.

And I am the one who has thrown them onto the battlefield. It will not go down as one of my finer parental decisions.

"Your father would never hurt me like that," I say. I don't add, but think, that the way he has hurt me is just as bad. The bedside phone rings, jarring us all. Josh lunges for it before either Alex or I can stop him.

"Hello? That was my mom. She comes from a long line of Vikings." He nods vigorously then hangs up. "Front desk. You're too loud, Mom. You're disturbing the guests." In Italy less than twenty-four hours and the Italians are telling me I'm being too loud. The Italians.

"Kids, please," Alex says. They look to me. I nod. Reluctantly my children slink back into the living room. I walk over to my suitcase and dig out a green sundress. Alex watches me put it on.

"What are you doing?" he says.

"Going out."

"Where?"

"None of your business."

"I don't want you wandering around in the dark."

"You should have thought of that before."

"I'll leave. You stay here with the kids."

And let you run back to your mistress? "Absolutely not," I say. "I'm going out, and you're going to stay with the kids." I feel free. Terrified. Like anything can happen. Alex walks onto the balcony. I hear something buzz. It's his cell phone. It's dropped from his pocket onto the bed. I pick it up, slip it into my purse, and walk out.

I stand in front of the hotel, looking down the dim, narrow street. I am a fool. He loves *her.* He wants to live with *her.* What am I supposed to do and where am I supposed to go right now? If I only knew where she lived, I would go to her flat this instant. Alexandria might have Alex fooled, but I know exactly what a conniving little tramp she is. She deliberately made me watch the two of them kiss, and Alex still wants to be with her. My footing is gone; everything I thought I knew about my husband has come unraveled. What if this woman is trying to scam

Alex? Does she think he has money? Or is there some kind of prestige to being with an American professor? I highly doubt it. Men are one thing, but how a woman can cheat with someone else's husband mystifies and enrages me. What happened to sisterhood?

I start walking away from the hotel. I need to think, figure this out. It's slightly cooler outside than it is in the hotel, and out here the warmth feels nice. It smells like someone is doing his or her laundry. How peaceful; how ironic. I don't dare look up at the hotel windows; I don't want to see the kids' faces pressed against the window, worried about me, although the most likely scenario is that the kids are glued to the television, oblivious to my absence. And what is Alex doing? Lying in bed dreaming of his mistress, or is he in the living room trying to repair the damage with Rachel? Has he realized his cell phone is gone? I reach the corner of the street, stand under an old-fashioned street lamp, and flip it open.

First I check for text messages. There are none. Either they are not into sexting or Alex has cleared out all the messages. I cross to a darkened stoop across the way and sit. Slowly but surely all of the earlier anger and adrenaline have drained from my body, and I realize I am exhausted. I have to look at his call log. But first I look back up at the street lamp. What a beautiful city. And me, in this foul mood, I am like a cancer, invading it. I wish Megan were here; I could use a friend. Especially one who was there with me when I first fell in love with Alex. Megan was a witness to the fact that he once loved me very, very much. Where does love like that go? And if it can disappear, just like that, then did he ever really love me in the first place? After all the times I dreamed of being in Florence, now that I'm here, I'm sitting on steps thinking of my dorm room in college. How I burst in the door and flopped on the bed across from Megan.

"I met the man I'm going to marry," I said. Megan was painting her toenails neon green and chewing purple bubble gum.

"It's only our first week. You should sample the rest of the offerings first."

"Don't need to. I come from a long line of Vikings. When I want something, I go for it."

"Well, I come from a long line of Georgia peaches. When we want something, we let it come to us." I laughed even though I could tell Megan was a hundred percent serious.

"Are you going to be my bridesmaid or not?"

"Men are hunters. If he wants you, he'll come after you."

"Then I have to get him to hunt me." I moved to my closet and took out my giant sketchpad. I propped it up. "Help me come up with a nine-point plan to make him chase me," I said. Megan groaned, dug in her desk drawer, and held up a colorful glass pipe. As she lit up, I drew a huge circle on the canvas. A bull's-eye. And in the middle I wrote **ALEX.**

I should have listened to Megan. Who would I be now if I had never married him? I was going to have to buy a calling card soon and talk to Megan. Surely if there was any occasion when you could call your dear friend up at all hours of the morning, this had to be it. When I did finally land Alex, Megan was jealous. Even after she got married, she complained her marriage wasn't as steamy or passionate as mine with Alex. Some good that did me. Megan was still in a steady marriage. Her husband, Martin, was just not the type you could ever imagine cheating. Or getting off the couch for that matter, but at least Megan always knew where to find him. Did Alex know when he took the job that our marriage was at risk? Had he taken the job just to end it?

I push off the stoop and head down the street with the lamp at the corner. Most of the street names are carved into the corners of the buildings. I am keeping an eye on where I'm going so that I can find my way back home. Compared to the earlier revelries, it's fairly quiet. Stores are closed, but restaurants and bars have their doors thrown wide open, and the closer I get to the center of the city, the more people I see. A cluster of boys and girls stumble past me, all clad in Italian football jerseys. They are young and jovial. Several feet behind them, an old woman pushes a cart. A skinny black kitten trots at her heels.

An old man leans against the wall of a building, smoking a cigarette. His face is severe and heavily lined. He looks weathered
and tested by life. He looks like the type of man who had a mistress in his day. I wish I had the guts to ask him.

I reach the end of the street. I need a direction. A revelation.
A lightning bolt striking me with the answer to my prayers. I
need my husband to love me again. In the near distance I see
the Ponte Vecchio bridge spanning the Arno River. It's a beacon, and I head for it. Alex's phone rings in my hand. Is Alex
calling me from the hotel? Calling to apologize, tell me what a
crazy mistake he'd made, how he didn't mean it when he said
he loved her and not me?

The letter **"A"** flashes on the screen. Was this Alexandria?
The proverbial scarlet letter? How dare he. At least now I have
her number. I click open the phone, but don't speak.

"You still here? I tell you! I will kill you!" It's a deep male
voice. He's Italian.

"Who is this?"

He doesn't answer right way, but I can hear him breathing. I
frown. Drunk? "I am Marco," he says. "Who are you?"

Mi chiamo Marco, I mouth. "Lena."

"Lena." I like the way he says my name. Lingering over it as if
he's considering awarding me some kind of grand prize. "You
are the wife?"

It's all he needs to say. I know instantly he is the husband. Or
the boyfriend. I did not see this coming either. "I am the wife."

"I want to kill you husband." I almost laugh. And not because
I think another man threatening to kill my husband is funny,
but because of the way he says it, like a bad actor on an Italian
soap opera. I've never seen an Italian soap opera, but I imagine
soap operas are all the same. Amnesia victims, and handsome
surgeons, and beautiful women unknowingly in love with their
half brothers. Hot, macho, shirtless Italian men standing on ve-
randas overlooking the Tuscan hills, throwing an accusing finger to the heavens and shouting, "I want to kill you husband."

"Are you the husband?" I say.

"No, no, no. I am the lover."

"Well, let me tell you something, lover, if anyone gets to do the killing, it's the wife and the mother. *Capisce?*"

"How long you marry?"

"Sixteen years." It sounds like a long time. It makes me sound old. Whoever this "lover" is, he's younger than Alex.

"Do you still love him?" he asks me. He is very forward.

"Of course I love him. Very much. He has two children who love him very much. You might think it's funny to go around saying you want to kill somebody, but I don't." My voice echoes through the cobblestoned streets. I had better be careful; my temper is flaring again.

"*Si, si, si.* I no kill him. I only say I want to kill him."

"As long as I'm clear. I am the wife. I am here in Florence, and there will be no killing." This is ridiculous, as if we were actually negotiating this.

"Welcome to Firenze!" he says as if he is my personal tour guide.

"*Grazie.* I'm hanging up now." But I don't; I hold the phone to my ear as I walk, wondering what he looks like. Alexandria doesn't seem like the type to go for ugly men. I wonder if he is as beautiful as she is.

"You are the wife, and I am the lover. This makes us friends, no?"

"No. Bye now."

"Wait, wait." I hear a rustling noise, and the opening and shutting of a door. He has changed locations. That's right. He's calling me on her phone. That means he stole it like I did, or he's with her. Maybe I should indulge him a little longer, see if I can find out where she lives.

"Where are you?" I say. I realize it sounds too familiar, but given everything he's blurted out, I figure I can get away with it.

"I am in his flat. She is here too. I am here, in his flat, with her. You tell him."

"What do you mean, *his* flat?" There is obviously a language gap here, but I still want to keep this murderous Romeo on the phone as long as possible.

"*Scusi, scusi.* Is your flat too, no? You are wife, so it is yours too."

"Alex lives in the university dorms," I say. "It's Alexandria who has a flat."

Marco laughs, throaty and deep. "Alexandria afford flat on her own?" He lets out a string of Italian, all the while laughing. He ends with a word I recognize. "*Impossibile.*"

Alexandria, afford a flat on her own, impossible. "You're saying that this flat is rented by my husband?"

"*Si, si.* Through the American university."

Alex has a flat; Alex has a flat; Alex has a flat. Where he keeps his mistress. Why that big, fat liar.

"You tell him. He no answer his *telefonino* tonight, so she ring me!"

"First, I have his *telefonino.* Second, that's bad, Marco."

"What does this mean?"

"You shouldn't go running to her the minute she calls." What was the Italian word for doormat? I didn't need it; Marco caught on pretty quickly.

"Ah, *si, si.*" He sounds disappointed. "But I am only here as friend. She cry, cry, cry, and now she is like angel, sleeping."

"Seriously? How many 'angels' do you know who sleep with married men?" My God, all they need is a gorgeous face and body and the rest really doesn't matter, does it?

"You are jealous," Marco says.

No shit, Sherlock. I wonder how you say that in Italian. "She's sleeping with my husband."

"Ah. Maybe this will not last."

"Maybe we can help end it."

"How do you mean by this?"

"Why don't you slide into bed next to the little angel and take a picture with your *telefonino?*" I say it partly because I want to see if he will do it, and partly because I am starting to like saying "*telefonino.*"

"Ah. *Si! Si!*"

"Then send it to me—to this number." I would make sure

Alex saw it. I am close to the bridge now, and I can see colored lights reflecting off the river. I gasp.

"What is wrong?"

"The Ponte Vecchio bridge. The lights. It's so gorgeous."

"Firenze!"

This time I feel every ounce of his passion. "I've only seen it during the day," I say. "It's magical."

"I will meet you." He has lowered his voice, and he is talking to me as if we are lovers. Suddenly, I want to meet him too.

"Okay," I say. I am afraid to say more.

"You stay near the bridge. I come."

"I'll wait in the middle of the bridge," I say. "And don't forget to take that picture." I hang up, and I am smiling. I keep smiling until it really dawns on me that I have just invited a complete stranger, who wants to kill my husband, to meet me at night in the middle of a bridge.

CHAPTER 10

I stand directly in the middle of the bridge, looking out onto the shimmering Arno River. I will gather strength from this ancient, yet sturdy beauty. Ponte Vecchio. It means, "Old Bridge." The three arches supporting the bridge were built to allow boats to easily pass underneath. During World War II it was the only bridge spanning the Arno left untouched by the Germans. Instead of blowing it up, they blocked passage by taking down medieval buildings on either side, but I am grateful it remains. It gives me pause to remember that you can never be untouched by war, and often both sides will be destroyed. Just like Alex's affair has already injured the kids and me. I must stop the damage. Even if he can't see it, his mistress has declared war.

Bands of light reflect in the river, along with a whimsical mirror image of the bridge, and shops, and glittering lights above. I have always dreamed of this city glowing in the night, and it does not disappoint. People are everywhere, gathered as if there were a festival, enjoying the sights and sounds of the evening. Gold and jewelry shops, built into the side of the bridge, attract tourists from all over the world. Now, at night, their shuttered brown and green eyes reflect in the Arno River. Tucked into an alcove along one side sits the bust of Benvenuto Cellini. He was a famous Italian goldsmith, painter, sculptor, soldier, musician, and writer. In the Loggia dei Lanzi, I showed the kids his bronzed masterpiece: *Perseus with the Head of Medusa.* Typical overachiever. If I sound bitter, it's because Cellini was known to have taken some of his female models as mistresses. I imagine a bust of Alex on this bridge, watching over all the beautiful young girls who pass by below, while I am nearby, immortalized in bronze, holding a severed head in my sculpted hand. *Lena with the Head of Alexandria.* Hey. A girl can dream, can't she?

I shouldn't be engaging in such destructive fantasies. Not here! In Firenze, the beautiful beating heart of Italy. Once again I can't help comparing Italy and America. The Italians just seem to grasp incorporating beauty and leisure as an essential part of daily life. They are older and wiser, and we, America, are the younger child, forging ahead without much thought to what we might be trampling underfoot. I cannot think of a single pedestrian bridge back home where people gather like this on a nightly basis. Italy is like an older grandmother, whispering in my ear. Slow down. Eat. Look. Walk. Listen. Live. Alex's words echo through me.

My wife hasn't been happy in a long time. Who has time to be happy? Obviously, the Italians do. Sure, they have their share of miseries. They have been affected by the economy, like the rest of the world. And Alex told me something recently that startled me. Despite having the third largest economy, Italy has the highest percentage of children in poverty, compared to all the other European nations. Like many places, there is a divide. The thriving north and the withering south. But here, in Florence, I only see the golden side of Italy. Ancient cathedrals, and regal arched bridges, and magnificent statues. Gelato instead of ice cream. The Tuscan sun over tanning booths. I am just as in love with Florence as Alex. Could it be that he's projecting his love of this city onto Alexandria? I would have easily lived here in Florence with Alex. How can he think that he's the only one who feels as if he could be somebody else here, somebody better?

A musician plays his guitar in the middle of the walkway. Soon, a man with an accordion joins him. Their tune is lively and melancholy at the same time, and as the notes filter through the warm night air, they send a thrill through me, and even my fingertips seem to tingle. Tonight feels like it is my night, and anything is possible. As I wait, and watch, I count at least five pairs of clasped hands. All the lovers coming out at night. When was the last time Alex and I held hands? It's insane that I can't remember and even crazier that it might have been the last time we ever will. I would have wanted to know, so that I could have memorized the feel of his palm against mine, so I could have squeezed it gently, so I could have stopped all of this from happening. I study the hand-holders pair by pair. A tall man with a woman so tiny I think she is his daughter until she lifts his face to his and I see they are both in their fifties. An old man and woman; he is holding not only her hand but also a bag full of something. Perhaps they are on their way home, and I pray they have been married for fifty plus years, and they will have fifty plus more. Or are they married to other old people, who are hiding away at home, either not knowing or not caring at this point that their other halves are still getting some on the side? Where is this Marco? How many times have Alex and Alexandria passed through here holding hands? How many pairs of eyes looked at them and said, "What a lovely couple"?

I think holding hands is one of the most intimate things you can do with your lover. It means, "I'm with you," and "You're not going far from me," and "I am linked to you," and maybe, most of all, "I've got you." I used to slip my hand into Alex's every chance I got. Once, when Rachel was only nine months old, we went hiking. Alex had Rachel in a pack on his back, and we came across a log over a river. Athletic Alex had no problem crossing it, even with a pudgy toddler on his back, but halfway across I lost my balance and started to slip. I cried out, and in lightning speed, Alex was in front of me, holding my hand. *I've got you,* the gesture said. Hand in hand we finished crossing the log. Alex walking backward, me inching forward. Rachel's round face stared at me from behind Alex's head. I must have had quite the stricken expression on my face, for Rachel stared at me intently, then suddenly tilted her head back and roared with laughter. It was a deep sound, as if emanating from a tiny gangster instead of a tiny toddler. Alex and I were so startled, we both slipped into the stream. Luckily it wasn't too deep, and Alex was able to keep Rachel above water. The only reason it took us a long time to reach the shore was because of how hard we were laughing. That was real. Whatever else, we had that; no one can take it from us, and it was real.

But my memories feel corroded now, like a beloved bike left out in forty days of pounding rain. If not Alex, I can't imagine holding anyone's hand ever again.

I don't know what I will be able to salvage of my marriage, of the man whose hand I have been holding for sixteen years, but I do know one thing. Alexandria slept with the wrong woman's husband. She will not get to sneak away gently into this Florence night. I am coming, and she will be forced to face me.

A half-moon dangles over the bridge, tipped sideways like a beloved hat. I look up, and the minute I see the tall, younger man striding toward me, I know it is Marco. The Italians have a saying, *La Bella Figura,* the beautiful figure, a philosophy they strive to live for—putting your best foot forward. It's not just looks; it's presentation; it's creating an aura of beauty. And Marco is demonstrating it to a tee. First, he is all smiles. His stride is confident. He is wearing a dark blue blazer with black shirt, designer-faded jeans, and shiny black leather shoes that look as if someone is following him around all day with a polishing rag. He is a beautiful man, and even though I suspected as much, the confirmation sends a shock of pleasure through me. As if I am somehow deserving of his beauty.

He has soft chestnut curls, hanging a little past his ears. I might have said it was too long for a man, but it suits him. He is making a beeline for me. How is it we know each other when we've never met? It is probably just the shiny shoes and blond hair, but either way, I register this fact, that we simply know. As he draws closer, still smiling, I notice little imperfections that in a weird way make him even more beautiful to me. His eyebrows could use a tweeze, and he has a little mole to the left of his chin, and a crooked top left tooth. He also has flawless tan skin and hazel eyes and lashes too long for a man.

"*Ciao, bella,*" he says. He leans in and kisses first my right cheek and then my left. "You are even more beautiful than your pictures," he says.

For a second I think he has the wrong girl. Maybe this isn't Marco. It's a man on a blind date. Meeting someone who looks like me? Not here in Italy. "My pictures?"

"Alexandria has a picture of you," he says. He leans in close to me, even though he is already standing closer than an American man would. His cologne is fresh, and I like it. His breath smells of mints. I suddenly wish I had put more thought into what I look like. Of course I had no idea I was coming out to meet the lover of my husband's lover, but in the future I make a note to expect anything and everything.

"Where did she get a picture of me?"

"She stole it from your husband's wallet."

I knew it. She's a total psycho. Did Alex even realize it was missing?

"I think she's jealous," Marco says. "Now I see why." Ah, the ease at which Italian men toss out compliments. Like Frisbees on a beach. I look closely at him for signs of sarcasm, but I see only open admiration, and I drink it in. I don't like admitting this, but I need this right now. My pride has been drained, and he is already filling it up with his words. Alexandria, jealous of me? This is an interesting development, and I tuck it away, like a secret ingredient that I can't wait to use.

"Did she wake before you left?" I say. I hope I don't sound too eager to learn everything I can about my enemy. I assume Marco is feeling the exact same way I am and is on my side, but I can't be too careful.

"No. She is heavy sleeper. Also she drank much wine and cried. Tears exhaust her."

Tears exhaust her, I repeat silently. As if they refresh the rest of us. She certainly knows how to wrap men around her finger, doesn't she? And what the hell is she crying for? Because Alex went one day without contacting her? I want to march over to the flat—Alex's flat—and yank her out of bed by her hair. I will get the address out of Marco before the night is through.

"I'm starving," I say. "Would you like to take to me to dinner?" Marco's grin widens, and I find myself grinning back. To passersby we might look as if we are on a date. I am being brazen, and it's only because I could care less, and I like it. I was this way with Alex when I set my sights on him, oh so long ago.

"But of course. Firenze has some of the best *ristoranti* in the world." He offers his arm, and I take it. Then he tucks me in close to him, and we walk. Soon we are over the bridge and navigating narrow side streets populated with lively places to eat and drink. I will have to count on Marco to lead me back to the bridge. From there I will know how to get back to the hotel.

Unless I don't go back to the hotel. Wouldn't that teach Alex a lesson? If I just disappeared? The thought teases me, but I push it away. Instead I feast my eyes on the string of shops closed for the evening, and the restaurants whose seats spill out onto the sidewalk. Establishment doors are thrown open, illuminating light and laughter within as well as out. Marco stops in front of the liveliest restaurant on the block. I wonder if he's trying to impress me. I am dying to eat outside, but the patio is overflowing. Waiters are opening bottles of wine table-side and navigating the small spaces with plates of food that look like works of art. Marco leans in.

"Don't worry, *bella*. There is a private garden in the back. You will love it." His smile shoots right through me. He knows I need this, and he is giving it to me full force, pretending we are on a date. I am married. I am a mother. And I am on a pretend date with my husband's mistress's boyfriend. It makes me feel prickly, and slightly sick, and excitingly alive. Marco takes my hand, the hand that mere minutes ago I thought would never be held again, and leads me inside as if I belong.

The hostess, a tall, leggy thing with a mane of dark hair, lets out a whoop when she sees Marco. She hugs him, and he actually picks her up and swings her around. I step back, fearing she's going to hit one of the candles on the little tables or me, but to my amazement, she clears it all. Obviously, they've done this before. I take note that I feel like a prized toy quickly discarded for something new.

"Marco, Marco, Marco," the hostess says, back on terra firma. She rattles off something in Italian, and he rattles off something in Italian, and they throw their heads back and laugh in the universal language of mirth and merriment. *I want to kill you husband.* What am I even doing here? I should have called the police, not invited him to dinner. Should I make a run for it, while he's busy with the hostess and her big eyes? Suddenly, they both look at me as if they know what I'm thinking. I don't know what to say or do, so I just smile. I feel inadequate.

Marco touches the small of my back, and a waiter leads us down a hall and out a back door to a garden patio. In the center is a cherub spitting water. Gorgeous flowering bushes line the perimeter of the cozy space, and a violinist plays quietly on the sidelines. Almost every table is full, but unlike outside, there is plenty of room between the tables. Everyone here seems gorgeous, at least to me. Designer shoes peek out from underneath almost every table. I glance down at my feet. I am wearing flip-flops. I am an American eyesore. *I didn't know I'd be here, folks,* I try to submit telepathically as we are led to our table. *My husband is having an affair!* I think of the one pair of heels in my suitcase and imagine them appearing on my feet. They do not. It doesn't matter; everyone is looking at Marco anyway. A few people even nod and smile as we pass. He must come here a lot. The waiter leads us to a table in the center of the patio and whips off a "Reserved" sign. From here, we have a panoramic view of the little oasis. A bottle of wine appears within seconds of our sitting down.

"Okay," I say as I smile across the table at him. "Who are you?"

He grins, puts his hand on his heart. "I am Marco."

"Do you own this restaurant?"

His laugh is loud and genuine. "No. I do not own this restaurant." He seems to be digesting my words, the vocabulary, the rhythm. "But I am, how do you say, a regular."

I nod, and he grins. Then he rubs his hands together and signals a waiter. "Your first meal out in Florence, is this true?" he says without taking his eyes off me.

"Yes," I say, holding his gaze.

"*Buono.* We will dine the Italian way. Four courses. Starters. *Primi. Secondi.* Dessert."

He holds up his thumb and fingers as he lists them. I nod and smile, even though I still cannot imagine putting food in my mouth. This is a meeting. We have common enemies, so it makes sense that we have common goals. This is part of the negotiating. We will chat. We will eat. And then we will get down to the business of systematically destroying the relationship of Alex and Alexandria. Italians may know a few things about love, but nobody can do revenge like the Vikings.

CHAPTER 11

The glow from the candle strikes my wineglass, and the contents shimmer like rubies. I take a small sip and let the flavor spread over my tongue. "Oh my God," I say. I sound so American. *"Belissimo,"* I add. Marco winks. It is strange to be winked at by a man who looks fifteen years my junior, but I must admit, it's nice. Little plates land in front of us along with a basket of bread and flask of oil. Edible works of art. Marco begins to point and narrate.

"*Prosciutto e melone.* Octopus salad. Buffalo mozzarella and tomato."

"My first meal with Alex was in a college cafeteria," I say. What was I doing? Bringing up Alex too soon, as if we're here to wander down memory lane. Fruit Loops. Our first meal together was post-sex Froot Loops in the cafeteria. I am in Florence, with edible works of art in front of me, and a beautiful man across from me, and I am not going to talk about Froot Loops. Or how we didn't even eat them together; rather Alex sat with other TAs, and I sat with the rest of the ignored freshman.

"Tell me," Marco says. He is being sweet.

"I'm sorry. Who cares about that, right? This looks incredible."

"You met Alex in college?"

"Grad school. He was my TA." Marco keeps smiling, but frowns at the same time. I have never seen someone pull this off. He is really very cute. I can't see why Alexandria needed to steal my husband if she has him. "Teacher's assistant."

"Ah. You were hot for teacher?" He repeats it as if he's watched one too many American movies. I laugh.

"Teacher's assistant. Anyway. It was taboo for us to be dating. You know—I think he liked the sneaking around." I guess he still does. Was that why he was with Alexandria? The thrill of sneaking around again?

"You haven't tried a bite," Marco says. "You don't like?" He looks genuinely concerned. I will not ruin this dinner by thinking about my cheating husband. Tears are running down my face. Before I can do anything about them, Marco is gently dabbing them away with his napkin. "I feel this sadness too. Together we do something. I promise. But tonight, *bella?* Tonight is for you to enjoy. No?"

"Yes," I say. "Yes." Marco picks up a fork, lifts the prosciutto and melon, and offers it to me. Am I actually going to let him feed me? Then again, the fork is right there by my mouth. I'm not in Rome, but for the first time in my life, close enough. I lean in, he guides the fork in, and I gently close my mouth around it. It's sweet, and silky, and melts in my mouth. Marco's smile widens into a grin, and he gives me another wink. Then he drizzles olive oil over the buffalo mozzarella cheese that lies on top of fat tomato slice topped with a sprig of fresh basil. He smiles at me across the candlelight, then squeezes lemon on the octopus. I reach for the fork, because I really am not the type to sit here and be fed all night. Luckily, he does not argue, as I taste first the mozzarella and then the octopus for myself.

"Oh my God," I say.

"*Oh Dio mio,*" Marco says.

"*Oh Dio mio,* is right. This is just the first course?"

"Yes, this is the starter." Just the beginning of tearing down Alex and Alexandria? "The first course, *il primo,* will be next. A pasta dish." My eyes wander around the patio as he explains the four courses. I am slightly buzzing from the wine. I see now, how easily it can be happen. Seduced by wine, and candlelight, and beauty, and private gardens, and four-course dinners, and winks from strangers. It does not excuse Alex, but sadly, I can see it.

My eyes land on the back wall of the garden. It is lit by a string of white lights hanging just above the patio. And it's filled with chalk drawings. The same face I destroyed on the street the other day, the neon-colored renditions of Alexandria. These are all stunning. One with yellow hair, green eyes, and purple eyebrows. Red eyes, black hair, orange lips. Blue hair, pink lips, green eyes. She looks beautiful in every color. Every single one. Did Marco know they were here? Is he purposefully messing with me? I set my wineglass down with a thunk, throw the napkin on the table, and screech my chair back a few inches. Marco turns to see what's captured my attention.

"Ah," he says. "Your face should be on that wall."

"I've seen one of those before. On the street near the Duomo."

"And what do you think?"

"I heard they were all over the city. A walking tour."

"Yes. They are all over, in secret locations all over Florence."

"Doesn't she remind you of someone?"

"Art is in the eye of the beholder. We see what we see."

"You don't see it?"

"I did not say that."

"So you know what I'm talking about?"

"You sound as if you are upset. Would you like more wine?"

"No. It's her. It's Alexandria." I stand. I don't know why, but I just can't sit. Why does he look so bemused? Does he really not see that it's her?

"Please. Don't let them upset you." Marco stands too. People are starting to glance at us. I don't care.

"Just tell me you think it looks like her too."

"Yes, yes, yes. Exactly. Exactly like her."

"Alex knows the artist. Giovatti. He's obsessed with your little girlfriend too; did you know this?" Marco nods and gestures for me to sit back down. I do, and he follows suit. "I dumped gelato on the one by the Duomo."

"That was you?"

"You heard about it?" For a second I am stricken. Was I reported on some kind of Italian news program?

"I mean this to say—you did this?"

I have to remember there is a language gap before I jump down anyone's throat. "Yes. I did. And I wish I could destroy all of them."

"Really? How?"

"I don't know—just—smear them all or something." *Spray paint WHORE all over them.*

"Maybe you would like to switch seats?"

"Oh God. I'm coming off like a crazy woman, aren't I?"

"No, no. You are passionate. I like this."

"No, I'm ridiculous. They're beautiful. I just can't believe my husband's mistress is the face of Italy. It's maddening."

"You are beautiful. Your face should be on that wall." He holds my gaze. What is he doing? Trying to take his revenge on Alexandria by seducing me? It's tempting, but I am not going to win Alex back by sleeping with Alexandria's boyfriend.

"I'm not going to sleep with you," I say. Marco tilts his head and studies me as the waiter clears away the starters and sets down the first course.

"Spaghetti all'Aragosta," Marco says. "Pasta with lobster and tomato." He watches me take a bite. "Fished straight from the Tuscan sea," he says with a wink. I don't know whether or not he is joking, because I don't have a clue what lives in the Tuscan sea, but I'm too in love with the dish to even care. We settle into a comfortable silence. The second course, or *secondi,* is a medium rare Fiorentina steak with asparagus and Parmesan cheese. As I bite into it, I feel a jolt of guilt. My kids are in a hotel room watching television. What do I think I'm doing?

But wait. They are with Alex, whom they haven't seen in six months. They need this bonding time. And I am trying to get their father back, for their sake, for our family's sake. I will make this up to them tomorrow. We will find a way to make this a nice holiday as well. The kids will thank me for it someday. *Remember when we went to Florence to confront our father's evil mistress? You still managed to make it fun. We've never forgotten that.* Somehow the bottle of wine disappears and another one takes its place. I would lift a finger to protest, only I'm too busy digging into dessert, a soft cake with vanilla liquor and strawberries. If Alex could see me now. I am in Florence, and my first meal out is with a man I have just met, who wants to kill him.

Music from the violin swells into the warm night air. There is no reason for me to be crying yet again. Tell that to the tears streaming down my face.

"I'm sorry," I say.

"No, no, no."

"It is so beautiful here. And you are so kind. But I cannot enjoy it. He's ruined everything. I don't think I'll ever be happy again."

"No, no, no."

"Yes, yes, yes. I have to go. Believe me. I want to stay. I want to enjoy this. It's amazing. But I'm married. I am supposed to be here with my husband."

"I like your passion."

"Tell that to the hotel. I screamed at Alex so much they called and asked me to keep it down."

"You should not be quieted down. Not here in Italy. You should let go. This is what you deserve." Marco grabs my hand and pulls me up from the table. With his other hand he swipes up his dessert plate, which, unlike mine, has most of his cake left.

"Come," he says. Where is he pulling me? Does he want to

dance with the cake and me at the same time? Is this some kind
of strange, Italian tradition? Instead, he leads me over to the
wall of faces and hands me the cake. "Throw!" he says.

"What?"

"Throw cake in her face." I glance around. We have everybody's attention. Although oddly none of them make a move to
stop him. Maybe they all hate these faces.

"I can't," I say.

"Here." Marco scoops up a bit of cake and throws it at the
face with the yellow hair. It lands in her nostrils.

"Marco." I am thrilled. "That's vandalism."

"Now you," he says with a nod to the plate.

"I can't." He takes another swipe and throws it. This one
lands in the chalk girl's eye. I try to go back to my seat. Marco
catches me by the wrist and swings me around.

"What are you going to do, Lena?" he says. "Come here and
hide? Or come here and be your passionate self?" He takes my
hand and turns the plate of cake upside down over it. I look at
the glob in my palm, then look at the wall. I pull my arm back
and hurl the cake at the chalk drawing with the blue hair. It
splatters all over the entire face. I hoot. Suddenly the noise
level on the patio drops, and the violin cuts off.

"Belissimo," Marco yells. *"Brava, brava, brava!"* Suddenly a pa-
tron from a nearby table lifts his plate, loaded with pasta and
meatballs, and hands it to Marco. He hands it to me.

"Throw."

"It's his dinner."

"I buy him a new one. Throw!" I glance at the man who is
without his *primi*. He nods his encouragement, kisses three fingers, and blows them up to the heavens. Before I can talk myself back to sanity, I catapult the pasta onto the last chalk face.
Meatballs stick where the eyes are, strands of spaghetti slide
down her cheek, and a pepper sticks above her mouth like a
mustache. To my surprise, the patio erupts in applause.

"They love it," Marco says. "I love it."

"She's a whore!" I shout. The patio patrons cheer and applaud. I am smiling until I glance up and see the leggy hostess standing in the center of the patio. Legs spread, arms crossed. She isn't smiling. Soon a very large man in a dark suit sidles up next to her. They both glare in my direction. I lean into Marco. "How do you say 'Run!' in Italian?"

CHAPTER 12

Marco takes my hand, opens a latch in the fence of the patio, and together we run. He's fast, and I'm still dizzy from the wine but also riding on the adrenaline stirred up by throwing cake and meatballs at Alexandria's chalk faces. I wonder about my purse, as an image of hanging it on the back of my chair rises to mind. I paw blindly at my side, and there it is, bumping off my hip. Soon we find ourselves in a narrow alleyway between stone buildings. Shadows bounce off a single streetlamp illuminating a dumpster. Its lid is near bursting. Is this a seedier side of Florence? If so, it still beats most cities I've ever seen.

"Stop, stop," I say. Marco stops and swings me into his chest as if we are doing the tango. I can feel his heart beating. We are both out of breath. Slowly, one of his hands slides up my back. I hold my breath, but only for a second. I gently place my hand on his chest and take a step back. He drops his hands. "We have to go back," I say. "We have to pay."

"Pay for what? Our sins?" He says it with a grin. But as I stand looking at him, it hits me. I am in a dim alley with a total stranger.

"We didn't even pay for dinner. I can't accept that. I have to go back."

"No. Come. I will make everything all right." Marco begins walking through the alley with his confident stride. I glance back. I don't think I can face going back alone, and I realize I don't have enough money on me to pay our bill anyway. Alex is cheating, and I am stealing. I follow Marco. He waits for me at the end of the alley.

"I mean it. I feel terrible."

"You hated the drawings. You took revenge."

"It's not like me. I love art. And artists. I was going to be one once upon a time."

"Tell me."

"Nothing to tell. It was college. You either experiment with other girls or art. I went for art." I am joking, to a degree. Marco is looking at me so intently, and I can't go around telling people I'm an artist. Especially Florentines. I might have had a little bit of talent at one time, but as a stay-at-home mom, the only art projects I've done lately involve pipe cleaners and macaroni.

"You are either an artist, or you are not." Marco says. "It is not like a shoe that you slip on and off." He begins walking again, and I follow. It's dark, and I'm tired. I will find the restaurant tomorrow and pay our bill. It makes me think of Alex's spending money on Alexandria, putting her up in a flat. He's still lying to me. After all this, he didn't tell me about the flat.

"I think sometimes you have shoes that you keep in the back of your closet, but just haven't worn for a while," I say. "I used to sketch 24-7. Even Rachel remembers it. She said the chalk drawings reminded her of the faces I used to sketch."

"And so you dump gelato on her." Now he sounds like he's judging me. Wasn't he just the one egging me on?

"I lost my mind. I haven't felt like myself since finding out about the affair." We are finally coming to a main street. In the distance, I can once again see the Ponte Vecchio bridge. I am relieved. I need to go back to the hotel. I need a bed.

"You are not the same since the affair. And neither am I. I can't sleep. My work is different now too. I am pacing, pacing, pacing all the time. Until tonight. Until you. I think you saved me." His face contorts into a desperate sadness. I've seen that look before. In the mirror lately.

"How long have you been with Alexandria?"

"All my life. My family live near her family. Together, we grow up."

"Oh. Well, how long did you two date?"

"Date. That is funny American word. Date. We have been lovers for eight years. Since we were twenty-one."

"You're twenty-nine?"

"*Si.* How old are you?"

I laugh.

"What is funny? You are young too. Not as young as me, but you are still young."

Young and carefree. "What happened? I don't mean to get too personal, but why do you think she's with Alex and not with you?"

"My work. It is everything lately. I treat my work like my lover, and my lover like my work."

"What do you do?"

"This is another very American thing to say."

"I'm sorry."

"Ah, *prego, prego.* I like your American way. But I don't want to talk about work. Alexandria lives to be the sun. I forget this. I was careless."

"But why Alex? Why not you?" Marco stares into my eyes as if I have just revealed that I think he is one of the sexiest men I have ever met and I cannot believe Alexandria would pass him by for Alex. I feel as if I've just reached over and put my hand on the zipper of his jeans. I'd better bring the focus back. "Or why not this genius artist—Giovatti?"

Marco shrugged. "Maybe he is ugly."

"You've never seen him?"

"Yes, of course. I know him very well." Marco spits on the ground. "But in Florence, everyone is beautiful, and everyone makes art."

"Like Hollywood, where they're all actors or screenwriters."

"Movies! Yes. I love to go to Hollywood."

"You should. You're very handsome." We're strolling along the streets again; it's so easy to stroll in Florence. "You should be a movie star."

Marco laughs and shakes his head. Then, he stops and poses. "I'd like to thank the Academy."

"Ah, it's an international fantasy, I see."

"Remember *Life Is Beautiful?* Roberto Benigni?"

"Of course."

"He accept award; he do this." In two steps Marco is in front of me. He puts one hand behind my neck and soon his lips are on mine. I mean to pull back immediately, but I lose myself in the sensation of being kissed, really being kissed by a man for the first time in six months. His lips are soft but insistent. He is not a bit shy, not a bit like a man ten years younger than me. He presses harder, and I let go. Our mouths open, and his tongue gently probes mine. A yearning shoots through my solar plexus. Hunger, for a total stranger, rises up in me. We are bonded by neglect and betrayal. Just as I start to fear how far this will go, he releases me. We stand for a moment and stare at each other as if equally stunned. "You remember?" he says. As if the kiss were all about the award show.

"I do," I say.

Marco looks away. When he looks back, he is smiling. Just as I'm wishing he would kiss me again, he pulls a single key out of his pocket and dangles it in front of me.

"A key to your kingdom?" I say. *Or your heart? This is probably moving a little fast, even for European standards, but whatever it is, I'll take it.*

"It is the key to your husband's flat."

"Where he keeps Alexandria." The messy apartment from the video. With the leopard-print lounge chair and messy bed. It is not hers. She does not belong there.

"Alexandria is a lot of things. 'Kept' is not one of them."

I turn the key around in my hand. "You stole this?" A hot-blooded jealous lover with the keys to the flat. Had Alex been in real danger here? Was he still? If anything happened, it would not look good in court that I was dining with, and vandalizing with, and kissing this man. But for now, in this sliver of time, we are still the victims.

"I did not steal. I made a copy."

"Does she know?"

"No. It is our secret."

Our secret. How quickly we crossed into the land of secrets. The land of plotting. He does not seem concerned to give me, the jealous wife, the key. Perhaps I do not look the type who could harm anyone. I certainly haven't come out and threatened her. Although I am destroying chalk-drawing her. "The picture of you and Alexandria in bed. Did you send it to my phone?" I tuck the key in my purse and dig out Alex's cell phone. The picture is there. Two heads on a pillow. Close-up faces. Marco, eyes wide, grinning. Alexandria, asleep. She looks peaceful. I want to disturb that.

"Listen. Thank you for the key. I don't know what I'll do with it. But what you said about wanting to kill Alex?"

Marco puts his hands up. "You are here now. He is your job."

"I'm going to get him back. I'm going to keep them apart. But I'm not going to physically harm anyone."

"You are a gentle woman. A good woman."

"I need to hear you say that you aren't going to resort to violence either."

"I am offended."

"I'm sorry. I just need to hear you say it."

Marco leans in, takes my shoulders in his hands, and stares at me. "You are the wife. Revenge is in your hands, m'lady. I am here only to help you."

"Play hard to get with Alexandria. No more rushing over to her flat to comfort her."

Marco smiles. Winks at me. "*Si,*" he says. He is laughing.

"I don't think any of this is funny. I'm serious." Marco begins to bob around me until he is on his knees on the cobblestone street. He takes both my hands in his. A passerby would think he is proposing.

"I promise. I am all talk. Italian men, we have much bravado. I will not hurt your husband. Or my lover." He stares at me until I nod. He kisses my hand. He stands and looks into the distance. "But if you were to do anything," he says, "I would make it look like an accident."

"Marco!"

"I cannot help. I am little devil. Come. I will walk you to the hotel."

"Just the bridge please. I can find my way from there." We walk in silence. Our steps echo in the night. The streets are still bustling and probably will be long after I go to bed. I imagine walking around in the morning, when just the bakers and street sweepers are awake. *I would make it look like an accident.* Marco's words echo through me. At the bridge he kisses me on both cheeks, then plants the third one on my lips before strolling away. He does not look back. I walk along the river, then lean over and gaze down. I should throw away the key. Toss it into the river and be done with it! *Take your wedding rings off and throw them in too.* I don't. I walk away from the river, tracing my path back to the hotel.

Alex pays the bill. Which means it is my flat too. And then it hits me. Marco didn't give me the address. I still have no idea where the flat is. I will have to find out on my own. Perhaps Marco does think me capable of harm, and he doesn't want to incriminate himself by giving me the key and the address. Or perhaps he is playing a game, teasing me. Maybe he wants me to get violent. He's giving me the key to the flat and telling me to make it look like an accident. He is using me to hurt his lover. He encouraged me to vandalize those drawings, practically forced me. And then of course we ran from dinner without paying for a single thing. I am ashamed. I vow once again to find the restaurant and pay the bill. I vow to handle this much better from now on. I will not stoop to their level. I cannot change the past, but from now on, I will handle this with dignity. I will still make sure that Alex is never with Alexandria again, but I will do it with dignity.

As I begin the journey back to the hotel, some of my guilt fades. It's replaced by a sense of excitement. My God. Am I actually enjoying this?

My reminders help me navigate the yet unfamiliar streets. I turn when I see the old-fashioned lamppost. I pass the Da Vinci Museum. During the day a wooden bicycle sits out front. One of his many inventions. I turn next at the carving of a stone angel just above the entryway of a building. It's better than following breadcrumbs, and soon I am at the entrance to the hotel. I am worried I will find the front door locked, but it is open. The lobby is pitch black. Now I am worried that they do not lock the front door. That isn't safe.

Make it look like an accident.

I grope in the dark, pawing my way to the staircase. Guess they aren't afraid of lawsuits like they would be back home. It would be easy to slip, and fall, break my neck. I grip the bannister and slowly ascend. If I slipped and fell, and died, would Alex even care? He would be upset for the kids, of course, but would there be a part of him that felt free? How long before he introduced our children to his mistress? How long before they bonded with the younger, more beautiful mom?

I make my way to our hotel room door. No wonder guests complained about me. They are all early to bed; the place is as silent as a tomb. I use Alex's phone to illuminate the door, then open it with the key. It's wild to me, a hotel room that does not use a card key, and I love it. The door squeals as I enter. I stand for a moment, allowing my eyes to adjust. I see a shape bouncing in the dark, heading for me. Stella. I drop to my haunches and fold her big orange body into me, then kiss her on the head and allow her to lick me in return. I do not understand people who do not like dogs. This girl is nothing but love. I could take a lesson from it. Maybe I should let Alex go. That damn saying. If you love something, set it free. It is my choice how to handle this. But I do not want to set him free.

Where is he? In our bed? I can make out a lump on each

sofa. Josh is snoring quietly. Alex doesn't snore. I always bragged about that. Isn't that silly? Petty? How lucky I am that my husband doesn't snore. I never thought to brag how lucky I was that he wasn't putting his penis into other women. Lesson learned.

I shut the door as softly as possible, lock it, and head for the bedroom with Stella at my heels. As I round the sofa, I see Alex lying on the floor behind it. An icicle pierces my heart. He does not want to share the bed with me. Of course there is no other way he could have played it, is there? Yes, he could be sleeping on the floor of the bedroom. In the bedroom would mean he was hoping for a reconciliation. Wants to take me to bed after six months of being without me. Wants to make love to me and not her. Here we are in Florence, after all these years, and we aren't going to sleep together. It's a new shock. I've been receiving a series of them, several new jolts of painful realizations per day. How can I survive this? Why should I be expected to?

I want to kick him and spit on him. I also want to kneel down and kiss his neck and hold my Alex. I want to whisper in his ear that I forgive him, I will forgive him if he swears he loves me and not her, and promises never, ever to do this again, and insists we all get on a plane tomorrow, go home, and begin the process of putting this nightmare behind us.

He is fast asleep. Not worried about me. Not tossing and turning. *You didn't tell me you have a flat,* I say silently as I hover over him. *And I have the key.*

I hurry into the bedroom before I do anything violent or passionate, and once inside I step out onto the balcony. The revelers are gone. It is dark. I don't see a single lit streetlamp along this stretch.

Tomorrow is a new day. I will give Alex a choice. Take us home now and leave all this behind.

Or?

I think of the key in my purse. I can't think too far ahead. But if Alex won't listen to reason, then I will use it.

Make it look like an accident. But it already is. This entire affair is a colossal train wreck, one giant accident, and I am standing in the aftermath, trying to pick up the pieces, identify the bodies. But with damage like this, I have no idea where to even begin. At this moment, I have what I need. I click open Alex's phone, and there it is, a picture of Marco and Alexandria, two heads on a pillow. She is sleeping; he is wide-eyed and grinning. I tiptoe into the living room and set Alex's cell phone on the floor beside him, then take off my dress and crawl into bed, mostly nude, and alone.

CHAPTER 13

The flat must have weighed on my mind during the night, for I wake up in the middle of a dream about the first place Alex and I lived in together. This was before marriage and babies, and we were renting. I had just quit grad school, and Alex was working as a waiter while he applied for positions as a college professor. We were renting the left side of a brick, two-family townhouse. I thought it was lucky that we got the left side; after all it's the left hemisphere of the brain that's responsible for creativity. I often made proclamations like this, and Alex would shake his head and laugh, but I would often hear him repeating my Lena-isms to his friends and later his colleagues. It always made me feel loved whenever I would hear Alex repeating something I'd said.

We never officially met our neighbor on the other side of the wall, just glimpsed his large figure clothed in sweat suits when he headed out for his morning jogs. We were big *X-Files* fans back then, and Alex took to calling him The Jogging Man. Alex was so funny back then, and I was an appreciative audience. I thought this boded well for us too, our ability to have little inside jokes that made us both break into hysterics whenever the other would mention them. Other than his morning runs, we only knew The Jogging Man by the weights we would hear him dropping in the mornings after his run. I used to love to sit with my coffee and the carrot cake Alex always brought home from the restaurant. I wasn't against exercise; I just liked eating carrot cake while someone else engaged in it. How that changed when I had children and realized I'd have to fight to keep my figure. And some good that did me now. If I had known that Alex was going to cheat on me anyway, would I have worked as hard?

Our home was small and furnished mostly through hand-me-downs and thrift stores. Alex and I used to love trolling flea markets, and farmers' markets, and yard sales on Saturday mornings. He didn't have to go into work until four p.m., so we would spend our time making love or taking walks to the various markets or sales. Other than that we watched a lot of television together, and had brunch when his schedule allowed it, or even better stayed in bed with the Sunday paper, and coffee, and carrot cake. We celebrated all of our first holidays as a couple in that townhouse, and Alex indulged my desire to make them all as big of a deal as possible.

We decorated our little flat for Halloween, Thanksgiving, Christmas, Valentine's, Saint Patrick's, Easter, and Fourth of July. We didn't have a yard, but we had a little side patio with a few feet of dirt in which I planted flowers, herbs, and a few vegetables. Alex bought me a huge barrel for tomato plants and a used grill. While he waited tables, I worked at an art supply store just three blocks from the house. It was one of my most productive years, given that I had a fifty percent discount storewide. I painted the patio with the tomato plant and the grill. I painted our entryway with coatrack and yellow umbrella propped in the corner. And as the flowers grew, I painted them. Snapdragons, Jewel Box, black-eyed Susans, and peonies.

One afternoon I snapped a picture of Alex walking off to work. Then I painted his tall figure, his broad shoulders, and the back of his head. I gave it to him for his birthday. He hung it above our bed. Life was simple back then. We worked our jobs, hung out with each other in our free time, made love almost every day, sometimes several times a day, and dreamt of our future, one in which things would get progressively better. I wish I could capture those days in a jar, like fireflies, keep their lights blinking as long as humanly possible. They were some of the best days of our lives. And right now, they are behind us, lost forever.

I sit up in bed and listen for sounds of life in the living room. There is no digital clock beside the bed; this place is old school. I wonder if Alex dreamt of me last night. Somehow, somewhere, we've gotten off track. Maybe in retrospect, instead of painting him walking away, I should have painted him coming toward me.

I lie back down for a few seconds, and next thing I know Josh is jumping on the bed. I know it's him—too frenetic and light to be Rachel. I open one eye.

"Dad said to let you sleep," Josh says.

"Way to follow directions."

"What time is it?"

"Where were you last night?" Rachel accuses from the doorway. She has her hands on her hips. "Did you get drunk and get a tattoo?"

No. But I had dinner with a sexy man ten years my junior and threw a plate of spaghetti and meatballs on the chalk face of your father's mistress. "Is that any way to talk to your mother?"

"Did you?"

"Yes."

Her eyes widen, and she steps up to the bed. She looks me over as if she's suddenly discovered I am human and I can be cool. "Really?"

"No," I say. "Is there coffee?" Voices filter in from the living room. If my kids are in here, who is out there with Alex? Florence might be magical, but I highly doubt Stella has been bestowed with the gift of speech. And there was no way SHE was in there, was there? Because I would kill her. Him too. I wouldn't even worry about making it look like an accident. For a sick second I hope she is here. I want to feel her slim, olive neck underneath my hands. I want to squeeze. I look down to see my hands are curled into fists, gripping the bedsheet. I look at Rachel.

"Mr. and Mrs. Lucas are here with their brood," she says. She purses her lips and flutters her eyes at me. Everyone talks about how terrible it is when your kid becomes a teenager, but it's not. I love seeing Rachel develop a little bit of an attitude. She has brilliant expressions. She makes me laugh. Although right now I can't fully appreciate it.

Jean and Harold. This early. Unannounced. Great. "Oh God. Shut the door." Rachel goes to shut it. Josh cuts in front of her and slams it.

"Du—you mind?" Rachel says. I catch the intention and the "save" and let it slide. I was just admiring her spunk; I don't want to fight.

"What time is it?"

"Nine a.m." Josh says. "We've been up since seven."

"What are they doing here?"

"They want to take us on a *family* outing," Rachel says. "What do you think of that?" She gives me a look that's way too wise for her years, and I want to take it back; Forget the spunk, I want her to stay an innocent little girl.

"Cool, right?" Josh says as he resumes jumping on my bed.

"Shoo. Both of you. Let me get dressed."

"Get out du—do get out," Rachel corrects. "I have to talk to Mom."

"You're grounded," I say. I lie back down and put the pillow over my face. Maybe I will just smother myself. Is that even possible?

"You can't ground me in Italy! Besides, I didn't say it."

"You almost did," Josh says. He's starting to get that I don't like it, and he's starting to use it to get attention. Parenting is like a series of little paper cuts. Try to correct one thing and something else gives you a little slice. It's not only the hardest job in the world; it's nearly impossible.

"Almost doesn't count."

"Does it count, Mom?"

"I want coffee," I say.

"Dearest brother, will you please scram?"

"Is she allowed to say 'scram'?"

"Please, please just both of you go and play with one of Jean's kids." I can't remember a single one of their names. Josh shrugs, then bounces out of the room. Rachel shuts the door after him and leans against it.

"Are you guys getting a divorce?" Gone is the attitude. She sounds shaky. I am out of bed and over to her in seconds. I take her in my arms.

"Shhh. Don't worry. This is nothing you have to worry about." We are not getting divorced. Not over *her*. Not here and not now.

"I hate him."

It slices me. I don't want her to hate him. I know how much he loves her. I can see him holding her in the hospital, a look of wonder and pride and protection in his eyes. He has never stopped. I know this. "Don't say that."

"He's screwing some girl. You think I don't know what that means? I know what that means!"

"It's over. It's never going to happen again." I say it as if I am Alex, begging for forgiveness, reassuring. "You cannot believe how sorry he is." I don't know why this is coming out of my mouth. He doesn't want to save this family; he wants to be with her. But I want to save this family, and he is not in his right mind.

"But you're not going to take him back, are you?"

"Honey, one step at a time."

"What does that mean?"

"Let me do the thinking. And the worrying." *And the planning, and the punishing.*

"Are you going to cut his dick off?"

"Rachel!"

"Chloe said that's what you should do."

She was telling her friends? I don't want her to tell her friends. But I hold my tongue. I have been spilling it to total strangers, so how can I ask Rachel to keep this bottled in. I take a deep breath. "How are you even talking to Chloe from here?"

"There's a computer with Internet in the lobby."

"Okay. Well. No. Nobody is cutting anything off of your father."

Rachel nods, but her bottom lip is quivering. I try to hug her, but she pulls away, wipes her nose with her sleeve, and disappears out the door. She is imitating me, I think. My steely resolve. Seeing it in someone else is startling. It's not natural. We should be allowed to feel. I can't believe she just asked me if I was going to cut Alex's dick off. Where is this going to end? We have to go home. I'm going to insist that we go home. As soon as I have a look at the flat. I just need to look. I don't know why. Call it closure. Once I see it for myself, and look Alexandria in the eye, and tell her her reign of seduction is over, then I will have a tiny bit of closure, and we can go home and pick up the pieces. Of course it means convincing my husband that he wants to remain with us, and not her. I don't care what it takes. I want him back. His children need a father at home, and I'm going to do whatever it takes to make sure they get one.

CHAPTER 14

When I emerge a half an hour later, dressed in a simple skirt and tank top, Jean Lucas is in my living room drinking a mimosa. Everyone else is gone, even Stella. Jean is a tall and thin woman, her hair a vibrant shade of auburn, cut short but trendy. Unlike me, she is designer-dressed: cropped silk pants and a lace-enhanced matching top. The outfit looks plucked from one of the many trendy shops that dot the Florence streets. She's in her late forties, I suspect. It's wild to me that she had all five children pretty late in life. I wonder if they were conceived in vitro, or even adopted, or by surrogate? We've never talked of anything but the university, and a few odd jokes about our husbands. I'm not going to start getting chummy now, especially with the current drama. I wonder, as I watch Jean sip her mimosa, if she and Harold know anything about Alex's affair. Alex admitted they might.

Jean is a strong and attractive woman. A woman of the world. What would she do if she were me?

"They're all downstairs in the garden," Jean says, following my gaze around the room. Jean stands, picks up another mimosa from the coffee table, and with one in each hand, holds out her arms as if to hug me. I ignore the hug, but take the drink and just look at it. She does know something. Why else try and get me liquored up so early in the day? Or was this just Florence?

"Actually I was thinking coffee," I say.

"Oh, go on. You're in Italy. Live a little."

I down the mimosa in one go, then hand it back to Jean. "Have I earned a cup of coffee now?"

Jean laughs. "I always did like you."

"Ditto. Anyone who can raise five children has my respect." *At your age,* echoes in my mind. Definitely shouldn't have had the mimosa.

"Six," Jean says. "You must count Harold."

"Six it is then," I say. I don't like playing this game, chatting as if my life isn't falling apart around me. Whatever she does or does not know, Jean Lucas is definitely someone I would want to have in my corner. I need to find out if Jean knows something without giving anything away.

Jean finishes her mimosa, sets it on the coffee table, then heads for the door. "We're going to take you to the most fabulous lookout today, and then on to the Uffizi Gallery, and then—"

"Actually," I say, "I was hoping you could take the kids for a few hours. Alex and I have some catching up to do."

"Catching up," Jean says. "What a way to put it." She digs sunglasses out of her purse, then perches them on her head. She puts one hand on the doorknob and the other on her hip.

"I'm sorry?"

"Darling. I'm sure the kids miss their father too. You too can have some alone time later." She winks. I want a cup of coffee, but if I had one now I'd be torn between drinking it and throwing it in Jean's face. How dare she tell me that the kids need to see their father? Even though it is true; they definitely miss Alex and deserve time with him. Quality time. Especially with Rachel, Alex needs to repair some damage and quick.

"Come with us to the lookout," Jean says. "The view is breathtaking. I'm telling you, there's nothing like getting a higher perspective on life." She is definitely looking at me as if she knows something.

"Where are you staying?" I ask. I pick up my purse, take out a compact and lipstick, hoping to stall until I find out exactly what Jean does or does not know about my most private pain.

"Oh, you'll have to see it. It's a lovely little villa. It's only a house really, but villa sounds sweeter, doesn't it? We even have a back garden."

A back garden. Just like I dreamed of having. Jean has a villa with a back garden. She also has a husband who presumably isn't sleeping with a gorgeous young Italian woman on the side. I feel petty, and broken, and jealous. "Did the university help you find it?"

"Of course. They have an extensive list of places available to rent."

I put the lipstick away. I am quickly running out of ways to stall. "And do they keep records of where all the professors are staying?'

"I suppose so. Why do you ask?"

"Oh, we're just thinking of finding a place for the summer as well," I say.

"Thank God."

And there it is. The tone. The admission. Jean knows. "Thank God?" I say.

"I'm just so glad you're staying. I think it's the right move."

I drop my purse on the sofa and head for the minibar. "Is there any more champagne and orange juice?"

"Sit down darling. I'll pour." Jean tosses her purse on the sofa, gently pushes me into a sitting position, and picks up our champagne flutes.

"So you know that Alex is having an affair," I say when Jean hands me my second drink. Jean sits on the coffee table so that we are eye to eye.

"Harold and I have been married twenty-five years," she says. "And let me tell you, it's been a picnic."

"Oh. How wonderful." Why on earth did Jean think I would want to hear about her great marriage right now?

"Ants. Rain. Rocky ground. Forgot to bring the picnic blanket. Spoiled food—"

"I see."

"Spoiled kids. You name it."

"Okay. I will name it. Has he ever cheated on you?"

"Harold's always had a wandering eye. He has websites he visits a little too often. Actual infidelity? I don't think so. But it's not because he's some kind of saint. In fact, he'd probably try it if he thought anyone would be interested. Let's face it—your Alex is much better looking."

"That's hardly comforting."

"Marriage is hard. Raising a family is hard. Honey, I know what it's like to be a university wife. Especially when they send our men here. Without us. Am I right?"

"Apparently."

"Men are stupid, Lena. They're visual creatures." *Creatures,* I think. Of *the black lagoon variety.* Wait. What is she saying? Is this a comment on how pretty Alexandria is? "You're a beautiful woman," Jean continues. "But sometimes men just react to something a little younger. A little newer."

I slam my glass down. "I can't believe you just said that to me."

"Darling. I've offended you. I'm so sorry. I just meant—well, it happened, and it's horrendous, but you're here now, and he's a man. Why don't you show him what he'd be missing? Take his credit card and go crazy. Get a makeover. Get a sexy dress and high heels. The Italian men will follow you to the ends of the earth. Let Alex get a look at that! Then you'll lay down the law and make him pay—I'm a firm believer in making them pay—but you're a wife and a mother, and you're going to stand your ground and fight for what's yours, and I just wanted to tell you, darling, that Harold and I are completely on your side."

"How long have you known?"

"Pardon?"

"I'm just wondering how long you have known that my husband was sleeping with another woman?"

"I'm not sure why that matters."

"Well. You say you're completely on my side. Yet you never bothered to contact me to let me know what he was doing."

"That's hardly our place. No good can ever come of that. But we're so glad you know. Now you can do something about it."

"Actually, there's nothing I can do. He says he's in love with her and wants to be with her."

"Don't listen to that nonsense. I'm telling you—it's a fly-by-night affair. You have to fight for him. You have to lay down the law. You are the wife and the mother. No pretty young thing can compete with that."

"Have you had the two of them to your villa?" I can see it. Alex and Alexandria having drinks on the patio with Jean and Harold. Laughing about me, the clueless wife back in the States. Something a little newer, something a little younger, two things I will never, ever be. I've been wrong about Jean. She's not a woman of the world. She's not classy and sophisticated. She's a traitor. If only she had spoken out against what Alex and Alexandria were doing. Picked up the phone and called me and warned me. I am racking up enemies by the second here in Florence.

"Pardon?" Jean says.

"Have you had the two of them over to your villa for drinks or dinner on your lovely patio?"

Jean sighs, stands up from the table. "Yes. But only to figure out what was going on. So we could help."

"I see."

"Please hear me. I am a mother. I am a wife. I am on your side."

"Good to know."

"So I need to give you some advice."

"Oh, I heard your advice all right. Fight for him. Get a makeover. Lay down the law."

"Yes, yes. But also."

"Yes?"

"You need to keep this quiet. We can't have the university finding out about it."

"Excuse me?"

"It's a scandal. Scandals and universities do not mix."

"She's not a student, is she?"

"No."

"So why would the university even care?"

"Because of Giovatti, our artist in residence."

"Here we go again with this artist."

"Alex told you about him?"

"He's a genius. He's in love with Alexandria too. That's why he's been putting her face in chalk all over the city. Hardly a compliment if you ask me."

"He *is* a genius. They're calling him the next Michelangelo. Young and very hot, and a bit of a bad boy, and he's got this incredible range, although portraits are his favorite. Faces in particular. He's getting all the Florence artists excited about his work, and with the talent—past and present—in this city, that's saying something."

"I really don't see—"

"And the young kids! They're so inspired too. The university is sponsoring him, and he's bringing in a ton of money. I mean a ton."

"I still don't—"

"Have you seen his chalk drawings about town?"

Visions of splattered yogurt and pasta and meatballs float through my head. Chalk girl's big neon lips. *I am fucking your husband.* "Yes. I've seen them."

"Giovatti's on fire right now. And because he's on fire, the university is on fire right now too."

"What does this have to do with Alex?"

"Alexandria works at the university. Alexandria is at the university helping out Giovatti. Do I have to keep coloring the lines in?"

"Just a few more please."

"If the university knew Alex was having an affair with her, standing in the way of their moneymaker—"

"They'd fire him?"

"Guaranteed."

"So why doesn't this Giovatti just 'out' Alex?"

"I don't know. I thought it was coming to that, and then suddenly, he backed off. He's a bit strange. I think he almost enjoys the competition."

"So all this—you asking me to keep my mouth shut—you're just doing this for Alex's sake?"

"No, of course not. Harold and I have our lives wrapped up in the university. A scandal like this would cause tremendous damage. They'd come down hard on all the professors. We'd probably lose our privileges, like the villa—they might even replace all the teachers."

"So you don't really care about my sixteen-year marriage or my children. You just don't want this affecting your standing in the university."

"Harold is up for a promotion. Dean of the university."

"Good for him."

"Not if Giovatti pulls his support and Alex ruins all of our reputations with his little indiscretion!"

"Maybe you should have thought of that before you wined and dined the two of them in your backyard."

"Keep your friends close and your enemies even closer. Surely you understand the importance of that?"

"Jean. I am here to see if I can salvage my marriage. With all due respect. Your reputation is the least of my worries."

"I see the feisty in you. Alex has always mentioned it, and I thought he was exaggerating. I don't care if you want to take your anger out on me. I'm a mom, you're a mom, and I can see how confused you are. Don't do anything rash. Think about your children."

"I think about nothing else."

"So then you know. Even if you divorce Alex—especially if you divorce Alex—you'll want him employed so he can pay child support and alimony, won't you? So when your kids are of college age they can go to the university free of charge. So you'll all have health insurance. You're a stay-at-home mom. Do you want this to destroy the financial security of your children's future?"

"Of course not." I am going to cry again. Shit, shit, shit, shit.

I shouldn't have come. This is too much. I am in the middle of a soap opera, and I'm not even the star. Just the sad, stupid wife.

Jean puts her arms around me. "Whether you repair your marriage or leave it is up to you. I'm only trying to help. Please. Don't talk to anyone affiliated with the university. Don't make any sudden moves. We'll figure this out together, okay?"

I am numb, and I want to get out of this room, and I never, ever want to see anybody from the university, ever. "Okay," I say. She studies me, then hands me her sunglasses. I hesitate, then put them on. Now I can cry in private.

"A few more cultural things you should be aware of. Don't associate with any Americans wearing white tennis shoes, and don't mention the mafia, ever."

"Got it."

Jean smiles and claps her hands. "Now, shall we go and do a little sightseeing?"

"Not quite. You've asked a few favors of me; now I have a favor to ask of you."

CHAPTER 15

Jean's directions are easy to follow. The apartment building is in the middle of a narrow, dead-end street. Everything in Florence looks quaint to me, even this slightly rundown slice of domestic Italian life. This street seems mostly comprised of apartment buildings. Several stoops have toys scattered about, but eerily no one to play with them. A fat yellow cat eyes me from his perch on a paint-flecked windowsill. Other sills have clothing draped outside, drying in the remaining scraps of the sun streaking in through gaps in the overhead trees. In front of the building where I am headed stand a stooped-over elderly woman and a scrawny boy. The woman is sweeping off the steps with a broom so old it looks as if it were made to deposit dirt instead of sweep it up. Her face is tan and heavily lined, accentuated by a red bandana wrapped around graying hair. The boy, who looks to be about five years old, clutches a dustpan in one hand and the woman's blue housedress in the other. I smile at him. The woman tilts her head and looks at me through one dark brown eye, then she snaps her focus to the steps as if worried the broom might try to flee. The boy stares open-mouthed. Has he never seen blond hair before? Probably not, I suppose. I smile again. *Run away,* I want to warn them. *The flat above you could be a future crime scene.*

"*Buon giorno,*" I say as I take the steps. The pair does not answer, nor do they take their eyes off me. I forget that here they prefer the casual "*ciao*" to "*buon giorno,*" but I don't think that's the reason for their silence. I am underwater, out of place. I look up, and three floors above spot the red flowerpot and green balcony rails. Just as Jean said. Nothing appears to be growing in the flowerpot, I like to think it's because Alexandria is incapable of caring for another living thing. No matter. I have found the lair. Eenie meenie miney mo. Catch a mistress by the toe. Only this mistress, Jean assured me, will be at the university at least until late afternoon.

What if she isn't? What if she's so heartsick over Alex's not calling her back that she's up there right now, sobbing? What would I do? Leave? Spit on her? Punch her? *Make it look like an accident.* No matter what I do I can't get Marco's words out of my head. What if he's here too? I am not going to chicken out. I am going in. I don't have a key to the front door of the building, but when I turn the knob and push, it opens with a creak. I step into a small hallway and head directly for the staircases in front of me. I climb three flights, then pause to catch my breath at the top, her floor. I find the correct door, put my ear to it, and listen. All quiet as far as I can tell. Alexandria, like me, doesn't seem the quiet type. I insert the key and open the door as if the flat belongs to me.

"Honey, I'm home," I call out. This is definitely it, the tiny place I saw on her computer screen. The blue movie starring my husband. The bed is to my immediate left when I walk in, as unmade as I remember it. Barely big enough for two. At home we have a king-sized bed. Our kind of mess is different. Often filled with one or the other child, the dog, art catalogues, the Sunday paper. This isn't a family bed; it's strictly a lovers' bed. The small bathroom where Alexandria held up Alex's shaving case is to my right. A sink, a toilet, and a small standing shower. Alex has showered in there with Alexandria. The thought fills me with rage. Not me, the wife, but her, the mistress. I slam the bathroom door shut as if that will be enough to shut out images of their wet bodies entwined in embrace, slathered with generic Italian shampoo.

A leopard-print chaise lounge in front of the bed has women's clothing draped all over it. A round wooden table delineates a small kitchen, still littered with empty wine bottles. There on the refrigerator, held together by a magnet of the Duomo, is a picture of Alex and Alexandria. It's the same picture Josh had printed out, with her hair plastered to his neck, only she isn't cut out of this one. Alex is looking forward, smiling, but his head tilts toward her, and she is on her tippy toes, whispering in his hear. She has a beautiful profile; she is a beautiful woman. Why is that enough in this world? Does nothing else count?

I rip the picture off the fridge, stand over the sink, and tear it into as many pieces as I can. My hands shake. Behind one of the empty bottles of wine is a full bottle of Limoncello. I have never had Limoncello. I unscrew the cap and take a swig. Strong, strong, strong, lemony and syrupy. A coughing spasm grips me, and it feels good. The choking is a relief from all the thinking. I grab a book of matches, strike one, and drop it into the sink on top of the remnants of the lovers. "How could you?" I say to Alex's left ear just before it burns. "You've killed me." I take another slug from the Limoncello. It is not my favorite drink in the world, but right now its bitter-strong taste is just what I need. Only I am going to have to drink a lot more to drown out Alex and his lover.

Slobs. Adulterous slobs! Alex is a neat freak. How can he stand this tiny, messy space? In somebody else's hands, it could be charming. Two wood-shuttered windows overlook the street. I set my purse on the table, walk over to the windows, and throw them open. Daylight filters into the room, scattering dust particles in the air. They gravitate to the beam of sun and swirl joyfully in the spotlight. I watch them, mesmerized, then jeal-

ous. I am jealous of dust particles. Somebody help me. Next to
the left window is a doorway covered by a dirty cream curtain.
The entrance to the balcony. I push the curtain aside, open the
door, and step out.

Heaven. Big enough for two and Sunday brunch. The red
flowerpot is filled with cigarette butts. A week ago I would have
told you my husband doesn't smoke. But it's becoming appar-
ent there is a lot I don't know about him. If they share cigarettes after sex, it looks as if they have done it hundreds of
times. Even though I am only three stories up, I have a view of
the entire street. Could someone die if she fell from this
height? Probably not, but surely she could be seriously injured,
crippled even. Crippled! I like the thought of crippling Alexandria. I don't like myself for having the thought, but it's true, at
this moment, I like the thought.

Standing here, I am infused with a sense of adventure. *I will
not let them destroy me. This is my balcony now.* Imagine stepping out
onto my little balcony in Italy every day. In the morning with a
cappuccino, in the evening with a glass of wine. Somehow it feels
more comforting than even my own backyard, which requires
mowing, and planting, and the picking up of dog poop.

Although Stella is worth the effort. I could bring Stella here!
But I won't. Alex will have to take her. Alex has to go home with
the kids, and the dog, and he will have to be the mom and the
dad, and take Rachel to dance, and Josh to soccer, and Stella to
the vet, and sleep in a bed with an empty spot, and cook all the
meals, and clean the house, all while I live here in Florence in
my own little flat. Maybe I will even take a lover.

Marco?

Polo, my brain answers, and I laugh out loud. I am laughing!
I didn't know I could still laugh. Maybe another shot of Limoncello is in order. I am going to live here—take over this flat—
it's the solution to everything. Well, maybe not the solution to
everything, but the thought of it coats me with a gooey warmth;
it's the first feeling of hope I've had in days.

I hear Drew Carey from *The Price Is Right. Lena Wallace! You've lost a husband! But you've gained a flat in Florence, Italy! Come on down!*

I walk back into the studio and look at the messy bed. An image of Alex and Alexandria making sweaty love on the bed accosts me. It has tangled red sheets with a white down comforter, adorned with red, loopy stitching along the edges. I scoop the comforter and sheets into my arms and march to the balcony. And even though I hold the pile as far away from my nose as I can, the bedding gives off a powdery musk scent. It is *her* scent, perfumy and sickeningly sweet, and Alex loves her. I cry out. Why isn't inflicting this kind of pain on someone punishable by law? The street is deserted. I dangle the bundle of bedding over the edge, then let it go. As I watch, I hope to see it billow to the ground like a parachute. Instead it falls straight down and lands in a heap in the middle of the sidewalk. I go back for the pillows and toss them over the edge and onto the pile. It feels much better to look at a stripped bed. Calmer. Now what? The pile of clothes on the chaise lounge, how about that? And right underneath it, high heels and a thong. Screw her! I scoop up the clothes and then use one of the heels to pick up the thong. Disgusting. Little black things with a pink bow. I quickly move to the balcony where I toss them onto the growing pile. Are there curb alerts in Italy? How long before people realize there is a pile of free stuff up for grabs?

It would be nice to have a copy of the lease with Alex's name on it, in case the police are called. But now that I've started, I don't want to stop. I am going to find every single item of Alexandria's and toss it overboard. It's a small space; it won't be long until it is free of her. Then I will clean. And then? I survey the space again. Then I will need to get the locks changed.

"I'm staying," I tell the flat. "Until the end of the lease." As soon as I say the words, it's like the bird of freedom flies down and gives me her wings. I feel giddy, and I laugh some more. Alex can take the kids and go home. He will be far away from his mistress; he will reconnect with his kids, and I will get Italy. I will get romance, and adventure, and hot sweaty forbidden sex. *This is your fault, Alex, and I don't care who hates me; I'm doing this.* Because inside, there is still a little part of me churning. I feel as if I am rotting from the inside out, and I am barraged with violent images. Alex, dead, bludgeoned, covered in blood. Alexandria flung off the balcony, lying spread-eagled on the street, her leg bent in an unnatural position. These violent thoughts scare me. I should probably tell someone, get some help. But wait. I am doing something, and didn't I say I already feel better? I am going to become someone else, just for a few months. Not the unappreciated mother. Not the jilted wife. Somebody new. Somebody not rotting inside.

What if Alex's colleagues see me around Florence? It doesn't matter. It's not against the law, is it, to summer in Florence? I can buy a few hats, stick on my big sunglasses, and no one will be the wiser. Maybe I will follow Jean's advice and get a new look as well.

I open the closet. It is stuffed with HIS and HER clothes. In one closet. At home Alex hates it if I even open his closet door, and now he is sharing? I grab hangers and pile as much as I can into my arms. Alexandria has beautiful clothes. Silks and laces, and pretty designer frocks in very small sizes. Frock her. Frock them. I make trip after trip to the balcony. By now the old woman and the little boy are standing over the piles. The broom is nowhere in sight. Good for you, I want to shout. Let that dirty, old thing go! "Watch out!" I say. They look up. Then move back. I let the clothes drop.

It only takes twenty minutes to empty the closet and the bathroom. On the shelf in a closet I find a shoebox of family photos belonging to Alexandria. It just doesn't seem like good Karma to destroy family photos. I am about to save them, let them sit untouched on the shelf, when I come across another photo of Alex and Alexandria. They have their arms around each other and look as if they are standing on the edge of a cliff. No, I think. *Please, God, don't let this be Cinque Terre. Please, God, no. See how much I've endured. Don't let this be Cinque Terre. Give me some little piece, some little peace.*

Tall emerald trees and pink and purple sky soaring high above the Italian Riviera. The edge of the world, their hair blowing in the wind. I hold the picture, but close my eyes, and permit the memory to intrude.

"Cinque Terre?" Alex says, lifting an eyebrow. I am lying on my stomach on the bed that we have just bought at Sears. I am wearing nothing but my wedding veil. It is bad luck to see the bride in her wedding dress, but nobody said anything about the veil. I roll over. Alex lies on top of me, and it feels so good, and so right, and I am dying to tell him about the special place we are going to visit as husband and wife. Cinque Terre, five little villages built into cliffs hovering over the Mediterranean Sea. Soaring above the earth. When we finish making love, I snuggle up to him and tell him about the magical place I've heard of, the perfect place to honeymoon.

"Can you imagine? You walk from one village to another. I've been talking to people, and they say we have to go there. We have to."

"Oh, you've been talking to people?" Alex kisses my neck, my forehead, my lips. "Five little villages?"

"Five little villages. Just for us." He finds five little villages on my body to kiss.

"On the edge of the world?"

"On the edge of the world."

He kisses lower, then I pull him up. "Say yes."

"Yes, my bride." And then he is inside me, and I close my eyes and imagine the two of us suspended above Cinque Terre, the five little villages on the edge of the world.

I turn the picture over. Cinque Terre. 2013. With her. He's betrayed my deepest dream. This hurts just as much as finding out about the two of them in the first place. Maybe more. Now it feels like she's stepped right into my place, my place as wife, my place as new bride, my place at the honeymoon table. I take the entire shoebox of photos over to the sink, then dump them in. I grab the book of matches, strike one after the other against the phosphorus strip, and burn every photo, bar one, over the sink.

CHAPTER 16

I have five hundred euro on me, and a key to the flat, but if I don't find a locksmith, the entire plan will be a bust. It is good to have a plan, but I step outside a little less sure of myself than I'd been seconds earlier. There is still a crowd gathered around, but most of the clothes and items are gone. I see a little girl wearing one of Alexandria's black negligees over her own outfit. She sits on a stoop gripping some of the material in her hand. I silently apologize to her mom. I walk past with a smile. Can I really and truly do this? I don't care if Alex doesn't like it, but I don't want to upset the kids. I can picture them on a therapist's couch years into the future, blaming all their problems on me. "Remember when Dad cheated on Mom with that beautiful young Italian girl (You mean Dad's wife?), and Mom totally abandoned us in a foreign country? That's the exact moment when deep inside I turned into a heroin addict." Rachel, most definitely.

"Yes, but if she hadn't, would we now speak Italian and wear such fine leather shoes?" I don't know if the future Josh of my imagination is straight or gay, and it doesn't matter; what matters is these future children have apparently never spoken to me again.

Relax, Lena. It's a summer. One summer. I will get a locksmith, go shopping, clean the apartment, then call Megan. I can't remember when Mom and Frank will be home from the cruise. I guess I've been a little preoccupied lately. I can use the support. I'll call my father too; he can go visit the kids while I'm gone. I'd invite him to Italy, but Dad has never left the East Coast and has stated numerous times that he doesn't want to. It may be one of the reasons it didn't work out between my parents, but my mom knew this about him when she married him. I thought people were supposed to accept other people, warts and all. Alexandria doesn't have any warts. At least not on the outside. At least not that I've seen.

I hold my head up as I stroll the streets of Florence, trying out what it feels like to belong. With my white-blond hair, I stand out like a beacon. Many men I pass turn and flash their bright Italian smiles. I smile back.

You weren't happy. Come on, Lena. You know you weren't happy.

"Buon giorno," an old lady calls out to me. "Good morning," she adds in English with a gap-toothed smile. Is it still morning? It feels like afternoon.

"Buon giorno," I reply. Enjoy the moment. It's exactly how I will live the rest of the summer, moment by moment, happy. Or at least trying to be.

Three young boys convene at the corner on their bicycles. I ask them if they know where I can find cleaning supplies and a locksmith. They don't answer me, but speak to each other in rapid Italian, then laugh, then try to push each other off their bicycles. I'd be happy to do that to them myself, but I walk on. *Note to self: Do not ask little boys in Florence for help.*

Along this section of town there are clothing boutiques, jewelry stores, and upscale restaurants, or *"ristoranti."* Every turn leads to new sections, new discoveries, hidden little enclaves. I could get used to this. Maybe I could fall in love here. With the city at least. Should I turn right or left? Where is Alexandria now? I have to make sure I get back to the flat before she does. I am pondering my options when I spot an electronics store. Cell phones dangle in the window from invisible strings. I need a cell phone. I can buy a cell phone, ask for a phone book (Do Italians use phone books?), and call a locksmith. After that, I just need cleaning supplies and wine. I can clean and drink wine while waiting for the locks to be changed.

I come out a few minutes later, a proud owner of an Italian cell phone. The kid in the store didn't have a phone book, or know the name of a locksmith, nor could he advise me on where to buy cleaning supplies, but I have a new phone, an Italian phone, and it makes me feel like I belong. I bought some calling cards so I can call Megan, and my parents, and I am already rehearsing what I will say to each of them. For the next three months, I am living here, Firenze!

Back in the flat, I open the bottle of wine I purchased after the cell phone. It is heaven. Much less than I would have paid in the States and top-notch quality. I decide to drink straight out of the bottle. I hope I'm not cheapening it by doing that, but that's what my instincts lead me to do, and while I am here I am just going to learn to follow my instincts. Things progress nicely. On my hands and knees I scrub the kitchen and bathroom, and living room floors. Dust particles are no longer dancing. Everything that has a surface is now shining. I even remove the dirty cream curtain. I will buy something fresh and new. Fresh and new, just like the new and improved Lena. *This will not cannot kill you; this will not cannot kill you; this will not cannot kill you.* I take stock of my new belongings. I have a round wooden table, a chaise lounge, and a bed. The bathroom is also clear of Alexandria and Alex, as is the closet. The locksmith has come and gone, and now I am the only one who has keys to this flat. I'm pretty sure he gave me a good deal, although I'm not quite used to the exchange. But how lucky was it that the locksmith boy has been cheated on too!

Of course he was young, and it wasn't a wife who cheated on

him, but pain is pain, right? He was quick, and efficient, and totally sympathetic. I kissed him on the lips when he left, but in a European way. Not as deep as I'd kissed the hotel boy, and not quite as scandalous, but still, I kissed him on the lips. Just a boy. I would have to be careful how far down the rabbit hole my instincts wanted to hurl me. Still, today is an exception. I have a mistress to smoke out. Speaking of smoke, I also cleaned the flowerpot. This weekend I will find an actual plant for it. Everything is basically done. All I have to do now is wait.

I go through all the kitchen drawers. I find a pack of cigarettes, and now I am looking for a lighter. I won't smoke until I see Alexandria coming, and I will see her coming, because I am perfectly positioned on the balcony to see anyone who turns down the street. I want her first image of me to be one where I have smoke coming out of my nose. I'm not sure I can actually blow it out of my nose, but I am going to try. Just when I think I've cleaned out everything and I'm about to assume stakeout position on the balcony, I notice one last kitchen drawer all the way at the bottom left of the cupboard. I slide it open. Inside I find a stack of papers. They are emails printed from Alexandria's computer. Is she keeping them as some kind of "evidence"?

Alex,
I hate being here alone. When are you coming?
Alexandria

A,
I won't be too late. Six? We'll go out for a bite.
Alex

Alex,
I'm going crazy. When are you going to tell your wife? If you don't, I just might!
Alexandria

Alexandria,
We've talked about this. I know you are frustrated, but this is not
something that can be handled on the phone or through a letter. You
need to leave this to me. Please take this very seriously.
Alex

Alex,
You're not working at all this weekend, right? I need you.
Alexandria

Alexandria,
Not only am I NOT working this weekend, but I have a surprise for you.
Alex

Alex,
If you don't come, I'm going to do something drastic. I swear.
Alexandria

Alex,
Work, work, work! Your wife sounds sexy when she says hello. Is she
sexy? Do you still love her? I'm thinking I'd like to talk to her. Your
daughter answers most of the time now. I shouldn't be calling your
house. Please stop ignoring me. I found a great little restaurant. I can't
wait for you to take me there.
Alexandria

Alex,
I've never felt love like this before. We have to be together. How much
longer is this going to last? I'm telling you. I can't take it. I can't. I
can't be alone much longer. I won't. You need to marry me.
Alexandria

I cannot believe it. I never even thought about all those
hang-up calls we'd been getting. How dare she. But this is better than gold. She actually saved these? They're having this
much tension already? Marco is right. She needs to be the cen-

ter of attention. If I send Alex home and give the impression I am going to be just fine without him—even better—here in Florence for the rest of the summer, she will go ballistic, and he will get back to reality, and by the time I'm ready to come home he will have seen the light and never want to see Alexandria again. And all I have to do is stay here and have as good of a time as I possibly can, considering.

I don't know how Alex will be able to make all this up to me, but as of right now, I am looking at it as if he has a disease, and her name is Alexandria.

What other explanation is there for Alex's putting up with things he hates? Messes, and drama, and jealousy? I remember the first time I got really jealous. Alex had been tutoring a student a year younger than me. Her name was Lacey. She had long red hair, and big breasts, and the loudest laugh on campus. The biggest aphrodisiac for a man is for someone to think he is funny. I had been dating him a year by now and had grown used to all his material. I didn't realize that my relationship would thrive on my ability to keep laughing at his jokes. Until I heard Lacey laughing with Alex in the empty study hall. It was just the two of them in a sea of red auditorium chairs, heads bent toward each other, and I stepped into the hall at the very minute when Lacey threw her head back and laughed. I could see her breasts jiggling even from a distance. That's when I realized I'd messed up big time by no longer laughing at anything Alex said, and once in a while rolling my eyes. Why don't relationships come with owner's manuals?

When he came to my dorm that evening, I picked a fight.
"How was your day?"
"Good, good. Yours?"
"I saw you."
"Excuse me?"
"I saw you in study hall with that girl."
"Which girl?"
"Don't play dumb. The redhead with the double Ds."
"I was tutoring her."

"She was practically sitting in your lap."

"Were you spying on me?"

"No! I came to see if you wanted to have dinner."

"Lena. I like you. You're my girl. But, please listen to me. I lived with a jealous mother. I loved her, but she harped, and whined, and emasculated my father every single day. If you don't trust me, I can't be with you. No matter how much I love you. I tattooed a Viking hat on my ass for Christ sakes. But if you pull this kind of paranoia on me, you will lose me."

And so I never did. And now I've almost lost him anyway. But this new plan is going to work. I can feel it.

Where are the kids and Alex now? I wonder if they are still sightseeing or if they are back at the hotel. Does he wonder where I am? Is he worried about me? Most likely he's relieved. Who wants the scorned wife traipsing around?

I step out onto the balcony. I am getting a little bored. It's hard to enjoy your revenge plan when nobody knows about it. I sit on the balcony and light up the cigarette. Maybe it will make somebody come. I miss Josh and Rachel already. And Stella. Who do I think I am all by myself? I feel like a failure at my new life, already bored and missing my old one. And so I sit. And I keep waiting.

Someone is coming up the street. Oh God, it's her. My heart begins to tap dance. I'm in third grade again, a bare tree being shoved onstage. All this waiting, and now that she is here, I do not feel ready. She is alone and chatting away on a cell phone, walking in the highest heels and shortest skirt I've ever seen. Could Alex have picked more of a stereotype? This embarrasses me, as if the *type* of mistress is a reflection on me. It reminds me of an old joke about a Victorian era woman looking through her opera glass. She spies her husband's mistress, then the neighbor's husband's mistress. "Ours is better," she says with pride.

I crush the cigarette on the railing and dive into the flat. So much for smoke coming out of my nose. Forget going down with the ship. I hide inside the apartment, only one step from diving under the bed. My heart is pounding. I feel as if I'm about to be caught doing something wrong, breaking into someone's home. This is my flat too!

Soon her footsteps can be heard on the outside stairwell. Pound, pound, pound. She certainly isn't dainty walking up the stairs in those high heels. Her voice is still going, rattling on in Italian, still on the phone. She can't be talking to Alex; I don't think his comprehension is that good. Seconds later I hear the sound of her key being placed in the lock. Seconds after that, the doorknob starts to rattle. And then the cussing begins.

It's in Italian, so I can't be sure, but it definitely has the ring of someone swearing up a storm. Key, rattle, cuss. Key, rattle, cuss. It goes on for quite some time. My heartbeat starts to slow, and a smile creeps over my face. This is better than the smoke thing. And then, she is back on the phone. This is the part I really want to hear, for she has to be calling Alex. From the sound of it, he isn't picking up the phone. Two for two. I am winning this round. I am also filled with a giant sense of relief. Alex is ignoring his mistress. I lie in the chaise lounge and light another cigarette. I want Alexandria to smell it from underneath the door. It's better than smoking after sex, which I've never done, but I can imagine it. I take my first drag and have a quiet coughing fit into a leopard pillow.

"Alex?" she says through the door. "Marco? Who is smoking? *Ciao? Ciao? Ciao?*" It takes ten whole minutes before I hear the click clack of her heels as she makes her way back down the stairs. I want to see what she does, but I don't want her to see me. I put the cigarette out, then drop to my hands and knees and crawl out onto the balcony. She is there, just below me, talking to someone else on the phone. She must have a lot of contacts. She is not happy, and she is loud. We have that in common.

Trying to go slowly, I creep my head up like a gyroscope until I can see Alexandria. She's not looking my way at all. I stick my head up even farther. It's the very moment Alexandria chooses to look up. Maybe she can sense me. Our eyes lock. Her hands fly up to her mouth. Her nails are painted tangerine orange. She points at me. "You," she says.

I rise to full height. "Me," I say. Then, "Fuck you."

"You change the key?"

"I did."

"My things, you cannot keep my things."

"You were robbed. Your things are gone." I'm not sure she understands all of what I say, but from the expression on her face, she understands enough. Those frown lines will give her future wrinkles, and for this I am happy.

"Gone?"

I hold out my hands in a giant "What are you going to do?" shrug. "Everything. They took everything."

"You are lying."

"When Alex is here to escort you, you can see for yourself." I'm not letting her in.

"I want my things. My clothing, my shoes, my makeup, my jewelry."

I want my husband back. "Gone, gone, gone, gone," I say. Boy, does it feel good to repeat that word.

"Steal? Somebody steal?"

"Italy is beautiful, but there are a lot of thieves."

"Alex there with you?"

This one, I don't want to answer. If I say yes, it means Alex is such a coward that he doesn't even want to face Alexandria. That might infuriate her, which is good, but if she goes ballistic and calls the police, that is bad.

"Alex is with his children. *Bambinos.* He's married to me. Leave us alone."

"I want my things."

"They are gone, gone, gone, gone."

"I want to see."

"Then bring Marco or Alex." Alexandria's eyes pop open at the mention of Marco. She puts her hands on her hips. "Marco? You know Marco?"

"Oh yes. Marco and I are very good friends." I lean over the balcony on the word very, and let Alexandria see that I too, have plenty of cleavage. Good enough for seducing her ex-boyfriends anyway. Maybe I should make it a point to meet this artist who loves her too. Maybe I can steal him away as well. "I live here now, Alexandria. Your things are gone. My husband is mine. If you want to keep Marco all to yourself, then I suggest you get out of my sight."

Alexandria isn't listening. She's on the phone again. No doubt calling Marco. And even though I still can't understand a word, her tone is different with Marco. Softer. Someone who sounds vulnerable. Is she just playing him? She nods while she is on the phone. I wonder what he's saying to her? Pretty soon she hangs up and marches off.

Huh. Now what? I wander back into the flat. I could go out and buy myself a nice dress and a bouquet of flowers. But I need to conserve the money I have left. I will go on a shopping spree after I work out some kind of financial arrangement with Alex. Speaking of which, I think it's time to call him from my new phone. Good thing I've memorized his number. I dial, and he picks up right away.

"Hello?"

"Alex, it's Lena."

"Lena?" There is a lot of noise in the background. They are still out sightseeing. "Where are you? Are you okay?"

"I'm at the flat."

"What flat?"

"Your flat, Alex. Or should I say, 'ours.' "

"Oh God."

"Are you and the kids still with Harold and Jean?"

"Yes. We just left the Mercado, which I really wanted you to see."

"Oh, I'll have plenty of time to see things."

"You will?"

"Tell Harold you have to go check on something at the office. Meet me here."

"Lena, I don't think you should just hang around the building. Why don't we meet back at the hotel?"

"If you go to the hotel first, will you grab my things and bring them here?"

"Lena, I just said I don't want you hanging outside the building."

"Oh, I'm not hanging outside. I'm inside the flat." At this I hang up. It will drive Alex crazy. Now he will have to show up, just to see what I'm up to. From now on, I will not let him steamroll over our conversations. It's Italy on my terms now.

CHAPTER 17

Alex is calmer than Alexandria. He stands in the flat, surveying all I've done. He's speechless. I light a cigarette.

"You're smoking?"

"Yes."

"Please don't."

"All those butts in the flowerpot? Weren't you smoking with your lover?"

"No. Friends of hers. Alexandria doesn't smoke. Neither do I. And neither do you." Alex walks over and grabs the cigarette out of my hand. I sit there as he takes it over to the sink and douses it with water. He still cares. A warm sensation works its way up to my heart. Alex stands against the sink, arms folded across his chest. I've always thought he was sexy when he was angry. I glance at the bed. I wish he would take me to it, make love to me, not take no for an answer. I can't imagine never sleeping with him again.

"I'm sorry you found out this way," he says.

I stand and face him. "Are you?" We have a staring contest.

He knows what I mean. He had ample opportunity to tell me about this flat.

"How did you?"

"How did I what?" I'm not going to make any of this easy on him.

"Find out."

"Alexandria, of course."

"That can't be true."

"Oh, it is. She couldn't wait to tell me. I told you, she's very disturbed. And you just can't see it." I wonder if he's seen the photo of Marco and Alexandria on his phone? I can't ask, because it will give my part in it away. He doesn't even know I've met Marco. I like having secrets from him. I don't think this bodes well for who I'm becoming, but I do, I like it.

"She sounded very surprised that you were here, Lena. Alexandria is not that good of an actress."

"She's better than you think."

"But how did you get the key?"

Darn professors. Always thinking. "Is that all you have to say to me? I should have found out about this place from you! You secured this flat through the university. I wonder what they would think of your keeping your little mistress here?"

"I don't want to hurt you anymore. Please, believe that. I have no idea anymore how to make any of this remotely better."

"You can start by telling the truth. All of it." Alex simply stares at the floor. "Unless you don't want to repair trust?"

"Of course I do. You are the mother of my children."

"And your wife, Alex. My God. I am your wife. Six months in Italy and you've completely forgotten our sixteen years of marriage?"

"Of course not."

This was not my plan. My plan was to be easygoing Lena. Live and let live, Lena. Send Alex home, Lena. Let distance and an Italian makeover make me new and exciting again. Let Alexandria be the one whining and demanding things of Alex. After seeing those emails, I know I have to stay cool. Act like I don't care. Not an easy feat when every instinct in me wants to fight, to hurt him as much as I'm hurting.

But getting worked up is only going to make me scream and then cry. I've done enough of both. I take a deep breath. I smile, because I read you can eventually make yourself feel better by smiling even if you don't feel like it. Given that I can't imagine genuinely smiling for the next ten years or so, if then, I'd better keep my lip muscles working. "What's done is done. I've decided to stay." I walk toward him. He stands still for a moment, and I'm so close, as if I'm going to touch him, and he stands there waiting to see what I will do. I reach around him and pick up the teakettle. When I move to the sink to fill it with water, he goes to the table and sits down. I wonder if he thinks I am going to make him a cup. I am not. I don't even like tea, but I need to show him this is my place now.

"Stay where?" He's looking at me again.

"Here." I say it lightly. I smile.

"Here."

"Yes. I'm staying here, in this flat, and you are going home with our children."

"That's not a good idea."

"It actually is, Alex. It's the best idea I've had in years."

"What about my job?"

"You are going home. How you break it to the university is your business."

"I don't want to leave them in a lurch like that."

"Yet you'll do it to me."

"We'll all stay."

"No. I'm staying. You and the kids, and Stella, are going."

"And if I say no?"

I am ready for this. And I have practiced it. Alexandria may not be a good actress, but I'm discovering I have a knack for it. Who knew? I have to convince him without coming off too heavy-handed. I keep my voice soft and vulnerable. And if I cry this time, they will be soft, pretty tears, and I will let them flow. That part will be for real. "I know I haven't been the perfect wife. I'm feisty. I'm too sarcastic. I didn't always say what you needed me to say. But I could stand here listing my faults until Tuesday, and it still wouldn't excuse what you've done."

"I know that."

"I wanted to come here on our honeymoon so badly. I had it all planned. And not only have you broken my heart in the most hideous way imaginable, you've done it here, in Florence. And not only Florence."

Alex looks stricken. "What do you mean?"

I go to my purse and take out the only picture I saved, the only one I didn't burn. Alex and Alexandria in Cinque Terre. I hand it to him. The tears have started, and now I wish I hadn't confronted him, because I'm not sure I can stop the waterworks. I still can't afford to lose it. Alex just stares at the picture, and then his eyes well up too. I know he must be thinking of our time in bed, me fantasizing about Cinque Terre, how passionately we made love after.

"I can explain," he says. He can barely choke out the words.

"Don't."

"Her family wanted—"

"I said DON'T." I mean it. This is not up for discussion. This may be the one thing I can never forgive. "You couldn't have hurt me more if you took a rusty knife and stabbed me in the heart. If you have any feelings at all—not just for me, but as a *human being*—if you want to give me any chance of healing—even just the tiniest bit—then you will give me the summer in this flat, and you will go home with our children, who I have been parenting solo for the past six months, and you will do it without making me go all kinds of crazy on you or make threats that I do not want to make."

Alex is still crying. "Okay," he whispers.

"Okay," I say. "Now let's go and tell the children, and get you guys on the next flight."

Alex doesn't move. I sense there is something else he wants to say. I wait. "Her things," he says. "I don't care about mine. But what did you do with her things?"

"Nothing," I say. "I think you were robbed. And I didn't have a key, by the way. I didn't need one. When I got here the door was wide open, and the place was stripped. All I did was change the locks and clean."

Alex stands up, wipes his eyes, looks around. "Robbed?" he says.

"Is there anyone else who is upset about you and Alexandria?" I say. It's probably not nice to throw Marco under the bus, but I'm sure he wouldn't mind. Alex goes over to the closet, opens it, stares at the empty hangers.

"Pictures," he says. "Where did you get the one of Cinque Terre?"

"It was on the fridge," I say.

"Just that one?"

"Yes. It was as if somebody wanted me to see it. I thought it was Alexandria."

Alex walks up to me and takes my hands. I'm too shocked to pull away. He grips them tightly. "I heard you," he says. "And I'll do whatever you want. But I don't think you should stay here. Whoever broke in, what if they come back?"

This is unexpected. And thrilling. Alex is worried about me. I can use this. I don't want us to stop holding hands, but I pull away. "I changed the locks," I say. "And there's nothing left for them to steal."

"Please, Lena. I don't like it."

"There's a lot I don't like lately, Alex. I guess we're both going to have to get used to it."

Alex and I walk to the hotel to wait for Josh and Rachel. I don't want the kids in the flat. It feels wrong somehow. When we arrive, Jean and Harold are waiting with Josh and Rachel; Jean and Harold seem all too relieved to be going back to their own little villa. Jean gives me an approving look. Is my new plan yielding confidence already? I realize I am excited about staying here; not all of it is a ploy to keep my family intact.

"Are we going home now?" Rachel says.

"Pretty please," Josh says. I don't know how to tell them. Suddenly I feel like the one who is doing something wrong. Alex looks at me and nods. He steps up.

"Guess what?" he says. "I'm going home with you two. I'll be

calling the airlines in a little bit." Rachel and Josh whoop. I
don't remember them ever whooping for me. Rachel suddenly
stops mid-whoop and looks at me.

"What about you two," she says. "Are you getting a divorce?"

"We're taking a little break," Alex says. I am grateful Alex is
doing the heavy lifting. I am suddenly exhausted. I don't even
know if I have the energy to pack my bag. I sink down on the living room sofa. There are moments, like now, when I expect
someone to tell me this has all been one huge joke. The prank
of the year. *We can't believe you fell for it!* everyone would say. *You
actually thought Alex would cheat on you? You're crazy!*

"What does that mean?" Rachel says. "A little break?"

"Like Ross and Rachel on *Friends*?" Josh says.

I raise my eyebrow. I didn't even realize he'd been watching
the reruns. I need this over with. I need to take a twenty-year
nap. "It means, I am staying in Florence for the summer so your
dad can spend time alone with you two." My children stare at
me as if I am speaking Italian.

"That's right. Your mom is going to stay here and regroup
while we go home and have a great summer," Alex says. His
voice cracks at the end. At least he's really trying.

"You're staying here?" Rachel says. "But dance camp!"

"Your father will take you to dance camp," I say.

"And soccer?" Josh.

"And soccer," Alex says.

"Who is going to walk Stella? And cook dinner?" Rachel
looks worried it is going to be her.

"Me again," Alex says.

"You burn toast," Rachel says.

"I've learned a thing or two living in Italy," Alex says. "Now I
burn paninis." He is the only one who laughs.

"I'll be back by the time school starts," I say.

"But why? Why do you want to stay in this old hotel?" Rachel
again. Alex and I exchange a look. It feels both familiar and
startling to be in on something private with my husband.

"The university is going to help me find a place to stay for
the summer," I say.

"Why? You don't work for them." Rachel seems to have a never-ending string of keen observations.

"Fringe benefit," Alex says.

Rachel flings herself into my arms. "I'm sorry, I'm sorry, I'm sorry. Don't stay," she says. "You don't even have to divorce Dad." I squeeze Rachel as hard as I can, then pull back and brush my daughter's hair out of her face. She's so young, I remind myself. She has her whole life ahead of her.

"It's just for the rest of the summer. It will be over before you know it."

"I want to stay with you."

"You have dance camp," Alex says.

"I don't care. I won't go. I want to stay with you, Mom."

"Not me," Josh says. "I'm going with Dad." I have to laugh. God bless that kid, he has no filter.

"You can Skype me every day," I say. "Tell me how you're doing at dance camp."

"This is happening, kids," Alex says. "Although I have one request first, Lena?" I wait. Even Rachel stops her theatrics. Alex glances at the kids, then gently pulls me into the bedroom. He looks me in the eyes. "I think it would be good if we all went out tonight. As a family. Just one night out?"

My heart quickens. I want to hug him. I want to say yes. For the kids. For the memory. But I have a plan. And if the request along with the pleading look on Alex's face is any indication, it is already working. "No," I say. "I just can't."

I leave the hotel room feeling like a puppet whose strings have been severed. As if I don't know how to even move on my own. Without my family! Who do I think I am? Why didn't they put up more of a fight? They don't seem traumatized at all. They are going to have a fabulous time; it's going to be all ordering pizzas and playing video games, and Alex is going to fly Alexandria home, and I am going to come back to obese children who have forgotten how to talk in complete sentences. Is Alex going to laugh every time Rachel demeans her brother? I should turn around right now and call this whole thing off.

I stop in front of a squat stone building. It looks medieval. It is sandwiched in between larger sandstone buildings, tucked slightly back. A cross hangs above arched wooden doors that are propped wide open. People file inside. I follow them and stand in the entryway. A series of tiny candles flicker behind the last row of pews. Organ music plays long and low. The floor is simple, faded wood planks, and there is one stained-glass window, and a single statue of Mary, as well as one painting of Jesus. I love it. The simplicity makes me believe. I've never really gone to church. Ornate, large rooms overloaded with statues and glass overwhelm me. To my surprise, I find myself heading for a pew and taking a seat toward the back.

I lean my head back and look at the low, domed ceiling where wood planks criss-cross like an art sculpture. I'm sure there's an architectural reason, but to me it looks like they're banning heaven. Maybe only sinners look up and see this; maybe others look up and see the sky. If that's the case, I should be grateful I'm not looking into a ball of fire. I didn't realize how much anger I've been holding in my body, until I start to feel some of it slide off. I live here, I think. I am free.

A hiccup escapes me. I throw my hand over my mouth and look around. No one is paying any attention. I hope I can stop them. I close my eyes and hold my breath. And I troll through my memories of Alex and me, dusting them off, shining them up. Because he has forgotten, and I must make him remember.

CHAPTER 18

After church I buy a bottle of wine, and I go straight to the flat and pour myself a glass, and sit on my balcony and continue down memory lane to the first time I saw Alex outside of the classroom. If I could go back now, would I change anything?

I was strolling the quad with my sketchpad. My nine-point plan to win his heart was already in play; he just didn't know it yet. He was spread out on the campus lawn, long, lean body, elbow propped up on the grass, strong chin resting against his fist, staring down at his textbook. I stood very close and observed him. For the longest time, he didn't even know I was there. I had my sketchpad propped against my hip, and I watched him as if he were a blade of grass or a patch of flowers. Studying the subject of my future sketch, I felt more than just an artistic inclination; I was flooded with desire. Couldn't he see we were meant to be together? I could picture us so clearly, sharing a breakfast table, having children, becoming a family. It wasn't the plan I had for myself when I entered grad school; it really wasn't. I was going to be a famous, bohemian artist. I was going to remain single at least until my thirties and travel the world, sketching as I went. But here he was changing my destiny, and he wouldn't even look up from his statues. I had never chased a man up until this point in my life. Men chased me. They chased me for my white-blond hair, my tall and slim figure, my pale blue eyes and ivory skin. I didn't know how this kind of unrequited desire felt until I saw Alex lying on the ground and I wanted nothing more than to walk over and straddle him without so much as saying hello. And so, as if in a dream, where you follow every strange thought that pops into your mind, I moved closer.

This time, of course, he noticed me. Since he was lying down, his first view was of my pink toenails and aqua flip-flops, then of my shaved calves, then my short skirt, underside of my breasts, and I could only hope he wasn't looking up my nostrils. Even if he was, he didn't linger. His eyes drifted lazily up my body, his gaze so cocky and self-assured, and then instantly they were back on his book.

"Yes?" he said. A smile played at his lips, one he was trying to conceal.

Who does that? Who says, "Yes?" like that? And that smug little smile! He knew. He knew I wanted him. It would destroy the plan. I was supposed to make him think he was chasing me. What had I done? Why was he smiling? I was suddenly angry with him. After all, shouldn't he have come to the same conclusion by now, that we were meant to be together? Shouldn't he be chasing me?

"I want to sketch you. I'm going to call it 'Portrait of an Asshole.'" I couldn't believe I'd said it. It certainly wasn't what I meant to say. But Alex didn't miss a beat.

"Well, if you're going to do it, then kindly stand somewhere else. You're blocking my light." It was true. I stood between him and the sun.

"Forget it," I said. "I've changed my mind." I walked away. I tore up the nine-point plan. I didn't look at him during lectures. A week later he knocked on my dorm-room door. I had never told him where I lived. I was in sweats and a T-shirt, no makeup, hair piled on my head and held with a pencil. Expecting it to be Megan who had already lost her keys three times this semester, I threw it open and shouted, "Hey."

It was him. I couldn't believe it. Alex Wallace was standing in front of me, and I had just shouted HEY.

"Hey," he said. His voice was quiet, almost timid.

A rush of endorphins flooded me. He was here. He knew we belonged together. The nine-point plan was working, and I hadn't even gotten beyond the first point. "What do you want?" There I went again, saying the opposite of what I was feeling inside.

"I want you to sketch me."

"No thanks."

"Please."

"Why?"

"Christmas is coming. I have no idea what to get my parents. I figured 'Portrait of an Asshole' would at least be original. Unless of course you reproduce it so it can hang on living room walls all over this great country of ours."

"My birthday is on Christmas," I said. "Come in."

"Now?"

"Now or never."

"Now it is."

He's mine, I remind myself. He was then, and he is now. Alexandria means nothing. Alex will come back to me. I feel someone staring at me. It's more of a sensation than a sighting, but it makes me look down. A shadow quickly passes; I hear a rustling and see the back of someone running away. Dark clothes, and even a cap, and running shoes. Is it Alexandria? It's definitely a smaller frame, but it could be a man, or a boy. But I don't know of any men or boys who would be stalking me. Just one very disturbed girl. She wants her things. She wants her pictures. She wants my husband. What if she tries to hurt me?

I will not, cannot let her. I am the one who is coming for her. I go back into the flat and find myself staring at the mattress. Even stripped of the bedding, it's still the place where my husband lay with another woman. Rage is back, battling inside me. I set my sights on the mattress, and I grab a corner, and I pull it off the bed. The opposite end lands with a thunk and jostles a bedside table. I drag the mattress onto the balcony, knocking into the chairs and table that I should have moved out of the way first. It's like wrestling an elephant, but I manage inch by inch to teeter the center of the mattress onto the rail of the balcony. Breathing heavily, hair sticking to my face, my God, how humid it is in Tuscany. I look below. I do not see anyone down there, but what if the small boy decides to dart out at the last minute? Could a mattress falling from three flights above kill a child? I cannot take the possibility, or the Karma. I drag it back inside, then open the door and begin to drag the mattress down the stairs. It feels good, channeling all my rage onto this beast. The steps are uneven, and the cream walls have cracks, and I could slip and fall and get a concussion. Imagine!

I've made it down one flight; now I am going for two. I wouldn't mind having a concussion. I wouldn't mind not knowing. Maybe then I would be dining alfresco and meeting new friends instead of dragging stained mattresses down shoddy steps. By the time I am at the main door, I am drenched in sweat, and my hands are red and raw from grasping the edges. I have to lean the mattress against the small entryway in order to open the door. I haul it outside, into the fresh night air, drag it down the stoop, and leave it in the middle of the sidewalk. I hope Florentine dogs come and pee on it in the night. I stand there staring at it, as if it's going to do something. Maybe I should drag it to the *Fountain of Neptune*. Throw it in the fountain. Then set it on fire. The Burning Bed. Instead I walk back up the three flights of steps and go to lie down. Except there is no longer any bed, just the simple wood frame, like the outline of a body. I curl up in a fetal position on the leopard print chair, brace myself for the tears that are coming, and pray they never did it on these soft, velvet spots.

The next morning I head out with the sun. I navigate the streets, preparing to feast on the routines of those who live here, beginning their day. So far, all is quiet; only the street sweepers have crossed my path. I soak in the quiet of the historic city, basking in the glow of the first morning light. It makes the terra-cotta roofs shine, and I can only pray some of the beauty and peace of this city will rub off on me. I soon find a market that houses a long espresso bar. A tingle of excitement hits me as I step into the lively place. Here, it is not quiet; there are voices bantering back and forth, and glasses clinking, and espresso machines frothing. It is also part food market, part gift shop, and I'm in love with it. Baskets and cured meats hang from the ceiling, and past the espresso bar shelves are lined with glass bottles, and jars, and cheese, and pastas, and I feel almost drunk taking it all in. The store is longer than it is wide, and every space from the tiniest corner to the tallest shelf is filled with something.

But for now, all I want is a cappuccino. Italy, the founder of the coffee bar concept. As I expected, people are standing up along the bar sipping on their espressos and eating pastries. I work my way in, convincing myself I belong. I will have to learn to ask for my cappuccino in Italian. A robust man behind the counter with a white apron gives me a backward glance as he stands at the espresso machine. "Ticket first," he says. I open my mouth. Where do I get a ticket? Tears spring to my eyes. Everything makes me cry. A thin man with foam on his mustache looks at me, then points his entire body to the cash register directly across the way.

"You pay first," he says. "Then you come here with your ticket."

"*Grazie,*" I say. I bite the side of my cheek, staving off the tears with the pain. I will learn all the customs, and I will fit in. I stand in line, pay for my drink, and return to the counter. The man with the apron approaches me and holds his hand out for my ticket. I grin and give it to him.

"*Ciao, bella,*" he says, just like you hear in the movies.

"*Ciao, bella,*" I repeat, before realizing he probably does not want to be called beautiful. But he winks at me, so maybe he does.

"You are American," he says, as if he needs to remind me.

"Pretty obvious," I say with a nervous laugh.

"I am Angelo. What is your name, *bella?*"

"Lena."

"You are on holiday? With *la famiglia?*" He slips in the Italian word for "family" as if gently schooling me.

Before I can even bite down on the pink inner flesh of my cheek, the tears are streaming down my face. "My husband is having an affair," I say. "With an Italian woman. I am making him go home with our children. I am alone." Angelo looks at me, really looks at me, even though people seem to be shouting for him both in front of and behind the counter. He has heavy jowls and a thick middle, but a youthful face underneath, and brown eyes that radiate kindness. His hands are thick too, I imagine from kneading dough, and I suddenly realize I would love to paint him. I haven't picked up a brush in fifteen years. I want to paint everything in this shop. I want to paint the refrigerated cases of meats and cheeses. The bottles of olive oils and sauces. The salami hanging from the ceiling. The gleam of the espresso machine with the steam coming off it. But most of all I want to capture, forever, the kindness I see in the eyes looking so intently into mine.

"Cappuccino," he barks, then starts, as if realizing he is the one who has to make it. He whips up a white cup, throws it under the machine, and begins to sing to himself as he prepares my drink. I watch, fascinated, the tears gone. When he presents it to me, it's with a huge smile and another wink. "You are not alone," he says. "Now you have me, and you have a cappuccino." And then he is off to the next person before I can reply. I nod as if he has given me an order and take a sip. It is still hot, but it tastes like heaven. Rich and creamy. I have only had a sip, and I'm already mourning it, dreading when it's gone. Why can't anything last forever? How do we stop everything from spinning so far away?

It's too early for these kind of crazy thoughts. Besides, I can always order another one. I can stay here all day; I can drink as many as I want. There are no mouths to feed, no dogs to walk, no places to drive, no laundry waiting for me to fold. I have to stop telling people about Alex's affair, but my mouth is always racing ahead of my mind. I force myself to drink slowly. For the first time in my life, I can actually live in the moment. I can pretend I am the free-spirited girl I once thought I would be. If I had never approached Alex on that lawn, if I had been more in love with art than I was with him, if I hadn't had a nine-point plan, who would I be right now? A famous artist? Would I be creating art on the streets of Florence instead of destroying it?

Despite my trying to go slow, the cups are small, and I am almost finished with my cappuccino. A man standing to my left begins to edge his way in my direction. The personal-space zone is much smaller here than it is in America, and it's one facet of life where I wouldn't want to adopt the Italian way. Mistresses are another. Regardless, this is a café, not a crowded train station, and really, does he have to be so close? His cologne is overpowering. Did he pour the entire bottle over his head? I do not want my last sips of heaven to taste like canoe, or musk, or shotgun, or whatever else they're naming colognes these days. He's darker than a lot of locals I've seen; maybe he's Spanish. I wonder if he is going to hit on me. I move a few inches in the other direction, in the guise of shifting. It's too early to be hit on. Besides, if I'm going to engage in romance it would be with Marco, wouldn't it? At the thought of him, I am filled with a rush of warmth, and a spontaneous smile appears on my face. Oh God, is this how it began with Alex and Alexandria? I hate the thought of him standing in his classroom and daydreaming of her. I hate it! The man to my left has moved in even more. I will have to just leave. I glance down to leave a tip, when I notice what he's reading. It's a brochure of the chalk-drawing tour. I can't believe it. He's looking at the picture of Giovatti on the back.

All you can see is the back of Giovatti; he is on his haunches as he renders one of his drawings on the cobblestone streets. I wish to see his face, this mysterious artist. Maybe I should follow the faces today, face them all, pun intended. I realize I still have the same brochure in my purse. It's sitting on the counter in

front of me, with my right hand resting gently on top. I look up
to see Angelo standing at the other end of the counter. He is
looking at me and the man who is practically on top of me. He
frowns. Maybe my Italian barista is protective of me? Maybe
he's right; maybe I'm not alone. Just when I'm about to reach
in to get a bit of change to leave on the bar, the stranger's hand
shoots out and he grabs my purse right out from underneath
my own hand resting on top of it!

He's like this ocean-dwelling shrimp creature I saw on a nature documentary. Quick as lightening and no fear! He tucks
my purse underneath his armpit and runs. He's left the
brochure on the counter. I grab it, shove it in my pocket, and
take off after him. "Hey, hey, hey," I yell. "Help." I glance at Angelo. He throws both hands up and shakes a finger at the back
of the man's head as he runs out. Maybe this is why they make
you pay first in Italy. "Stop him, stop him," I scream. He's already out the door of the shop. The streets are a lot more
crowded than when I came in. Morning rush hour. He knew
exactly when to steal my purse. I hurry after him. "Thief, my
purse, get him." I wish I knew how to say "Stop, thief!" in Italian. Or Spanish. As if only a simple language barrier is responsible for his taking off with my purse. Should I call someone? I
reach for my purse as I run. Not my finest hour. He's too far
ahead now; I can barely make out his green pants and brown
shirt through the crowd. I sprint full on. Everything is in my
purse. I knew better; why didn't I leave most of it in the flat? It's
too late; I didn't—it's all there. Close to five hundred euro, my
passport, my wallet, my new Italian cell phone. The keys to the
flat. My God, the keys to the flat! "HELP!" Nobody seems disturbed by my screaming or sprinting. I note expressions of curiosity and even annoyance. What's wrong with these people?
I'm still running full on, but the man has disappeared. My
lungs are on fire, as well as the balls of my feet, and my heart is
tripping. He's gone. My purse is gone. The keys to my flat are
gone. My children are gone. My husband is so, so far gone.

I am nameless. Sweating. Burning. I stop. My hair sticks to
my face. I bend over and try to breathe. Shit. I don't have a

thing to my name. I could go back to the hotel and see if Alex is still there, but surely they are at the airport by now. I only had one debit/credit card, and it will have to be canceled. I limp in the direction of the hotel, angry with myself. One morning on my own and already robbed! I'd been warned about this. Gypsies, and thieves, and con artists. I'd heard of a scam in which a woman throws a baby at you. In panic you open your arms to catch it. Meanwhile someone is behind you, cutting off your purse strings. By the time you realize it's a doll, the purse is gone. How evil, to throw a fake baby at someone. Even knowing the trick, of course I would have to catch it. How could you risk it? I was on the lookout for flying babies, not swarthy little men. Not only did I get robbed, he wasn't even very creative about it. I'd tell him this, if I could just get my hands on him.

CHAPTER 19

Alex and the children have checked out. I knew this, yet it still hits me like a punch to the stomach. The girl at the desk is embarrassed by my tears, and she lets me use the phone and the computer. I send Alex an email telling him I was robbed and ask him to wire money. He'll know if there is a Western Union or some such place nearby. I tell him I will check this email frequently. I call my bank and cancel my debit card. There is already an unauthorized purchase. Italian bras and panties. Beaucoup bucks. I can't believe it. What kind of a thief would immediately go and buy bras and panties with my credit—?

The mistress kind. Alexandria is behind this. She has to be. The thief must be a friend of hers. Was that Giovatti? I stand outside the hotel, furious, my mind spinning. If it is her, she now has the new key to the flat. She thinks I still have her pictures, or she just wants to exact a little revenge. I march back into the hotel and fire off another email to Alex.

* * *

Alexandria had my purse stolen and she is already using the debit/credit card.

There. Let him deal with that. Of course I don't have solid evidence, but that doesn't bother me a bit. I know in my gut it was her. I need to find the young locksmith. At least he'll remember me. But of course his phone number is in my phone, which was in my purse. I could go to the university and see if Alexandria is there, or I could just hurry and find the locksmith. Hopefully she won't attempt to get into the flat until after work. It gives me all day.

Except that I have no money to pay him. Or to eat. Or to get something to drink. I am homeless in Florence. I look to the sky. What now, God? Did I get too big for my britches? Enjoy my cappuccino a little too much? *Is it my new lot in life just to suffer, and every time I get a little scrap of happiness you're going to yank me back to misery?*

I need to calm down. I need to remember what is important. None of this really matters. What else can Alexandria take from me? My clothes? She can have them. I need a new wardrobe anyway. I am going to go do something right now to get my mind off this. I'm going to do something touristy. It has to be free though, given the current situation. But I am in luck; this is Florence, where the outdoors is a walking art museum. I know where I will go. I will go somewhere on the chalk-face tour.

I take the brochure out of my pocket and stare at it. The first stop is at the very top of the Piazzale Michelangelo. I don't know what I expect to get out of this, but it's as good a thing to do as any.

The climb to the overlook begins at a tower at the base of a hill. A tour guide is speaking to a small group. I nudge in so I can listen. "This is the Piazza Poggi. Named after the architect, Giuseppe Poggi, who in 1869 built the monument at the top in honor of Michelangelo." The guide, a short man with suspenders and a fedora, pauses here as if waiting for questions or applause. He gets neither, but continues with a nod and a smile as if he had. "Now. If you look up at the slats under this tower, kids, you'll see there are four soccer balls wedged up in there." This time the crowd makes appreciative noises as several tourists move forward to confirm the existence of soccer balls wedged into the slats. *Ah, tourists. Monuments built in 1869, survey says NaaaaaaaaaaaaaaaH. Soccer balls stuck in slats, survey says ding!ding!ding!*

Alex would have made a great tour guide. He could make everything seem cool, and fun, and exciting. Because that was him. He was that guy. The guy who walks in, and suddenly what was a bunch of coeds standing around with sweaty plastic beer cups is now a party. I married that guy. And he was going to continue being that guy without me. He will be that guy for everyone else. He is that guy for Alexandria. I glance up at the wide stone steps ascending toward the Piazzale, and I feel dizzy. I am going to cry, or scream, or both. My purse has just been stolen. My husband has been essentially stolen! And I am standing here, in Florence, Italy, listening to people ooh and aah over soccer balls!

"Are you okay?" I feel a cool hand on my hot shoulder. When did it get so hot out here? A woman in a wide-brimmed hat is looking at me with concern.

"Would you like some sunblock, dear?" the woman says. I must be sunburned already. I should have worn sunblock. The kids need to wear sunblock every day. Will Alex remember to put sunblock on them everyday? I have an urge to run back to the hotel to email him again just to tell him this.

"Sunblock," I say with a nod. My throat is parched too, and I want a bottle of water, which I would have been able to go and buy, if not for the thief who wanted a bra. The woman pulls a huge bottle of sunblock out of her purse. Two children, about Josh and Rachel's ages, also in hats and sunglasses, stand patiently behind her. Of course. Because mothers who care carry industrial-sized sunblock in their bags. Big fat tears run down my cheeks. *"Grazie,"* I say, even though the woman is obviously American. Without even using it, I hand the sunblock back to the woman and start up the hill.

The climb culminates in a large, open parking lot with a 360-degree view of Florence and the Arno valley. The main building is a monument Poggi built in dedication to Michelangelo, and it's set off by a divine nineteenth century-style terrace. It was originally intended as a museum for Michelangelo's works, but for some reason that never came to fruition, and now it is a restaurant.

In the distance an ancient stone wall parades up the lush Tuscan hillside, its ridgetop dotted with evergreens and the occasional villa, and umbrellaed by a bright blue sky. The parking lot is littered with vendors, streetlamps topped by globular white balls, and a replica bronze statue of David, who looks as if he's just hanging out saying hello. To the west the view looks over the series of three bridges lying across the Arno River: Ponte Vecchio, Ponte Santa Trinita, and Ponte Alla Carraia.

But my favorite vantage point is looking toward the city. Here the Duomo and the clock tower rise bravely above the rest, as if all the other buildings are shy maidens, too modest to flash anything but their white bodies and their red-brick roofs. According to the brochure, the chalk drawing is up another hill just before you reach a little church and graveyard.

I pass cozy houses and lush green gardens on my ascent. Soon I reach the San Miniato al Monte. It is yet another sweet little Tuscan church, but the view is the true miracle. It is less crowded up here, and I feel my breath expand. Tucked behind the church is an ancient cemetery, but I do not linger among the headstones; I do not want to think about death. I am too close to it myself.

I find it in a small section of pavement in front of the church. Alexandria's big chalk eyes and chalk lips. This one is done in red, white, and blue. How ironic. I sit down next to it. I stare at it for a few seconds before touching the tip of my toe against Alexandria's chalk chin.

"Listen, adulteress," I say quietly. "I'm going to get you for this." I grind my toe, just a little. When I pull away, the chin is good and smudged. Then I scoop up some loose dirt and arrange it above the lip until she has a handlebar mustache. Like the villain in a melodrama. Laughter rolls out of me.

Perfetto! Taking advantage of still being the only one up here, I scoop up more dirt and give her really bushy eyebrows. Take that! I hear voices just over the hill. It sounds like the tour group I passed on the way in is coming. I run behind the church, and like it or not, here I am among all the little headstones. Pretty soon the group will come upon the altered chalk drawing. I am like Marcel Duchamp putting his touch on other people's works and claiming it as his readymade art. I think for a second of the artist, and feel a twang of guilt. It doesn't last long. I'm doing this man, this Giovatti, a favor. He needs to fall in love with somebody else. His muse is rotten. She doesn't deserve these "love letters" written in chalk.

But the group doesn't even stop to look at my handiwork. They enter the little church instead, with the tour guide yammering on. Maybe they'll notice it on the way out. Either way, I can't stay. I have a lock to change once again and a mistress to catch.

I feel lost now. I just want to go back to the flat, but Alexandria has seen to it that I cannot. I go back to Angelo at the espresso bar. The last time he saw me, I was screaming for help, and I'm not sure what kind of reception to expect when he flies out from behind the counter and envelops me in a hug. He smells like dough and sweat and espresso, and I have never been so happy to be touched.

"Sit, sit, sit," he says. There are no chairs at the counter, so I'm not sure what to do. I want to please him, but I don't think sitting on the floor is the right move. So I lean into the counter instead. "Thieves!" he says. "Steal right from under you nose!"

"My husband's mistress," I say. "It was her." Angelo frowns and stands in front of me wiping sweat off his brow with a stained linen napkin.

"I see a man. Not woman," he says.

"I know, I know. But she was behind it. I'm sure of it." Angelo raises one bushy eyebrow. He looks like he doesn't quite believe me, so I nod very seriously, and after a moment he follows suit.

"I'll just go pay for a cappuccino," I say. Except I can't; I don't have any money.

"No, no, no," Angelo says. "Cappuccino is only up until eleven in the morning. After that, no cappuccino."

"But the machine is right there," I say, pointing.

"Italian way," he says. "You follow Italian way."

"All right," I say. Mainly because I've no way to pay for it. Angelo winks and makes me a shot of espresso. It looks good. I wish I had money. He slides it in front of me.

"I can't pay," I say, on the verge of tears again.

"Of course you cannot pay. Thieves! Right out from under you hand."

"I'm telling you, it's Alexandria. But it's okay. I just introduced one of her faces to the bottom of my shoe." I sip on the espresso while Angelo frowns. I find the large creases in his forehead comforting. If I'm going to learn not to drink cappuccinos after eleven a.m., he's going to have to learn that I have a sarcastic bent. I wonder how soon Alex will get my message. If he doesn't wire enough money for a locksmith, I'm going to have to go to the university and confront Alexandria. She's the one who should pay.

"What are you going to do, *bella*? In Florence, you need money."

"I know, I know. My husband will send it."

"The one who cheat on you?"

"Yes. But it's not like I'm asking him for a favor. It's our money."

"My wife. She take all my money too."

"How long have you been married?"

"Forty-five years." I choke on espresso. Angelo pounds me on the back. "If you cannot imagine it, it's probably not for you," he says.

"What's your secret?" I say when I can talk again.

"She's the boss," he says. "I work, I pay, she happy."

"I'm sure there's more to it than that," I say. Angelo smiles and shakes his head.

"Is simple, love. You work, you pay, that's it."

"Well. Good for you. I worked. I paid. And now, for me, that's it. Same story, different ending."

"You want the secret to love, *bella?*"

"Of course."

Angelo waves his napkin at me. "Choose neither a lover nor linen by candlelight." He throws his head back and laughs. I laugh with him.

"Good advice." I met Alex under stage lights and then under the vibrant glare of the sun. I keep this to myself.

"You no look for love, *bella.* Let it find you."

"You sound like my friend Megan."

"She is wise, this friend."

"Hunt it down and kill it. That's more my style."

"You wait. It will find you. For now, you love Firenze."

"No offense, but if the Italians know so much about love then why do all operas end in tragedy and death?"

"Because the tickets they are expensive, no? If you pay big, you want to see someone die. This is just the way."

I finish my appropriate after-eleven beverage. I am hopped up on caffeine and revenge, eager to confront Alexandria. Angelo puts a hand on my arm. "I call locksmith," he says. "You pay me later. This woman, she's not worth your time."

Oh, but there is no better way to spend my time. I keep this to myself and gratefully accept his offer to call a locksmith. When Angelo gets off the phone, he tells me the locksmith will be at my flat in about an hour. Then he takes my hand, turns it palm up, and plants twenty euro in it. I kiss him on the cheek and try not to blubber as I profusely thank him and promise to pay him back as soon as I can. He waves me off, then points to his other cheek and leans in for another kiss. I laugh, oblige, and leave with tears running down my face. I take my time walking home, winding through new streets, looking in the windows of shops, imagining what I will buy when I am solvent again. I will get one outfit. From head to toe. And I've no choice but to get a new purse. Definitely a trip to the hairdresser. Maybe I will shock Rachel on our next video call by getting a tattoo. What would I get? A heart with a knife plunged through it?

I arrive home, stand in the street, and look up at the balcony, half expecting Alexandria to be standing there. Lucky for her, she is not. I sit on the stoop and wait. It is really hot. I'm too fair skinned to just sit here baking like this. I move to the closest tree and sit on the sidewalk underneath it. I fall asleep under the Tuscan shade. When I wake up, a short man with a long toolbox is staring down at me. After figuring out that he's not here to kill me, I take him up to my flat. Instead of young and cute, this locksmith is old and cranky. He doesn't seem to like me watching him, but it's a tiny place, and there's nowhere to hide. He keeps muttering to himself, his hands flying. Maybe he really wants to be a dentist. He gestures with his hands that the lock is new. Why am I changing it?

"My husband's mistress stole the key," I say. "And my purse." This time I should leave a spare key somewhere. With Marco? It might be fun to give him a key. Not that I know how to get ahold of him, and not that I would if I did. For all I know, he was in on my purse being stolen. Yet another man doing Alexandria's bidding. This girl either needs her own Broadway musical or she needs to be taken down a few notches.

Before the locksmith leaves, he mimes putting a purse on diagonally across your body and holding it tight. Very tight. His eyes are all squinted up, and he's holding it so tight he's turning red. I wonder if I'm supposed to play the thief and grab it? I just nod instead. Once he's gone, I kind of miss him. I'm still without identification and money, but at least Alexandria won't be breaking into the flat. And I've had enough of this. There's only one place to go now.

CHAPTER 20

I find a tobacco shop, indicated by a large *T* on a black sign, and then, as Angelo instructed, look for the orange A.T.A.F. sticker in the window. I feel a sense of pride when I spot it, then go in and buy a bus ticket and pick up a schedule. The stop I need isn't far, and I find it easily using the map provided with the schedule. Less than ten minutes later, I board a bus to the university. Ready or not, Alexandria, here I come. The very thought is making my breath come in shallow waves. If it comes to a physical fight, I think I can take her. But she's so popular around here, it would probably be like punching Mary Poppins in the kisser. Whatever else happens, I am not going to let her hang on to her angelic reputation. I take a deep breath, then look out the window at the hillside dotted with terra-cotta roofs. So pretty. I should be taking this ride with Alex and the kids; he should be touring me around the campus, proudly introducing me to everyone. Will I get a glimpse of this famous Giovatti while I am there? Oh God. What if somehow he knows what I've done to his chalk drawings? What if the kids told Alex, and Alex told Alexandria, and she told Giovatti? Relax. He doesn't know what I look like. Unless of course he's with Alexandria and she recognizes me, and tells him who I am, and he goes to wring my neck with giant, chalk-dusted hands.

My thoughts are interrupted by the bus's bouncing over a pothole; for a second, I am out of my seat, and then I am slammed back down as we labor uphill. The engine wheezes and labors, and it sounds like we're not going to make it. I imagine the bus careening backwards; maybe this is where my story ends, in a giant fireball, at the base of the hill. But we make it after all, and the bus leaves me off just a few feet from the entrance to the university.

The campus sits hillside a little north of the center of the city. I'm in awe as I approach the forty-acre estate. It consists of six gorgeous villas, the largest of which is a stately fifteenth-century stone building. The stone has been painted a cheerful yellow, a color that literally pops out because of the green trees and gardens surrounding it. Alex has talked about it so much, I feel as if I've been here. The huge villa includes a fifty-room museum. I will not be taking a tour today. Alex has ruined a lot of tours for me. The grounds are bordered by stone fences, and decorated with black iron benches, and once again, everywhere I look there are statues in various states of repose and undress. They look at me like I know nothing of life, these cherubs, and maidens, and scholars. Get naked, lie back, grab a fig leaf, think about someone other than yourself for a change, they taunt me. Rows and rows of olive trees form a neat little square in front of two of the villas. It doesn't even seem real, such beauty. So besides his gorgeous mistress, this was where Alex was spending all his time. Poor hubby.

Several students mill about, with books and backpacks. I see at least two students with easels, painting the olive groves and scenery. I am both envious and protective of them. Mostly protective. *Don't marry the first boy you fall in love with,* I want to warn them. Instead, I smile, but they are not looking at me, rather through me; among the very young I do not exist.

* * *

As I approach the arched doors I feel as if I'm bypassing the life I could have had with Alex but didn't. I would have moved to Florence if that were what this was all about. Maybe Alex couldn't bring himself to ask me, or even dare to dream it himself, so he slept with Alexandria in order to force some kind of crisis that would allow him to live here year-round. It's not very logical, but the question—How could he do this to me?—will not be answered with logic. I am dealing with raw impulse—Alex morphed into a caveman. All I need to do is expose Alexandria for the rotting person she is on the inside, and Alex will see the light.

After opening the massive door to the main villa, I step into an expansive room covered in deep, rich wood, and museum-quality artwork. By the front door is an easel with a poster propped up. I don't stop to read it. I am being watched by a girl whose desk is flanked by two scholarly bronze heads. There's almost too much art and history in Florence; I am becoming immune to it. I don't even want to read the plaques to see whose heads merit guarding the desk and the pretty young girl who sits behind it. Just like art, there is no shortage of pretty young girls. If it hadn't been Alexandria, would it have been someone else? I smile and approach.

"Can I help you, ma'am?" the girl says. She is young and blond and American, and in the moment I want to slap her. Does she call Alexandria ma'am? How old is ma'am anyway? There should be an official memorandum on the subject. The Italian version, *signora,* sounds slightly better.

"I'm Lena Wallace. Professor Alex Wallace's wife." The girl's whitened smile doesn't change, but she suddenly springs from her seat.

"Oh my God. We love Alex. Professor Wallace. He is the best."

If by "best" you mean "cheating bastard" I totally agree. "Thank you."

"No, seriously, he's everyone's fav."

"I'm sure he is." *Alexandria's in particular.*

"You're so pretty."

I absentmindedly touch my hair, taken aback by the compliment. I still need a new look. "Thank you."

"Are you staying for the summer?"

"As a matter of fact I am. And I need to speak with Alexandria."

"Miss Cosetti?"

So that's her last name. It startles me. I hadn't even thought of her as having a last name. Or anything else a human might have. This is how killers operate. They de-humanize their victims. *Remind them you have a name!* Good advice if you wake up chained to a pole in some psychopath's basement. Who is this woman turning me into? Correction: Who is Alexandria Cosetti turning me into? If she marries Alex she will be Alexandria Wallace. Or AW. Awwwwwwww. People will feel sorry for her even then!

"Yes. Miss Cosetti," I say as if the name doesn't stick in my throat. *The husband-stealing witch.* "Is she here?" Enough with the chitchat. I have come to face her, and I'd better do it while this adrenaline is coursing through me. I stare intensely at the girl, looking for any sign that she knows about the affair. But her expression doesn't change even a smidgen. She glances at the poster by the door.

"They're in a meeting."

I wonder what the poster has to do with the meeting. "Sounds important."

"More like scandalous."

"How so?"

"I'm sorry. I shouldn't have said that. Can I take a message?"

"Don't worry. I'm always saying things I shouldn't too."

"Really? Everybody tells me I have a big mouth."

"Nonsense. We all do. If it makes you feel any better, I'm really good at keeping secrets." *So is Alex.*

"The artist is freaking out a bit." She glances at the poster again. I turn to it, but I'm still too far away to read it.

"Giovatti?"

"You know him? Of course you do—Alex—Professor Wallace worked closely with him." This is the second time she has uttered his first name, then corrected herself. Did Alex flirt with all the girls? *Call me Alex.* Was he the predator and Alexandria the innocent victim? The thought makes me ill, and I can't do this, I can't read evil intent into everything he did, or it will destroy us. "Don't you think he's like, totally brilliant?" For a minute I think she is talking about Alex, another smitten victim, and then I remember she is talking about Giovatti.

"Totally. So what's the scandal?"

"I really don't want to get in trouble."

"How about I tell you a juicy secret, and then you tell me, quid pro quo."

"Deal."

"You know Alexandria?"

"Of course. She's like totally gorgeous and totally famous, which is why she's—" The girl stops, looks shocked.

"Why she's what?"

"I almost spilled. See, I do have a big mouth. You haven't told me the secret."

"Swear you won't tell."

"I swear."

"She's having an affair with a married man," I say. The girl literally gasps, and for some reason it pleases me. It is shocking. It's just nice to have someone else confirm that.

"Seriously?"

"You can't breathe a word."

"I won't, I won't. Who is it?"

"It's your turn." She looks disappointed. "One secret. That was the deal."

She nods; she is the type of girl to whom secret-swapping is sacred. "Giovatti wants to replace her face."

"What?"

"He doesn't want her to be the chalk-drawing face anymore. He wants to erase all of them and start over. He has a new muse."

Well, well, well. It's good news and bad news. Good news because Alexandria is vain enough that this is totally going to crush her ego. Bad because if Giovatti is doing this, it's because she's not responding to his advances. Which means she's still after my husband. "Wow. How's she taking it?"

"She's totally freaking out!"

"Good!"

"Good?"

"I'm sorry. It's just—as a wife and a mother myself, I just can't feel bad for someone who would wreck somebody else's happy home, you know?"

"Totally. Except."

"Except?"

"Well, how happy could it be if the husband is having an affair?"

"So you're blaming the wife?"

"No. God, no. Except."

"Except?"

"Well, it takes two, doesn't it? He might be cheating, but like he wouldn't if he were happier. These things don't just happen in a vacuum."

"How do you know? Do you even have a boyfriend?"

She turns red. I didn't mean to say it. I need to be careful. I reach my hand out and pat hers. "You will. You're gorgeous. You'll definitely meet some Italian hunk." She would love Marco. *She can't have him,* reverberates through me. I realize I need Marco to get through this. I need his flattery and attention focused solely on me. Not to mention he's my partner in crime. I need his help taking down Alexandria. It's okay to use whatever I have to help me get through this. I wonder if he's thinking about me. I wonder how I can go about seeing him again. The girl is still smarting from my comment. If I want her on my side, I have to do some damage control, quick. "You're probably right, about the wife. I mean there were probably signs. Maybe if she hadn't ignored them—"

"No, no. You're right. We can't blame her. Imagine finding out your husband is cheating with Alexandria of all people."

"Why her of all people?"

"You know, because she's drop-dead gorgeous. It would be like how Jen felt when Brad left her for Angelina."

"Tramp." It just flies out of my mouth. "I'm sure that's what Jen was thinking," I say.

"But now she has her man, and Brangelina are still together, so maybe it was meant to be!"

"Don't say that."

"I'm sorry?"

"No matter what. No woman says *'til death do us part* and then just says, 'Oh well, wasn't meant to be.' "

"I guess you're right. God, I don't know if I'll ever get married."

"Don't. Live your life."

"But you and Alex are happily married, right?"

"Professor Wallace and I? We're college sweethearts."

"You make such a nice-looking couple." She blushes again. She is smitten with Alex, although I don't feel threatened. Some girls are able to have crushes and not act on them.

"So how long is this meeting going to take? I really need to see her." From down the hall a door slams. Footsteps, then raised voices. A man strides ahead, and from the way everyone is following, I assume he is Giovatti. But all I can see is the side of him, and I'm not even interested in getting a good look, because right behind him is Alexandria.

"Alexandria," I say. My voice is wobbling. She doesn't even hear me. Giovatti, if it is him, is already opening the main door. If I don't act quickly, she'll be gone. I yell her name again, as loud as I can. This time the entire group stops, everyone but the man at the door; he takes advantage of the interruption to disappear. Alexandria turns and stares at me. Her mouth opens. Someone else is staring at me too: Jean Lucas, hands on hips, stands in the center of the little group. I remember all of her warnings. I don't care. I walk over to Alexandria, listening to my heels echo and clack on the marble floors. Alexandria stands still, and for a second I can't help but admire her courage. But only for a second.

I don't know what I'm going to say or do. Tears are threatening, and I cannot cry. Not in front of her. She is very, very beautiful, and it makes me livid, and it makes me like her, and it makes me sick.

"He's mine," I say. "This ends now."

"I'm glad you're here. I forgive you."

"Excuse me?"

"For my things. My clothes. My furniture. My jewelry. At first I want to kill you. But Alex remind me that what we do to you hurts very, very much. I am sorry for this. But my pictures. Please, please, give me back my pictures."

I am taken aback. This isn't how I expected this to go. There are tears in her eyes. They look real. And I actually feel guilty. A sick feeling crawls over me as I remember the faces of strangers I burned in the kitchen sink. I shouldn't have done it. I wouldn't have done it if it hadn't been for the picture of Cinque Terre. But I am not here to defend myself to her! Is this what she does? Manipulates people into doing her bidding?

"You were robbed. I didn't take your clothes, or your jewelry, or your pictures."

"Those pictures. My parents. They're all I have." She puts both hands on her heart. So she's an orphan, it sounds like. Great. Little Orphan Alexandria. I envision her as she was on my computer screen, purposefully staging the scene so that I could watch her kiss my husband, and all empathy I feel for her turns to stone.

"If you ever so much as email my husband again, I will kill you."

"Lena!" Jean grabs my arm and pinches the back of it really hard. "This way," she says, dragging me toward the door.

"No!" Alexandria says. I jerk away from Jean and whirl around. "I no listen to you. You steal my things. My family pictures. And somehow you make Giovatti want to draw your face. But Alex and I are in love. He is coming back to me, and you can't stop him!"

"Giovatti?" I say. Everyone in the group is staring at me. I look from Alexandria to Jean. She is not pleased with me. This could only be worse if I were wearing white tennis shoes and shouting "Mafia!" at the top of my lungs. But this, Giovatti's wanting to draw my face? I didn't have anything to do with that one, and I can't even wrap my head around it. "Why would he want to draw *my* face?"

"That's the question I've been asking myself all morning," Jean says. "Care to enlighten me?"

"Maybe because you run to him crying! You make everyone feel sorry for you." Alexandria is yelling now. Good. Let them see her for the temperamental little shrew she is.

"I've never even met Giovatti," I say.

"Liar!" Alexandria shakes her head. "You think I'm so bad for falling in love? It is love. You cannot tell your heart whom to love. But you! You are worse. You do nothing but lie, lie, lie."

Heat floods my face, and my fists curl at my sides. She's winning them over. These people actually think I am the bad guy here. I might have told a few necessary little lies, but I had nothing to do with this. Wait a minute. Marco said something about Alexandria's having a picture of me. Did Giovatti see it? Does he know who I am? Maybe he's doing it for revenge. I'm starting to like this guy. But I'm not going to float that theory here. And I'm not going to let Alexandria stand there and make me look like the bad guy. "Jean. I swear. I've never even met Giovatti."

"Are you sure about that?" Jean asks. Her voice is ice-cold. What is wrong with her?

"I swear on my mother's grave," I say. *Sorry, Mom.* But it's okay because I'm telling the truth. I miss her. I even hope she's having a good cruise. I have to forgive her; I need people on my side. "Did you hear me?" I say. "I just swore on my mother's grave!"

"I heard you," Jean says. "How could you? Your poor, poor mother."

"What the hell is that supposed to mean?"

"Oh, you know what it means." Jean is really rattled. She's not a woman you want as an enemy.

"I don't. I don't know what it means. I'm telling the truth."

"Lena. He's famous around here. You can't go sneaking around with him and expect not to be seen. I told you Florence is tiny."

"I was not sneaking around with him! I've never even met him!"

"What an act! You're the one who started destroying the chalk paintings. It's your fault he's doing this."

"I don't know what you're talking about! I've never met the man in my life!"

Alexandria steps forward and points at me. She actually points at me. "No wonder Alex fell in love with me. You do nothing but lie."

I am really considering going for her now, and I don't care if it lands me in an Italian prison. I want to grab her hair close to the roots and shake her. And I'm moving toward her, I don't care anymore, I'm going to hurt her, when the front door swings open and in waltzes Marco. It's not an exaggeration to say the crowd literally parts. And I don't blame them. I'd forgotten how charismatic and beautiful he is. He's like Alex in the sense that he changes the energy of a room just by walking in. I am so relieved to see him. He will take my side. He will tell them I've never met Giovatti.

"Marco," I say.

Marco grins. It makes my insides feel on fire. I grin back. *"Ciao, bella,"* he says. In one swift move, he is kissing first my right cheek, then my left, then my right. For a moment I want him to kiss me on the lips in front of all these people. I want to make out with him like mad; I want it to get back to Alex.

"See!" Alexandria says. "Liar."

Several people in the group are looking back and forth between me, and Marco, and the poster. When I glance at it, Marco actually steps in front of it. I shake my head, gently push him aside, and step up to it. It's a promotional poster for Giovatti. In the picture he is standing in front of an olive tree in faded jeans and a T-shirt, holding a paintbrush in his right hand, casually, down by his thigh. Behind him is a giant canvas propped against the tree with the rendering of one of the many faces of Alexandria. But for once, I'm not looking at her face. I'm seeing double, and once again I do not mean Alexandria. Giovatti, it turns out, is the artist's last name. Marco is his first.

FIRENZE
MONTH TWO

Lingua di miele è cuore di fiele.

A honey tongue and a heart of gall.

CHAPTER 21

I cannot believe I have been in Florence for exactly thirty days.
It feels like a lifetime ago that I saw my kids, and I miss them
more than ever. I've been calling every day, on the computer.
Even though I can tell they want to get off the phone, I make
them talk to me for at least an hour. They are having a good
summer, they say. Alex is doing what he is supposed to be
doing, I guess. Being a dad. Taking them to dance, and soccer,
and parks, and movies, and ice cream. I am sad. I should be
there. I never ask to speak with Alex. A few times I've seen him
standing in the doorway, listening to me talk. He never moves
closer to the screen, and I never acknowledge that I can see
him. But when I know he's there, I force myself to sound more
upbeat than I feel. I wonder if he misses me. I want to ask
Rachel to spy on him for me. I want proof that he's not speaking to Alexandria. But I can't put her more in the middle than
she already is, so I don't ask. Knowing her, she has already
taken it upon herself to spy on him, and if there were any evidence that he was still carrying on with Alexandria, she would

tell me. I'm so happy to be able to see the kids every day, but more and more I end the call and feel hollow. I know I am supposed to be home with them. It's like coming home and finding all your furniture rearranged. We are the same, but we are in the wrong places. I know one thing. Alex wouldn't be listening in on our conversations unless he missed me. It is working. I just have to have faith. Another couple of months and he will see more than ever what a hideous thing he's done, and he will want to spend the rest of his life making it up to me. I am making progress; I just have to stay the course.

I know conversational Italian now. I can ask simple directions, and inquire about the restrooms, and tell them I am Lena from America and my husband has a mistress.

I have developed routines. I visit Angelo every morning. I drink two cappuccinos, and he complains about his wife with a twinkle in his eye. I roll my eyes and shake my head when the tourists try to order directly from him, and silently point to the cash register. I have been to all the food markets and flea markets about town, and I have been to the Pitti Palace, and the Boboli Gardens, and all the piazzas, and every morning I discover a new street to walk down that still sends a thrill up my spine. I've discovered where all the craftsmen have their little shops, and I take a stroll by most mornings after Angelo's. I buy ingredients from the market and routinely make Tuscan beans on bread with tomatoes, with a touch of salt and garlic, and olive oil. It's amazing that's all you need. Alex is sending me plenty of money, and I'm not even feeling guilty about spending it, much. I still haven't had my big makeover. I'm saving that for right before I go home. I want Alex to see the new, sophisticated me. For now I simply window-shop and imagine myself in this designer dress or that, with very high-heeled shoes, or perhaps that pair of long leather boots that always catches my eye. I will go home a new woman, one he will almost not recognize, but one he will not be able to stop staring at. He has also sent my birth certificate and social security card, but I have not tried to get a new passport or ID. I'm not sure why, other than that it feels like power.

And then, there is Marco. I sit on the balcony with my glass of wine, treasuring my weekly conversations with Megan. I tell her how I haven't spoken to him since that day at the university when he became just another man lying to me, making a fool of me.

"He sounds kind of exciting though," Megan says.

"I just keep remembering that night—throwing pasta at his artwork, Megan. Every time I think of it, it's third grade gym class all over again." I wore a skirt the day we had to climb the rope. I still think the teacher should be sued for child abuse for not stopping me from climbing all the way to the top.

"But he was the one encouraging it," Megan says. "I think it's kind of sexy and outrageous. Isn't that just the distraction you need right now?"

"I just can't trust him. Plus he said he wanted to kill Alex." I am repeating myself now. Poor Megan.

"It's like a movie. *The Wife, the Husband, the Boyfriend, and the Mistress.*"

"Mistress. I hate that word."

"Understandable."

"It makes her seem glamorous, mysterious, beautiful."

"And she's not. She's hideous." Megan has seen pictures of Alexandria. She is lying through her teeth. I appreciate it.

"I wish it was a movie. At least then I'd know there was going to be an end."

"So if you're not having fun, why don't you just come home?"

"Because I think it's working."

"What's working?"

"My plan. Alexandria is outraged over Marco's substituting me as his muse."

"He's actually drawing you all over the city?"

"Not yet. He's still destroying the ones of Alexandria. But rumor has it he's then going to draw me."

"That is unbelievable. How can you not go out with a man who is going to draw you all over a city?"

"Because it has nothing to do with me. He's just trying to get back at Alexandria."

"Are you sure about that?"

"He's madly in love with her. Just like everyone else."

"I don't know. I think he really likes you."

"What is this—junior high?"

"Hey. Lena. Don't bite my head off."

"I'm sorry, I'm sorry. He doesn't like me. I mean we might be a little attracted to each other, but that takes a backseat to revenge."

"Uh huh."

"I'm serious."

"Well, I think you should forget about Alex and Alexandria and spend the rest of your summer getting it on with Marco Giovatti."

"How can you say that?"

"Lena, I love you. And I've tried to keep my mouth shut since this whole thing started—because I can't imagine how painful this must be. But would you even want Alex after what he's done to you? I could kill him myself. I think you should fall in love with Marco and tell Alex you don't give a damn what he does."

"Sixteen years. I can't throw away sixteen years."

"I know. I'm just telling you what I wish you would do. I love you."

"I love you too." We say our good-byes. I gaze into the distance, realizing I didn't even get to the conversation I wanted to have with her. I've been going to an Internet café nearby and doing some research on scorned women. All normal women, like me, who went absolutely insane after their husbands cheated on them. One woman poured boiling water on her husband's private parts while he slept. I couldn't wait to tell this to Megan because I can predict her response—

I bet he wasn't sleeping for long. And then we'd both laugh, even though it really isn't funny, and I wouldn't do that to anyone no matter what. But I can't deny that I feel good reading about how others have gone off the rails; it makes me feel normal. Another woman auctioned off her cheating husband's condom (size small) and the woman's underwear (size large). Then there was the wife of a dentist who first got a ton of plastic surgery to make herself look better and when that didn't work she ran him down with one of their luxury cars. He's dead, and she's in prison. They are cautionary tales, and I wanted to prove to Megan that I'm handling this remarkably well.

Make it look like an accident. I realize, with a start, that I miss Marco. He's my partner in crime. Alexandria is already twisting in the wind over this, and Alex is listening in every time I call the kids. Maybe it is time to pretend to take a lover. Just because we aren't really going to be together doesn't mean there isn't a lot of leverage to be had by making people think we're together. And so what if I'm attracted to him as well? Who wouldn't be? And of course it would be a nice escape to have an affair with him. It would make me feel better. In the moment. But I'm not after a moment. I'm trying to save a marriage.

I go back to the Internet café and Google him. Marco Giovatti.com. His page is filled with photographs of his paintings. He has quite the range. Abstract splashes of color. Realistic sketches. Gorgeous landscapes. But by far—faces. Marco loves faces. And he's amazing at capturing them. A little old woman who looks stunningly beautiful. A child's face, looking as if she has just laid eyes on the best gift in the world. A boy, one who appears to be on the verge of turning into a man. The kind of man who will turn heads and break hearts. My God, no wonder everyone was raving about Marco. His chalk drawings were just a teaser. He is extraordinarily gifted. Desire flares up in me as I replay that evening with him. This talented man was attracted to me. Infatuated with me even. But he is the one that deserves all the focus. I think he must have loved being with someone who wasn't just interested in him because of his fame. And of course he wanted to destroy the Alexandria faces just as much as I did. There is a contact button on the website. Before I can talk myself out of it, I send him an email.

Going to the Sant'Ambrogio Market this afternoon.
Lena

*   *   *

I decide to go shopping in preparation for my meeting with
Marco. How can you come to Florence and not do a little retail
therapy? Of course I have no idea if Marco will read the message in time, or if he does, even want to see me. But it's a good
excuse nonetheless. Alex sent me a new credit card, and although we may have different interpretations of "emergency
only," I feel I am in the right. I still don't know how many things
he's bought Alexandria. For all I know he's still buying her
things, replacing the items I destroyed.

I enter a jewelry boutique first, drawn in from the window by
a bracelet on display. It's a thick band of wood and copper
painted various shades of greens and blues with tiny turquoise
jewels. It looks like something a confident, powerful woman
would wear, and I can't wait to see it on my wrist. It's a nice surprise, anytime I get these little jolts of joy. My body is used to
crying and grief lately, so that anytime happiness finds it way in,
I light up like a rocket ship. I reach for my new bracelet, and,
from a few feet behind me, the pinched saleslady lets out a
shriek. To my astonishment, she flies out and smacks the back
of my hand as if I'm a naughty schoolchild. I haven't even
made contact with the bracelet.

"No touch!" She points to a sign next to the bracelet. It's in
Italian. For all I know it says, TRY ME ON! I stare at the back of
my hand, expecting a red welt, and once again I'm overtaken
by a flash of angry tears. She hit me first; this is my chance; I
can belt her one. I decide to start with my words.

"I'm trying it on," I say. "I want it." I know I sound like a
spoiled child, and I suddenly want to go home. I don't want a
bracelet. I want my children, and my home, and Stella, and my
goddamn husband. I stand shaking with rage. I want my husband. What do I have to do? *Make it look like an accident.* The
woman remains nearby with her hands on her hips, but she's
not completely immune to my tears, for her mouth has relaxed
slightly. "My husband is having an affair," I say. "And I want him
back." I whisper it. As if saying it too loudly would be a sin.

"No touch," she says.

"Do you want people to buy or do you just want to yell at people and slap the back of their hands—what are you, a nun from the 1950s? You want me to slap you?"

"*Scusi, scusi, scusi.* The artist. She no like you to get your fingers. Is copper, see? Copper no good to put fingers all over. You want to try on, sure, sure." The woman picks up the bracelet and puts it on my wrist. I hate it now. She's ruined it for me. It feels like a shackle.

"I'll take it," I say. I slap down Alex's credit card. I want him back; I want him back; I want him back. Somebody, please just tell me what to do, and I'll do it. I'm going to call him. As soon as I get out of this tin can of a store, I'm going to call him and beg him to take me back. Maybe I'll actually get on my knees on the cobblestone streets and wail like a character in an Italian opera. Maybe if he doesn't immediately tell me he wants me back too, I'll slit my throat as the Tuscan sun sets.

The woman looks at the name on the credit card. If she asks me for ID I'm really screwed. I could have replaced it by now, but I like being without it. It makes me feel as if who I might become is wide open.

"Is this him? He cheat on you?"

"Yes." I sniff, dab my nose, and lift my chin. "With an Italian tramp."

She watches me for what feels like an eternity. "*Pronto.* I know what to do. We need to find a necklace. And some earrings to match."

The next store I go into is manned by two Italian men dressed in suits. Unlike my recent experience, the welcome is instant. *Ciao, ciao,* kiss, kiss. It is strange to be kissed by two strange men, cheek, cheek, cheek. Strange, but I kind of like it. The boutique is populated with designer dresses, shoes, and jackets. The mannequin in the window is wearing a playful navy-blue dress. It has satiny material that begs to be touched. My husband wanted to touch another woman, and I want to touch all these designer Italian clothes. I want to touch them, taken them into me, morph into someone else. Someone who remembers how beautiful she is. Someone who has her whole life in front of her. Someone who is going to meet an eccentric, sexy artist in the market in just a few short hours.

I step closer to the dress and imagine myself wearing it. The short sleeves sit just off the shoulder, the neckline plunges, the middle hugs the stomach, and the bottom is flared and fringed, perfect for showing off sexy legs. I would need a pair of high heels. I am good at walking in high heels, even on the cobblestone, so why have I resigned myself to flats?

With matching high heels, it will definitely turn heads. This is not just frivolous; I need this. I need to show myself that I can still attract as much attention as Alexandria. Aren't I the new face of Florence? Well, of the streets of Florence anyway. And, true, nobody knows it yet, because Marco isn't unveiling yet, but soon I will be the face of Florence. I am going to start dressing the part; I am going to fake it until I make it, and I definitely want to be wearing this, or something like it, the next time I see Alexandria. She had so many pretty clothes and high heels. Damn Alex. If he wanted me to dress sexier, why didn't he just tell me? Or did he not even know it himself until he saw how glamorous Alexandria looked?

"*Bella, bella,* this would look so good on you." One of the salesmen lifts the dress off the mannequin and holds it out to me as if handing me a baby.

"You are perfect to wear this," the second agrees.

"Please, try this on."

"We have shoes." They produce them. Satiny high heels that match the shade of the dress exactly. "Quickly, quickly." They usher me behind a curtain.

I try the dress on, and it's as if it's made for me. I step into the heels, and the lift does me good. Except my hair is too shaggy, and my eyes are rimmed with dark circles. Have I not looked in a mirror lately? How can Marco like this face? Well, he's going to like it today. After I leave in this outfit I am going to get my hair and makeup done. I hope I have enough time. I step out of the dressing room.

"Oh my God."

"Oh, *bella*."

"It's stunning."

"Where is your husband?"

"He's in America," I say. "But my boyfriend is here." The men throw their heads back and roar with laughter. I like them. They are stylish and funny. I can't tell if they're gay or just European.

"You must go to nightclub in this," says one.

"She will," says the other.

"With her boyfriend. He is Italian?"

"He is."

"He's going to rip this off you."

"I'll take it," I say. I look at the price tag for the first time. It's eighteen hundred euro. I try and do the conversion in my head. It's over twenty-five hundred dollars for the dress alone. This is not like me. I still wear clothes I bought in high school. Our mortgage isn't even this much. Emergencies only. I turn and look in the mirror again. I like this woman better than I like the drab me I've been dragging around. I take out Alex's credit card, and before they can ask me for ID say, "My husband has been sleeping with his Italian mistress for the past two months. I kicked them out of the flat, and now it's my turn to exact a little revenge. I'm going to wear this home." I return to the dressing room, pick up my old sundress, and dump it in a tiny garbage can next to the cash register. "I also need a purse since mine was stolen. I was so busy looking out for flying babies I let my guard down."

Within seconds they come up with the perfect purse. As one takes my credit card without any hesitation, the other hands me a glass of wine. And then a cigarette. They sit me down on a cushiony bench.

"Give us the details," one says.

"From the beginning." The other.

"And then you will drink. And then you will smoke, and then we will bring you more delicious things to try on, and then we want to hear about this new Italian boyfriend."

"And while you talk, I call the hair dresser," the other says.

"I need makeup too," I say. A nod of understanding, phone calls to the right people, and this glass of liquid rubies. Maybe God hasn't completely abandoned me; maybe he's telling me that no matter what, everything is going to be all right.

Make it look like an accident, reverberates through my head. I think I still have a ways to go.

CHAPTER 22

I am straight from the salon in my heels and new outfit. The makeup artist even seemed able to rid my eyes of puffiness. It's as if I haven't spent the last month in constant tears. My cut is shorter than Alex likes it, and that makes me feel a bit edgy. Take that. There is freedom in realizing that everything you've done for somebody else was for naught. I will no longer consider his likes and dislikes when it comes to my hair or how I dress. Not that I was ever any kind of Stepford wife, but it's natural to want to lean toward the thing that your partner likes. But now, I'm just me, and my hair is shorter than it's ever been, and my heels higher, and I'm way overdressed for a food market, but I'm going, and I'm dying to see if Marco will like the new me.

The Sant'Ambrogio Market, located in Piazza Ghiberti, is where the locals go to haggle over colorful fruits, vegetables, meats, and cheeses. There is an indoor and an outdoor section of the market. Inside are meats, fish, and cheeses in refrigerated cases; outside are tables tucked underneath white tents selling fruits, vegetables, and wares. Outside, I stand back and watch three little old ladies haggle in Italian with a robust man standing in front of crates piled high with apples, oranges, lemons, and bananas. He bellows words in Italian. I wonder if he is naming the fruit or singing a song. Could be either. The three old ladies answer back with hands flying, heads shaking, and a chorus of guttural mutterings. I presume his prices are too high, and I love these old ladies. The man picks up several bright oranges, cradles them in his arms, then rocks them like a baby. He does this until the women eventually laugh. Instantly their elderly faces turn bright-eyed and beautiful. They shoo him away with their hands, but this time with less vigor and smiles playing at their lips. He laughs in return, a robust sound that comes from his diaphragm.

One by one, the women snatch the oranges out of the man's arms and return to their bargaining dance. I drink it all in. They all seem absolutely out of their minds, and I love them. Maybe I will grow old here. Rachel and Josh will visit, stand where I am standing now, and watch me. Maybe it will take a while for them to realize the crazy lady in the flowered bandana yabbering in Italian and arguing about prices is me. Maybe they will each take an arm and guide me home, as I point out this and that architectural or artistic tidbit about Florence as we pass. I would ask after Alex and Alexandria: Where are they living again—Michigan? Cleveland?

For a few seconds I feel something that feels like joy spread in the center of my chest. And then it twists. Jealous. I am jealous of three little old ladies. God, they seem so happy. I wish I were one of them, standing with them, flailing my arms, wearing a bandana around my hair, negotiating. Knowing exactly what I want out of life—that orange there, no that one, the one underneath, just give it to me, don't throw it, you'll bruise it— and more important I would know exactly what I was willing to pay, and I would actually get it.

Could I, should I, have done that with Alex before things got so out of control? Negotiated with him, flailed my arms, bargained until he agreed never to sleep with another woman?

Keeping my arms to myself, I step closer to the table bursting with fruit. The vendor doesn't even look at me. The old ladies are gone, and he is reading a newspaper. Not even a glance. Does he not like Americans or just me? I lift my arm. *"Ciao,"* I say. He turns one corner of the paper down and peeks at me with one eye.

"Ciao," he says. Then he rattles off several other things in Italian. I can tell by the raised eyebrow that he is testing my comprehension.

"Grazie. Scusi." Although I have picked up the odd phrase here and there, I don't know enough to enter this haggling dance. I give him euros, and he gives me change, and I am happy to have the orange. I peel it as I walk away, and when I bite into it, it tastes like a tiny burst of citrus hope. I would have paid four times the amount! It is all relative. In my mind, I got a bargain. I will remember this orange for the rest of my life. I lift my arm and give a little 'hey.' Loud enough for my own ears, but quiet enough that I won't draw any attention to myself.

"I do not know why you celebrate. You overpaid for that orange." Marco's voice sends a shiver of delight down my spine. He's talking to me from behind. Did he recognize my ass? He came. I whirl around and smile.

"Marco." He grabs my orange, tosses it in the air, and throws back his head as if to catch it in his mouth. He has a beautiful throat. The orange comes back down and sure enough lands in his mouth. When he brings his head level again, the orange protrudes from between his lips. I clap. He spits the orange out of his mouth, lets it hit the ground, and takes a bow.

"Brava, Marco, *brava,"* I say. "Or should I call you Giovatti?"

"Let us buy some rotten tomatoes," Marco says. "We can ruin the next face. It is here, just behind the man selling the leather."

"No." I stop. "I don't want to ruin any more of your artwork. I'm so sorry. I had no idea."

"Of course you didn't. That's what made it so fun."

"I saw your website. You are an incredible artist—"

"Please. Don't become one of them."

"One of them?"

"I do not like fuss. Art is about passion. It is a living thing. What we are doing—destroying Alexandria—it is art too." Marco speeds up, still holding onto my arm. Seconds later, I am staring at another Alexandria. This one is done in pinks, and purples, and greens. Several people are standing around it, photographing it. They speak excitedly in Italian. Marco laughs.

"What?" I ask. Marco leans in to whisper to me. His shirt brushes against my arm. It is white, and starched, and unbuttoned several buttons. His chest looks tan and smooth. He smells inviting, of a fresh dab of cologne. I want to lean in and kiss his neck. Marco looks in my eyes as if he knows what I'm thinking. He smiles. I have to remind myself that we are just using each other. Teaming up to take down our cheating lovers.

"They are wondering when the vandalism will strike. Three times the number of people have come to see my chalk faces since you started your path of destruction." Marco laughs. It is a nice, deep laugh with childish undertones. I give him a soft punch on the arm, which I instantly regret as too much of an American thing to do. "I covered my street drawings, all of them. I was going to start over with a new face, until I realize, destroying the old ones is also an art form. You taught me that."

I taught him that. As if I'm the artist. Maybe I am. That part of me has been buried for so long. And I am the one who buried it. I cannot blame it on Alex, even though I would like to. So I'm not going to be the new face of Florence. As long as we are destroying the old ones, I'm good with that. "We can't destroy it in front of people," I say. "It must be done in secret." I'm not even sure what I'm saying except I like the thought of having a secret with Marco. We are the ones destroyed by the affair. Destroying the chalk drawings is an intimate, private affair. I want to keep it that way.

"I should draw you right now. Right here," Marco says. "You look so beautiful."

His words send a rush of pleasure through me. He noticed. And he commented. For years now Alex and I might notice things about each other, but we hardly ever say anything, unless it's slightly sarcastic.

"Are you hungry?" Marco says. I nod. Marco knows of a little trattoria in the market. We have toasted crostini bread with cheese and olives and some kind of fresh white fish, beans, tomatoes, and garlic.

"Oh my God," I say after the first bite. I can't help it. How can something so simple taste so amazing? I could eat this and nothing else for the rest of my life. I suddenly feel guilty for all the peanut butter and jelly sandwiches I've ever fed my kids. A pang of sadness hits me. I wish they were here now so I could force-feed them these delightful Tuscan sandwiches.

"Oh my God." Marco mimics me with a silly grin.

I laugh. "I sound very American, don't I?"

"You are to be adored."

"Flattery will get you nowhere," I tease.

"That is okay," Marco says, staring at me. "I am already where I want to be." There is another long moment during which we look into each other's eyes. Marco looks away first, and stares instead at a young man standing in front of a cheese case reading a newspaper.

"Do you know him?" I say.

"No," Marco says. "But I think I know what he's about to do." Just then the man peeks out from behind the newspaper, opens his mouth, and begins to sing in an operatic baritone. Next, an older Asian woman passing by with a full cart of fruits and vegetables stops and sings back to the man, also in a perfectly trained operatic voice. I glance at Marco. He grins.

"It is called Spontaneous Opera," he says. People begin to circle around, and heads whip this way and that to see who will be next. Maybe because of how I am dressed, a few people look at me. Marco laughs. He is standing behind me now. Seconds later I feel his arms around my waist as he pulls me into him and holds me from behind. I was not expecting it, and for a moment I freeze. It feels good, to be held. Is this part of the plan, let people see us together in public, let the rumor mill grind, wait until our lovers hear that we are an "item"? Surely it's okay to stand here for a few minutes and allow myself to be held? Although from the feelings coursing through me, if I gave in to my desires, I would want much more. Marco lifts my arm with his and points to a young man behind the cheese counter. He is wearing an apron. Sure enough, he too begins to sing. A young girl sitting at a table nearby answers him.

The performance is short, but refreshing. When they are finished, we and the rest of the crowd erupt in applause. The small group holds up signs: *Viva musica. Viva l'arte.*

"You like?" Marco asks.

"I love," I say. I take the moment to break away from Marco. We are going to have to talk about this, aren't we?

"Do you want dessert?" He is staring at me as if I'm dessert.

"God, no," I say. "I am so full." There, a little talk of bloating should cool our jets for a moment.

"Buono, buono," Marco says. "When the stomach is full, the eyes can see."

"What the hell does that mean?"

Marco throws his head back and laughs. "You. America. I like you." He takes my hand. "We walk," he says. "And then we feed our eyes."

He's taking me to the Uffizi art gallery. Alex talked about it so much, I didn't think I could face going without him. I wonder if Marco senses this, for as he takes me to the front of the line, he squeezes my hand. The woman handling tickets lights up when she sees Marco, although her smile dims when she notices him holding my hand. She waves us in past the crowd.

"Benefits to being an artist," Marco says. When we enter the museum, a tiny door in my heart slams shut. Alex had his chance to take me here, and it is gone. I will not let that stop me from enjoying it.

There isn't a single corner of the art gallery that doesn't have something to feast your eyes on. The frescoes in the ceiling. Statues in the hall. The marble floors beneath our feet. We turn into a hall where a wall of windows stretches along the Arno River, inviting the outside in, blending the spectacular beauty of each. The gallery is one of many legacies left by the Medici family. It was originally built in 1851 as offices for Florentine magistrates. Slowly, it began to swell with artwork and sculptures owned by the family, then it officially became a museum in 1765. There are over forty-five rooms with masterpiece paintings from the 1200s up to the present day. I've read so much about this place, but I do not tell Marco. It feels as if it's between me and Alex, and I do not want him to intrude on this date.

Not that it's a real date, but as fake dates go, I am enjoying myself.

God, no wonder Alex loved it here. Why couldn't he have loved it with me? Will I ever stop thinking about him, obsessing on every little thing?

"The galleries are in chronological order," Marco says. "The early masters are first." I must look a little overwhelmed, for Marco gives a soft laugh, then brushes his lips against my ear as he leans in to whisper. "We can come back any time," he says. "Today we see as much as we want to see, and then we are done."

After that, time ceases to exist for me. Four hours fly by. My favorites are Botticelli's the *Birth of Venus* and da Vinci's *Annunciation*. I don't need Alex's lectures; I have a real live artist giving me his take on everything. Yet he also knows when to stop talking and let me simply take in some of the work in silence. Alex's lecture would have never stopped. At some point I would have just tuned him out. The reality makes me feel guilty, but strangely free. Marco has an easygoing way about him. I wonder what exactly happened with Alexandria. He seems like the perfect man. Why does she want Alex instead? If I had met Marco at the same time as Alex—and at that time he was the age he is now—whom would I have chosen?

I find myself wandering back to the *Birth of Venus*. The Venus, born of the sea foam, stands on a seashell. Her long, orange hair covers her nether regions; her hand delicately shields her breast. To the west are Zephyr and the nymph, Chloris, both of whom are rendered in other masterpieces. To the right Pomona, goddess of Spring, prepares a flowered mantle for the Venus to wear. The light coming from the pale water is ephemeral and timeless.

"The allegory of spirituality and nature," Marco whispers in my ear.

And lust, I think. Human lust. There is no avoiding it. Marco's whispering is driving me crazy. Can I really blame Alex for giving in to this?

Yes. Of course I can. I will not give in to this. Alex didn't have to give in to this. Look at the price you pay. Isn't that what separates man from beast? The ability to recognize our base instincts, our lust, and still walk away?

I tell Marco I am ready for a break, but first I want to go back to da Vinci's *Annunciation.* It's one of his early works. The archangel Gabriel kneels before the Virgin Mary. She has been reading, and the interruption startles her. The archangel carries a white lily.

"Symbol of virginity," Marco whispers. It sends another tingle down my spine.

Technically, Alex has already ruined our marriage. I would not be just like him if I slept with Marco. Marco gently pulls me aside to show me how the painting is meant to be viewed. From below and to the right. At this, Marco sits on the ground and pulls me down with him. At first I am embarrassed, but soon I follow Marco's finger as he narrates the painting. From this vantage point the keystones on the building align, and the foreshortened arm of the Virgin, along with the height of the lectern, take on the correct proportions.

Just like life. Maybe I have been viewing mine from the wrong angle.

"What do you think?" Marco asks, touching me lightly on the small of the back.

"I think prayer and loincloths were certainly important back in the day."

"You are very funny."

"Actually, when I take in all this beauty—all this talent, all this culture—I think, what have I done with my life?"

"Don't you see? Art? Life? It is one and the same. Your art is your life, Lena. If you don't like what is happening, you start a new canvas."

CHAPTER 23

"I need to go outside," I say. "I can't breathe." It's too late. It's too late for a new canvas. What if I make a mess of it, just like the first? Without even checking to see if he is following, I start walking as quickly as I can toward the entrance. I need air. I'm going to have a panic attack. Why did I stop painting? Because of Alex? Because of time? Because I wanted to be the perfect wife and mother?

Outside, on the streets of Florence, I can finally breathe. I can feel Marco behind me, silent but very present.

"I want to paint you," Marco says, turning me around, and drinking in my face with his eyes. "Not just in chalk, in the street. In acrylic. On canvas. In my studio."

"No," I say.

Marco looks as if he's never heard the word. "Why not?"

"Because I don't want to be just a subject in life anymore. I want to do."

"You can do me!"

"You're not very subtle, are you, Marco?"

"I am saying. You can paint me. I will lie on the sofa. You will do all the brush strokes."

I don't know if it's purposeful, how everything out of his mouth sounds sexual.

"I'll keep it in mind," I say.

"We go now," he says.

"I don't think so."

"You said you wanted to do. So we do!"

"I know. But it's been a long day." Actually I need to get away from Marco right now, and his intense gazes, and his whispering, and his nice-smelling cologne, and how if I wanted to, he'd take me somewhere right now and make love to me.

"Okay, so you paint me another time. But you are in Florence. What would you like to see? Boboli Gardens? Tuscany? We could take the train to Venice and be riding a gondola by sunrise."

We begin to walk. *We could be in a gondola by sunrise.* We had already spent an entire day together, and night was descending. He didn't want me to leave. Another manufactured memory rises to my mind. Alex and I. Newlyweds. Riding through the canals, passing under ancient bridges, serenaded by a gondola driver, kissed by the Venice moon. I am here and Alex is home, and we will never have a honeymoon. Marco and I near the Ponte Vecchio Bridge. The lights glow in the dim light. We stop, and I gently put my hand on Marco's chest. He immediately covers it with his, keeping my palm trapped against his beating heart. It would be so easy to take him home.

"I have to go," I say. "I have to call my children." Rachel and Josh deserve at least one parent who is thinking with her head. Marco gently moves his fingers along my hand. He brings it up to his lips and kisses it. Then he backs up, bows, and starts to walk away.

"Marco," I say. He turns and waits. I want to ask him if he's still speaking to Alexandria. I want to ask him if he knows whether or not Alex and Alexandria are still speaking.

"Thank you for a lovely day."

"Jazz," he says.

"Jazz?"

"Next time. No market. No lunch. Drinks, and jazz. Wear that dress."

Jazz? I would love to listen to jazz. Why am I running away? It's too late to call the kids anyway. And I am in a new outfit with great hair and makeup. *Start a new canvas.* "Forget next time," I say. "Let's go now."

He knows just the club, located in Santa Croce. Music is already underway in the intimate space we enter. Marco weaves his way to a table that is in the front of the room, but off to the side, offering both the best viewing but privacy at the same time. A "Reserved" sign sits on the table. A waitress rips it off with an eager smile as Marco slides into the booth and then gestures for me to do the same. The waitress gives me a look I am becoming familiar with. *Why is he with you and not me?* I am wondering the same thing, except, right, I remind myself, Marco and I are in cahoots.

A saxophone and a keyboard serenade us with the kind of tune that conjures up a claw-foot bath brimming with candlelight and bubbles. A young, shaggy-haired kid on the drums keeps the rhythm going. Soon, we have a bottle of wine. As the waitress pours it, Marco scoots very close to me. We are on a date, I think. A real one. The minute I have the thought, the crowd applauds, and even though it's for the keyboard and sax players, I take it as a sign of approval. We might just be playing around, but I still want to kiss Marco tonight, and if I'm honest with myself, it's not just because of revenge.

"What are you thinking about?" Marco asks me. And here I am, thinking about kissing him.

"Do you get reserved tables wherever you go?" I tease.

"But of course," he says. Spoken like a truly spoiled man. Although, maybe he has a right to be. I've seen his work; he *is* something special. "Do you want to know what I was thinking?"

Marco looks deep into my eyes. Then, he moves closer. He feasts on my hair, my face, my lips. *Damn you, Alex.* Marco goes in for the kiss, but just as he's about to seal it, I put my index fingers on his lips.

"I can't," I say. "It would be revenge kissing."

He pulls away, cocks his head, and smiles. "Revenge kissing?"

"Yes. To get back at Alex."

"I like this," he says.

He moves in again, and I block him again. "Don't you want me to kiss you for real?"

"But of course."

"It wouldn't be real; it would be to get back at Alex."

"Why can't it be both?"

"Do you still love Alexandria?"

"Why do you ask?"

"Because, what are we doing?"

"We are living life."

"I thought we were supposed to be keeping our lovers apart."

"Alex is in America. Alexandria is here. We are here."

"You make everything sound so simple."

"It is simple."

"No. Because if anything happens between us, we'll be cheaters. Just like them."

"Ah," Marco says. The music picks up tempo. Several couples get up to dance.

Please don't ask me, I think. I can't dance.

"Would you like to dance?"

"I can't."

But Marco is pushing me out of the booth.

"Come, come, come," he says. "We'll call it the revenge trot." I have to laugh. Who can say no to the revenge trot? Marco, I soon discover, is an excellent dancer. He spins me around the floor like he owns it. I wonder exactly how many women he's performed the revenge trot with? I let out a spontaneous whoop as he twirls me around. Just as quickly, he spins me back in, and I slam into his chest. He grins, thrusts our arms straight out, and we walk forward in dramatic tango fashion. When the song ends, Marco dips me, lifts me back up, and before I can protest, plants a kiss on my lips.

"I have to use the ladies' room," I say.

"I will walk you," Marco says.

"Not necessary."

"Are you sure?"

"Of course." Marco is about to walk away when I grab his shirt collar and gently pull him forward. Then, when his lips are close to mine, I lean in and plant one on him. It is different from the bellboy and the locksmith. This is a real kiss. Marco lets me control the pace and the strength, although I can feel the power beneath it; all I would have to do is yield, and he would take over. When I pull away, Marco is grinning.

"Revenge kiss?" he says.

"No," I say. "Thank you kiss."

"Ah, *grazie*. But for what? What did I do for this thanks?"

"You made me forget myself for a moment," I say.

"Then I wish to make you forget forever," Marco calls after me as I thread through the crowd to the ladies' room.

I grin as I apply lipstick in the small bathroom. Studying my smiling reflection, I shake my head and talk to myself. "You're acting ridiculous."

"I couldn't agree more." Startled, I look up to see Jean Harris standing behind me.

"You scared me," I say.

We look at each other through the mirror. She's looking at me as if I'm her teenage daughter caught sneaking in after hours. "What in the world are you doing?"

"What do you mean?"

"Marco. You. In plain view. Like you're not a professor's wife."

"Did you follow me here?"

"This city has eyes," Jean says. "It talks."

"It *stalks* is more like it."

"You need to think about your future."

"Jean. With all due respect. Leave me the hell alone."

"If Alex gets fired where will you be?"

"Marco and I are just friends," I say. "There's nothing going on."

Jean eyes my hair, my dress, my recently applied lipstick. "Do you want this to get back to Alex?"

Yes. Tell him! Call him right now. Make sure you emphasize how good I look and how Marco and I danced the tango across the room. Do you have your phone? I'll dial for you. "What part of 'Leave me the hell alone' did you not understand?"

Jean puts her hand on my shoulder. "What do you think is going to happen here? You'll fall in love with Marco and live happily ever after?"

"I'm listening to jazz. Enjoying the company of a friend."

"Let me be that friend. We'll go somewhere. Drink wine. Figure this out together."

"No thanks. I'm on a date."

"Don't be so sure."

"What's that supposed to mean?" She doesn't answer. Instead she stares. I can feel her judgment chipping away at my good mood. I may have started a new canvas, but now it has been slashed with black. I open the bathroom door.

"You'll thank me later," Jean calls as I walk out.

Thank her for what? What a nosey woman. I'm going to leave all right. With Marco. I'm going to take him home and let him have me. Paint me. Whatever he wants to do. I head back to the table. Marco isn't alone. Sitting next to him is Alexandria.

You'll thank me later. Jean brought her here.

I stand in the recesses of the club, watching them. Marco was right about one thing. Jazz had cured all my obsessive thoughts. What he didn't tell me is that when they came back, it would be with a vengeance. What is she doing here? How dare she? Why isn't he pushing her out of the booth? He knows I'm just in the bathroom. Does he really think I'll come back if I see her sitting at my table?

They are sitting close and talking. About what? Did the plan work already, and she wants Marco back? I don't want her to have him either. She doesn't get Alex, and she doesn't get Marco. If I had special powers I'd follow her around for the rest of her life and make sure she didn't get anyone. Look at me. Bitter and wicked. I can't help it. She doesn't get to do a hit-and-run on my life. I want to throw something at her. Jean is right. I am acting the fool. Marco isn't even looking around to see where I am. All he can see is her. All any of them can see is her. I stride out, into the Florence night, without a backward glance. I keep hoping, as I walk home, that he will race up behind me, lift me into his arms, and carry me back to the flat. After all the Italian cuisine I've been eating, I would probably be too heavy to carry for long, but I don't let that bog down my fantasy. I should have stayed to take pictures to send back to Alex. How can I exact revenge if I get sidetracked by Marco's flattery, and his kisses, and his cologne, and the thought of what he might do to me in bed? I want to lie naked, and I don't want him to paint me, I want him to paint on me. I want his fingers covered in oil paints, and I want a parade of color splashed all over my body.

I'm the fool. He's following the plan; he made her jealous, and now she's sitting in the booth with him. She's keeping both of them on a string. Of course she's going after Marco now that Alex is home. And if all I want is to break up her and Alex, why aren't I happy that she has now nuzzled up to Marco? Why didn't I snap their picture and send it to Alex? My plan seems to be working. And I've never felt worse.

CHAPTER 24

I sit in a cyber café, so grateful for this technological advance, being able to see and talk to my children on the computer screen. Of course it's hard to have an honest conversation in an Internet café. But nobody is paying attention to me; they are immersed in their own lives, and pages, and emails, and calls. Rachel and Josh look as if they are being forced to sit in front of the computer. Squirming, elbowing each other, rolling their eyes. They answer my questions as curtly as possible. Dance is okay; soccer is fine. I press for details. I don't get any. Except that Dad is never late taking Rachel to dance, and he doesn't yell like I do at the soccer games, and he lets them order takeout all the time.

"Where's Stella?" God, I miss her big orange head. I realize I want somebody, anybody, to beg me to come home. Even if it's just Stella's pleading brown eyes.

"She's with Dad," Rachel says. "In the backyard."

"Oh." Even the dog likes Alex better. "What are they doing in the backyard?"

"Mowing," Rachel says. "We're having a BBQ this Saturday."
A BBQ. Without me. I was always the one pushing Alex to
have a BBQ. Why have such a beautiful backyard if you're not
going to use it? I should know; I've been the one taking care of
it for the past six months. Didn't I want this? Alex to go home,
bond with our kids? "I'm sure the three of you will have a great
time," I say. I keep my voice as cheery and light as possible.

"It's not just the three of us," Rachel says.

"It's a huge party," Josh says.

"Who's coming?" I know I don't sound so happy now, but I
just can't help it.

The kids start listing neighbors and friends. They sound
happy. Even Rachel.

"I kind of like being the only girl in the house," Rachel says.
"Except for Stella."

"So you don't miss me?" I ask. It's a dangerous question. I
can tell Rachel is mad at me, and if she picks up on my hurt
feelings, she could use them against me. She shrugs. That's
when I realize this is the worst technological invention ever.

"Stella doesn't pee in the house anymore," Josh says.

"Josh!" Rachel says.

"Well, it's true."

"It's *technically* true," Rachel says.

They are winding up to an argument. I cut them off at the
pass. "Sounds like everything is just perfect without me." Two
sets of eyes stare back, unblinking. "Will you get your father?
I'd like to speak with him." Josh zips off the chair and out of the
room. Rachel continues to stare.

"You look different."

"I miss you two," I say.

"Then you should have kept us," Rachel says.

"I'll be home soon."

"Whatever."

Tears come into my eyes. "Please," I say. "I need you." For a
second Rachel's face softens. Then she abruptly stands up,
leans into the screen, and yells.

"I had to buy a bra the other day. Without you. DAD had to take me to buy a bra! I hate you! I hate you!" Several people in the café turn to look at me. The owner gestures with an index-finger-across-the-throat motion. He looks like he could have mafia connections, but I will not ask.

"Rachel, Rachel, Rachel," I say. "I'm sorry." She whirls and runs out of the room. I put my head in my hands.

"Lena?" Alex is in front of me.

"She hates me," I say.

"She's a teenager. They all turn at some point. The only thing you can hope for is that they eventually turn back."

What about you, Alex? Are you going to turn back? "So. You're having a party."

"I'm just trying to keep things upbeat."

"This is a nightmare. I can't take this anymore, Alex."

"I'm sorry. I was really hoping you could just enjoy your time in Italy."

"Really? Were you?"

"Yes. I mean it, Lena. You deserve it."

Lena. Not Llama. He does not care anymore, and all this pain, and rage, and worst of all, love, is all on me. My burden to carry. Panic claws at my insides. I don't know how to fix this. Please, somebody, anybody, tell me how to fix this. I would do anything. "We were supposed to be a family."

"We are. Maybe not the same as before. But we'll always be a family."

"Are you still speaking to her?"

"Lena."

"Are you still speaking to her?"

"Yes. Okay? I'm still speaking to her."

"Why? Why? Why?" They're looking again. If the owner comes over here and shuts this computer off, I'm going to lunge for his neck with my bare hands.

"She's fragile, Lena."

"Fragile? Are you kidding me?"

"If you're going to get hostile, I'm hanging up."

"She threatened me, Alex." The words just flew out of my mouth. I've got his attention.

"What?"

"She's been harassing me. Telling me it isn't safe for me to stick around."

"Isn't safe? She said that?"

I nod and swallow. "Marco said she's unhinged."

"Marco? Giovatti?"

"Now that you're gone, she's after him again."

"That's not true."

"I'm sorry, but I was there."

"You were where?"

"Marco took me to the Uffizi Gallery and then to a jazz club."

"Did he now?"

"You were right about the Uffizi. It's amazing. And it was such a treat to go with a real artist."

"I know what you're doing. It doesn't suit you."

"At the jazz club, Alexandria showed up. She saw us together. We were just enjoying the music. A little dancing. She threw a huge fit. Really made a scene."

"Lena. This isn't helping anything."

"I just thought you should know what your mistress is up to."

"Please don't call her that."

"Well, don't you worry. Marco doesn't want her. He wants me."

"Look—if you want to take up with someone, I don't have a right to tell you otherwise. But Marco Giovatti is the one who is unhinged. Why do you think Alexandria tried to leave him?"

"Tried to leave him? What does that mean?"

"It means he started drawing her face on the streets. It didn't start out as some kind of art project. It was a pathetic attempt to woo her back. He's obsessed with her."

"Not anymore. He has a new project now." *Me. Take that, Alex.*

"What's that?"

"It's not important. I'll stop talking to Marco if you stop talking to Alexandria."

Alex sighs, runs his fingers through his hair.

"Did you ever love me?" I ask.

"Of course. You know that."

"Do I?"

"I hope so."

"Then listen to me. I'm still your wife. You're not going to do this to me. You're not. You are not going to be with that girl. Even if you leave me. Not her, Alex. I won't be able to take it. If you ever had any feelings for me at all—or even respect—you will not do this to me."

"I don't want to talk about this right now."

"I swear to you, Alex. You will not be with that woman. I won't stand for it."

"Lena."

"I will do whatever I have to do so that doesn't happen."

"What does that mean?"

"It means what it means."

"I don't even know you right now."

"Right. I'm the total stranger. Your little girlfriend just threatened me, and I'm the psycho bitch."

"I'll talk to her."

I pound the table. The owner comes from behind his desk and walks toward me. "No," I say. "You won't. That's the whole point."

"I'm hanging up now."

I stand up and scream at the computer. I know the whole café can hear me, but I'm past the point of caring. "I'm going to sleep with Marco. I'm his new project. And I can't wait to get him into bed."

"Nice, Lena. Real nice." Alex is fuming. I know my husband. I've done it. I've gotten to him. For a second it feels good. And that's the worst feeling ever. Love isn't supposed to go sour. You aren't supposed to get a thrill out of hurting someone you love. Alex is right. I don't even recognize myself. All I know is that

I'm filled with pain and I can't take the burden alone anymore. Alex reaches his hand toward the screen. Then he is gone.

He hung up on me. He wasn't on his knees, apologizing. They aren't falling apart without me. Rachel bought her first bra. Stella is no longer peeing in the house. They are having a party. He is still talking to his mistress. I am lost, I am lost, I am lost.

I walk out, feeling as if everyone is staring at me and wondering how I've messed my life up so spectacularly. I gravitate back to the bridge, my center of gravity in Florence. As I gaze out at the water, I think of another body of water, another trip I took, this one with my family. It was early in my marriage, when Rachel was just two years old. Alex and I took a trip to Maine. We had the best time. Walking along the ocean picking up shells, visiting lighthouses, trolling the little shops, and especially eating lobster at restaurants with stupendous ocean views.

One such night, we sat dipping soft white lobster chunks into hot butter. We watched the waves crash against the rocks as the sun started to set. It was one of the prettiest sunsets I had ever seen, leaking red, pink, and purple stripes across the sky. I looked over at Rachel's chubby, angelic face, then at my handsome husband, and I remember feeling like the luckiest girl in the world.

Just then an older couple sitting at a table in front of us broke out into an argument. In their seventies or eighties, they were paying no attention to the food on the table, or the waves outside, or the miraculous sunset. Instead, the wife was relentlessly nagging the husband about something, and he was grumbling right back. Alex and I exchanged a look. *Thank God, that's not us. That will never be us.* He reached out across the table for my hand. Then, we each grasped Rachel's tiny hands, covered in sticky kernels of corn.

"My girls," Alex said. "I love you."

"We love you too," I said. I said it loudly, wanting the couple to overhear me. I wanted to run over to them and shout. "If you can't be happy here, you'll never be happy anywhere."

I lean over the bridge. How easy it would be to fall in. I'm just like that old woman. Unhappy in Eden.

Alexandria. She is still manipulating Alex; that much is clear. She is the reason I can no longer be happy. If Alex won't listen to me, then I have to see to it that she does. I may have lost my husband. But she will not have him. If it's the last thing I ever do, she will not have him.

CHAPTER 25

If I am going to confront the enemy, I am going to have to get to know her a little better. Keep your friends close, but your enemies closer! Don't shoot until you see the whites of their eyes. Revenge is a dish best served cold. The last one I totally don't get. I want my revenge white-hot. Steaming. Since I am no longer welcome in the cyber café, I enlist Megan's help snooping onto Alexandria's Facebook page. I promise her that no matter what happens to me, I would never give Megan up to the Italian courts. I may be a little overdramatic what with barely any sleep but plenty of wine.

"I don't think the Italian court cares if we look at Alexandria's Facebook page," Megan says.

"I just don't want any record of looking her up."

"That doesn't sound good. Why don't you come home?"

"Please. Just look at her page."

"How? We're not friends."

"She's a narcissist. She's going to have a public profile. Mark my words." I never thought I'd turn into the kind of woman who said, "Mark my words," yet here I am. I sigh as I hear Megan typing in the background.

"Oh my God," Megan says.

Apparently, she's found the page. Alexandria probably has a million skimpily clad pictures of herself. I don't have to see it to imagine it. "Public page?"

"Yes. I'm on."

"I knew it. Didn't I know it?"

"Oh, honey. I'm so sorry."

"Why? Because she's like a supermodel?"

"You don't deserve this. This would drive any woman over the edge."

"Are you saying I'm over the edge?"

"I'm saying, if you were, it's totally understandable. I mean she's completely flawless!"

"Thank you."

"I'm sorry, I'm sorry, I'm sorry."

"Moving on. Did she post anything about Alex?"

"I'm looking," Megan says. "She has a lot of friends. And her posts are all in Italian."

"Great." I hear a little gasp. "What? Tell me!"

"Do you really want to know?"

"Abso-fucking-lutely."

"Okay, Mr. Big. She has a ton of pictures of Alex." I can see it. Smiling, happy pictures. Sharing a single string of spaghetti between their lips. Riding a gondola at sunset. Toasting the clueless wife with a nice bottle of Chianti. I even imagine family pictures—mine—with my face cut out and Alexandria's pasted in. Alexandria holding Rachel. Clapping at Josh's soccer games, drawing smiles from all the parents, especially the fathers. Rubbing Stella's big orange head.

I imagine darker pictures. Alexandria shaved bald. Alex bending over as if in testicular distress. Alexandria in a body bag. This is probably what cracking up feels like. I always thought it was just an expression, but now I can feel it. Little cracks forming all over my insides. "Is Alex still 'friends' with her?"

"You don't need this. I'm not going to do this to you."

"Tell me."

"Yes, he's still friends with her. And he's 'liked' all her pictures."

"That son of a bitch. What about Marco?"

"Nothing immediate." That was something, wasn't it? So much for Marco's being obsessed with Alexandria. One down; one to go.

"Do you catch the names of any places she might hang out?"

"I mentioned it was all in Italian, right?"

"Anything. A description of a picture. A sign. Anything."

"Tell me your plan first."

"I just want to talk to her."

"Lena."

"It will be therapeutic."

"Come home instead."

"To what? A husband who's in love with another woman?"

"Your home. Your friends. Your children."

"I need to confront her."

"You have confronted her. Several times. It always makes you feel worse."

"I still need closure, Megan. I won't do anything drastic. I swear."

Megan sighs. I know she's going to help. She's all I have left. "There's a bar—café—it's called Minotti's."

"Minotti's." I write it on the palm of my hand. "Thank you."

"Alex isn't worth this."

"I know. But I am."

"Call me if you're tempted to do anything stupid."

"I could never afford that many minutes."

The little wine bar isn't far from the apartment, which is probably why Alexandria started going there to begin with. I am wearing a black dress, heavy makeup, and my hair is tucked into a green fedora. I bought it at the market because it looked mysterious. And I can't very well spy on Alexandria if she spies my white-blond hair. It's a beacon, especially in Italy. Maybe next time I will get a wig.

The bar is cozy and dark, and in addition to the wine, serves a large variety of appetizers. The list of little bites you can get with your vino fills an entire book. Not that it matters; I can barely read at the dim bar. Another reminder that I am not exactly young anymore. But the servers are. They are all young, and somewhat standoffish, which suits me just fine. If anything crazy does happen between Alexandria and me, surely none of them will remember a single thing about me. Not that I plan on doing anything crazy.

I just want her to see me. I want her to think I will never go away. I drink three glasses of wine and taste four appetizers before calling the first night a bust. I'm going to gain weight if this surveillance keeps up much longer. I take a longer route home, hoping to burn a few calories. I'm not sure why I even care. I should just let myself go. All these years of trying to keep in shape for Alex—and he's still gone off and found someone else. I should just eat and drink myself into an early Italian grave. *Here lies a betrayed and bloated woman.* In the window of a little shop I watch a man bent over, welding something. I want to march in and take over, push him out into the streets, and force him to live my life instead. I would do it. If only I knew how to weld.

"Would you like more?" The bartender hovers, wine bottle poised and ready to pour. It is my third night back. Three times is the charm. Plus I'm really starting to like it here. I like to sit at the bar and pretend I'm an unemployed cabaret singer.

"No thank you," I say. "I think that's enough for tonight."

"Grazie," he says with a nod. What is he thanking me for? Getting out of here? Am I that bad? Maybe I don't look as mysterious as I think I do, sitting here night after night in my fedora. Maybe I'm just an American idiot.

On my fourth night, I am on my second glass of wine and third appetizer when Alexandria appears. I zap to attention. I feel electrified. The kind of adrenaline that can lift cars. I look at her sideways, wondering if the entire place can hear my heart beating out of my chest. Alexandria is surrounded by a small posse. When I hear her brash voice, the little hairs on my arm rise. Alexandria and her friends commandeer a small table off to the side. I have a clear view through the mirror on the back wall of the bar. If Alexandria is devastated that Alex is gone, she certainly isn't acting like it.

She is holding court, laughing the loudest, talking the most. I watch her in the mirror, and she looks like such an innocent, nice girl. It's infuriating. I want to see her shriveled up and crying in the gutter somewhere. The bartender notices me looking at Alexandria. Some spy I would make. He walks up and points.

"You know her? She is an actress? A model?" Great, another one in love.

"She's a whore and a thief," I say.

"Wow," he says, even more enamored. I could probably have said she chopped puppies up into little pieces and he would still be drooling. It wasn't fair. People were always jealous of me because of my looks. Not that I ever asked for anyone's admiration; it was just thrown at me, like rice after a wedding. And now I'm fading into the woodwork, and out rises this Italian goddess. Maybe I should just pack it up and give up. Let her win. Let her walk away with my husband.

I am thinking of leaving when the door opens and in walks Marco. I catch my breath, and my heartbeat quickens. What is wrong with me? He has to be my partner in revenge, nothing more. He doesn't even notice me. Instead, he arrives at Alexandria's table, scoots in next to her, and puts an easy arm around her. I watch it all through the mirror. Et tu, Marco? Rejected again, for the same woman. What really makes me furious is that if my husband were here right now—my husband—he would be jealous. Of Marco and Alexandria. Not the chick at the bar with her hair tucked into a fedora, trying to figure out who she is now that her other half has ripped himself away from her. There is something fundamentally wrong with that. I understand the raw emotion of a revenge opera without having to attend. This shit hurts. Why in the world should I be the only one who has to pay?

"Her boyfriend?" the bartender says, clearly disappointed.

"Check, please," I say. When he slides it to me, I throw money at it and then push away from the bar. But I'm too angry, too forceful, and instead of scooting back, my chair tilts to the floor. I scream and try to grab onto the bar, but it's too late. I tuck my chin into my chest and try and protect the back of my head with my hands. The chair whumps to the floor, and my knuckles take a hard hit. I lie on the floor, staring at the ceiling. It has pretty little baskets hanging from it; I hadn't noticed that before.

Suddenly someone is kneeling down beside me, jabbering away. I turn and look.

"Lena," Marco says. He has such big eyes. And long eyelashes.

"Not fair," I say.

"Not fair?" he parrots. And then he throws his head back and laughs. It makes me laugh too. I am having a really good time.

"Let's get you up," he says.

"Why? I like it down here." People are always trying to get me off the ground. Maybe I do like it down here. Leave me alone!

But he puts his arms around me, and I encircle his neck with my hands, and he lifts me into a standing position. To my surprise, the little café breaks into applause. Apparently, the Italians like a little damsel in distress on a Thursday evening. Is it Thursday? Or Wednesday? I don't even know. Now that my life isn't dictated by lessons, I can't keep track. Marco and I still have our arms around each other. We're dancing to no music. He is smiling like he is really happy to see me, and he doesn't seem to remember he came here to see Alexandria. I lean in and kiss him, in full view of the bar, and more important, in full view of Alexandria. I pour all my pent-up longing for Alex into the kiss. He should be the one getting this, but since he is not, it has to go somewhere.

When I pull away, the café applauds again. *"Brava, brava,"* one person yells. Another yells something in Italian. I wonder if it's the equivalent of "Get a room!" Marco stares at me, and I have to say, he seems a little stunned. We've kissed before, so why is he looking at me like this? There is something vulnerable in his gaze, and it sends a shot of fear up and down my spine. We cannot let emotion ruin our partnership. Alexandria rises; confusion marches all over her pretty face. And then it hits me. She doesn't recognize me with the hat. This person who has consumed and spit out my life doesn't even know who I am. I take off my cap and shake out my hair. Alexandria slaps her hand over her mouth. Her nostrils actually flare. For the first time, I see that there are times when she can appear rather unattractive.

Alexandria advances slowly, looking only at Marco. I can't believe she's going to approach me. I think this is going to get physical. I think this is the night when I rip her hair out by the roots.

Marco steps behind me, wraps his arms around me, pulls me into him. Does he know what I'm thinking, and he's going to try and hold me back? Let me at her! She comes to within a few feet, stops, and says something to Marco in Italian.

"Speak English, tramp," I say. Marco drops his hands. When I turn around, his mouth is open. "What did she say?"

"Alexandria!" A little old man pops up in front of her, blocking the path my fist wants to take. Next, a little old woman steps in. They look like a stereotypical Old World Italian couple. Short, round, gray hair, tanned, wrinkled faces, beaming, slightly crooked smiles.

"Nonno," I catch Alexandria saying. "Nonna!"

"Grandmother and grandfather," Marco whispers in my ear, in case I'm still considering a smackdown. Great. Saved by the sweetest little Tuscan couple I've ever seen. Will this be Alexandria in fifty years? Will she shrink down to something adorable and nonthreatening? I can't wait that long. And I'll probably be dead.

But I can't let her have it right now. Not in front of Nonna and Nonno. No-no is right. The hugs are over, but it looks as if the touching, and gesturing, and exclaiming are going to go on forever.

Just when I think it's finally over, Nonna reaches up and put her hands on Alexandria's face. She smiles and makes more loud exclamations and moves Alexandria's face side to side in her exuberance, then pinches each cheek before clapping her hands, keeping them tucked under her chin with a big grin.

"How long has it been since they've seen her?" I whisper to Marco.

"She lives with them," Marco says. Alexandria glances at me, causing Nonna and Nonno to spin around to see who she is looking at.

Oh God, they're moving in, grinning; they want to touch me too. I try and step back, but Marco is still holding me, keeping me in place. But even though they get so close I can see gold in both their mouths, they don't actually touch me. Nonno turns to Marco with a grin and a wag of his finger.

"E la tua ragazza?"

"He wants to know if you're my girlfriend," Marco whispers in my ear.

My heart tap dances. I want to ask him what he's going to say. I don't. He answers them in Italian. Their expressions remain happy. What did he say?

"Did you say I'm the wife of their granddaughter's boyfriend?" I say.

"No," Marco says. "I told them you are my girlfriend."

I whirl around, and Marco and I engage in a staring contest. A sly smile plays out on his lips. This man wouldn't mind at all if my temper flared. I think he gets off on it. "Why would you say that?" I want to know the answer, and my body is doing all sorts of signaling and firing, but my brain can't figure out what I want that answer to be, or what I'll do with it when I hear it.

"You want to spy on Alexandria?"

"Keep the enemy close," I say.

"You won't get any closer than Nonna and Nonno." He's got

a point. They seem to like me, and Alexandria looks downright sick. She's pale, which with her olive skin tone means slightly yellow-looking. I smile at Nonna and Nonno. How much do they know about this sordid tale? Have they ever met Alex? Has Nonna pinched his cheeks with her soft, wrinkled hands? Nonna turns and speaks with Alexandria, all the while looking at me and gesturing.

"I suoi capelli sono come il sole," Nonna says.

"She says your hair is like the sun," Marco whispers. His lips brush the tips of my earlobes. "I agree," he adds. Lust invades me. I want Marco. I want to make love to Marco. How could you do this to me, Alex? Aren't you going to stop me?

"Grazie," I say to Nonna. I turn to Marco. "How do you say— 'Your granddaughter is a whore'?' "

"Dové Alex?" Nonna says.

A small rusty pick hovers in front of my heart and begins to hack, hack, hack. "Alex," I say. "She just said Alex."

"Keep it together," Marco says. "If you want to spy." Alexandria begins to cry. She is crying at the mention of Alex.

"Alex is my husband," I say. Nonno and Nonna do not understand. Alexandria's tears alarm them.

"Andiamo. Mangiamo!" Nonna says. She slips her arms into Alexandria's and mine. I am one arm-link away from the woman who is destroying my life. Nonna steers us to the door while Nonno hurries over to open it.

"Marco?" I say. I throw him a look over Nonna's head.

"It is useless," Marco says. "She has decided to feed you."

We traverse back street after back street, and soon arrive at a building in the Santa Croce area. The outside is made of old stone, the color of cream. It sports twelve evenly spaced, arched wooden windows, drawing your eye up to the roof where a giant bell sways in the evening breeze. Marco leans in to tell me it was a monastery in the seventeenth century. To the left is a small courtyard guarded by an iron fence. Marco sees me looking at it. "Never lean on that fence," he says. He slides his left-arm sleeve up and shows me a long scar. "I took the fall," he says. Alexandria keeps glancing at me, waiting for me to put an end to this charade. It is precisely because she wants me to that I do not. Instead I turn up my smile and pretend to be thrilled. I like the fact that I am now invading the second place she calls home. If I have my way, she will feel under scrutiny every place she goes.

We enter and take the stairs to the third floor. The interior of the apartment is quite simple and beautiful. The floors are terra-cotta, and the ceilings are a series of slanted wood beams. I have had too much wine and immediately upon entering, I excuse myself and escape into the restroom.

It is small, but quaint. The floor is tiled in colorful blue and green squares. The window above the tub is open, and a breeze blows a soft linen curtain in and out; it's as if the curtain is a willowy paintbrush creating its own masterpiece. What do you know, even Italian curtains moonlight as artists. If a curtain could practice painting, why can't I take it up again? The toilet flushes rather loudly. I stand at the little sink and consider not washing my hands. I can sit next to Alexandria and infect her with my bacteria. I wash them anyway, just in case Nonna is listening outside the door.

Except for a makeshift curtain that can be pulled to separate them, the living room and the kitchen blend into the same cozy space. At the far end of the room is a dining room table situated near a single window offering a partial view of the Duomo. How incredibly lucky, to live here and gaze upon that every day. A memory of speaking with Alex on the phone sneaks in. It was shortly after he arrived, that small window of time when we were so eager to speak to each other and bridge the gap between us.

"I was invited to a real Italian home for dinner."

"Cool."

"It is. It's actually a big deal. Florentines don't invite foreigners over too often."

"They must really like you."

"Their dining room looks out on the Duomo." I don't remember where the conversation went from there. Perhaps I started complaining about something unrelated. Could anything I said have stopped all of this in its tracks?

Am I standing where it all began? The unraveling of my marriage in this quaint little flat with Nonna and Nonno? I stare at a block of knives on the kitchen counter. The grandmother catches me looking around, then waves me away as if I had been contemplating helping with dinner. I feel as if I am an evil person, a person capable of things nobody could ever imagine.

What am I doing here? I need to make an excuse and leave. Or just leave. Walk out the door and never look back. A couple of middle-aged uncles sit on the couch like rotund bookends watching football and cheering, it seems, for opposite teams.

"Ole!" one yells.

"Auuuguh!!" the other responds.

Except for the occasional cheering or booing, it's as if the men have been shot with tranquilizer darts, while the women are amped up on speed. The men are butts-on-couch, staring at a blaring television, while Alexandria and Nonna whirl a path between the kitchen and the men, bringing them snacks and beers, and emptying ashtrays as fast as the men can fill them. And of course, in between, they are cooking dinner. *You've got to be kidding me.* Even Marco has morphed into a lump of Jell-O, his body melting into the couch. Stunned, I stand in no-man's-land between the groups.

"*Mammonis,*" Alexandria says as she passes me. "Mama's boys. All Italian men." None of them even glance up. "Did you know Marco lives with his mother?" Alexandria announces.

"Very funny," I say.

"I am not joking. This is all Italian men. They are either with their mommies or their wives. She even irons Marco's underwear."

"Marco," I say. He doesn't even glance up. "MARCO." He finally looks at me.

"*Si?*"

"Do you live with your mother?"

"Ah. *Si, si.*" He smiles and goes back to watching television. Alexandria shoots me a smug look and goes back into the kitchen. I have an urge to ask Marco to drop trou just to see how ironed his underpants are. I feel more out of place than ever. *Mammonis,* a whore, and a grandmother I can't understand. I don't fit in with any of them.

Under different circumstances I would have jumped at the chance to observe an Italian grandmother in the kitchen. Besides the dizzying speed at which she works, Nonna peppers her conversations with loud bursts of Italian, reaching out to touch my hair at every opportunity. Touch Alexandria's hair, I want to shout. Pull it out from the roots!

I'm not sure how to do it, turn an Italian *nonna* against her granddaughter, but I am determined to try. In the meantime, it appears that Nonna has a plan of her own, namely to kill us all with food. Every surface is being used to chop, heat, stir, or roll out dough. Is she making homemade pasta? There is an actual tomato plant sitting on the kitchen floor, and every once in a while Nonna plucks one up with her thick fingers, chops it in seconds flat, and drops it into one of the pots. It's like a well-choreographed ballet. Alexandria chops and stirs as well, but with less finesse, and she is doing her utmost not to make any eye contact with me.

I wander away from it all, stumbling slightly even though I've yet to be offered anything to drink. I soon find myself in a small hallway littered with family photographs. Will I find one of Alex among them, smiling as if he belongs? If so, I will lose it. All bets will be off. The largest picture in the grouping is centered in the middle of the wall. I edge closer. It features a young, smiling couple. I remember this couple; I burned them in the sink. It is the same exact spot in Cinque Terre where Alex and Alexandria stood. On the edge of the cliff. These must be Alexandria's parents. I can certainly see a resemblance.

Suddenly, I feel someone staring at my shoulder blades. Nonna is directly behind me. Startled, I turn around. Nonna adjusts her head scarf, scattering fragments of flour like snowflakes, then pats a red linen towel slung over her shoulder. She grabs my hands, thrusts them atop her ample bosom, and begins to wail.

"What's happening?" I say. "Marco?" Sobbing. I can't pull away. Nonna is rocking and squeezing the life out of my hands. It feels like an eternity before Alexandria finally comes over and speaks quietly to Nonna, who eventually drops my hands. She then gestures to the photos and wails in English. "My baby. Dead."

"I'm so sorry," I say. "Your daughter?"

"My parents," Alexandria says. "They were killed."

"When?" It comes out a little too harshly, but once again, I hear Alex. *She had a family tragedy. I was there to comfort her. It just happened.*

"Three months ago," Alexandria says quietly. She is crying. Nonna is crying.

"I'm sorry," I say. I direct all of my sympathy at Nonna, not wanting any to spill over to Alexandria.

"They crashed their car," Alexandria says. "It went over a bridge." I glance over at Marco to find him staring at Alexandria with concern. "We spread their ashes in Cinque Terre," Alexandria says.

"I see," I say. So that's why Alex was there.

"It was their favorite place in the world." She points to the picture. "In fact, this is where they stood when my papa proposed to my mama." She looks me in the eye, tilts her chin up.

She and Alex recreated the photo. I know what she's getting at, and even though I know it didn't happen, I can still play along.

"You can't really get engaged if one person is already married," I say. Alexandria whirls around and then retreats to her chopping corner. Marco's eyes land on me.

What? I mouth.

You're beautiful. I stare at him, warmed by the silent compliment, but also worried. Does he know anything about this?

Does she really think she and Alex are engaged? And why is Marco looking at me like that?

Alexandria trots to the couch with a couple of beers for the bookend uncles, and one of them points at Alexandria's belly as she walks away. Then, he catches me staring at him, open-mouthed. He grins and mimes a pregnant belly. I cry out. Everyone's head whips toward me. I whirl around and stare at Alexandria's stomach. Sure enough, she has the beginnings of a pouch.

"Are you pregnant?" I say.

CHAPTER 26

Marco is at my side in a flash, although he does not touch me. I spy a full decanter of wine on the kitchen table, and I head straight for it. I lift it to my lips and drink for a long time. When I finish, even the rest of the *mammonis* are on their feet staring at me. I put down the wine and advance on Alexandria.

"Are you?"

"Maybe I am just fat."

"You do not want Nonna to catch on to what you are saying," Marco says.

"Your granddaughter is a pregnant, husband-stealing whore," I say to Nonna. That's when I notice she's clutching the picture of Alexandria's parents to her chest.

"Boom!" she says.

"The car exploded," Alexandria interprets.

"Oh my God," I say. *"Mi dispiace,"* I say. I'm sorry. "I'm leaving," I tell Marco. "Are you coming with me?"

"Marco would never leave my home before dinner," Alexandria says.

"Why? Because I am a *mammoni?*" He glares at Alexandria,

then goes over to Nonna, takes her hands, and begins speaking to her quietly in Italian. She looks over at me several times. I kind of smile and shrug.

"Are you happy now?" Alexandria says.

"What is he saying?"

"Learn Italiano," Alexandria says, then marches out of the room. I want to follow her with a pee stick. Is it possible? Does Alex know? Did he propose? Is that why? I am sick, sick, sick. I don't care anymore what Marco is saying, I just want out. He must have mentioned leprosy, for Nonna doesn't even try to hug me when we leave.

"Where are we going?" Marco says.

There is the slightest chill in the air, or maybe it's just me. "Did you know?" I say as we begin to walk.

"I did not know. I still do not know. You and me, we are in the same boat."

"Or the same gondola."

"Yes. I understand. That is very funny."

"And it's sinking."

"*Bravissimo!* You are right. Our boat is sinking."

I ignore his misplaced enthusiasm. "You've known her your whole life. Do you think she's pregnant?"

"It would explain a lot. But maybe she just eat more since you took her lover away."

"He is not a toy. I did not take him away." Okay, well maybe I sent him away. And it wasn't like I had him anymore either. A baby. How can I take revenge out on a woman carrying a baby? Alex's baby.

"I'm sorry I asked you to come with me," I say. "I need to be alone." I don't know what to do. Call Alex? Don't call Alex? What if she's lying? What if she's playing games?

"I understand," Marco says. "*Ciao, bella.*"

"I thought that's hello."

"I'd rather say that than good-bye." We look into each other's eyes. He has feelings for me, and I him. I am about to ruin it. But I have to know.

"If she is pregnant. Is there any chance the baby could be yours?"

"No," Marco says. "We have not slept together since she met your Alex." Tears well in my eyes. Marco notices them, and his face softens toward me, but he lets me be. I turn and walk away.

"Pregnant?" Megan says. "Are you kidding me?" This is what I need, to hear someone else's outrage. I'm walking through the city with my second new cell phone, and even though it is going on midnight, the streets are active and every streetlamp seems to glow. It feels strange to feel so sad in the midst of such beauty.

"I don't know for sure," I say. "But she didn't deny it."

"Because she's evil. She's an evil, little liar."

"That's what I thought."

"You don't anymore?"

"Three months ago her parents were killed in a car crash."

"Oh God."

"I know. I guess the car went over a cliff and exploded. They spread the ashes in Cinque Terre. That's why Alex was there."

"Three months ago?"

"Guess who was there to comfort her."

"It doesn't exactly make Alex smell like a rose."

"I went there too. But I know my husband, Megan. He's not a bad man. He wouldn't have used her parents' death to seduce her."

"What are you saying?"

"That maybe Angelo is right about love."

"Pray tell. What did Angelo say about love?"

"Something about looking at the linens in the light."

"What?"

"I don't remember. Oh! And—'You work and pay' Something like that."

"I'm underwhelmed."

"It sounded better in my head. The point is—we love who we love. Just because I don't like it doesn't mean it isn't true."

"Are you saying you're going to let Alex go? Be with her?"

"Do I have a choice?"

"It's just quite a turnaround. This wouldn't have anything to do with Marco, would it?"

"What do you mean?"

"He sounds exciting. And you've already said he's young, and talented, and handsome."

"I'm grieving my marriage."

"I know, sweetie. But nobody would judge you." I stop. I have moved away from the main streets. It is quiet here and dark. I don't recognize the curves of the buildings or the stones beneath my feet. I am lost. Literally and figuratively. I suddenly want to find the little church where I sat just after I announced I was staying. And tomorrow I will go see Angelo. Drink a cappuccino. Eat a biscotti. I stand a little straighter, surprised with myself. I expected to be more devastated. I'm just slightly numb.

"Thank you, Megan," I say. "I'm going to go."

"What are you going to do?"

"Go to church," I say.

"Go to church?" Megan sounds as if she's choking.

"It's comforting. There won't be a service. Just candles and soft music."

"Okay. And then?"

"Go to bed. Get up and go visit Angelo."

"I mean about Alex. The baby."

"I still don't know if there is a baby."

"You have to find out."

"How? Follow her around with a pee stick?"

"Just follow her around in general. Wait—when you saw her at the wine bar, was she drinking?"

"As a matter of fact—yes! At least she was holding what looked like a wineglass."

"There you go."

"Some pregnant women drink. This is Italy—they let kids drink wine with dinner."

"I think you should follow her again."

"You're the one who tried to talk me out of it the first time."

"That's before I knew about this latest scheme."

"You think she's lying?"

"She's capable of it. Don't you think?"

"Absolutely. But even manipulative liars tell the truth sometimes."

"What do you think Alex would do if she were pregnant?"

"I've been thinking about that."

"And?"

"And I think he's going to flip out."

"Really?"

"He did both times I was pregnant. Just because Alex is notoriously responsible, doesn't mean he likes it. That's why he wanted to be here without the kids and me. Mr. Free and Single again."

"Well then, let's hope she is pregnant."

"Megan!"

"I mean it. Let him pay the piper while you run off with Marco."

"If this were an Italian opera, we'd all end up dead. Except maybe the baby."

"Well, be thankful it's not. It's just a regular old soap opera. Which means you end up in the bed of the hot Italian man." And before I can protest, she is gone.

I leave the church feeling much more peaceful and am almost home when my cell phone rings.

"I'm sorry," Alex says when I answer. For a moment, I am struck dumb. Did Alexandria call him? Is this about the baby? "It's your mother," he says. My heart stops.

"Is she okay?"

"Yes, yes, nothing like that."

"You scared me."

"Sorry, again."

"Well, what is it?"

"She made me tell her."

"She already knows. Rachel told her."

"What?"

"About you?"

"No. Not about me." Alex sounds ashamed. Good. "About where you're staying."

"Why does that matter?" I say. I am nearly to my building, taking out my keys. I hear laughter ring out a few feet away. I stop in my tracks. "Oh God," I say. "She's here?"

"Sorry."

"Shit."

"Sorry, sorry."

"How could you?"

"Your mother's like a bulldog when she wants something."

"Coward." It comes back, easily; my affection for him is like muscle memory. I didn't just love my husband; I liked him too.

"Mea culpa." For a moment we are bantering like we used to. At first it feels like a shot of morphine coursing through my blood, taking away the pain, and then as silence falls between us, it all comes rushing back.

"Alex," I say. "We need to talk."

"I know, Llama," he says. I stare at the distant hills, the tree-tops, the brick and stone flats. Joy shoots through me like a hit of heroin, but it doesn't last more than a second before I crash and feel nothing but pulsing, raw pain. Llama. What the hell are you doing, Alex? Why are you calling me that now? I see my mother now, standing with Frank, and two enormous suitcases, at one a.m. in front of my flat.

"Surprise!" my mother says.

"Sorry," Alex says.

"Your girlfriend is pregnant," I say. And then I hang up.

My mother and Frank shove their way into the espresso bar and immediately start ordering. I am standing in line for the cashier, having already tried to tell them the routine. Angelo is shaking his finger and his head at them, and they still do not understand.

"Mother!" I say. Finally, she looks at me.

"We'll get this, darling," she says. "If this rude man will just wait on us."

"He certainly has the sign language down, doesn't he?" Frank grins and begins waving his hands in the air, mimicking Angelo. Angelo looks at me, and I mouth, *mi dispiace.* He winks at me and then shakes his head at my parents. I want to marry him. I have to get out of line and go over to them, take them by the arms, and steer them in the right direction.

"We have to pay in this line first," I say.

"Well, that's just inconvenient," Frank says. He is a tall man with a booming voice. Every time he speaks, he sounds as if he's auditioning for a game show. I miss my quiet, polite father. How could she choose this man over him? Are we all just completely insane when it comes to love? I can no more change her mind about who to love than I can Alex's.

I know, Llama.

Whatever momentary affection for me that was is probably gone. Zapped away by my prematurely announcing Alexandria's pregnancy. Surely, he's called her already. Is he happy? Does he think the news means he can just walk out on us and start a new family with her? Oh God, I hope he doesn't tell Rachel and Josh without me. I will kill him. I wonder what Angelo would think if I asked for brandy in my cappuccino? We finish paying, but by now the counter is shoulder to shoulder.

"Makes you wish there were a Starbucks around the corner, doesn't it?" Frank booms.

"Do the Italians have something against sitting down?" my mother says.

"We should have made coffee at your place," Frank says. I stand behind a row of customers, begging Angelo with my eyes. He begins rearranging people up and down the line until there is room for the three of us to squeeze in, and he serves us our beverages in record time. I am grateful.

"He thinks he's going to get a big tip from us," my mother says.

"Plant your corn early," Frank booms.

"Should we go on a gondola ride?" my mother says.

"That's Venice," I say. "But you two could take the train and be there in a few hours," I say, brightening at the idea.

"Nonsense," my mother says. "We're here for you." She throws her arm around my shoulder. "And to tell you the good news."

Oh God. I definitely should have asked for alcohol. "What good news?" But she is already flashing an engagement ring in my face. In fact, she takes my hand and puts our rings side by side, as if I'm happily married, as if I we will swoon and whoop over her news like a couple of schoolgirls.

I yank my hand away. "I can't believe you."

"Lima," my mother says. She always called me Lima Beans as a little girl. I always hated it. I still hate it. She looks upset. I've ruined her surprise.

"My husband is leaving me," I say.

"Nonsense. It's just a spat. You two will work this out."

"You call sleeping with another woman 'just a spat'?"

"Keep your voice down. The locals are staring. I just thought our news might cheer you up. Give you hope."

"Have you told Dad?" I say. I feel like a child again. How can she do this to him? To me? Now of all times? Here of all places?

"Your father will handle it just fine. He stopped loving me a long time ago."

"How can you say that?"

"Darling, I can say it because it's true. We were never as in love as you and Alex."

"He never cheated on you either." My mother pales. I don't like having this argument, no matter what I think of him, in front of Frank. But we're standing here having it anyway.

"We'll be on our way, then," my mother says. "We certainly didn't come here to bother you with our happiness."

"I'm sorry," I say. "I am happy for you. I am." I hug her. She is stiff at first and then hugs me back. I hold out my hand for Frank to shake.

"Come here, you," he says. He pulls me into him, and I slam against his chest. He smells like sharp soap.

"I'm taking you out for a special dinner tonight," I say. "To celebrate." And I mean it. I can't take anymore bad Karma when it comes to love.

"That's wonderful."

"I'll bring a friend," I say.

"Oh?" my mother says. "Who is she?"

"Just someone from the neighborhood," I say. My mother adores Alex. She wouldn't even come to dinner if she knew I was inviting another man. Once he's there, she won't leave. She's too polite. And I need him there. My partner in crime. My buffer. As we head off for a couple of museums, I text Marco, invite him to dinner, and pray he says yes.

CHAPTER 27

My mother and Frank stop to make out in front of the Santa Croce church, while Marco and I stand back and pretend we don't know them. Watching your mother make out like a teenager with her husband-to-be is one thing. Sitting with them and my husband's mistress's boyfriend at a romantic table in Florence, while they feed each other across the table, is hell with a makeover. I drink a lot of wine as they talk about the ports of call in their wonderful cruise: Turkey, Greece, Spain, Portugal.

But the world is in such financial ruins right now, I find myself thinking. How can they be enjoying it? Or am I just seeing everything through adultery-colored glasses?

"The people of Greece are so nice," my mother says. "Their lives are so, so simple. That's the way to do it."

"The people of Greece are bankrupt, Mother. Bankrupt." I've been holding my tongue since she arrived; the wine is starting to loosen it.

"I know, dear. All the more reason I was terribly impressed. Have you ever been to Greece, Marco?"

"*Si, si.* Mostly when I was a boy. Lena is right; it is a tough time all around."

"Tough times just prove how resilient we all are, don't you think? People's lives come crashing down around them all the time, but do they roll over and die?"

"Mother."

"No. They're still fishing in their little boats, and smiling at tourists, and sweeping their sidewalks, and cooking simple, yet delicious meals. I had no idea how satisfied I could be eating nothing other than buffalo mozzarella and a tomato with oil and vinegar, but you know what? I was!" I slide my eyes over to Frank, who has buried himself in the bread basket. I watch as he dips the bread in olive oil, then vinegar, then back to the olive oil before plopping it into his mouth. The only thing that will make it worse is if—

Oh God. He's doing it. He's licking his fingers. This is the man my mother wants to marry? Instead of my father?

My father, whether at home or a restaurant, would never eat bread before everyone else had been served their entrée, and even then, he certainly wouldn't eat it like a savage.

"So, Marco," Frank booms when he finishes licking his fingers. "Did you ever watch *The Sopranos*?"

I glance under the table. Frank is wearing white tennis shoes. Doesn't my mother notice any of this? She doesn't look like she does; in fact, she's busy checking out Marco, and not in a good way. I stare at her until she notices.

"I think it's wonderful you have a little friend here," she says. "Enjoying the city. Relaxing. Hopefully getting some much needed perspective." *And we're off.*

"Is that what you think I'm doing? Vacationing?"

"Look around you, darling. What would you call it?"

"I'm on my honeymoon."

My mother looks at Frank, then Marco. "She always has a sharp tongue, that one. Her father put all those things in her head about Vikings."

"My father is the nicest man I've ever met." Oh God. Hurt is pouring out of me now like I'm ten years old and my parents have just divorced. Is this going to be Rachel and Josh twenty years from now? Picking apart any man I date after Alex? As long as they're doing it with him too, I'm all right with it.

"If you like sitting around making birdhouses and watching *Ice Road Truckers,* he's a catch."

"Mother!"

"I'm sorry, darling. But there's no need for the histrionics. Your father is happier than he's ever been." When did she start calling me darling? She's going through some kind of life stage, playing the part of a thirties movie star. Maybe she and Dad were a bad match. He does like those birdhouses. I don't think he even likes birds. He's like a surgeon who doesn't want to interact with his patients unless they're knocked out on his table. Matter of fact, he's never even hung one in the yard.

"Too messy," he said when I asked after it. We, on the other hand, have three of them in our yard. I wonder if Alex is remembering to refill them?

"I'll be home soon," Mom says. "I'll take the kids."

Where are the waiters in this place? We have wine and bread. Maybe that's all we're getting. And nobody but Frank is molesting the bread. At least we have wine. I've lost my appetite anyway, but I feel some strange sense of pride about Florence, as if it will reflect poorly on me if they don't like it. "What do you mean, 'take the kids'?"

"So Alex can join you. Make it a honeymoon for two."

"I'm sorry. Did you not get the memo? Alex had an affair."

"It happens all the time, darling, Marriages survive."

"I don't think you're listening to me. It wasn't just a hit-and-run—a one-nighter—he's been carrying on with this woman for two months."

"There really are some pretty women here," Frank says.

"We probably shouldn't do this here," my mother says.

"He was paying for the flat she was staying in."

"The place we're in now?" Frank says. "It's a little small."

"Frank," Marco says. "Would you like to join me outside for a smoke?"

"Oh, I don't smoke. Unless you have a Cuban?"

"No, no, just a cigarette. But it's European. Maybe you will like it."

"Filthy, filthy habit. Why do so many Europeans still smoke?" my mother says. Even though I've only sampled a few revenge cigarettes, a curtain of shame descends on me.

"We live, we eat, we smoke, we love," Marco says. He looks at me on "love." It's not a normal look, either. It's filled with testosterone, a bull about to charge. It's the kind of look that would make even my mother want to smoke.

"Alex loves you," my mother says. Marco's gaze stays on me, but it softens. The bull is gone. He is checking to see if she's hurting me. It's been so long since a man has been this tuned in to me. It's the biggest aphrodisiac in the world, knowing someone is on your frequency, watching out for you so you don't get short-waved or whatever bad things can happen to frequency. I really don't know anything about frequencies. Or electricity. Except for the kind I'm feeling with Marco. My mother is right. I am a married woman. What am I doing?

"So can you buy Cubans in Florence?" Frank says.

"The cigar or the people themselves?" Marco says. I burst out laughing. Marco keeps his expression deadly serious, and Frank is trying to work it out.

"What do you do for a living, Mark?" my mother says.

"It's Marco," I say.

"Americans," Marco says. "This is a big question with you, no? What do you do?"

"Marco is an artist," I say. "In fact, he has a public art exhibition all over Florence. He's famous."

"The exhibition is currently closed," Marco says with a slight smile.

"Why?" Frank says. "Because of the heat?"

"No. Because I was inspired to change the project."

"Lena mentioned you," my mother says. "You drew with chalk on the streets? Like hopscotch?"

"Mother!"

"What is hopscotch?"

"I never said hopscotch," I say. "They're faces. Gorgeous colors—I can't believe it's chalk. They were magnificent. And very, very popular."

"Alex knows everything there is to know about sculptures, doesn't he, darling?"

"He's certainly done his share of sculpting here," I say.

"Are there any waiters in this place?" Frank says. For once I have to agree. The place isn't even busy, and we're being ignored. It's probably the white tennis shoes. They glow from underneath the table.

"It is true; this is not good," Marco says. "I can speak with them, or we can go somewhere else."

"We've already had wine," my mother says. "We can't leave now."

"And bread," I say, looking pointedly at Frank. I want to follow it up by licking my fingers one by one, but I resist the impulse.

"I will speak with them," Marco says. He disappears to talk with a waiter. My mother doesn't waste a second.

"What is he doing here?"

"I asked him to come."

"Why? What would Alex think?"

"I can't believe you. After all this, and you're still taking his side."

"Darling. Taking his side is taking your side. He's your husband."

"He's fucking another woman!"

"Don't be crude."

Marco arrives at the table, but doesn't sit. "I ordered the best dishes on the menu. They are very sorry. It is, how you say, on the house."

"Splendid," Frank says. He lifts the empty basket of bread. "Do you think we could get more?"

"I spoke with Alex," my mother says when Marco goes off again with the bread basket. "He's worried about you."

"That's just rich."

"Please. Tell me you aren't sleeping with this Mark."

"It's Marco."

"Lena!"

A thought occurs to me. "Did Alex *send* you here?"

"He thought you might like some support." Interesting. He sends the most devious of all spies. My mother. She's always taken his side. Was this actually a good thing? Was he thinking more about me than Alexandria?

Marco is back with a full bread basket. God bless him.

"Lena. You've had your fun—" my mother starts to say. I push back from the table.

"Fun? I've had my fun?"

"Come home, darling. Your family needs you."

Marco stands with me, quietly in the background.

"I have not abandoned Rachel and Josh. They are with their father. He's the one who left for six months. He's the one who has destroyed us."

"Don't be so dramatic. You can fix this!"

"I didn't break it!"

"You are not a quitter."

"She's pregnant. With Alex's baby." I turn and glance at Marco. He raises an eyebrow, but does not refute me. I appreciate this. In fact, he's been nothing but great. I am going to have sex with him. Wild, passionate, take-that sex.

My mother stands up too. She's clutching her napkin. She doesn't know what to say or do. I reach out and take her hand.

"You should be enjoying yourself," I say. "Thank you for your support. But I need to figure this out on my own."

"There has to be a way. This is just a setback."

"No, Mom. It's a complete roadblock."

"Alex is your husband. For better or worse, remember?"

I laugh, glance at Frank. "I remember," I say.

"Your father and I were never a good match. And I at least waited until you were grown. Think of your children!"

"That's exactly what I'm doing."

THREE MONTHS IN FLORENCE

"Doesn't look like it to me."

I give my mother a hug that she does not reciprocate. I salute Frank. "Tell Alex this was low. Even for him." I take Marco's arm. "Get me out of here," I say.

"*Ciao, bella,*" he says. "Where would you like to go?"

"Anywhere but your mother's," I say.

CHAPTER 28

As Marco and I walk, I realize I wouldn't want all of my life to be like it is here in Italy. Imagine still living with my mother. And Frank.

"Sorry about all that, Mark," I say. Marco laughs, and as we walk, he slips his hand in mine. A tingle runs through me. I'd forgotten this, how erotic it is to hold hands with someone new. Not just someone. Someone you can imagine going to bed with. A lover. I stop and gently pull my hand away.

"Marco." We have a backdrop of old buildings and cobblestone streets and undulating hills.

"*Si?*"

"My life is a complete mess. I'm a complete mess."

"You are a beautiful mess."

"The Beautiful Mess. La Bella whatever-mess-is-in-Italian. They'll be lining up to buy tickets."

"Then we should celebrate. I'm taking you to my studio."

"Marco."

"Polo."

I burst out laughing. He smiles. His eyes really do twinkle.

He is adorable. And mine for the taking. "I don't want to use you."

"Then don't."

"It's not possible. My heart is destroyed. I couldn't fix it this fast even if I wanted to."

"So you don't want to see my studio?"

"I do. And I want to do other things. But I don't want to hurt you."

"We are in this together, remember?" Marco places his hand on his heart. "My heart was for her."

It hurts. I know it shouldn't, but it hurts. I don't realize I've lowered my chin until Marco gently steers it up with his index finger. "Meeting you has been like a salve. On my heart. Opened me up to new things. I am done with her."

"You don't have to say that."

"I just did."

"But I'm—"

"Still married."

"Yes."

"And broken."

"Yes."

"*Bella.* I may be much younger than you, but I am a big boy."

You live with your mother. I keep this to myself.

"Shall we go?"

"Yes," I say. And this time, as we continue our journey, I slip my hand in his.

Marco's studio is part of the university, set way back on the property, far away from the main campus buildings. As we walk through the olive grove, and take in the sun going down on the gentle green countryside, I realize I want to see more of Italy. I want to explore the smaller villages in Tuscany. I want to go to Venice, and Rome, and Milan.

Marco's studio is a small, stone cottage. I am surprised to see a couple of chickens loitering around the doorway. I can smell paint as we approach. It brings back memories; I remember that smell from my own art days. Marco opens the door, and all

I see are canvases, covering the small space. He seems nervous, as we step in, and it is the opposite, I am in awe. Once again I think that Marco's work should be hanging in galleries. Seeing his work on the website was one thing, but it's truly stunning in person. A close-up of an old woman examining a lemon. A young girl sitting on a sidewalk, legs splayed out, hair sweaty, lip curled in a pout. He has captured her post-tantrum. A boy on a bicycle, face flushed and determined, as if he were jetting off on a rocket and not pedaling his heart out. Two old men playing chess. It is like looking at color-enhanced photographs. I can see every detail down to the dirt under the old man's fingernails as he holds up his queen, pondering where to move next. I feel for him. I am afraid of my next move too. I know where I want to go, but it will put my marriage in checkmate.

"Marco. I'm truly in awe. A lot of love went into these paintings." Marco gives a little shrug, but a smile plays on his lips.

"I don't paint love," he says. "Love paints me."

Love paints me. The sexual chemistry is already at an all-time high, and then he has to go and say, 'Love paints me.' He is romantic and passionate. We are on a dance to the bed, and I'm not sure whether or not I am going to stop it. "Alex was right. You are a genius."

"He said this?"

"He called you another da Vinci or Michelangelo." Marco shrugs again, but his grin grows slightly wider. I suddenly feel exhausted. I sit on the floor, near all the beautiful canvases. After a moment Marco sits down beside me.

"I pursued Alex," I say. "I was so determined to have him."

"You chased him down?" Marco says. "He was not already running after you?"

I laugh. "He was interested. But I was the one with a nine-point plan on how to get him."

"A nine-point plan? I would love to see this. I would use it on you."

I laugh again. "Don't bother. I got away with it for a while, but look at me now. Right from the beginning, I was the one who was more afraid, the one holding on too tight. I didn't let love paint me. I forced it. I colored in every single little line."

Marco gestures around him. "Life is not one canvas. It is many. Sometimes I even use the same canvas and paint over it."

"But you still know what is underneath."

"That is true."

"How do I possibly start over? I have children. *We* have children. A mortgage. A dog. Sixteen years' worth of a canvas. Don't you feel this way? You said you've loved Alexandria since you were children. Aren't you the man who called in the middle of the night saying 'I want to kill you husband?' You seem totally normal now. What happened to all of your rage?"

"I met you," Marco says softly.

"Stop this."

"I do not control this. I cannot stop this."

"You don't even know me."

"I know what my heart tells me."

"Well, your heart is wrong. You love Alexandria. Just like Alex."

"Now, I love her like sister. You are the one I want to tear the clothes from your body." We are sitting side by side not looking at each other, not touching. Slowly he moves his hand, touches my fingertips, then places it on my thigh. It feels heavy, and soft, and there is just enough pressure to ignite me.

"You're shaking," he whispers. It's true. We look at each other. He brushes my hair aside, then leans in and gently kisses my neck. I still don't touch him. His arms encircle my waist. I lift my head, and his lips are on mine.

We kiss. We lie on the floor. We knock over canvases and a can of paintbrushes without stopping. Soon he is standing, pulling me up, and guiding me to a little cot in the corner of the room. I hit the cot first, and he stands over me, staring with a look of hunger in his eyes. He is looking at the buttons on my blouse.

"Rip it," I say. He smiles, but does not make a move. "I'm serious. Do it." Swiftly, he reaches down and with both hands rips it right down the middle. The sound of fabric tearing and buttons popping turns me on even more. I reach up and grab his T-shirt. It's way too hard to rip. He half growls and pulls his shirt over his head. He is lean but strong, and I pull him down into me.

I feel his chest against mine, skin against skin. I can feel all of him pressed into me, and I feel as if I not only want him, but I need him. And that's the reason, maybe the only reason, I can't do it.

"Stop," I say. He does. Immediately. He pulls back, looks into my eyes, cups his hand against the side of my face, and waits. "I'm sorry." Marco leans in, kisses me softly, then pulls back and hands me his shirt. Silently, I put it on, close my legs, breathe. It smells like him. Fresh, with a nice, soft cologne. If I were a normal person I would grab him and climb on top of him and allow his beautiful body and hands and mouth to erase my pain at least for a little while. I look at my wedding ring. I do not want to cry, not in front of Marco, who should probably be hopping in a cold shower, but I am weak, and grief is relentless. Marco hands me a tissue. I think he's the sweetest man on the planet. "It's not about Alex. It's me. I made a vow. If I do this then it's like the past sixteen years I've dedicated to my family don't mean anything."

"It's okay. I understand."

"I'm really sorry, Marco, and I really, really wanted to."

"I know, *bella*. That kind of passion? It takes two."

"Maybe someday." I smile, wipe my eyes.

He puts his hand on his heart. "*Si batterà per un giorno,*" he says.

"What?" I whisper it.

"It will beat for some day," Marco says. I kiss him gently on each cheek and then on the lips. "I am going to smoke a cigarette," he says. "Would you like to join me?"

"Do you have any Cubans?" I say.

Marco offers to take me home, but I need to be alone. I walk far enough away from the studio that he can't see me, then slide to the ground underneath an olive tree. One of the chickens has followed me. It stands a few feet away, head cocked, staring at me with one black pin of an eye. I pick up an olive from the ground and have an urge to throw it at the chicken. It swivels its head, then turns back to the studio and totters off. Italy is beautiful, I think. And I am a freak. I throw the olive in the direction of the chicken, knowing I will miss, but wanting the satisfaction of doing it anyway.

I rest my head against the tree and close my eyes. It wouldn't be so bad to die here, I think. Olive, I answer. *I'll live.* Josh would love that joke. I wish he were here so I could share it with him. He'd spend the next week making me repeat it. Every day he would say to me: "Are you okay, Mom? Are you going to die?"

"No, honey," I'd say, holding up one of the little greenish-black gems. "Olive."

I laugh until I start crying, and I stay there, for quite some time, until it's getting dark, and cool, and I pick myself up and head for home.

"My husband's mistress might be pregnant," I say into my cappuccino. It is the next morning, my mother and Frank are off to Rome, and I can't get ahold of Alex or the kids. Why did I tell him? I don't even know for sure. Did my mother say something to him about Marco? Why isn't he answering the phone? Since I've arrived, he's picked up every single call. Making up for all that sneaking around. But now there's a huge hole of panic again. What if my mother told him I'm sleeping with Marco, and now Alex thinks we're even?

Even if I had slept with him, we wouldn't be even. And I didn't. Wanting to doesn't count. Or it counts in the opposite way: I can't believe how much I wanted to—and I didn't.

"Bambino!" Angelo's face lights up, then does a free fall as he realizes what this means for me.

After this joyous reaction, I sort of want to take back my twenty euro which I finally remembered to repay him. Who would have thought that having my purse stolen would become one of "the good old days"?

"Yes, this is complicating things. But you no worry," Angelo continues. He leans over my drink. "You want another?" he whispers. "You no have to pay." I shake my head. I'm already shaking; more caffeine is not the answer. "Maybe it's not his," Albert says. He pats me on the hand. Then holds his fist up. "Maybe she is a liar!"

"Right? She could be lying." I don't tell Angelo that she has never come out and said she is pregnant, because I think explaining her inferences would be too complicated with the language barrier.

"You play detective. See if she is really pregnant!"

Play detective. See if she's really pregnant. And then what? "Angelo?"

"Si, mio amore."

"If your wife cheated on you, would you forgive her? Take her back?"

Angelo leans back and laughs. An all-out belly laugh with his hand on his large stomach. "My wife she no tiger in the bed, if you know what I am saying. Cheat on me! I would like to see this."

"Just—suppose."

Angelo puts his hand over his mouth, as if it will help him think. Then he stretches both hands out to the side. "Once my heart is break, it no go a back."

"I hear you." I know he thinks he means it, but it's different when it actually happens to you. It's different when your entire future is on the line. Did we have anything left fighting for? "What about the man? What would you do to him?"

"I would ask him. How does he get my wife in the mood?"

"Angelo!"

"All right, all right. You Americans, you no like joke. I kill him! That what I do. I kill him dead!" Angelo leans in. His breath smells like onions. Hoping it's not too obvious, I lean back as far as I can go. He dangles something in front of me. A set of keys.

"You want to follow pregnant mistress?"

"Possibly pregnant. Presumed pregnant."

"Tomato, tomato." He pronounces it exactly the same way both times. He jingles the keys. "You need this."

"What is it?"

"A *motorino.*"

"A scooter? A Vespa?"

"*Si.* Vespa, Vespa."

"I can't afford it."

"You no buy. You rent by the day."

"Do I need a license?"

Angelo shrugs. "If you no have, you no need."

"Oh. Okay."

"Just don't let police pull you over. If they pull you over, then you very much need."

CHAPTER 29

I had no idea it was so hard to drive a little scooter. I have to lean my body one direction or the other to steer it, and I keep leaning the wrong way. I am surprised how fast it can go, although everyone else must think I am going slow, for I've never been beeped at so many times in my life. Beeps, angry gestures, vocalizations from Italians without the patience to allow for my first time riding a scooter. I am dying to ride it up on the sidewalk, but I would probably kill a kid or a cat. The dips and holes in the road and the steep curves terrify me. I have to lean into the curves in order to hug the road instead of veering into traffic.

I have to admit, I am proud of myself as I zoom along the streets of Florence, becoming a living breathing part of the architecture and the hills. Even if the scooter is old and chipped, and loud, and spews exhaust, and most of the time it feels as if it is going to flip me over, I am still doing it. Holding onto the handlebars, leaning this way and that, trying to get it to go faster, and sticking to the road. There is no way I am ever going to start weaving in and out of traffic like some of these lunatics.

All I can pray is, if I do spot and want to stalk Alexandria, that the girl will travel in a straight line. Otherwise, I'm screwed.

I bought a laptop with Alex's credit card. I'm sick of being thrown out of Internet cafés. Now I can sit in the flat and yell at him all I want. "I'm driving a motorcycle now," I say. I am on video chat with Alex. Lately, I've taken to calling him just to wake him up. It is three in the morning his time. He has yet to complain about this, but I can see frustration in his eyes. He lifts his sleepy brows.

"A motorcycle?"

"A *motorino.*"

"A scooter? Like a Vespa?"

"I'm quite good."

"You bought one?"

"I'm renting one."

"Huh."

"Have you talked to Alexandria?"

"Lena."

"Have you?"

"I've tried. She's not talking to me."

"Why not?"

Alex sighs, wipes his eyes with his hands. It reminds me of a younger Alex, coming home from that first year of work, excited but exhausted. I wish I could go back to that time and say or do something different, so we wouldn't be here. "I might have come off a little harsh when I asked if she was really pregnant."

"Why? What did you say?"

"I said, 'Are you really pregnant?' "

I stifle the urge to laugh. Not because any of it is funny, but because I know his impatient tone very well, and I can imagine Alexandria wouldn't feel very welcomed by it.

"Listen. Coming home was the best thing I could have done. It's like I was under the influence—in Italy. The Alex in Florence was a totally different man. I'm ashamed. It's not Alexandria's fault either—it's all mine. And I decided. I will not continue the relationship. Even if—even if—I'll always have these feelings." He's still in love with her. No matter what I do, no matter how much time he's had to process it, no matter what the consequences. He is still in love with her.

"And the baby?'

"Are you sure she's pregnant?"

I sit back and look at him, really look at him, digesting his question and his tone. He knows Alexandria is devious. He knows. The very fact that he's asking me that question is proof. He is starting to see what she's really like. "No. But I'm going to find out."

Alex sits up straight, completely awake. "Don't," he says. "I don't know what you're thinking, but please. Just don't."

"On another note," I say, "Florence has been good for me."

"Good. I'm glad."

"Not that you're forgiven. But, now that I'm here, I don't feel like a married woman either."

"Okay." He sighs. He thinks I'm just doling out abuse, and he's trying to be the bigger person by not having an emotional reaction. I'm not going to let him get away that easy.

"Marco would rather have me than Alexandria. Isn't that ironic?"

"Are you sleeping with him?" It's his jealous voice. And there it is: Whether it matters or not, part of him still cares. I waver on answering.

"I came close."

"Lena. Please. Come home."

"I wanted to see if it was possible for a person to stop himself or herself. For a full mature person to be attracted to someone who is not his or her spouse, and then stop himself or herself. Guess what? It's possible."

"I'm sorry. I'm sorry. I'm sorry. I can't take it back."

"You've got that right."

"The kids miss you. They need their mother."

"Funny you should say that. They sound like they've been having a blast with you. Doing things I could never get you to do when we were a family."

"We're still a family, Lena. Please. Come home. I'll cut it off. Okay? If you stay away from Marco, and just come home, I'll never speak to her again. I swear."

I stand up. "You'll never speak to her again? She could be having your baby."

"What do you want me to do?" Alex stands up too. I've done it now; I've gotten to him. It doesn't feel as good as I thought it would. He's also on the verge of tears. He is not going to be a good parent if he's this messed up. I will have to stop these phone calls.

"Where's Stella?"

There is silence, as Alex just looks at me and shakes his head.

"They're all with your mother for a while," he says.

"What? When did that happen?"

"Yesterday."

"Thanks a lot for that by the way."

"You know your mother. I couldn't stop her."

"Why would Mom take Stella? She hates dogs."

"I just needed some time alone. To think."

"Unbelievable. I took care of them by myself for six months. And you can't handle—what? Forty-five days?"

"You dropped a bombshell on me, Lena. You think the thought of having a child right now doesn't scare the shit out of me?"

"You should have thought of that," I say. "You should have thought of a lot of things." I click off without saying good-bye. My small act of revenge. So Alexandria isn't talking to Alex. Exactly what is she up to? My little Vespa and I are going to find out. But first, I have another brilliant idea. And for this, I'm going to have to wake Megan.

I sit on my balcony with a bottle of wine, light a cigarette, and begin punching the calling card numbers into the phone. Megan answers on the third ring. "Thank God," I say. "I need you to do me a huge favor."

"Are you in danger?"

"No."

"It's three-thirty in the morning."

"I'm sorry, I'm sorry." I'm cracking up. Alex deserves to be woken at this hour; Megan does not. I honestly, completely forgot.

"Are you smoking?"

"Oh my God. How can you tell over the phone?"

"It's been twelve years since I quit, but I can hear a smoker a million miles away."

"I'm only smoking a few a day. On my balcony. With wine."

"It only takes a few to get hooked."

"My life is falling apart. Some days these few cigarettes and wine are the only things that keep me from jumping off this balcony."

"One crisis at a time. What's going on?

"I need a huge favor."

"Will it land me in prison?"

"If anything goes wrong, I won't mention your part in it."

"Lena, I was kidding. Wait. What are we talking about here?"

"I need you to go over to my house."

"Okay. Is something going on? Are the kids okay?"

"No, they're fine. Except that they're with my mother and Frank."

"You want me to break Alex's kneecaps?"

"Would you?"

"It would be my pleasure."

"I'll keep that in mind. No. I want you to try to get in when the house is empty. I keep a spare key in a fake rock by the front door."

"Really? People still use those?"

"It looks exactly like a rock. And I colored on it with chalk like it's something the kids picked up to play with."

"That's a nice touch."

"Once you're in, I need you to go into our bedroom."

"I'm liking this less and less."

"Alexandria and Alex are starting to have problems. Alexandria sounds like she's on the edge."

"Surprise, surprise."

"And I'm going to give her the push she needs to go over it."

"Are we talking a literal push here?"

"No. I need you to steal all of Alex's dirty underwear and mail it to me."

"Oh my God. No. No way. You're kidding, right?"

"And if there are any hairs around the sink, grab those too."

"I am going to give you the name of my therapist. She's pricey, but she knows her shit."

"Oh, and dirty socks too. Grab a few of those."

"The answer is no. You can hear me, right?"

"And if you happen to see his reading glasses lying near the couch somewhere, grab those too."

"You think she'll be disgusted by his reading glasses?"

"No. But he goes crazy when he can't find them. I mean like totally crazy. So the glasses are just for me."

"How much wine have you had?"

"I, in turn, am going to drop the little care package on Alexandria's doorstep."

"Okay, funny. Ha, ha."

"I'm deadly serious. I've washed his dirty socks and underwear, and cleaned up his little hairs around the sink and tub for sixteen years. She can do it once. See how romantic she feels toward my husband then."

"You are serious, aren't you?"

"Yep."

"Why don't I just send you some of Martin's, and you can pretend it's Alex's? His are nasty. I mean really, really—"

"She's been sleeping with him for months. I think she knows the real thing when she sees it. See? Even that thought is making me burn up. You have to do this for me. You have to." I exhale and watch curly wisps of smoke travel over the balcony rails and disappear. I crush the cigarette out on the bars and then toss it into a tin can I set on the table. Eight cigarette butts. Four days. I wasn't doing too badly. The wine bottles were a different matter. The last time I took them to the garbage, a neighbor was standing there. She started talking about what a wild party she once had. Cheated on, party of one, but the neighbor didn't need to know that. "Megan? Are you still there?"

"This is the most disgusting, horrible thing you've ever asked

of me. You want me to get on a plane, fly to your town, rent a
car, drive to your house, steal your husband's dirty socks and
underwear, check for hairs around the sink, then mail all of it
to you in Italy so you can drop it at his mistress's doorstep."

"You got it. And send it overnight. I'll send you a check."

"Lena, listen to me. You're in freaking Italy! Go shopping.
Go to a museum. Take the train to Rome or Venice. For God's
sake go out and pick up a hot Italian man, then screw his brains
out. I'm telling you. You have to stop thinking about that
woman!"

"I can't. Megan, you know me. I just can't."

"Why don't you explore the Tuscan countryside? Find an old
house to buy and renovate. Get a bicycle and an Asian best
friend. Remember how we loved *Under the Tuscan Sun*? And *Eat
Pray Love*? Your version is starting to sound like *Smoke, Drink,
Stalk,* and you need to stop it right now!"

"You have to do this for me. They are this close to totally losing it. It's my chance."

"You're the one who's losing it."

"I'll never, ever ask you anything ever again."

"Lena."

"I would do it for you. I would steal Martin's underwear right
off his body if you asked me to."

"Martin would be very turned on right now."

"Please. I'm begging you. I'm literally on my knees on my
balcony." I'm not, but what's a little exaggeration between
friends?

"I'm blogging about this."

"It would make a great blog! You'll get tons of new followers."

"Fine. But only because I sense what a fragile emotional state
you are in, and I do not want to be responsible for sending *you*
over the edge."

"Thanks, Megan. Don't forget to overnight it. I love you!" I
click off before Megan can change her mind.

CHAPTER 30

I have been lurking around for three days now, but still haven't spotted Alexandria around town. On the fourth day I am back at the open-air market when I spot Jean Harris. I've been dodging her dinner invitations, and I certainly don't want to get into it with her this morning. I duck behind a table of peaches. The next thing I know, Jean is standing over me.

"Lena?"

I look up from my crouched position and pretend to be surprised. "Jean. How are you?"

"What are you doing down there?"

"I dropped a peach." The fruit vendor, who is standing all the way over at the other end, suddenly materializes and with a frown begins surveying the ground for dropped fruit. "My mistake," I say, getting up and holding my hands up. "Not a peach to be found." The fruit vendor bares his teeth at me; he's missing the two middle ones.

"You buy?" The wind whistles through the gap as he speaks. *All I want for Christmas. . . .*

"Yes," I say. I grab a bag and start stuffing peaches into it.

"Are you making a cobbler?" Jean asks. She sounds amused.
"No, no. I just like peaches." Jean puts her hand on mine, then takes the bag of peaches and dumps them back into the bin. The vendor starts screaming in Italian, and the whistling picks up.

Jean speaks to him in Italian. Whatever she says calms him down. He waves us away. *"Grazie, grazie,"* Jean calls, hauling me in the other direction.

"What did you say to him?"

"I said you were a patient from a mental hospital and I had to get you back to the bus."

"You did not."

"You'll never know."

"Where are we going?"

"We're going for a walk."

"Right." I could make an excuse and leave, or heck, even outrun Jean, but part of me is relieved. I don't know what I would have done with all those peaches. I don't think I'm taking the news of this possible pregnancy very well. I have to find out, one way or the other. But for now, it's nice to see a familiar face. Jean is practically speed walking through the streets of Florence. Soon we are at a bus stop.

"Where are we going?"

"You'll see." We stay on the bus for four stops. "Here we are," Jean says as the bus pulls up to the Pitti Palace.

"I've taken the tour," I admit. "I don't think I'm up for it again today."

"We're going to the Boboli Gardens, darling," Jean says. "Just behind the palace."

The sixteenth century Italian gardens are just as beautiful on my second visit. Statues and shrubbery, and flowers, and manicured grounds, and fountains. A feeling of peace settles on me as I stroll. I wish I had a peach. After twenty minutes or so spent in silence, Jean sits on a bench.

"Are you going to tell me what's going on with you, or am I going to have to drag it out of you?" Jean says.

"What do you mean?"

"You've been seen lurking about town in one disguise after another."

"You can't possibly know that."

"You're a pretty blond woman making a scene trying to drive that scooter. Everybody knows."

"I'm getting better."

"What are you up to?"

"Just being a local."

"This wouldn't have anything to do with Alexandria, would it? She's stopped coming to work. So has Marco."

"You can't blame that on me."

"Oh, yes, I can. They never missed a day of work before you got here."

"Maybe Marco is off working on his chalk drawings."

"Another thing that you've ruined."

"I thought he was working on a new angle." Destroying every one of her pretty little faces.

"Nobody knows what he's doing. Nobody has seen him do anything lately except run around town with you."

"Jean. This is none of your business."

"I lied to you," Jean said.

"About what?"

"When Harold and I had only been married a couple of years, and I was pregnant with our first evil little gremlin, I came home to find the maid fellating my husband." I sputter, choking on my own saliva. "Didn't see that coming, did you?" Jean says. She pats me on the back. "Neither did I, my dear. Neither did I."

I might not have seen it coming, but I'm not surprised. Harold has "letch" written all over him. Alex doesn't. Alex was the nice one, the stable one, the boy who was kind to his mother. He doesn't tell dirty jokes in public like Harold does. He doesn't gawk at other women in public. He doesn't turn every comment into a suggestive romp. Still, none of that diminished Jean's pain. "That's awful," I say. "What did you do?"

"I turned the hose on them," Jean says. She puts her hand over her mouth and laughs.

"What?"

"They were on the back patio."

"Oh."

"Didn't even hear my approach."

"Ah."

"When the water hit her head—she bit down."

"No." I wouldn't have dared laugh, except Jean was laughing, and soon we are both cackling on the bench. I try not to glance at the statue next to me, whose penis is incredibly close.

"I had to drive him to the emergency room just so they could check it out."

"You did not."

"I did. She didn't bite through or anything, but there was blood."

"I can't believe you drove him."

"I can't either. But he was making such a racket. 'She bit me, she bit me, I'm bleeding, I'm bleeding.' The maid—or the girl I should say—she was Brazilian, ran out as fast as her feet could carry her. It was either drive him to the hospital or finish what she had started—and I don't mean the pleasurable part—so I drove."

"Wow."

"I know. I didn't go in with him. I threw him out at the emergency entrance and zoomed off. I got home, packed my bags, called a lawyer, and went to my mother's. In that order too."

"Good."

"I thought that was the end of my marriage for sure."

It would have been for me. "Why did you go back?"

"My mother had a long talk with me about men," Jean says. "Especially those who are about to become fathers. They're perpetual boys in a way. They never learn to tame the beast in their pants. Sometimes their urges just take over, and they do foolish things. Put themselves and everyone they love in jeopardy."

Especially those who are about to become fathers. Did she know some-

thing about Alexandria? "That sounds like a fancy way of saying 'Boys will be boys,' and, I'm sorry, but I don't subscribe to that. Women have just as many animal urges as men, and not all men act on theirs either. That's what separates us from the animals that walk on four legs; we're supposed to be able to control ourselves."

"Well, it would be nice, but come now, Lena, you live in the real world. Stress, distance, pressure, and—I'm sorry—I still think men are more easily distracted by their apparatus than we are by ours." She too glances at the statue. We both look at it for a minute. Such a small thing—relatively—to cause such big problems. "I'm not condoning the behavior," Jean continues. "I'm simply saying that it happens. A lot. It's not even whether or not it happens to you and your marriage; it's what you do about it that will dictate the rest of your life."

"I'm sure."

"And I didn't just take him back without any consequences. Nor did I go back right away. But we had a child coming, and we owed it to him to try and work it out."

Alexandria might have a child coming. So did he owe it to her to work it out?

If Jean had left Harold, I can only imagine the talk with her children when they were old enough to ask why their parents got divorced. You couldn't exactly look your child in the eye and say, "He asked the maid to give him a blowjob."

"I had my terms. He went to counseling. Then I went to counseling. Then we went to couple's counseling. I'm not even sure it was what mended us. All I knew was that Harold hated going to counseling, so I kept making him go. As far as I know, he's never touched another woman."

He just undresses all of us with his eyes. Heck, we're probably all giving him blowjobs in his imagination. "Well, I'm glad it worked out," I say.

"The best part is, he was so freaked out about being bitten, that ever since, the last thing that man ever wants is a blowjob."

"Sounds like a win, win." I want to stop imagining Harold and blowjobs.

"Oh, for heaven's sake, darling. Go home. To your husband. Your family."

"Did Alex call you?"

"No. Why?"

"Because he's jealous, that's why."

"Darling. Marco needs to get back to what he does best. Making art. Not love."

"I haven't even seen him lately."

"Well, neither has anyone else. And his gallery opening is only a few weeks away."

"Nothing happened. Exactly. And even if it did, it's over."

"Oh dear God. He's obsessive about love. I told you this! I warned you!"

"He's a grown man."

"If it's over, then what are you still doing here?"

"Alexandria might be pregnant."

"Oh dear God. No." She sounds genuinely shocked. "You think, or you know?"

"It's a possibility."

"I bet she's faking it. Just to yank his chain."

"I don't know. I've been trying to find out."

"That's what all the hats, and scarves, and sunglasses have been about?"

"Yes." That and hiding swollen, hungover eyes.

"And the scooter?"

"I thought it would be cool."

"Oh, honey. It's not." She pats my leg. "Let me talk to Alexandria."

"No. This is my fight. Mine."

"All right."

"I mean it."

"I said all right. Now will you lower your voice?"

"There is something you can do for me."

"Take you shopping?"

"No. Give me Alexandria's address." If only I had been paying close attention when I went to her home with Marco.

"Whatever for?"

"I'm going to go over there and get everything out in the open. Is she pregnant or is she not? She won't even return Alex's calls. I'm not going to let her run the show anymore."

"I don't think it's a good idea."

"It's either that or I follow her on my scooter."

Jean looks out into the distance, contemplating. "Okay. If you do something for me."

"What?"

"Do whatever you have to do to convince Marco that he must follow through with the art show. No matter what."

"Okay. If you do something for me."

"What? No. I'm already doing something for you. I do something, then you do something. That's how these things work. Now it should be the end of anybody's doing anything."

"Deal," I say. Besides, I'm so fixated on Alexandria, I've already forgotten what she asked me to do.

FIRENZE
MONTH THREE

Non perdere tempo su aspetti banali trascurando l'essenziale.

Catch not a shadow and lose the substance.

CHAPTER 31

The box is sitting in front of my flat. Megan has come through. I almost open it when I remember that whoever tears into it first gets the first whiff. I will leave it on Alexandria's doorstep untouched. I tie it to my back with a makeshift backpack. I also pad my hat for a fall before hopping on the Vespa. When I am three streets away from Nonna's apartment, I park the scooter. Partly because it is very loud and I don't want them to hear me coming; partly because I forgot to get gas.

I walk toward their building, and immediately spot Alexandria and her grandmother gardening in the little courtyard. They are watering flowers and chatting away in Italian. Alexandria is eating a loaf of Italian bread. Not as in a little piece dipped in oil, but holding one end of the huge loaf and biting on it. Are these pregnancy cravings or heartbreak?

What is the Italian word for pregnant? I should have learned it so I could listen for it. This language barrier is really getting to me.

A cat from inside the courtyard notices me and trots up the stairs to greet me. Soon he is rubbing his scrawny body along the fence near where I am hiding. I try to gently nudge it away with my foot. It starts to rub against my shoe. This is a very needy cat.

I glance at the fence, bracing myself. I remember Marco's warning about leaning against it. How he took a nasty fall once. *Make it look like an accident.* This is my chance. The fence rests at street level, but the courtyard is at least ten feet below. The box is strapped to my back. I am padded, but if I don't fall correctly, I could still hurt myself. It's worth the risk. I slip the box off my back and hold it against my chest like a shield. I press my backside against the fence. At first, nothing happens. I take a deep breath and really lean into it. I hear a creak, and then the fence starts to move. *Relax your body; tuck your neck.* I do not have to fake the scream as I go down. The cat yowls and leaps over me, flashing its orange tail and unsightly hole. It's every man and beast for himself. I hear a sickening thud as the back of my head slams against concrete. Luckily, my padding takes some of the blow. I am still holding the box, looking at the Tuscan sky. It is a pretty shade of blue. I don't move.

I hear footsteps. Suddenly two big eyes, a waterfall of hair, and a half loaf of bread stare down at me. Soon the grandmother joins Alexandria. Cosetti—staring party of two. I want to laugh, but my lips don't. Alexandria and her grandmother start talking to me at once. Spit and bread fly through the air. Alexandria is now waving the bread closer to my eyes. What is she doing? Playing "how many loaves am I holding up"?

"LENA," Alexandria says slowly.

Whore, I silently answer. The back of my head really hurts. Something went wrong. I might be really hurt here. That's not fair; I was trying to fake it. Someone is humming. *When the moon hits your eye like a big pizza pie . . .* It's me. I'm humming. *That's amore. . . .* Stop that. I don't even like that song. The grandmother is gone. Is she getting a shovel? Are they going to whack me and then bury me? The cat is back, sitting beside my head, licking himself. *Fuck you, kitty.* Alexandria is talking on a cell phone. I close my eyes.

"No, no, no," Alexandria says. "Open your eyes." I try, but

I'm too tired. *When the moon hits your eye.* That's dumb. When does the moon ever hit anyone's eye? *Like a big pizza pie?* When has a pizza pie ever hit anyone in the eye either? I'd like to throw a big pizza pie at Alexandria. Now that would be cause for a song. I reach up for the bread. It's gone. Who took the bread?

"Here, kitty, kitty." I'm lying in something sticky. Sticky, sticky, underneath my head. I fell down and lost my bread. How did I get here? Where did I park the wasp? Somebody's fingers are on my eyeballs, peeling my eyelids open. That's rude! I try to slap the hand away, but my hands won't move. I do, however, manage to open my eyes. Thank God, the fingers are gone.

Alexandria looks at the ground near my head. Her hand is over her mouth, her eyes wide with fear. I lift my hand and bring it to the back of my head where it hurts.

"No, no," Alexandria says, turning away. My hand is really sticky. Wow, they aren't kidding about the humidity around here. Hoomiditty! I look at my hand as Alexandria shrieks. Red. My fingers are red. I reach out to show Alexandria. The girl screams and jumps back. "I can't touch it. I don't like blood."

Blood? She doesn't like blood? Well, that's okay, who does? Is she already worried about childbirth? Bloody, painful child-birth? I hear a siren. So loud. So insistent. So close. I want to turn my head and look through the gap where the gate used to be, but I can't. The gate. I am lying on the gate. I brought it with me, fell on top of one of its iron spikes. Well, no wonder my head hurts. I guess I did not think this thing all the way through. "Don't move," Alexandria says. "They are coming. Don't move."

Who is coming? I hear two doors slam. Smell cigarette smoke. Two men stand over me in matching medical outfits. One finishes his cigarette and crushes it with his big boot. He says something in Italian.

"Inglese," Alexandria says.

Lena could speak for herself! *"No parle* Italiano," I say. Wait, that's French. *Dové.* That meant something. *Grazie! Scusi!*

Espresso! Mama Mia! Mama's boys! *"MAMMONIS,"* I shout at
the Italian EMTs.

"What happened?" one repeats in English.

My eyes flicker to Alexandria. Then to her stomach. I point
at her. "She tried to kill me," I say. Forget accident, I am going
for attempted murder. *J'accuse!* I hold up the box of Alex's dirty
underwear and socks. "That's for you," I say to Alexandria. I
feel dizzy. I don't like blood either. And then, everything goes
black.

When I open my eyes, I am lying in a hospital bed. This is one
part of Florence I didn't expect to see. It looks pretty much like
an American hospital except the little signs and posters hanging
on the wall are all in Italian. There is a bandage wrapped tightly
around my head. I lift my arm and run my fingertips over it.

"She's awake." I turn to find Rachel, Josh, and Alex sitting to
my right. My family! I smile and spread my arms. Rachel and
Josh come running. Alex lingers behind.

"Do you know who I am?" Rachel says.

"My obnoxious teenager daughter," I say.

"Mom." Rachel sobs into my shoulder. I rub her back.

"My God," I say. "Don't tell me I've been in a coma for six
years."

"Three days!" Rachel says. "You've been sleeping for three
days."

"They had you on a lot of pain medication," Alex says.

"Do you remember me?" Josh says, edging his way over.

"Hello, Joshua. Come here." He piles on top of Rachel.

"Not too rough now," Alex says. "Come on, that's good." He
gently lifts the children off me. He is so handsome. I look at
him and smile.

"Hey, baby," I say. His eyes widen. I used to call him "baby" all
the time. Until we had real babies, at which time I stopped.

"Lena?" he says.

"Kiss me," I say. He leans in and kisses my cheek. I grab his
face, turn him, and kiss him on the lips.

"Dad?" Rachel says. "I think she has amnesia." Alex pulls back.

"Why do you say that?" I say.

"What's the last thing you remember?" Alex says.

Once again, I touch my head lightly, fingering the bandage. "I don't remember how *this* happened," I say. "Did someone push me?"

Alex leans in and lowers his voice. "Is that what you think happened? Are you saying this was Alexandria?"

"Alexandria?" I say. "Who is Alexandria?" I keep smiling, and smiling, and waiting.

Alex frowns. He crosses his arms across his chest. He swallows. "What's the last thing you remember?"

"Let's see. Josh had a soccer game. He scored. Didn't you, Josh?"

"That's right! She's right, Dad. I did!"

"And he didn't want me to yell. But I did anyway."

"You can yell, Mom. I'm sorry," Josh says.

"That was months and months and months ago," Rachel says. "Before."

"Before what?" I say.

"Let me handle this, kids," Alex says. "Llama. Do you remember anything else?"

"The fountain. We met you there."

Alex looks at the ground for a moment before looking back at me. "Right," he says. "And?"

"Ammannati. I finally got to see it. I think it's beautiful. I think Michelangelo was just jealous."

"Okay." Alex's eyes flit around the room.

"Oh God. I remember lying on the ground near the fountain."

"Yes," Alex says.

"That's where I fell? At the fountain?"

"She doesn't remember, Dad," Rachel says.

"Do you remember big boobs?" Josh says.

"Josh," Alex says.

"What happened?"

"Rachel, will you go see if you can find a nurse?"

"Alex, you're scaring me. Are you angry with me?"

"No, of course not." He leans down. "I'm very sorry this happened to you," he says.

"What did happen?"

"I'd rather talk to a nurse first."

"I doubt the nurse was there when it happened," I say.

"She can tell me about your memory."

"I can tell you about my memory."

"And you don't remember anything after the fountain? Nothing at all?"

"Is that bad? How much time has passed since the fountain?"

"Three months."

"Three months?" I try to sit up. My head throbs. "I've been here three months?"

"Not in the hospital. In the hospital only a few days. You've been in Florence going on three months."

"You make it sound like I've been here by myself. Where are we staying?"

"One more thing. They said you didn't have ID. Or even a wallet. Didn't you replace your ID?"

"I don't know. Maybe. Did I lose it in—the incident?"

"The incident?"

"Yes. Whatever happened to me. Was I hit over the head by a robber?"

"A husband-stealer," Rachel says. She really is my daughter.

"Rachel," Alex says.

"Where are we staying?" I repeat.

"Right. Well, you see . . ."

"Mom," Josh says. "You're staying—"

"Shut up, dufus." Rachel quickly looks at me, and I blink rapidly.

"We're going to move to a bigger place," Alex says. "The last one was too small."

"I don't mind small. Cozy."

"It's just. Not where I want to take you."

"Definitely not," Rachel says. She squeezes my hand so hard, I am afraid it is going to break. "I'm glad you lost your mind, Mom."

"Rachel," Alex says.

"Mom lost her mind?" Josh says. He holds up three fingers. "How many fingers am I holding up?"

"Three dirty ones," I say. "I think you need a bath."

"We'd better let you get some rest," Alex says. "We'll find a place, and it will be ready to go by the time you are. Do you mind if I look through your purse for the key to the old flat? I can pick up your things."

"Don't you have a key?"

"Of course. But I'll turn them all back over to the university when they secure our new place."

"Of course." I smile at Alex as he goes through my purse, then holds up the key. "Wait," I say as they are at the door. "What about work?"

"Work?" Alex says.

"Who's been teaching while you've been here—and with the kids?"

"They found a replacement for the summer."

"I'm so sorry."

"Please, don't apologize, Lena. Ever."

"Aren't you guys forgetting something?" I hold my arms out. The kids run up, hug me, kiss me. Alex lingers behind. I beckon him with a finger, and he approaches. I reach up and touch his cheek. It feels so soft and good underneath my hand. Alex grips my hand. Tears fill his eyes.

"I'm sorry," he says.

"What for?"

"Everything."

"I'm okay now. You guys are here, and healthy. We're a family. Nothing else matters, right?"

"Right." Alex can barely speak.

"Go on now," I say. My family. I watch them leave. God, my head hurts. I wonder if it's from all the lying. I wonder if the people who throw fake babies get massive headaches. And I really wonder, now that I have my family back, why I keep looking at the door and waiting for Marco.

CHAPTER 32

Here it is. My do-over. I've won. Our new apartment isn't glamorous by any means. Cream-tiled floors that I wouldn't want to clean full time. A small kitchen separated from the living room by a rod and a curtain, sparse but clean furnishings, and four separate bedrooms. Did Alex purposefully look for a place with four bedrooms or am I being paranoid? Each room is so small it can barely fit more than one person. But we are back to being a family, a unit. Alexandria has been wedged out. I used to believe that intentions mattered more than anything. I was wrong. Intentions are nothing without action. I did what I had to do for my family. I took action. Should I insist Alex and I share a room? If I truly had amnesia, I'd be horrified at the thought that we were sleeping in separate bedrooms. I should stick to the part; we should even make love.

But I don't have amnesia, and this isn't a romantic space. Although there was a time when Alex and I would have loved this tiny space, wanting nothing between us. Here I was still being faithful to him, a man who apparently no longer wants to share a little bed with me, or any bed at all.

"I thought you might like some recovery space," Alex says, watching me stand in the doorway and take in the bedroom situation.

"Are you crazy?" I say. I smile and walk toward him. He doesn't move to greet me, but he doesn't back away either. I have him very confused. Maybe he's afraid of going along with me, only to suddenly have me get my memory back. Standing here, smelling his cologne, being so close, close enough to touch, I want to cry. "I want to sleep with you." I say it with as much flirtation as I can muster. I listen to my own words as if they were uttered by a stranger. Do I sound sincere? Seductive? Am I sincere? Do I really want to sleep with Alex? Could I do it without grabbing a pair of scissors from the side table and plunging them into his back?

"Let's just put your stuff in here for now," Alex says. "And I'll put mine in the one down the hall. They just didn't make these rooms very big, did they?" And with a nervous laugh, he and his suitcases are out of my room. He doesn't want me. Even with a "do-over," he doesn't want me. *We don't paint love. Love paints us.* Damn you, Marco. I wonder where he is, if he heard about my accident, if he knows Alex and the kids are back in Florence. I kick my suitcase, then walk out into the living room/kitchen combo and take a deep breath. Josh walks in little circles in the living room, staring at the spot where there should be a television.

"When are we going home?" Josh says.

I smooth back my son's hair, grateful he is still at an age where he lets me touch him.

"We have Xbox at home, Mom. Do you remember what Xbox is?"

"Of course, Josh. Honey, it's only a few months of memories that I've lost. Everything else is still up here." I tap my head and grin. Rachel walks into the room wearing her red tube top as a dress again. "For example," I continue, without turning to look at her, "I remember telling Rachel there was no way she was ever wearing that dress in public."

"We're not in public," Rachel says. "We're in Italy."

"Fine," I say. "If your father approves, then I approve."

"Mom!"

"Or you can just stay inside the apartment all day."

"It's tiny."

"Well, lucky for us, the outdoors is very, very big." Alex comes in from outside. I can't be sure, but I get the feeling he's been on his cell phone. Was he talking to Alexandria? He rubs his hands and looks at me. I know that look. It's the one I see every time he has something to tell me that I'm not going to like.

"Lena."

"Yes?"

"We have to go to the police station."

"What for?"

"You accused a girl of hurting you. They're thinking of pressing charges."

She did hurt me. She hurt me more than I could have possibly imagined. This is my chance to have Alexandria put away for a long time. "Do they have her in custody?"

"No. But they're questioning her. They need to talk to you before they can clear her."

"I don't remember anything."

"Tell them that."

"Do I have to?"

"I don't think we want to get off on the wrong foot with the Italian police."

"What if she did hurt me?"

"The facts don't support it. It seems you were—leaning on an unstable fence."

"Why would I do that?"

"I really wish I knew."

"I don't mean why was I leaning on the fence. Why was I at this Alexandria's home? I must have known her somehow."

"We'll drop the kids off with Harold and Jean—"

"No. I want to stay together. As a family." I'm terrified of letting anyone out of my sight now.

"Okay then. We'll all go to the police station," Alex says. Rachel is eyeing us.

"Dad," she says. "Don't you think you should tell her?" She looks so worried. I don't want my daughter stuck in the middle of this. But if I suddenly get my memory back, it could ruin my chance to put things back together with Alex, which is for the greater good of the family.

"Tell me what?" I say. Alex looks like a child squirming in his seat.

"Look. Rachel. Lena."

"What about me?" Josh pipes up from the raggedy couch in the living room.

"You too, buddy." Alex turns to me. "Rachel thinks I ought to help you fill in your memory gaps. But the doctor suggested we wait and see if it comes back naturally. What do you want me to do?"

"I'm just confused," I say.

"I know. I don't want to add to that," Alex says.

"Am I in any danger?"

"What do you mean?"

"This woman. Has she been trying to harm me?"

"No," Alex says.

"That's not true!" Rachel says. "Dad you know that's not true."

"Rachel," I say. "Please don't get worked up. I trust your Dad to handle this." I go over, rub her shoulders, and lean down.

"Trust me," I whisper. She looks at me, wide-eyed, then as understanding seems to creep in, she nods.

"Let's follow the doctor's orders," I say. "I trust you."

"Can I wear this dress out, Dad?" Rachel says. "Mom said it's okay if you say it's okay."

"That was not what I meant," I say.

"It's what you said. Can I, Dad?" Rachel looks at him triumphantly. She's playing both of us.

"I guess I'll leave the fashion up to you girls," Alex says.

"Yes!" Rachel says.

"What?" I say. "No. No, you can't wear that. Alex, she looks like a prostitute. She's our child."

"I agree. I just—can't fight with her anymore. All she does is argue and whine and cry."

"I do not!" Rachel says. Her eyes fill with tears. "That's not fair." She whirls around, storms into her room, and slams the door.

"She's going through a hard time," I say. "It seems as if we all are."

"That's an understatement."

"Teenage years aren't going to be easy. But at least we can see the light at the end of the tunnel. God, can you imagine starting all over right now?" It slips easily out of me, and I purposefully keep my voice light and playful.

"It is hard to imagine, isn't it?" Alex says. He looks pained. I've hit my mark, but take no pride in it.

"That doesn't mean we can't practice," I say. My voice is a whisper, and I run my finger up his arm. "Maybe tonight?"

He hesitates. Swallows. Smiles. "I don't want to rush anything," he says. "You're still healing."

I nod as if it makes perfect sense. Rachel changes her clothes, and we walk to the police station as a family. I realize, as we travel in silence, that it's been a long time since anything in my life made any sense at all, let alone perfect.

"You have no charges to bring against Alexandria Cosetti?" The kids are out in the lobby of the station. Alex and I sit across from Alexandria and a uniformed officer. I study Alexandria before I answer.

She slept with my husband. She schemed to get pregnant. She ruined my life. She stole everything from me. "I can't remember what happened," I say. "So, no. Nothing for now."

"You fell. I didn't do anything."

The officer slides a piece of paper toward me. "If you decide to file charges, you have thirty days. You will need to fill this out. For now, we are dismissed."

"Can I have a word with this woman alone?" I say.

"Lena?" Alex says.

"It's okay," I say. "I just have a few questions for her. If she doesn't mind."

Alexandria looks at Alex for an answer.

The officer stands. "The room is yours, signorina, signora," he says. God, I want to kill him.

"I'll stay," Alex says. He nods to Alexandria. I put my hand on his.

"It's girl talk," I say.

"Do you remember something?" Alex says.

"Just fragments. Is there a problem with speaking with her alone?"

"No, no," Alex says. "I'll give you guys a minute." He goes to the door, then looks back. "I'll be right outside," he says. He starts to say it to me, but he glances at Alexandria before he finishes. Which one of us does he intend on being there for? I guess I wouldn't have to have this conversation with her if I knew. I'm starting to suspect that even he doesn't know.

For a long time, I just look at her. It makes her squirm. She does not seem like the cocky girl who was on my computer screen all those months ago.

"Just because I didn't file charges today, doesn't mean I'm not weighing my options," I say.

"You fell. I didn't even know you were there. I am the one who should be charging you with stalking me."

"Perhaps. But if you did that, then all the dirty details of your sleeping with an older, married professor will come out."

"You didn't lose your memory."

"No, I certainly didn't, although for the past several months, I've wished for nothing else."

Alexandria stands. "I'm going to tell Alex."

I rise too. "If you do, I will press charges so fast it will make your head spin."

"Go ahead. I didn't do anything."

"You didn't do anything? You destroyed a family. You caused

me pain I wouldn't wish on my worst enemy. Which, ironically means I wouldn't wish it on you. You hurt my children—"

"I didn't mean to hurt anyone! I fell in love."

"You purposefully wanted me to see you and Alex together. Without his knowledge. That is not love, my dear. That is pure evil."

"I was drunk. I am not a bad person! You see me. If I'm so bad, why does Alex love me?"

"Why, indeed. Your reign of terror is over, Alexandria. You are going to back off and let me try and save my family. You are going to cut all ties to Alex. If he tries to contact you, you are going to tell him it's over and that you never want to speak to him again."

"No. I cannot do this."

"Then I file charges. I would give it some thought if I were you. I don't think the university want the publicity of an American wife being attacked by her husband's mistress, do you? I would think they would want to make an example of the mistress."

"I am Italian. You are not. Plus I work for them. The university will be on my side."

"Maybe. But maybe not. After all, you are the same woman who broke Marco Giovatti's heart. Once they find out why— and with whom—do you really think anyone won't believe that you would want to hurt me?"

"I'm pregnant. You can't let Alex walk away from his own baby!"

"If you are pregnant—and don't think I will just take your word for it—we will need a paternity test. Then we will work out some kind of custody agreement."

"No. Never."

"Suit yourself. It will be up to you."

"Alex won't leave me."

"Oh, but he already has, Alexandria. And as long as you play your part, it's going to stay that way."

She looks at the ground. Her eyes are filled with tears. I wait for a few minutes to see if I feel anything at all. Any pity, or even rage. But I am empty. And I am done. I get up and start to walk out.

"He loves you," she says. I turn. It's not something I would expect her to say. I wonder what her angle is.

"He's my husband," I say. A sad little smile plays across her face, and she shakes her head.

"Marco," she says. "I was talking about Marco."

Alex waits for me outside. He is holding a bag and looks totally perplexed. "What's wrong?" I say.

"Alexandria's grandmother just handed this to me," he says. He reaches into the bag and holds up a pair of his underwear. They are folded, and bright, and look suspiciously ironed.

Damn. I never should have underestimated Nonna.

CHAPTER 33

Alex insists on taking me on a date. He's booked us all on a flight home for one week from now. Jean and Harold take the kids. Marco has called me a few times, but I haven't answered. That isn't easy, and just that fact bothers me. I should be thrilled to be back with my husband. I should not be tempted to take Marco's calls or feel guilty that I haven't. I'm sure Alexandria will fill him in. But I do have to tell Alex I have my memory back. We can't begin a new chapter of our lives with lies. But surely, he can forgive me this, if I'm willing to forgive his affair?

But am I willing to forgive it? Do I really want to do this? I've been so focused on revenge, on winning, that I don't know why I don't feel any joy. It must be all the lying. I will tell him tonight, and once things are out in the open, we can go back to being Alex and Lena, Professor and Llama, yet a better, stronger version of ourselves, for there must be something gained for all this pain. Tonight I will settle for a date with my husband in Florence.

* * *

I wear the dress I bought here, the one that Marco loved. I must remind myself not to connect every little thing to him. Of course it's natural; he's the one I spent time with while I was here. It's normal to be having such thoughts. I did not cheat. But I came close. Does coming clean with Alex mean telling him the truth about Marco as well? How did I become the one with sins to confess? Maybe I should wait until we are back home, until things feel normal again between us, and then get my memory back. No, I will face this, like a Viking.

I let Alex pick the restaurant, although I imagine the two of us on the patio, the same one where I had my first meal, okay, yes, with Marco, but it's Alex I am imagining myself there with. Maybe I just want to replace all the memories with him, starting with the first one. Alex and I do not hold hands as we walk down the streets, but he is talking to me, giving me the history of something, I'm not sure what, because I realize I have not been listening.

"Should we find a place with a nice private patio?" I say.

"I'd much rather eat inside. Wouldn't you?"

"Oh. I just thought—it's just so pretty out here."

"Yes, but it can get buggy outside."

It wasn't buggy with Marco. It was a beautiful, clear night. One of the best I've had in a long, long time. "I guess that's true."

"I know some places with great little interiors. You'll love them."

"Sure." Has he always done this? Blown right past my excitement and just decided for us? My God, I think he always has. I've just never really noticed. I don't want to go anywhere he's been with Alexandria, but I can't tell him this because I haven't confessed yet. Maybe I should do it now, but I'm thinking it will be easier with wine.

"See the cornice of that building?" I look to where he's pointing. It looks like an angel playing a trumpet.

"Beautiful," I say.

"Well, yes, but it's so much more. That corner represents the rise of man, but if we were to walk to the other side of the building—"

"Alex." I stop. He stops too, but looks confused. "Can you please not go into professor mode?"

"Sorry."

"No. I mean I love how smart you are. But I miss you. And I just want to spend this evening enjoying ourselves."

"This is me enjoying myself."

"Right. Just don't want you to feel like you're at work or anything."

"Not at all. Now do you see the etching above the statue?"

"Sorry. Did you not hear what I just said?"

"I told you. I don't feel like I'm at work."

"Okay, but I feel like I'm a student. And I just want to feel like we're on a date."

"I'm sorry. I didn't realize."

"I just want to talk about us. No statues tonight."

"Got it." We stand still, so I move in and kiss him. It feels strange, as if there is something wrong with my kissing Alex, as if I'm not supposed to. This is all Alexandria's fault. She is the reason kissing my husband feels like something I'm not supposed to be doing. His lips are cold and unresponsive. I want to throw him over the bridge. I'm surprised he didn't suggest a walk along it; it's so beautiful at night. He's sulking too, because he didn't get to finish his lecture. There's always been this aspect about him, a bit of a boyish reaction when he feels slighted.

We eat inside. The restaurant he chooses is bright and lively. There are no hidden corners, no flickering candles on the table, no fountains spewing love.

"This is a great family place," Alex says. He is right except we are missing the rest of our family. Did he come here with Alexandria, her grandparents, and the bookend uncles?

"I'm going to have to call Mom and see how Stella is doing," I say.

"What, now?" Alex sounds extremely alarmed. Maybe I've

been reading him wrong, maybe he does want to spend time with me. I'm sure we're here because of how amazing the food is. Alex never was one to think of candlelight and romance. Marco was more of a romantic—

"I see how Florence puts you under a spell," I say after we have been poured wine. I asked if we were going to have the four-course dinner, but Alex said a plate of pasta and a salad here is filling enough. I smile and nod, and I'm sure he's right. That's when it hits me. I'm still searching for the honeymoon we never had. Alex reaches into his pocket and checks his phone. Then shoves it back in. I wonder if he's checking to see if she's called. Alex taking calls from his mistress was never part of my honeymoon fantasy. Just what are we even doing here? I wonder if Alexandria is sticking to our agreement.

"Is it her?" I say.

"Who?"

"You know who."

He frowns. "Do you remember something?"

"I have to tell you something." Alex looks at me, waits. "We're only married because I chased you."

"You did not. I was the one who pursued you."

"No. You only think you did. It was part of my nine-point plan."

"Lena, what are you talking about?"

"I had a nine-point plan to win your heart." I laugh, remembering it, and start to go down the list. Alex reaches over the table and takes my hand.

"You didn't need a plan. I was crazy in love with you the minute you stepped into the auditorium."

"You didn't even notice me."

"Like hell I didn't."

"You didn't look my way. Not once."

"Of course I didn't. It was my first week as a TA. I couldn't concentrate if I looked at you. You stand out from a crowd. You always have."

I laugh. I certainly stood out here when I was throwing

gelato on Alexandria, or letting Stella pee in the fountain, or throwing spaghetti and meatballs on the wall.

"What's so funny?"

"Just thinking of all the crazy things Florence can make you do." Alex is smiling even though he doesn't have a clue as to the crazy things I've done, and I'm just looking at him, because I know all of his. After a minute, his smile fades as we continue to stare at each other across the table.

"You remember," he says softly.

"I never forgot," I say.

The food has arrived. It's horrible timing. I should have waited. Alex smiles and chats with the waiter in Italian, and I feel left out. This is a family place. The portions are huge. We should have the kids here. We should feel something other than this bitter divide between us. He hasn't even commented on my dress.

"Can we eat?" Alex says. "Or do we need to talk about this right now?"

"Let's eat," I say. He's angry.

"This is so simple, but delicious," he says, waiting for me to take a bite. And so I do. It does taste simple; I will give him that. "Well?"

"Mmm," I say.

"I knew it," Alex says. He begins to eat, and we settle into silence. I put my fork down.

"I made you Spaghetti Bolognese," I say.

"What?"

"The day you were supposed to come home. I was making Spaghetti Bolognese, and I hung a 'welcome home Alex' banner. It was in Italian too."

"I know," Alex says. He sounds appropriately mortified.

"You know?"

"The banner was still hanging when we went home." He's tearing up now, and it's not what I meant to happen.

"You're lucky I dumped the spaghetti," I say. We both laugh.

I think it's the first time we've laughed comfortably together since this started.

"You were faking amnesia?" he says. The mood is gone.

"I was," I say.

"Why? You had us so worried. I was blaming myself—"

"You should." It comes out harsher than I meant it. All these best-laid plans, all the times I practiced having conversations with him in my head, and it never turns out the way I expect.

"You faked amnesia to punish me?"

"No. I wanted to see. Never mind."

"Llama."

"Don't call me that."

"I thought you liked it."

"When we were in love I liked it."

"Okay." He continues to eat. I can't believe he can still eat. Why do I feel a storm brewing? Why do I feel as if I'm about to start another huge fight? Because I am not over this, and I don't know if I ever will be.

"Okay? That's it?"

"No, there's more, but I can't really say what I feel, now can I?"

"What do you mean?"

"I mean everything I say is moot. Because all you're thinking is, Alex is a cheater. And no matter what legitimate gripes I have, from here on out, those gripes will always be crushed by that hideous, irrefutable fact. I cheated on you. I cheated on the kids. I broke our marriage vows. And I'm never going to stop paying for it." I stare, open-mouthed. He resumes eating again as I simply watch him. "Tell me I'm wrong," he says.

"You might be right."

He laughs, nods his head, then shakes it. "I'm right," he says.

"Okay. Then for a brief moment, why don't I promise to suspend that little factoid so you can tell me what you were going to say."

"You swear?"

"I swear."

"I know what I did was unforgivable. So this is not an excuse. But I think you stopped loving me a long time ago."

"That's not true." Is it?

"I saw it again tonight. You didn't even want to listen to me talk about the buildings."

"You weren't talking, Alex. You were lecturing."

"There's no difference. It's who I am."

"But every couple gets on each other's nerves."

"True. But I didn't remember how it felt to be with someone who was really interested in me again, until I starting hanging around with Alexandria."

Like me with Marco. "You should have talked to me about it instead of sleeping with her."

"I know."

She's going to get sick of you too, eventually. I don't say it. Because what if I'm wrong? Doesn't he deserve to be with someone who doesn't roll her eyes at every statement he makes? And don't I deserve to be with someone who likes my passion? Encourages me to throw spaghetti and meatballs in public?

"What else?" I say.

"How could you make me think you had lost your memory? Do you have any idea how worried I was?"

I want to bite back—I have a million retorts. He is right. There is enough gas generated by his infidelity to drive to the ends of the earth and back. But I did promise. I suck it in. "I was only thinking that I wanted one more chance to remember what it felt like."

Alex stops. Waits. When I don't speak, he takes my hands from across the table. "Remember what *what* felt like?" He is speaking softly, gently.

"Us. Even if it was all pretend. I woke up in that hospital and, for a brief, glorious second, I forgot." It is hard for me to speak, because now I'm crying. "I looked over and saw my little family. And there was this rush of joy before I remembered. And it's not like it was a devious plan. I just wanted to go back to forgetting." I hang my head and sob. Alex usually hates any outburst in public, but I'm not going to be able to stop. He pushes his plate away too, then comes over, pulls out the chair next to me, and pulls me into him as I cry. He holds me, kisses the top of my head.

"I'm sorry," he says. "I would take it all back. If I could. I would take every single second of it back."

"I know," I say. And I do.

"Can I say one more thing?" he asks when I'm a bit more under control. I nod into his chest. "You look smoking in that dress."

CHAPTER 34

There are four days left. Jean and Harold are throwing us a good-bye party. We've been doing touristy things with the children and being super polite to each other. We're still not sleeping in the same bed. We don't want to rush anything, or confuse the kids, and the truth is the beds are really too tiny to do anything in them anyway. As soon as I have the thought, I imagine myself in one of the beds with Marco, and suddenly it doesn't seem small enough. I have to stop doing that, and I never did confess to Alex, but I figure it's natural; it's just me working out my anger over the affair. I am only human, and forgiveness is not going to come overnight. At least I'm no longer purposefully throwing it in his face.

We take a family trip to a nearby indoor food market to buy supplies for the party. I notice Rachel and Josh having a private talk next to a shelf of nuts. Rachel seems nurturing. Maybe something good has come out of this. Unless they're planning the destruction of the world. I sidle up to them and put my arms around them.

"What are you two talking about?"

"We want to see Stella," Josh says. Rachel elbows him.

"OW. MOM!" Ah, one step back.

"Rachel." I turn to Josh. "We'll see her soon," I say.

"Today?"

"No. We're going home in four days."

"But why can't we—"

"Josh," Rachel says. It has the tone of "dufus," but it is an improvement, so I let it slide.

"What's going on?" I say. Alex comes up. He puts a big smile on his face, but I can see the exhaustion and strain underneath. Maybe we should forget our last four days in Florence and just go home. I miss Stella too.

"I want to see Stella," Josh says. Alex's face does a weird contortion. I get the same feeling I got when I saw the roses from Alex and heard my mother's warning about men sending flowers.

"Alex," I say. "Where is Stella?"

"She's with a lady from the university," Alex says.

"Not with my mom?"

"She's here," Alex says. "In Florence."

"You didn't take Stella home with you?" I'm raising my voice. I cannot believe this. First, I would have wanted her if I had known she was here. Why didn't he tell me? What if something has happened to her?

"She's fine," Alex says.

"Why didn't you tell me?"

"I didn't want to upset you."

"Well, I am upset. Why did you just abandon her here?"

"She's with a great family."

"She already has a great family!"

"Do you know how much it costs to fly a dog?"

"As a matter of fact, I do!" We're both raising our voices now, and several people are looking our way. The bell above the door jingles, and Jean and Harold breeze in with their children. I realize, right here and now, I am never going to learn their names, and I don't care. Jean and Harold have an entire day of bonding and sightseeing planned. "We get Stella tonight,"

I say. "We bring her back to the flat, and we never, ever, leave her again.

"Okay," Alex says.

"Yes!" Josh says.

"I told him to tell you," Rachel says. She is worried. Every time Alex and I fight, she is going to be super worried.

"It's okay. Your Dad and I will get mad at each other sometimes. We'll work it out." I sound more mature than I feel. Right now all I want to do is get that adorable dog and disappear. Stella here all this time. I could have introduced her to Marco. There I go again. It's natural. Alex lied to me again. How was I ever going to be able to trust him if he didn't stop lying? As we weave around the store, following Jean and Harold and their gang, I pull up to Alex.

"Is there anything else?"

"What?"

"Anything else you're not telling me. Anything?" He shakes his head. "I mean it, Alex."

"No. Lena, there's nothing. And Stella has been perfectly taken care of—"

"Later," I say, because we're in public, and I can't think about the fact that he left Stella here without telling me. Besides—he was supposed to get a full dose of what it was like for me those six months and that included cleaning up dog pee. So that's why they said Stella didn't pee in the house once. Rachel, always skirting the truth, lacing it with sarcasm. She is going to be a handful these teenage years. I have to stay with Alex; I'm going to need support. That's what a marriage is. A support system for the family. Even if we're not the same couple as we were before Florence. He is my husband. He is back. And it's natural that we aren't very comfortable with each other right now. It will take time.

"Lena," Jean says, getting me alone. "You have to see the size of the salami in here. Size does matter, doesn't it?" I laugh. I never realized Jean can be just as raunchy as Harold. I allow her to guide me around the market. I'm going to miss this. Salami and other meats hanging from the ceiling, refrigerated displays stacked with hundreds of varieties of cheeses, shelves of olive oils, vinegars, spices, and candies, pastas in all shapes and sizes, and of course all the touristy items: a chocolate Duomo, a tin of the Giotto tower, and a licorice replica of the Piazza della Signoria, complete with a candied clock in the tower.

"I think we've lost them," Jean says. "Now I can tell you."

"Tell me what?"

"She's not doing well," Jean whispers into my ear.

"Who?"

"Little Miss Husband-Stealer."

"What do you mean?"

"Seems she's on a hunger strike. Can you imagine? With an Italian grandmother?"

A hunger strike? But what about the baby? There probably is no baby. This is just another Alexandria trick. That girl is diabolical. I am not going to fall for it. What is Jean even thinking, mentioning that girl to me? "Why are you telling me this?"

"I thought you'd be happy."

"Happy to hear about a pregnant young girl on a hunger strike?"

"You don't have to snap at me."

"Jean, why would that possibly make me happy?"

"Oh, she'll be fine. Marco is taking care of her." She eyes me now. There's almost a glint in her eyes. I feel a hollow spot in my stomach open up and start sucking all of the energy out of me. "I think they're back together," she says.

"Then why isn't she eating?"

"Who knows? I'm sure, with enough time around that hunk, her appetite will come back." This is how Jean has put up with Harold's crudeness all these years, I think. She lets her poison seep out everywhere else.

Josh appears behind us. "Can I have some candy, Mom?" he says. Yes, I think. My children deserve candy. We've been through so much. Is it ever going to stop? We deserve all the candy in the store. "Yes! Basket!" I say to Josh. For once he does what I say on the first try. I scoop up the chocolate Duomo, and the licorice tower, and the Giotto. I grab the biggest salami I can because size does matter, and have to slam it in the basket to shame myself for thinking of Marco, wondering what size his penis is, how it would have felt to make love to such a passionate man. We have to get out of Florence. Cheese. I need cheese. You have no idea how much cheese a person might need. What happens when we're home and I long for cheese and there is none except for crappy American cheese? I grab hunks and hunks of cheese.

"Lena?" Jean says.

"Wow," Josh says.

"Throw whatever you want in the basket," I tell him. Josh starts to take off. Alex is here, and he gently stops Josh.

"What are you doing?" he says to me.

"We've had a rough few months. We deserve it."

"Josh is a total weirdo on sugar," Rachel says.

"I am not," Josh says. "Am I?"

"All kids are," I say. "It's okay. It's okay to be a little weird. Besides, it's for our going-away party. Rachel, why don't you pick some things out as well?"

"What about the red dress?"

"Nice try." I continue throughout the store with my basket, throwing items inside. The gorgeous bottle of olive oil. The giant loaf of bread, a nice bottle of wine, along with an opener. A jar of olives. Marinated since the fourteenth century for all I know.

"Lena, can we talk about this?" Alex says. I feel a little feverish, but I also have this compulsion to keep filling the basket. It needs to be heavier. I'd rather carry physical weight than any more of this pain. If, in this moment, filling the basket makes me happy, I am going to fill the basket. Alex tries to take it from me, but I'm not done. Look at those cute little candles and tins. The basket is overflowing. I need two hands to carry it. I look back to see Josh and Rachel, and Alex, and Jean and Harold, and their children—what are their names?—staring at me.

"It's okay, Mom," Josh says. "I don't need candy." I suddenly see myself through their eyes. I'm crazy. I'm losing it. I'm not fit to be a mother. I set the basket down. Alex nods and steers me away from it, as if it's a bomb.

"We'll get candy later," I say. "The line is just too long."

It should feel good to be outside, in the sun, with my family. I wonder if I should tell Alex about Alexandria's hunger strike. *Marco is taking care of her.* Jean suggests we make our way to the Giotto tower. I can't help but be annoyed that Alex is purposefully walking up ahead with Harold. The kids travel in a pack like wild dogs, and Jean hangs back with me. I wish I could tell her to go away. I hope Marco knows I am only doing what I have to do. Right?

As Jean chats away, I realize I haven't heard a single word. There is a line to get up to the Giotto tower, but it isn't as long as the line to the Duomo. A tour guide speaks to a small group. I blend in so I can listen. He is explaining that it's 414 steps up to the campanile, or bell tower. He is full of energy and handsome, like Marco, and has a nice, bright voice.

"The tower is 84.70 meters high, sustained by four polygonal buttresses, one at each corner. If you look up at the building you'll notice how its four vertical lines are intersected by four horizontal lines, dividing this tower into five sections. Also, take note of the polychrome marble encrustations, and the statues built into the niches. Four in each direction: north, south, east, west. Giotto's tower rises in an angular, octagonal shape, running the whole way up, giving this building a considerable feeling of continuity."

That's what I want, I think. *A considerable feeling of continuity.* The kids complain that the line is too long, but I for one am going up. Jean and Harold give in to the whining brood, and that leaves Alex and me. He says he wants to go up too. I almost tell him that he doesn't have to do it just for me, but in the end, I simply let it be.

"We'll take the kids to get gelato," Jean says. "Just give us a text when you're down."

Up, and up, and up, and up we climb, stopping only briefly at several vantage points along the way. Alex seems to want to linger, as if he has something he wants to say, but I forge forward, because if I speak to him I'm going to have to tell him that his mistress is on a hunger strike. I am winded, but triumphant when I reach the top. It is glorious, another 360-degree view of Florence. Wave after wave of terra-cotta roofs. Undulating hills, the hazy blue and white sky, the domes and spirals. I feast on it all, trying to forget my life, just for a few seconds, when I feel arms slip around my waist.

"Incredible, isn't it?" He is touching me. He is whispering in my ear. He is acting like my husband. Can we do this? Can we make this work? Bridge the secrets that lie between us?

"I kissed Marco," I say. "Several times." His hands fall from my waist. He leans against the wall of the tower. I imagine it falling over, taking us both with it.

"And?" he says.

"And I just thought you should know."

"I see."

"I didn't sleep with him. But I came close."

"To punish me?"

"At first," I say.

"What does that mean?"

"It means . . . Look. He was there for me."

"Oh, I'm sure he was."

"It wasn't like that. He was hurting too."

"I told you to stay away from him."

"You can't tell me what to do."

"He's unstable."

"We're all unstable."

"Why are you telling me this now?"

"Because I'm sick of the secrets. If we're going to make this work—"

Alex grabs my hand. "We have to stop saying things like that," he says.

"Like what?"

"Like 'if.' We have to decide. This is happening. We are going to make our marriage work. No matter what."

Technology forcing, I think, looking at the Duomo. It worked for the church, but what will it do to us?

"Alexandria's on a hunger strike," I say.

"What?"

"Alexandria. She's gone on a hunger strike. Maybe you should check on her." Alex runs his fingers through his hair, turns away from me. Suddenly, he's back with an intensity I haven't seen in my husband in a long time. "Is this a test?"

"What?"

"I don't know what to do. You told me to stop seeing her, speaking to her."

"It's not a test. If she's truly carrying your baby, and on a hunger strike, I think you should know. That's all."

"Then come with me."

"Hell, no."

"Okay. Then I'll have Harold come with me."

"Do what you have to do," I say.

"I want to hit Marco. Can I hit Marco?" I stop and turn around. Alex stops short of running into me.

"Funny," I say. "Once upon a time I stopped him from killing you. So, no. You can't hit him. Let's just call it even."

"Even?" Alex calls after me as I start down the stairs. "Him wanting to kill me and me wanting to hit him? You call that even?"

"It is," I yell back. "Because I don't want to hit Marco. But I wanted to kill you too."

CHAPTER 35

We are together, my little family, on the sofa. Rachel to one
side of me, Josh to the other, and Stella lying on top of
me. Alex is out. The kids think he's running errands, but he's
off to see Alexandria. I wonder if I should text Marco and warn
him? Then again, Marco is a man who can stand up for himself.

"I miss Xbox," Josh says.

"I know," I say. "We'll be home soon."

"Mom?" Rachel says.

"Yes?"

"Are you and Dad really going to stay together?"

"Forever and ever," Josh says.

"Well," I say. "Nobody can say forever."

"Zombies can," Josh says.

I look at Rachel, smooth her hair from her sweet skin, kiss
her on the forehead. She is sweaty. Stella's fur is like a furnace.
None of us dare move. "It feels different somehow," Rachel
says.

"Different how?" I say. I know what she means, or at least I think I do, but I'm confused myself, and I want to hear what she's thinking.

"Remember that doll I had? Rosey?"

"How could I forget? You took her everywhere."

"Remember when her arm got ripped off?"

"Cool!" Josh says.

"Go on," I say. What she doesn't know is that I ripped it off. Hot guilt pours over me. I told her the neighbor's dog chewed it, but I actually ripped it off myself, in a moment of pure, overwhelming anger. I'd forgotten that. Things weren't perfect, even when Alex was home.

"You sewed the arm back on," she says. I did. Is she trying to say she knows I'm the one who ripped it off in the first place? God, I hope not. "And you did a really great job, Mom."

"Good," I say, knowing more is coming.

"But somehow, she just wasn't the same." It was true; Rachel stopped playing with her shortly after that. I thought she just outgrew her. It even lessened some of my guilt over what I'd done.

"We all outgrow our toys," I say.

"I know. It's just funny." She falls silent, her mouth clamped.

"What's funny?"

"Nothing. I don't want to make you mad."

"You're not going to make me mad."

"Swear?"

"Swear."

"It's just—I haven't felt that ever again. Until now."

"Now?"

"Now that you and Dad are back together. For some reason, I get that funny feeling in my stomach. Just like my doll. Mom, it just doesn't feel the same." She bursts into tears. I take her into my arms. I want to tell her it will be okay. I want to tell her it's normal to feel that way. I want to tell her things will get back to normal. And more than anything I want to tell her that I feel the exact same way. Instead, we sit, and we sweat, and I let her cry.

"Can I please wear that dress to the party?" she asks.

"Not on your life," I say. "Because some things will never change."

Jean's patio is exactly what I always dreamed of having. Strung lights and blooming vines, and sturdy, round wooden tables. It is the perfect place to say good-bye to Florence. Across the patio Jean is setting up several easels. As far as I know, she is no artist. I make my way over to her.

"What are you doing?" Instead of answering, she glances at the workmen setting up larger folding tables.

"Just a minute," she says. She holds her finger up, asking me to wait, and begins orchestrating the placement of the tables. They are each about nine feet long. We only know a small group of people here in Italy. Why is Jean setting up such large tables?

"What's going on?" I say. "What are these tables for? And the easels. You have nine of them. Why?"

"It's a surprise, darling."

"Jean. I have had enough surprises to last me a lifetime. Spill. Now."

"All right. I suppose I have you to thank for it anyway. Marco has decided to give us a special showing of his new paintings in advance of his gallery opening. Isn't that exciting?"

"His new paintings? What new paintings?"

"We'll find out, won't we?"

Why didn't he tell me he was coming to the party? Why is he coming to the party? What if these paintings are something horrible—some kind of revenge he wants to take out on me?

No, Marco isn't like that, and hell, even if they are, I probably deserve it. Did I break his heart? I never wanted to hurt him. I hope he knows that. It would be wrong to tell him how much I want him. Wanted him. Want him. I wonder how Alex is going to react to this surprise. It's definitely not going to be a dull evening, but then again, I haven't had such a thing since stepping on Italian soil.

I hear Angelo's booming voice behind me. *"Ciao, bella!"* I turn, thrilled to see him, in a brown suit, all cleaned up. Next to him is a round woman with a wide smile. "My wife," he says. He grins at me, and then over her head he makes a face. I laugh and allow her to hug me.

"You've got quite the catch here," I say to her.

"Ack," the woman says. She switches to Italian, voice heavy with teasing sarcasm, and I don't even need Angelo to translate. Complaining about a spouse is the same in any language. But there is an obvious and easy affection between them. Did Alex and I ever have that? Is it too late? Angelo and the wife are loaded down with food. He grins and holds the containers, as she begins to take them from him and set them on the table. Even in this simple act, there is love. I leave them to set up and walk by a man standing by a huge ladder propped up against the house. Jean is giving him directions.

"What's this for?" I ask.

"Checking for wasp nests," Jean says. "There's a nest up there somewhere. We just can't find it."

"Oh God. And you're still having the party here?"

"It's just a precaution. They won't disturb us unless they're disturbed, and if we can't find them, then we can't disturb them. If he finds them, he'll take care of it."

"Okay," I say.

"Why don't you go home and change," Jean says, looking me up and down. She's right. I'm hardly dressed for a party. The kids and Alex have their change of clothes here, but I didn't even think about mine. I don't know where my head is at lately. I go back to the apartment and sift through my outfits. I've worn my new dress way too much. Everything else, I had just shoved in my bag in grief, so unless I wear the black dress, I really have nothing. I am about to put it on when I pass Rachel's room and something bright red catches my eye.

Rachel's tube-top dress. *What all the women in Florence are wearing.* I can't believe I'm actually considering it. I couldn't pull it off. Could I? The only mirror in this flat is in the bathroom. I pull a chair in, teeter on it, and hold the dress up to me. The red makes my fair skin and blond hair really pop. Some high heels, some dark eye makeup, and I might even be able to turn a few heads.

In just a few short hours the patio has been transformed. A dozen checker-clothed tables bathed in candlelight. A small fountain in the middle of the patio is turned on, and another fat cherub spits water out of his mouth. An accordion player roams about, serenading the guests. I am standing in the recesses, afraid to walk out. The dress may have been a bad idea. It's quite possible that Rachel will kill me. Maybe this is worse than ripping the arm off her doll. The accordion player is openly staring at me. Suddenly, he wiggles his eyebrows. I laugh, remember the cab driver. Whatever happened to him? So many crazy people in this city. I think I love them all.

Marco is my Tin Man, I realize. I will miss him most of all. His paintings are set up on the easels, nine of them covered in dark green sheets. He's been here, I think. While I was gone. I tingle at the thought. I am dying to see him again. I wonder if any of the paintings are the ones I saw in his studio. Where it all almost happened.

"Well, well, well," Jean says, coming up to me. "Darling, you are an absolute showstopper." She thrusts a cocktail at me. "Drink up."

"What is it?"

"Homemade."

"Homemade what?"

"If you ask one more question I'm taking it back."

I mime zipping my lips and take a sip. If I had to guess: Limoncello and ginger ale. It's heavenly. "Oh my God," I say.

"Don't overdo it. They're lethal." I nod and begin searching the crowd.

"He's not here yet," Jean says.

"Who?"

"You tell me," Jean says, looking me up and down.

"Just looking for Alex and the kids," I say.

"You're going to stick with that?" she says. She takes a step closer. "He was looking for you too."

"You really like to stir the pot, don't you, Jean Lucas?"

"What's a party without a little fireworks?" Jean winks at me and disappears into the crowd. Suddenly, someone pinches my arm. Really, really hard. I yank my arm in and whirl around. Rachel stands in front of me, nostrils flaring, mouth open, death stare in full swing.

"My dress."

"How do you know it's yours? I hear all the women in Florence are wearing them."

"Mom."

"How do I look?" I twirl around as fast as I can. Which isn't very fast given how restricted my movements are in the skintight material.

"Actually," Rachel says, dropping her defensive stance. "You look pretty freaking awesome."

"Thank you, sweetie."

"Although you're totally too old to really pull it off."

"Stop while you're ahead." She is dressed in a much more appropriate dress, but there is still no doubt that she is becoming a woman. "You look gorgeous," I say. "I'll bet one of those Lucas boys is going to follow you around all evening."

"You still don't know their names, do you?"

"No. I don't."

"They're all gross."

"Where's your father?" I ask. Although that's not who I'm looking around for.

"No clue. But believe me, in that dress, he'll find you."

I beam. "I am so buying you a car when you turn sixteen." I touch Rachel on the tip of the nose. She rolls her eyes at me, and then walks away, a womanly wiggle in her step.

I spot Alex talking to a couple of other professor-looking types. A montage of boring faculty dinners flashes through my mind. Standing around. Fake smile plastered on my face. Listening to talk of curriculums, and budgets, and proposals, and test scores, and enrollments, and students, until I wanted to set something, myself included, on fire.

I am about to dutifully make my way over there when I stop. Funny. I don't feel obligated to go over there at all. It's a freeing thought. As I'm standing here, marveling at this change in me, Alex glances over and catches my eye. We stare at each other for a moment. Then he looks away. Just as my heart squeezes in rejection, his head snaps back. He didn't recognize me. He's gaping at me now, and his colleagues have all stopped to see what has captured his attention. Now all three of them are openly staring at me. One of them says something to Alex. I don't have to be a lip-reader to know the gist. *Isn't that your wife?* I grin, turn on my heels, and enjoy knowing they are all looking at my ass as I walk away. I have things to do, namely make sure all the right nametags are at our table. Sure enough, I have to scour the tables for the names I am looking for, set them all up at our table, and then put the ones I don't want in their place. Rachel is going to be mad at me again for not letting her sit at our table, but us grownups are definitely going to need to be alone to talk.

CHAPTER 36

Alexandria won't even look at me. We've been sitting at the table for fifteen minutes, and she's turned her seat completely around. Jean, outraged that I moved Marco's and Alexandria's nametags from her table to mine, keeps hovering above us to see if we need anything. Alex stares into his napkin. Marco is the only one who looks comfortable; in fact, if he doesn't wipe that silly grin off his face, he's going to make me start smiling.

Alex stands just as Jean is about to leave. "How could you?" he says to her.

"How could I what?"

"This," Alex says, gesturing at the table. "Invite them. Ask them to sit here." Alexandria bites out some kind of comment under her breath. I wish I knew Italian, although the gist is clear. She is not at all happy which thrills me. Alex is afraid to look at her. I wonder how their meeting went. I haven't seen her eating, but she's not fainting either, so I have to assume everything is okay.

"Jean didn't sit them here," I say. "I did."

Alex looks at me, stunned. "Whatever you're thinking," he says, "please, not here. Not now."

"I want to break bread and make peace," I say.

Alex eyes my drink. "How many of those have you had?" he says.

Finally, Alexandria looks at me. I turn to her. She is wearing a simple khaki dress, and her hair is off her face, twisted into a bun. For a second, I can see what she will look like as an older woman. I am no longer jealous of her beauty. "I want to go home," she says.

I take another deep breath, another drink. "Alexandria. Are you pregnant with my husband's child?"

Startled, Alexandria looks around the table. Then she slowly puts her hand on her considerable belly and stares at me. "Are you calling me a liar?"

"You've been known to tell a few fibs, darling, haven't you?" I'm not one to usually say "darling," but she needs a reminder that I have way more life experience.

"You're the liar. You tell everyone I try and kill you!"

"I cleared that up," I say.

Alex glances at Marco. "I hear you've been going around saying you want to kill me," he says. He turns to me. "This is us, breaking bread. Happy now?"

"I did want to kill you," Marco says. "Now I don't."

"Oh, really?"

"Yes. Lena changed all that." Marco's grin spells trouble. Maybe this wasn't such a good idea. "Now I am full of nothing but love," he says. "For her." Alex lurches across the table. Marco stands to meet the challenge, but Alexandria throws herself in front of him. Alex stops just short of coming into contact with her protruding stomach.

"Everybody, sit," I say. "This is my party. Alexandria. Answer the question."

Alexandria rubs her stomach. "I am having his baby. Are you happy now?" Marco helps Alexandria sit back down.

"You sit too, Alex," I say. His look is defiant, but he relents.

"Oh, gee, yes," I say, looking at Alexandria. "I'm so, so

happy." I look to Marco. "How do you say 'so fucking happy' in Italian?"

"*Così fottutamente felice,*" Marco says.

"*Così fottutamente felice,*" I repeat. I slam my hand down on the table.

"Lena." Alex's hand sneaks toward me. I pick up a fork.

"Do that again, and I will nail the back of your hand to the table," I say.

"I see the Viking now," Marco says. "I see it, and I like it."

"So what do you intend to do about this, Alex?" I say.

"Lena," Alex says.

"Let's clear this up. Right here, right now."

"You stay with me, Alex. I can't raise baby all by myself," Alexandria says. Alex swallows hard, then finishes his drink. When a waiter comes around with a tray of new ones, Marco takes the entire tray from the astonished kid and divides the drinks between us, except of course he leaves out Alexandria.

"I will support this child," Alex says. "I will be a father to this child. But Lena is my wife. And I can't begin to tell her how deeply, deeply sorry I am. I messed up everything. She's my Llama. She's my soul mate. It's you, Lena. I want to spend the rest of my life with you."

I glance quickly around the table. Alexandria stares defiantly, but now Marco is the one who will not look at me. His grin is gone. What have I done? Why didn't I think about his feelings?

"It's settled then," I say. "We'll support this baby." It's the right thing to say, but it also feels so wrong. I just want to go home. Marco stands and holds his hand out to me.

"Would you like to dance?"

"No," Alex says.

"Yes," I say.

He holds me close, and I am once again reminded what a good dancer he is. The accordion player keeps pace a few steps behind us, and romantic notes wash through us as Marco pulls me even closer. He smells so good.

"I'm sorry," I say. "I never meant to hurt you."

"You are the most beautiful woman I've ever seen," he says. "Do you know that?"

Then why didn't you paint my face all over Florence? I can't help but think. "Thank you. Marco. These last few months—"

"Shh." He puts his finger over my lips. I want to kiss it. *"Ciao, bella,"* he says.

"Ladies and gents," Jean says. "It's time to unveil the paintings." The crowd applauds. Marco stands beside his canvases, and I watch him from the shadows. I don't want anyone looking at me when I see his paintings, because I know I will not be able to hide how I feel. I love him. I am in love with Marco Giovatti.

The volunteers all whip the sheets off. Spotlights light them up, one by one. They are all of me. My face, close up. Different expressions. I step forward.

"I was originally working in chalk," Marco tells the crowd. "But for this, I had to switch to oil. For some things are meant to last."

Alexandria steps forward. "You painted her on canvas?" she says. "Her?" I don't even gloat over her obvious jealousy. I step up to the first one. He is an amazing artist. He has captured every detail on my face. In this one, I have a look of wonderment about me.

"It's the bridge," he says. "You hadn't seen me yet. You were looking at the water."

He captured what I looked like when I saw the lights for the first time. I move on to the second one. In this, I am flushed, excited.

"Throwing spaghetti," I say.

"Yes," he laughs.

Next I am looking a little bit lost.

"The market," he says. "When you wanted to bargain down the price of the orange, but didn't know how."

"But you didn't show up until later," I say. He smiles.

"I was working," he says. I look at him. Even though we are in a crowd, it's as if he only sees me.

"Working?"

"Watching my subject very carefully."

"Some might call that stalking."

"If I no paint, it is stalking. If I paint, it is working."

The fourth, I look rapturous. It is me taking in the paintings at the Uffizi. "Did you do all this from memory?"

Marco nods with a humble smile. He is truly a genius. "My head is like camera," he says. "I cannot get you out of my mind."

The fifth, I am looking up, as if I am on the ground. "The wine bar," I say. He laughs and nods. The sixth, a look of anguish. At Alexandria's when I found out she was pregnant. The seventh, it is pure desire; it is our moment at his studio; it is him almost taking me to bed. The eighth my face is stamped with guilt. I am fleeing. I am feeling guilty for in my heart I knew how much I wanted him. I finally step over to the ninth. I have never looked so sad in all my life.

"When is this?" I say.

Marco looks away. "Do not worry," he says.

"When is it?" I step up to Marco. "Is it when I said good-bye?"

"No," Marco says.

"When I followed Alexandria?"

"No."

"In the hospital?"

"No."

"Tell me."

He lowers his voice so only I can hear, although we have already been given a polite distance. Even Alex has kept away, and the others darn well better; if it were their faces up there, they would want the private tour too. "It's when he came back," Marco says. I nod, numb, and tears spring to my eyes, but it's not a surprise, because I knew it deep down in my bones, the minute I saw the deep grief on my face. It's me when I knew nothing would ever be the same in my marriage again, no matter what we did or said, or how sorry we were.

"When did you see me like this?"

"I came to the hospital. To see you. Your family was there. And I was happy for you, *bella*. Very happy for you."

"Until you saw the look on my face."

"It means nothing. Maybe you were still in pain from the fall." I take Marco's hands and look at him for a very long time. "It means everything," I whisper. *"Grazie."* I am about to turn away, for the crowd is applauding, moving in to receive him. "There are nine of them," I say. "Why?"

His shy little smile is back. "It was my nine-point plan to catch your beating heart in my hands," he says.

I look over to see Alex and Alexandria standing with their heads very close. Josh comes up and pokes me in the back.

"Mom," he says. "I got it from Emily. She said I could borrow it."

"Borrow what? Who is Emily?"

"Jean and Harold's daughter," he says. Shoot. I really didn't want to bother at this stage.

"Got what?"

"I'm going to get her."

"Get who?" I'm starting to sound like a one-woman Abbott and Costello routine.

"HEY," Josh roars. He lifts his right arm high into the air. He is holding a doll like a football. Why is he holding a doll? He winds his arm back, and something flies through the air, straight at Alexandria. She looks in time to scream and duck. The baby-doll hits the middle easel, and one by one, all the paintings to the right of it tip and fall like dominoes. The last easel hits the ladder that is still leaning up against the house.

"She didn't catch it!" Josh says. "I threw the baby at her, and she didn't catch it!" He throws his arms open. "I forget what that means!" he says.

"Dufus," Rachel says. "You were supposed to steal her purse."

"Oh," Josh says. "Why?" A murmur works its way through the crowd. And then, the distinct sound of buzzing. A dark, swirling pile rises from the corner of the house. Alexandria screams and points.

"*Vespa! Vespa! Vespa!*" The dirty cloud of wasps begins to spread, as if silently agreeing to span out, sting as many party-goers as they can. Alex lunges in front of Alexandria. He is protecting her. I watch it like I am an outsider looking in. The middle buttons of her maternity dress pop open. Inside, red, lumpy fabric protrudes. I am surprised, and not surprised. It changes nothing. For me, anyway. How it affects Alex is not my concern. She grabs the pillow out of her dress revealing her ridiculously flat stomach, and holds it up as a shield against the wasps. I am swept up in the crowd. Everyone is running, taking refuge inside the house.

Minutes later we are gathered in the kitchen, which is where all parties eventually end up. It's an open Tuscan kitchen, with stone floors, and sturdy pots, and a lovely view of the patio. It seems everyone is inside, and it's eerie to watch the wasps glide and dart among the empty chairs.

"Josh? Rachel?" I call.

"We're fine," Rachel pipes up from behind me. "No thanks to Dufus."

"What did I do?"

"You threw the doll at the easels, and the easels knocked down the wasps' nest."

"Oh. Right.

"It was an accident," I say.

"It was no accident," Alexandria yells. "I am allergic to *vespa.* He try to kill me!"

"Listen, doll," I say. "If anyone was going to kill you, it was going to be me." I glance at her stomach. There is no point in mentioning the pillow. Action speaks louder than words. Even Alex will have to see the truth about her now. I look around, but I don't spot him.

"My party is ruined," Jean says. "We're going to be the laughingstock of the university."

"It wasn't your party in the first place," I say. "It was mine."

"You've ruined everything since you came to town. You and your husband. Everything your family touches turns into a disaster!" Jean says.

"At least a maid never gave my husband a blow job," I yell.

"Lena!" Jean says.

"You told her about that?" Harold says. "How could you?" Just then, a man stumbles in the door from the patio. His face is covered with swollen, angry dots. His eyes are golf balls. Sealed shut. Alexandria isn't the only one allergic to wasps.

"Oh my God," I shout. "Alex. Alex." I run up to him. "911. Or whatever the hell it is in Italy."

"I can drive," Marco says. "Is much faster."

"Honey, can you hear me?" I say.

"Yes. I can hear you."

"Oh my God. Jean, do you have ice? Do we put ice on it?"

"Is he going to die?" Rachel says. "Daddy, I'm sorry, I'm sorry!"

"Nobody's going to die. Marco, let's go." The kids and I hurry with Alex to Marco's car.

"I'm coming too," Alexandria says. I want to say no, but we'll need two cars. At the hospital, Alex looks so grotesque they take him in immediately. The five us sit and wait in silence. It is almost an hour before Alex walks out. It's the moment I've been waiting for, the moment I need to see. He looks around. It is me he eventually walks toward. But it wasn't me whose eye he wanted to catch when he first came into the room. It was her.

"You still look terrible," I say. We are at the fountain, suitcases at our feet, saying good-bye.

"They pumped me with shots and painkillers," Alex says. "So I feel fine."

"Why can't Josh and I stay with you?" Rachel says. I go to her, put my arm around her and Josh.

"I swear to you. Next time you are coming with me. But there are a few things I have to do. A few more places I have to go."

"Yeah, yeah. But now you owe me two cars."

"I want a car!" Josh says. Alex pulls me aside. The kids pamper Stella who is woozy from the sedative. I hope she will sleep on the plane.

"Lena. I just want to know that you know—how sorry I am."

Our marriage is over. We haven't discussed the exact details, but soon Alex will be moving out. Perhaps he will return to Florence. Perhaps someday I will too.

"It's okay."

"It's not. But I'm going to always be there for the kids. Always."

"Of course you are," I say.

"What if we're making a horrible mistake?"

"We're not," I say.

"How can you be so sure?"

I glance at the fountain. I take in all the people milling about the square. I gaze out at the undulating hills. It's only been a few months, but in my bones, I feel as if I belong. "Because we don't paint love," I say. "It paints us."

CHAPTER 37

I go to Rome for three days. Stand in the Coliseum and feel as if I am part of history. Go to the Vatican and send up prayers. Eat incredible meals and drink amazing wine. Next, I go to Venice. Walk the piazzas. Take a speedboat to Saint Mark's Square. Go on a solo gondola ride through the little canals. The driver sings to me, and chats with me, and points out the buildings where the water levels have risen past the foundations. When I depart, he hits on me. Says he likes blondes and gets off at six. He wants to take me to dinner. I smile and say no.

I eat gelato and realize it's more fun to throw it. Listen to music. Take a tour of the islands. I return to Florence where my replacement passport is waiting for me. There is one more trip I have to take before I return home.

I stand on the cliff, hanging over the edge of the world. Cinque Terre. It is breathtakingly beautiful. Slowly, I ease my wedding and engagement rings off my finger. I cradle them in the palm of my hand. Alex and Lena. Lena and Alex. That portion of our life is over. I will miss Italy. But I will be back. I am going to start painting again, learn how to speak Italian. I gaze out at the glittering blue-green water and toss the rings as far into the air as I can. I imagine them hanging there for a moment. Suspended in time. Promising ever after, and catching the white-hot, unpredictable rays of the crazy Italian sun.

I take my time walking back to the bungalow, snuggled into the base of a cliff. Marco is sitting outside, leaning against the doorway with an easy smile. I catch his eyes and smile back.

"*Ciao, bella,*" he says. I show him my bare finger, and he kisses it. Then, he stands and searches my face as if to root out pain. It is there, I am sure, for you do not turn sixteen years of marriage off like a faucet. But there is something else; if he were to paint my expression right here and right now, there would be hope, and relief, and of course, knowing what we are about to do, there is, of course, desire.

I put my arms around his neck, lift up on my tippy-toes, and because I do not yet know how to say "shut up and kiss me" in Italian, I show him instead.

Please turn the page for a very special

Q&A with Mary Carter!

How much time did you spend doing research for this novel?

In June of 2012, I had a glorious eight-day trip in Italy. I went to Rome, Tuscany, Venice, and Florence. It wasn't nearly long enough, but between the trip, the Internet, books, and travel videos, I was able to conjure up a feel for Florence. Originally I wanted to live in Florence for a year, and would still love that opportunity, but it didn't work out this time around.

How did Florence compare to Rome and Venice?

I think Florence was my favorite. It's smaller than Rome, and a bit more bustling than Venice. If I were Goldilocks, I would say it was "just right." It's also so jaw-dropping—beauty on every corner. Every single piazza is an outdoor museum. That said, I really liked Rome and Venice as well. Some of our best meals were in Rome, and I loved my gondola ride in Venice. I can't wait to go back someday.

Did anything you experienced inspire the plot?

Readers may think that the chalk drawing on the street is a contrived or even absurd part of the plot. However, I saw such street paintings when in Florence. They were so good they looked as if they should be hung in a museum. Email me for the picture if you don't believe me! Also, Marcantonio Ninci (Marco) and his lovely family at the Villa San Lucchese in Tuscany, who showed me such hospitality and helped me book my train tickets to Venice, inspired a line of dialogue when he put his hand on his heart and said "Firenze! The heart of Italy." And, lastly there was a female shopkeeper who came flying out at me when I touched a bracelet in her shop in Florence. You would have thought I had just lit a match and set fire to the place. I was so taken aback by her behavior that I bought the bracelet—in part to prove a point. It's also a beautiful bracelet.

Do you speak Italian? What do you think of the Italian language?

No. But I listened to some beginning tapes before the trip and then looked up phrases as I was writing the story. Even after such light research, I think I could fall in love with the Italian language. Like the country, it's complex and beautiful. Guess lessons are on my "To Do" list!

Are people more romantic in Italy?

It feels like it when you listen to the language and the phrases they have for love. And the surroundings are so romantic, how could it not rub off? The food makes you swoon, and of course so does the wine. And everyone is well aware of the passion of the Italian people—from their food, to operas, art, and of course, *amore*. But, like everything in life, it is not all perfect. Italy has suffered from economic problems like the rest of us, and in some places outside of the major cities, poverty affects many, especially children.

THREE MONTHS IN FLORECE

Mary Carter

ABOUT THIS GUIDE

The suggested questions are included to enhance
your group's reading of Mary Carter's
Three Months in Florence!

DISCUSSION QUESTIONS

1. Lena and Alex met and fell in love in college. Is the demise of their relationship simply a product of outgrowing each other?

2. Lena began college life determined to become an independent artist. Let boys be her "playthings." Life quickly went the other way. Did repressing this artistic desire contribute to her problems in the marriage?

3. If Alex and Lena had taken their Italian honeymoon all those years ago, do you think the affair would still have happened?

4. Lena comments in the beginning that the affair would have been easier to forgive if it had been a one-night stand. Besides the obvious, what additional pain does a prolonged affair cause as opposed to a one-time thing?

5. Lena learns about the affair through the mistress. Do you think Lena's reaction would have been different if Alex had confessed to the affair?

6. Lena brings the whole family, dog and all, to confront Alex. Was this bad parenting, or a necessary step for the entire family?

7. Lena observes that affairs don't just happen to the adults, they happen to the kids too. How does Alex's betrayal affect Rachel and Josh? Do they react in the same way? Are the children the same at the end of the book as they were at the beginning?

8. From the moment Lena arrives in Florence, Alex's mistress is "in her face"—literally. If Alexandria were older and less attractive, would it be easier for Lena to deal with the affair?

9. If Alexandria were less beautiful, would the affair be easier for Lena to handle?

10. How does the setting of Italy and the Italian language affect the plot? How does Florence affect Lena? Is it harder to recover from an affair in such a beautiful place, or easier, or a little of both?

11. While in Florence, does any of the "younger Lena" start to come back? If so, how?

12. While in Florence, Lena meets Marco, the boyfriend of her husband's mistress. What role does Marco play in helping Lena come to grips with her new reality?

13. What are some of the cultural differences between Italians and Americans as portrayed in the novel? Do Italians know more about love than Americans? Do they express it differently?

14. What does Jean want from Lena? Does she have her best interest at heart?

15. Would Alexandria and Alex be happy together? Why or why not?

16. Is there any significance to the location where Lena finally rids herself of her wedding ring? Should she have hocked it instead?

17. What do you think the future holds in store for Lena? For Alex?